EXQUISITE HUNGER

At last they were alone. William's hands began to roam over Elizabeth's body, caressing, feeling. Soon he plucked impatiently at her shift, which had prevented him from touching her skin directly. He lifted her to carry her to the bed, but midway there fell to kissing her breasts. Elizabeth had to bite her lips to keep from screaming with excitement. She moaned and bit his neck. Then she gasped his name and the word "please," feeling she would die if she did not soon have some relief from the intolerable pressure of pleasure that was building in her.

"*SIREN SONG* is an absolutely fascinating book."
Dana Fuller Ross, author of the *WAGONS WEST* series

"Roberta Gellis is truly a wonderful storyteller."
William Stuart Long, author of *THE AUSTRALIANS*

"*SIREN SONG* is a great book and I look forward to reading all of the books in the Royal Dynasty series."
Michael William Scott, author of the *RAKEHELL DYNASTY* series

Siren Song

Roberta Gellis

**PLAYBOY
PAPERBACKS**

SIREN SONG

PRODUCED BY LYLE KENYON ENGEL

Published simultaneously in the United States and Canada by Playboy Paperbacks, New York, New York. Printed in the United States of America. Library of Congress Catalog Card Number: 80-82657. First edition.

Books are available at quantity discounts for promotional and industrial use. For further information, write to Premium Sales, Playboy Paperbacks, 747 Third Avenue, New York, New York 10017.

ISBN: 0-872-16692-9

First published January 1981.

CHAPTER 1

+-+

The elegantly clad court functionary looked down his long English nose at the ragged knight who had asked anxiously if the king or queen was in residence. The young man had a thin, dark face, a high-bridged, aristocratic nose, and light gray eyes, which were startling. His features and expression bespoke breeding, but his armor was covered with dirt and rust, his surcoat was stained, muddy, and torn in several places. Even the French he spoke was ragged, carrying an odd, rough accent. Another foreign beggar, Michael Belet thought with contemptuous irritability. Ever since King Henry had married, the court had been full of them.

"They are here," Belet said shortly. "What is it to you?"

The young knight smiled in relief. He had a sweet temper and, besides, was of such station that he did not notice subtle insult from a stranger, being unable to conceive that anyone would dare offer it. In fact, he rather pitied the elegant functionary, believing his bad manners to be an unconscious result of a lifetime in this barbaric backwater.

"I have already been to London and Windsor in hot pursuit," he said merrily, "and if I follow my aunt about much longer, my destrier and I will both need new shoes."

The courtier's lip curled even more scornfully. The young man looked as if he needed new shoes right now. He had been right. This was another office seeker close on the trail of some woman in the queen's service. Then that woman would beg the queen for a place for her nephew and the queen would go to the king . . . Belet's face flushed with rage. The young knight misread the

5

flush for one of embarrassment. He would have been embarrassed if he had spoken so crudely to the nephew of the queen. He smiled again.

"It does not matter," he said kindly. "Just point out the proper person to announce me—or give me his name."

"Announce you? To the king?" Belet's shock made his voice somewhat faint. He could only suppose that this tatterdemalion came from some tiny, jumped-up principality where the ruler was little richer or more powerful than the pauper knights he led. Before Belet could put the creature in its place, however, one of the queen's women came out into the hall.

"Sir Michael," she began, then stopped and goggled. "Raymond?" she gasped, "is it you?"

"Yes, indeed, Lady Blanche." The young knight smiled, and his eyes lit with mischief.

"Oh!" the woman gasped again, her eyes running over his soiled clothing and battered mail. "What has befallen you?" And then, before he could reply, "No, never mind. Come with me."

Belet opened his mouth to protest, but then he bit his lips together. That scarecrow would find a place—and a good one. Lady Blanche was one of the queen's favorites and had come with Eleanor from Provence. Nonetheless, one could not help liking Queen Eleanor. She was good-natured and a peacemaker between the king and those who had incurred his wrath for little things— and she did not interfere in great matters of state. Lady Blanche had pushed Raymond along a corridor and into the antechamber of the queen's apartment with all haste.

"How did you get into such a disgraceful condition?" she cried. "What happened to your clothes? Where are your servants? Why did you not tell Eleanor you were coming? Oh, Raymond, is something wrong? Your father? Your mother?"

Emotion flickered across the dark, young face, but it was gone before Lady Blanche noticed, and Raymond shook his head. "Everyone is well, very well. I have only come for a visit. I suppose I have outstripped the messenger or, likely, some accident befell him." Raymond's voice was stiff. In general he was a truthful young man, and he did not like to lie.

"But Raymond, where—"

"Raymond?"

The voice was warm, a little high with surprise. Both Lady Blanche and the young knight turned toward the inner doorway. Lady Blanche sketched a curtsy. Raymond bowed low, but the dark, beautiful woman who had come through the door did not wait with dignity for him to complete his obeisance. She ran across and threw her arms around his neck and kissed him.

"Raymond, dear, I am so happy to see you. How is my brother and your dear mama?"

"Very well, and the rest of us also. I understand you have had no word of my coming. I hope it is not in any way inconvenient to you."

"Of course not," the queen cried, kissing him again.

"And for heaven's sake, do not ask me where my servants are and what happened to my clothes," Raymond said, laughing. "Let it stay that I have come to no harm, that I was well pleased to be without them, and— that I do not intend to answer such questions as the answers would not be fitting for your auntly ears."

That was, of course, a jest. Eleanor and Raymond were almost exactly the same age, Eleanor being one month, to the day, the elder of the pair. She was the soberer of the two, however, and Raymond always teased her about being an "old aunt."

"Raymond, what sort of scrape are you in?" Eleanor asked characteristically, but when he only laughed again and shook his head at her, she sighed resignedly. "If you will not tell me, will you tell Henry?"

Raymond flushed slightly. "It is not a matter to trouble a king with. Truly, madam, it is of no consequence. I am here, safe and sound. Your husband has far more important things to think about than how I came here without clothes or servants."

Voices and footsteps interrupted and Henry, third

of that name to rule England, came in. Lady Blanche bit her lip. She had gone out to tell Michael Belet, the royal butler, to have a flagon of the king's favorite wine sent to the queen's chamber and, in the excitement of seeing Raymond, had forgotten her errand. Dropping a curtsy, she edged out of the room.

By the time Lady Blanche was in the hall, looking for Belet, Eleanor had introduced her nephew to Henry, who blinked. As far as he knew, his wife had only one sister older than herself, married to the king of France, but certainly not married long enough to produce a son of this age. Eleanor trilled with laughter at her husband's blank expression and explained that Raymond was the son of her half-brother, Alphonse d'Aix. The king's expression cleared. Of course, during the negotiations for his marriage, he had been told of the count of Provence's youthful indiscretion—but that had been -eight years ago and even at the time he had paid little attention. All he had cared about was that the natural son born of that union would not complicate the succession in Provence.

Now, taking in the young man's ragged appearance, Henry smothered a sigh. Apparently something had happened in Aix to reduce his wife's relations to penury. Why the devil could they not go to the count of Provence for help? However, Henry did not remain irritated long. It was flattering to his ego that he was known as so rich and so generous that Raymond would prefer to travel all the way to England from the very south of France to beg succor rather than go to his grandfather or— suddenly Henry smiled warmly at Raymond—rather than go to that sanctimonious, tight-fisted Louis of France, who was his other uncle.

"We are happy to welcome you," he said to Raymond, "and we hope you will be happy here at our court. Be sure you will be welcome to us as long as you wish to stay. What else can we do for you?"

"Sire—" Raymond began, but Eleanor cut him off.

"You can give him something decent to wear, for one thing, Henry," she laughed. "Really, he cannot show himself in this condition. Everyone will think that my family has fallen into ruin."

Since that was exactly what Henry had thought, he was much surprised by his wife's remark, and even more when the young man made a gesture as if to urge silence on his aunt.

"Er—certainly," Henry replied. "I am sure something suitable can be found." His voice held a note of petulance. He had been prepared to be generous, a bountiful lord to a poor suppliant. It seemed from Eleanor's light remark, however, that his bounty was not necessary. Her nephew's problem seemed to be a temporary embarrassment. Henry did not like to have his generous gestures frustrated, but fortunately, before he could begin to feel spiteful toward Raymond, Eleanor spoke again.

"And he is in some trouble, Henry. Do make him tell you. He will not tell me!"

Color flooded into Raymond's face. Henry felt better at once. Apparently his help was necessary. He smiled first at Raymond and then at his wife. "Very well, but if you want him decently dressed for dinner, I will have to take him away to my chamber now. It would scarcely be fitting if suits of men's clothing were to be carried into your rooms, my dear."

Eleanor agreed to this with laughter, although she was somewhat reluctant to part with Raymond when she had not yet really heard any news from Provence. To pacify her, Henry suggested that they have dinner together privately. Then he bore Raymond away to his own apartment. After he had seated himself and pointed out a stool to Raymond, he looked closely at the young man—who was still very flushed—and said, "Well?"

"I am not in any trouble," Raymond said. "It is only because I have come without servants and baggage—"

"Yes? Well, that is an odd thing to do," Henry remarked, with twitching lips. "Surely it cannot be a comfortable way to travel. And servants and clothing are easy enough things to obtain with money—so you have no money either."

Henry gave in and grinned, his voice was warm, his

blue eyes glinted with amusement. Raymond hesitated and then yielded to the charm that prevented Henry's barons from hating him, no matter how much he plagued them and exasperated them.

"You will think me ridiculous," Raymond sighed. "I have run away from home."

There was a brief silence while Henry wondered if his ears had played him false. Men in their twenties did not "run away from home"—unless . . .

"You are escaping from an unwanted marriage contract?" It was the only sensible thing Henry could think of, but Raymond shook his head.

"My mother will not let me *live*," he groaned.

"Your mother?" Henry's throat closed, and he could not get out the words: *wishes you dead.*

Henry had always adored his mother, passionately and hopelessly. He did not know his love was hopeless. Isabella said all the right words and made all the right gestures. Her voice was soft, her embrace graceful and scented. Nonetheless, Isabella could not or would not love, and Henry, although he would never admit it, felt the utter rejection of her frigid nature. Thus, he recoiled in horror from what any man with a more natural parent would have understood at once.

"This last matter was too much to bear," Raymond continued, so wrapped in his private frustration that he did not notice the king's reaction. "One of the vassals on her lands in Gascony had some idiot complaint and, instead of coming to my father in the normal way, flew to arms."

"That is normal for Gascons," Henry interposed bitterly.

"Yes," Raymond agreed, but without being deflected from his personal problem. "It was all arranged that I should give that idiot a firm setdown. It was *nothing*. One small keep and one small fool of a man bawling defiance. But my mother forbade it!"

"Does she not trust you?" Henry asked sympathetically.

"Trust me? What has that to do with it?" Raymond

raged, in full spate now. "Put on a cloak, it is too cold for you, Ray. Do not go into the sun, it is too hot for you, Ray. That beast is too wild, you will fall off your horse, Ray—"

Henry was beginning to understand, and he could not help laughing at the young man's fury of frustration. However, there was still a puzzle he wished to have explained. "I see," he said, grinning broadly, "that your mother is a little too fearful for your health and safety, but I do not understand how she could forbid what your father ordered. I suppose it was by your father's order that you were to go to Gascony?"

"Yes," Raymond grated. "Perhaps 'forbade' is the wrong word. She wept; she wailed; she held her heart; she could not breathe. . . ." He let his voice fade out at the king's smiling gesture.

"But your father—" Henry said.

"When it is a matter of real moment, my father endures. I understand he lived away from her for near six months when I was sent out to be fostered. But—but he loves her, and in other ways she is a good wife."

Henry nodded full understanding. Because of his mother's coldness, his wife's warmth had made him utterly her slave. Eleanor was a sensible woman, fortunately, but had she wept and wailed over something, Henry would have yielded also.

"I see that in a small matter like the Gascon business, he would surely give way for love of her. Still—" Henry's mind was devious. He would yield to Eleanor when she wanted something, but if she did not know she wanted it and did not ask . . . "Why did your father tell her? Or did you tell her?"

"We are not so stupid as that," Raymond replied. "I am not sure how she found out. Where I am concerned she seems to smell our intentions in the air. Six months ago I wished to ride in a tourney—only a tourney—and she fainted thrice and wept all night until my father told me to bide at home. I tell you, she will not let me live."

The king nodded sympathetically. He had suffered the same frustrations as a boy, although with him it was his guardians who held him so precious that they watched every breath in and out of his mouth. So, warmed by the memories, Henry liked his wife's nephew all the better.

"Well," he said, "you are welcome here, and no one will keep you from such action as is available and that you wish to engage in. But, I am afraid it cannot be for long. Eleanor will write, no doubt, to say you have arrived safe."

Raymond slapped a hand to his forehead. "What an idiot I am," he groaned. "If I tell her——"

"No," Henry said, "she will think only of your mother's pain and be the more hot to assure her of your safety if she knows of her ignorance of your whereabouts. And, even if I could fob off Eleanor with some tale, *someone* at court would write to some friend in Provence. I assume your mother would send first to your grandfather to ask whether you had gone to him?"

"Yes," Raymond sighed, then shrugged. "Oh well, I will have a few weeks at least."

Henry frowned, his eyes looking past Raymond. Then he said slowly, "If no one knew you were here, and I told Eleanor she must not write because you are engaged in some secret work for me . . ." His eyes focused on Raymond. "I have a little task—a minor annoyance but one for which I need a man truly trustworthy to me and yet not known to be my man——"

"I will do it if I can, and gladly," Raymond offered quickly.

The king smiled most sweetly, his eyes luminous with warmth. "It will mean that you must forgo your rank and name for some time longer," he warned.

Raymond laughed. "Nothing could give me greater pleasure."

"I have a brother, as you must know," Henry began, "whom I love most dearly, for he is a most excellent person. Some years ago, however, I noticed that Richard was at times cold to me and critical of what I did—and sometimes he acted even worse, berating me before my council. We have always been close, and such behavior hurt me to the heart. I could not believe it came of Richard himself, yet I believed also there was no one whom he loved that did not also love me."

Raymond had been so surprised by the mention of Richard, earl of Cornwall, that his face went blank and hid his feeling of recoil. He had expected, after their conversation, that Henry wanted him to perform some feat of arms, and it was with this expectation that he had pledged himself to do the king's will so eagerly and without reservation.

"Now I have heard," Henry continued, "through a trusty clerk, that a vassal of my brother's—no great man but only the holder of two keeps, albeit one sits on the Thames and the other commands a road of great importance—is the man who has poisoned Richard's mind against me."

"Is it likely that so insignificant a person could influence the earl of Cornwall?" Raymond asked stiffly, liking the turn of conversation less and less.

"I would not have thought so myself," Henry agreed, "but after the clerk named him I remembered that in the last years of my father's reign, during the troubles, and after, when Louis was in the land, this man's father—a friend of de Burgh—was castellan of Wallingford and had Richard in keeping quite often. The vassal, William of Marlowe by name, is of the same age— or perhaps a year or two older than my brother. They must have been, from time to time, playmates. Moreover, Richard mentioned to me that this William was squire to Rannulf of Chester."

"That is a high lord for a squire of so little note."

Raymond was growing less happy by the moment. Rannulf of Chester had been known throughout Europe as a man of the highest character—just, merciful, unwavering in his faith, fearless in advice, fine of purpose. Could a boy trained by the late earl of Chester grow up into a man who would maliciously seed discord in the royal family?

"That is true," Henry agreed, "but I believe he was taken because my brother begged for his company.

After the country was at peace and Chester was not every day in the forefront of battle, he was my brother's guardian."

Henry was a very self-centered person. Except for his wife, he rarely noticed what other people felt. This was not owing to coldness or indifference. Henry was a warm-hearted, loving man. It was merely that he was king, had been king since he was twelve years of age. By and large, people tried to echo and mirror the king's feelings and, if they felt differently, kept it to themselves. His guardians, of course, should have molded him better, but they were more concerned to teach the young king politics than to give him understanding of individual feelings. Thus, Henry did not notice the reservation in Raymond's manner and voice.

"Then the earl of Cornwall and Sir William are long-time companions," Raymond pointed out, trying to make the king see that the evil influence would have to be much older than a few years. The king's expression clearly showed he had not taken the point, and Raymond went on. "I cannot see, sire, what so small a man could gain from such a thing. And surely, he must risk all by speaking ill of you to the earl of Cornwall. It is well known, even in my land so far from here that the earl of Cornwall is most true and loving to you."

"Yet it was not always so." Henry's face darkened alarmingly. "When Richard Marshal raised rebellion against me thirteen years ago, my brother was very near to joining him."

The king, Raymond realized, feeling a little cold, carried grudges a long time. "That must have been a false tale told you by an enemy," he protested.

"Richard told me so himself, to my face," Henry snapped pettishly. "And only six years ago, when I gave my sister to the earl of Leicester—both of them came weeping to me and begging my help, for they were mad for love and had long tried to vanquish the feeling and could not—Richard spoke to me most foul in full council."

"Surely you cannot doubt your brother's love," Raymond breathed. "He has proved it again and again."

What had he made himself agree to? he wondered. Was this uncle, praised to the skies by his young wife, some kind of monster who intended to destroy his own brother?

But Henry's face had cleared. "No," he agreed, smiling, "I do not doubt Richard. He acknowledged his fault most handsomely and has supported me since then. But you asked me what such a small man hoped to gain. Is it not clear he hoped to gain a king who would raise him up among the mighty of the land?"

Raymond's mouth opened and closed without sound, his voice being suspended by horror. This time the emotion was so apparent that Henry could not miss it, and he laughed and shook his head.

"No, no, I am not accusing Richard of treason. However mistaken my brother may have been in his actions, he never thought harm to me. He thought, of course, that he would *save* me from harm by preventing me from some act that would anger my barons. But I do not think Sir William wished to save me from harm. He, I think, hoped Richard's action would so turn the nobles against me that I would be killed in war or by murder. Then he would sit at the king's right hand."

That made a kind of sense. Raymond frowned in thought. "Have you spoken to Earl Richard and—"

"You do not know my brother," Henry said. "He is the most loyal man in the world. You heard what I said just before. As Richard would not for any reward be disloyal to me, so is he to other men. If I spoke to him, he would defend his friend. No, I need proof. Hear me. I do not think this Sir William is a fool—Richard does not suffer fools gladly. He would not speak open ill of me to Richard—no man could do so and retain my brother's good will. He would say, 'The king harms himself much by this thing he does. For his own good, it would be well to curb him at all cost.' But perhaps among his own family and friends he speaks differently."

That, too, might be true, Raymond thought.

"I cannot act against Sir William because Richard would be furious. I have made enquiry and so much is true that they are frequent companions. Whenever Richard is at Wallingford, he spends some time in Marlowe or Sir William goes to him."

"Are you perfectly sure the tale is true?" Raymond asked.

"No. That is my second reason for holding my hand. I am this sure—that the clerk who carried the tale had no private reason to do so. He is not connected with Sir William in any way except that the abbey in which he was trained is nearby. It seems he heard by accident some talk that betrayed Sir William's purpose. Still, things overheard can be misunderstood. There is a chance, indeed, that Sir William is not guilty."

The feeling of being trapped by his own too-hasty offer of help, of being a dirty instrument used to cut a man down, receded. Raymond smiled. The king was well within his rights to weed out disloyal subjects. Raymond still felt a little uneasy about acting the spy. However, so long as his purpose was to discover the truth, not to find evidence by hook or crook to condemn an innocent man, Raymond was willing to gain his freedom by a small subterfuge.

"But I do not know this man," he pointed out, "nor even Earl Richard. What am I to say to him? I do not see—"

"Oh, I will give you a letter, saying—if you will forgive me the jest—that you come penniless to my court seeking succor. I will ask Sir William to take you into his household. As to why I send you to him rather than to another, I will say Richard has spoken well of him to me and so I thought he would be a kind master to a young man needing kindness."

At that Raymond laughed aloud with relief. He could scarcely be accused of spying if he came with a letter from the king. Apparently Henry did not wish to deceive his brother's vassal, only to discover the real truth.

"Excellent," he agreed. "I can be a simple Sir Raymond from Aix. That will not give me away. Every third man in Provence and Aix is named either Raymond or Alphonse."

"Perfect," Henry approved, and they laughed together like children over the mischief they were brewing.

Then Raymond's smile faded. "But how long am I to stay with Sir William? What if I find nothing that suggests either guilt or innocence?" He smiled wryly. "Sooner or later I suppose I must go home or at least tell my father where I am."

"I did not intend that you should spend the rest of your life as a hireling knight," Henry laughed. "I have not yet told you the end of the tale. There has been trouble in Wales. I will not take the time to explain that in full now; there is *always* trouble in Wales. But it grows more and more likely that we will have to march in with an army and lesson this David ap Llewelyn. What this clerk Theobald overheard was that Sir William's new plan for enraging Richard against me was to force me to attack him."

"Attack him?" Raymond said with patent disbelief.

"Not with an army, but to seem to persecute him," Henry explained. He paused, and his face darkened again. "I am always accused of unjust persecution. When I wished to free myself from being shackled like a slave to the will of Hubert de Burgh—that was unjust persecution. When I wish to obtain a see for a dear friend and a relation I am accused of persecution of Walter Raleigh. When Richard protects his friends— that is noble. When I do it—that is persecution."

Raymond was appalled. The king's voice had risen to a petulant whine as he recounted his wrongs, and there was nothing Raymond could say. What Henry complained of was both true and not true, according to the tales Raymond had heard in Aix. De Burgh had certainly become too great and needed a setdown, but Raymond's father said he thought the king had carried the matter too far and too long. It was the action, Alphonse d'Aix pointed out, of a young man who still feels the chain of tutelage when all others can see that it has fallen away. Thus he continues to strike out for freedom after the enemy has fallen and should be shown mercy.

In the matter of the see of Winchester, which Raymond had heard about in every hospice in France, Henry again was not totally innocent nor totally at fault. He had begun a perfectly legitimate campaign on behalf of a perfectly worthy man, but the see of Winchester had long been held by a great man of affairs who was more often absent from his diocese than in it. Those who held the right of electing the bishop claimed they had suffered neglect because their lord's attention was so much drawn away from them. Thus, when the king suggested to them another man much like Peter des Roches (the previous bishop), they said they would not have him and elected Walter Raleigh—also learned and wise but with no political interests or foreign connections.

Fortunately for Raymond, Henry did not expect a response to his complaint. Until he was made aware of the fact by near brutality, the king assumed that everyone to whom he spoke was in complete agreement with him. It was an unfortunate assumption and the cause of much pain because, when someone was finally forced to disagree violently enough to make the king understand, Henry was all the more shocked and hurt. This time, however, the long-dead de Burgh and the see of Winchester were side issues. Henry shook off his petulance to return to the immediate problem.

"Sir William's plan, as I understand it, was either to be so slow when called to fight in Wales that he would be fined or reprimanded or to cause such disruption in the campaign against the Welsh as to produce the same result. Then, when accused or blamed, to fly to Richard saying I wished to disseisen him or some such. That, on top of the Winchester affair and perhaps some other things of which I do not know, was to rouse my brother against me."

There was something wrong in what Henry was saying. If Sir William was Richard's vassal, it should be Richard who would summon him to Wales. However,

Raymond was aware that he did not really know whether the terms of vassalage were the same in England as in his country. Besides, he was not in a mood to examine things too closely. He was thrilled at the idea of a masquerade in which he would not have to play the rôle of a responsible heir of great territories. He nodded gleefully when Henry told him the Welsh affair would surely come to a head within six months. Six months would be a delicious spell of freedom. It would be a pleasure after that to go home and be cosseted. Then, if his mother still sought to shackle him, he would tell her plain he would be off again and see if that taught her wisdom.

CHAPTER 2

+-+

The keep at Marlowe was not very large, but it drew a look of surprised admiration from Raymond, for he judged it to be near impregnable if properly manned. It was set upon a hillside above the river, and below the two huge round towers that joined to make up its southern face, the hill had been cut sheer away and faced with stone. From the sides of the towers, the walls of the outer ward marched away east and west, curving back from the bank. To the west, which Raymond could see best, the walls ran down to the foot of the hill where a wide channel had been dug to provide a moat. This curved around toward the north and disappeared. Probably, Raymond thought, the moat did not go all the way around because of the rise of the land.

The drawbridge was down and a fair amount of traffic was moving over it—merchants on mules riding beside empty or near-empty carts coming out, servants and serfs who labored on the near sections of the demesne farm coming in. Raymond examined the faces of those he passed with interest. He was a little surprised at the general look of well-being and contentment and at the easy answers he had to the questions he asked the merchants. Certainly on the surface it seemed that Sir William was neither hated nor feared.

There were guards on the walls near the gate tower that controlled the drawbridge and portcullis, but they were lounging at their stations, idly watching those who came and went. When Raymond had entered, a man-at-arms did come forward, but he only greeted the young knight civilly and told him where to leave his horse. Guests were apparently frequent and welcome at Marlowe. On being asked, the man-at-arms assured Raymond that the lord was in the keep, and gestured behind him.

It was then that Raymond realized there was no inner ward. From his present position, he could see that two matching great, round towers made up the north face of the keep and that between them was a stretch of wall almost as strong that had been roofed over. It was not until he entered the building by a relatively flimsy wooden stair, which ran up inside the wooden forebuilding on the flat western face, that he realized Marlowe was not very old. It had never been four towers connected by walls that originally enclosed a small inner bailey but had been built in recent times just as it stood.

A remarkably ugly, deformed, but quiet-eyed elderly man advanced upon Raymond as he entered the hall and offered the hospitality of the house, introducing himself as the steward. Raymond thanked him without recoil. He was surprised at the position of influence that the deformed cripple held but not affronted by his ugliness. Such people were often used as buffoons or jesters. His mother had a little dwarf woman—although she was not near as ugly as this man. Raymond then asked whether Sir William could spare him a few minutes. The steward nodded and hobbled away, leaving Raymond to look around curiously.

The keep itself was very strong. The door passage was ten long strides deep and opened into a wide and lofty hall lit by deep window embrasures on both flat walls. On the two short walls between the towers north and south, huge hearths blazed with fire. At each corner, a doorway led into one of the towers. Raymond assumed that one contained a stairwell to the upper and lower floors. The other three might be private living quarters and were large enough for two large or several small chambers. Naturally Raymond did not expect to be accommodated in such luxury. For a hireling knight, a cot or even a pallet on the floor of the hall would be sufficient. He did not mind. He was not so far from his duties as a squire that he had lost the ability to sleep in comfort on the hardest floor.

A deep, pleasant voice spoke his name.

"Sir William?" Raymond responded, wishing to be sure this was really the man.

He asked because he was surprised again, and had to remind himself sharply that evil can often wear a pleasant mask. But Sir William's face had little of the mask about it. Square and, at first glance, uncompromising, it was softened by a surprisingly sensitive mouth, wide and mobile, and dominated by large hazel eyes that were shaded by laughably long, curling lashes. Moreover, the broadness of the face implied at first glance a stolidity that did not exist on further examination. Raymond, young as he was, could easily read the emotions that played across it—pleasure in a guest, curiosity, friendliness. He felt a twinge of doubt at the part he was playing, but reminded himself that the only deceit in it was the concealment of his real status and blood-relationship to the queen.

"Yes, I am Sir William. Can I serve you in some way, Sir Raymond?"

"I hope I can serve you, sir," Raymond replied. "I have a letter to you from the king that will explain."

"From the king?" Sir William's brows shot upward in frank amazement, but Raymond could detect not even the smallest hint of fear or anxiety, and his hand stretched out at once to take the letter without a tremor. He examined the seal before he broke it, but only cursorily, like a man of unsuspicious nature who also had no reason to fear any trap. His eyes skimmed the opening lines and came to the body of the letter, whereupon his mouth firmed, the corners tucking back in distaste.

That was all Raymond saw because Sir William turned away quickly, carrying the letter toward the nearest window. It was true the light would be better there, but it was quite sufficient where they stood. Raymond was sure Sir William had walked away to hide what he felt until he could control his expression. He was right. When Sir William returned, his face was blank, the mobile mouth set hard, and the expressive eyes hidden behind lowered lashes. That was suspicious, but Raymond felt no satisfaction, only disappointment and embarrassment. He had liked Sir William on first sight and had never before been in a place in which he, personally, was not welcome. If it had not been for his promise to King Henry, Raymond would have left right then, preferring to sleep in an open field and go hungry rather than accept grudging hospitality. He felt his color rise.

William had been rather surprised when Martin told him there was a young knight asking for him by name; but the mild surprise William felt at first was nothing compared to his amazement when the young man had said he came from the king. In spite of the fact that the king's brother was William's closest friend, he had never had much to do with Henry. He had always done his best to avoid the king. Since there were always large numbers of men striving for Henry's notice and favor, William had been quite successful in this purpose. In fact, until Raymond presented himself, William had believed that the king would not recognize his face and probably would barely recognize his name. He had first been thoroughly annoyed by the tone of the letter and by the assumption that feeding the flock of foreign scarecrows that followed the court around was the duty of every landholder in England. Now, however, seeing the painful flush on Raymond's face, William's irritation disappeared. At least this Raymond seemed willing to work for his keep. If all young Raymond had asked for was an introduction to someone who had place for a knight in his household, that was an honest enough desire.

Actually William did need just such a person as Raymond seemed to be. He had lost his squire to a virulent chill and fever the preceding winter, just as the young man was ripening into real usefulness. That loss had been the more painful because it came on top of the previous loss of the castellan of Bix, Sir Peter, who had taken over William's responsibilities when he was called away to war or foreign travel in Richard's tail. William had not replaced the castellan of Bix because he intended that place for poor Harold—and now Harold was dead and he had no one. William could only assume that Richard had passed this information to his brother and that the king had remembered when a likely candidate for such a place had appeared.

Now William was ashamed of the prejudice that had made him place the ugliest interpretation on an act of real consideration on the king's part. Henry had much to think of and to remember. It was truly kind of him to call to mind the infinitesimal problem of a minor subject probably mentioned quite casually. Just because I would have preferred an English-born man, William thought, I have no right to reject the king's kindness or make this poor young man uncomfortable.

"You are very welcome," William said, smiling now. "I was much surprised because I could not imagine how the king could have come to know my need. However, I suppose—"

William's voice checked as he saw Raymond's eyes fix on something past his shoulder. He turned his head and hastily raised a hand to hide his grin. Alys, his daughter, had just come into the hall. Alys always had that effect on young men, and the reaction invariably amused Alys's father. It was not that William did not recognize his daughter's beauty—he did; it was because her character was at such variance with her appearance of exquisite fragility. Sometimes there was no immediate cause for awakening, and a young visitor would ride away with a dream in his heart. More often, either deliberately or by accident, Alys displayed what she was made of, and a much chastened and wiser young man left the keep than had entered it.

Alys had hesitated when she saw her father engaged with a man in armor—thus one newly arrived, who might have private business with him. Not that any business William had was really private from Alys, but she had discovered that knowledge of that fact made many men uneasy, and she waited politely before finding out what she wanted to know. However, William gestured to her and she came eagerly across to him.

"This is Sir Raymond, Alys. My daughter Alys, Raymond. He comes to us all the way from Aix to take Harold's place—well, more than that of course, because Harold was not yet knighted—by the king's recommendation."

"The king's?"

William frowned a little at the note of distaste that tainted the simple surprise in Alys's voice. He had done his best not to infect Alys with the frequent exasperation Henry caused Richard and, through Richard, him—since it was not a safe feeling to hold—but he was never really successful in hiding things from Alys. He flashed a glance at Raymond, but the expression on the young man's face was still stunned and utterly fatuous, certainly not the look of a man capable of measuring shades of meaning in a voice.

"It was very good of the king to think of me," William said reprovingly. "Richard must have told him of Harold's death after that of Sir Peter."

"Would Uncle Richard tell King Henry a thing like that?" Alys asked doubtfully.

"He must have done," William replied. "Here, read his letter."

At the same time that he handed the letter to Alys, William cast another sly glance at Raymond. Sometimes the discovery that Alys could read, a skill that fit very ill with her delicate, feminine appearance, was sufficient to shatter a young man's dream. Raymond showed no signs of being disgusted, however. William's lips twitched. The arrow had struck him deep; he did not even look surprised—and it was surprising that the daughter of a simple knight should be literate. William would more likely than not have been illiterate himself—as his father was—had not he and Richard taken so strong a fancy to each other when they were boys. Yet, since Richard absolutely would *not* mind his book unless William, too, had to study, William was *very* literate. He could read and write not only French but Latin and English also.

Thinking back, while Alys read and then reread Henry's letter and Raymond gazed at her, William's lips twitched again. He and Richard had nearly fallen out over the question of education. William had been most unwilling to "waste his time" over so useless an accomplishment as reading and writing. What, he had asked, were clerks for if not to read and write for their noble protectors? He had angrily accused Richard of forcing him into spending hours crouched over a book or painfully scribing with cramped fingers on much scratched-over parchment just so that Richard would not be outstripped in feats of arms. Richard had turned red as a rooster's wattle—a thing he still did when angered—but he had not denied the accusation. His dark eyes had burned redly for a moment. Then the color had faded; humor sparkled in the eyes instead of rage, and Richard had agreed that William's accusation was true. There were some privileges to being a king's son, Richard had said, grinning, and not suffering alone was one of them.

William remembered also his father's fear when he crossed Richard. He had not understood it, and it had frightened him and made him uneasy so that he was careful in the future to quarrel with Richard only in private. Sometimes, of course, the results of a quarrel could not be concealed. One day he and Richard had returned to the keep well bloodied and still snarling at each other. Then his father had drawn him aside and told him never to anger the prince.

"He is the image of his father," old Sir William warned, "and John never forgot and never forgave a slight, no matter how small. Even if it took him ten years or twenty, he would be avenged, fairly or unfairly."

William had looked at his father in blank amazement. He knew Richard never held a grudge. He could be angry; he had a fierce temper. But once the matter was settled, it was ended for good. William judged things simply, and it was significant to him that, no matter how furious Richard was, he fought as fairly as his opponent.

Over the years it had been proven that William was right about Richard of Cornwall. Men who had known the old king well finally learned that humor rather than rapacity or spite burned in the dark eyes otherwise so like John's. Richard was eager for money and ambitious; there was a lust to rule in him and for that money was necessary, but neither greed nor ambition surmounted all other considerations as in the preceding generation of Plantagenets. Richard ruled in his own lands absolutely, and ruled very well. He took after his father also in his attention to the details of governing, in his lack of personal extravagance, in his ability not to be blinded by class in measuring justice.

For ten years at least, those who wished to see a land well governed and at peace with itself mourned inwardly that the wrong son was the elder. No one, however, had ever dared broach the idea that Richard should take Henry's place. Such a man would have died on the spot with Richard's powerful hands locked around his throat. The widest difference between Richard and his father was Richard's loyalty to anyone who deserved loyalty of him. And, whatever could be said of Henry, of his petulance, his vindictiveness, his shifting purposes and disloyalty to others, he never wavered in his love for his brother. No matter how furious each was with the other, neither ever distrusted the other.

"Papa?"

William came back from the past with a start. Richard had been right about the reading and writing lessons. William had acknowledged that soon enough and learned to take so much pleasure in books that he could not deny his one child, the apple of his eye, the joys and solace he found in reading. Thus, Alys was educated beyond her class. Raymond, of course, thought nothing of the fact that this miracle of grace and beauty could read. He would have felt her ignorance to be an imperfection. As one climbed the social scale, literacy became more prevalent, and in general, the south of France was more worldly, more cosmopolitan, more polished than England. Thus, Raymond's mother and sisters were literate, and he never stopped to think that they were very great ladies and Alys only the daughter of a simple knight.

She handed the king's letter back and made a very slight curtsy to Raymond. Startled by her movement in his direction, he roused from his trance and swept a deep, elaborate bow. William successfully controlled a grin. He felt a little sorry for Raymond but was not in the least worried about Alys. She knew her worth and her place and was not likely to be led astray by the blandishments of a hireling—of which she had plenty of experience.

"I bid you welcome," Alys said formally, which surprised William. Ordinarily she was very friendly and merry. "If you will come with me," she went on, "I will show you around the keep and introduce you to those who must know you. Papa, I know you wish to get back to your accounts."

"Wish to—" William swallowed the rest.

Reading might be a joy, but accounts were something else. Alys was actually better at them than he was and had done them for years. William had not been doing accounts but trying to think of a soothing way to answer a letter from Richard about the problems of the bishop of Winchester—and Alys knew it. Why had she not said, "You wish to get back to Richard's letter," or something of that sort? It was very odd, but Alys generally had reasons for what she did, so after a momentary hesitation, William finished by saying, "Yes, of course," and turning away.

Alys pulled her lips into a smile. "Perhaps you would like to be rid of your arms and into more comfortable clothing before you meet our people," she suggested.

Raymond flushed darkly. Somehow it was not so easy to appear a beggar before Alys as it had been before William. "I have no other," he admitted.

It was the truth. When he had stormed out of Tour

Dur, his father's keep, after he had been told he could not lead the Gascon enterprise, Raymond had been wearing just what was on his back now—a good suit of mail and a simple surcoat. He had ridden blindly for about twenty miles, stopping at last, when his horse began to flag, at an abbey. There he had left his shield, painted with his father's escutcheon and marked with the symbol for the eldest son of the house. He had also borrowed a small sum of money from the abbot, which he knew his father would repay on demand. A new shield bearing the device of a man's head without features—Raymond thought that was appropriate and a good joke—had eaten up most of that sum. What remained, Raymond had kept by him for emergencies, such as food on the road if he could not find a house to guest him.

To his surprise, Alys smiled at him much less formally and more warmly. "Never mind," she said cheerfully, "that is easily provided." A gesture brought the crippled steward to them. "This is Sir Raymond, Martin, who will stay with us now. He may go into the northeast tower room. He will want a bath. When that is seen to, come to me above and I will give you clothing." Then to Raymond. "I will see you at supper."

She tripped away and Martin stood quietly, watching Raymond's eyes follow her. "She is the lord's only child," Martin said softly, warningly, "the heiress of all he has."

Martin had not said, *She is not for the likes of you,* but that was what he meant. With an effort, Raymond pulled his eyes from the doorway into which Alys had disappeared and looked down at Martin. The steward was right, of course. It was completely out of the question for the heir of Aix to marry a little nobody from England. It did not occur to Raymond at the moment that that was a strange thought for him to have. Marriage had never come into his head before when he had been attracted by the daughter of an unimportant knight. His normal reaction had been to begin a campaign to get what he wanted.

Marriage had nothing to do with desire, or even with love, although, if one were fortunate, love grew out of marriage. Marriage was a thing planned and negotiated to tighten alliances, transfer land, or increase and consolidate power. It was not a thing a young man of Raymond's position considered on his own. In fact, Raymond had been betrothed for many years to the daughter of a Gascon noble. He was free only because the girl had died a few months previously.

Until this moment, Raymond had hardly thought of his betrothed's death. He had not known the girl, had never seen her. They had been betrothed six years ago, when she was two years old. Had she lived, she would have come to Aix when she was ten. Raymond would have married her when she was twelve, coupled with her after her first flux—if she had not yet begun her regular bleeding—and hoped they would grow fond of each other.

Suddenly, Raymond was aware of a violent distaste for such a marriage. He was shocked at the feeling, scorned himself for being so unseated from reason by a pair of bright blue eyes—yet he never once thought of taking for himself what it would have been natural to take in other circumstances. There was something in Sir William's manner, something in Alys herself, that said flatly, *These are not such people.* This girl was not for sale for money or advantage.

The knowledge brought a sense of loss, of something beautiful slipping away. To shake off the ridiculous notion, Raymond turned his full attention to the steward. He had been surprised when Martin first introduced himself but had not taken the time to wonder why so unsuitable a creature should be steward even of a poor knight's household. He had been trying to think of a speech to make to induce Sir William to accept him, if he raised any objections.

"Are you come in service to the lord?" the steward asked as they walked toward the northeast tower.

"Yes," Raymond answered.

The question seemed odd, but then he remembered

that Alys had not said he was a hireling knight, only that he had come to stay with them. Raymond's heart contracted. She was as kind and good as she was beautiful, for she implied that he was a guest so that he should be treated with greater honor than might be accorded to a knight in service.

"What sort of man is Sir William?" Raymond went on hastily, not thinking that it was a stupid question to ask a servant who obviously could not speak ill of his master. He was only trying to push the thought of Alys out of his mind.

"The kind of man who would find a place of usefulness and honor for such as me," Martin replied.

Raymond was shocked into attentiveness. The words could have been sneering and bitter, but they were not. There was passion in them, a passion of devotion. Martin's large brown eyes, his one beautiful feature, examined Raymond gravely, and then he nodded as if he had come to a decision.

"You were recommended by another lord, one who does not know my master well, I must suppose, or he would have told you how good Sir William is," Martin went on. "You would learn soon enough by being with him, but it is my pleasure to tell you. You see me, crooked of back and twisted of limb and face—so I was born and, being useless, left for God to care for at the gate of Hurley Abbey. There Father Martin took me in—he was abbot in that time, and out of his holiness he gave me his own name and did not let me die."

The steward paused. Raymond opened his mouth, but there was nothing to say, and he shut it again. Martin smiled at him, knowing that the young man was wondering whether the abbot had been cruel rather than kind. In his youth, Martin had also wondered. Now that he was old, he was grateful. With all his sorrows and suffering, he had been granted much joy in his life.

"I could not dig nor herd the sheep nor even clean the rooms," Martin continued, "but my mind was sound. The next abbot, Father Anselm, set me to counting the barrels of wine and salt meat and fish and testing the salt and spices that the abbey bought. I also saw to the necessaries that were portioned out—such things as a steward does. But I was never taken into the Church, for there was none to pay a fee for me and some thought I was not fit for that holy order. Then Father Anselm, being old, died. The new abbot thought my deformities an affront to God, a mark of sin, the seal of Satan. He put me out."

"But—" Raymond protested, horrified.

"It was his right." Martin shrugged. "I was not so calm and easy when it happened," Martin went on. "Now—now I see that it was a great blessing the Lord bestowed on me. It is very foolish to question the beneficent acts of God or to doubt His goodness."

Raymond stared. He was shamed that he should rail against strictures of too much love while this tortured being could praise the goodness of God with such deep sincerity.

"The act that thrust me out and left me to starve brought me to Sir William. In my first bitterness, I went off the abbey lands the quickest way, across the river. But on this side none knew of me and all shut their doors against me in horror. At last, I lay on the road, near dying. Sir William, going by, stopped to inquire what I was, for he is a careful guardian of the peace on his own land and feared lest I should rob or harm his people. In my extremity, I begged—and he looked at me and said, 'You are a stranger to the art of begging. What are you good for?' I told him, fearing that the abbot would deny my tale but fearing more to lie. 'God gave us a good meeting,' Sir William said then, 'for my lady is sick and such skills as yours are needful in my house.' He took me up, filthy and sick as I was, and brought me here. Seeing how all feared me—except my lady Alys who was then scarce more than a babe—he stood over his servants while they tended me, and then he set me over them in a place of honor. You asked me what sort of man he is—I have told you."

"I—then I have come to good fortune," Raymond said.

He could say nothing else, but he was appalled at the thought that he had come to uncover an act of treason in a man of such *caritas*. It seemed impossible that the father of Alys and the protector of Martin could be so flawed. Yet Raymond knew that one thing had no relevance to the other. Only, perhaps, Sir William was himself deceived about the king. The idea came as a relief. If that was the trouble, Raymond assured himself with the unconscious arrogance of youth, he could turn so good a man from that self-destructive path and save Martin his place and Alys—who had done all the kindness in her power to one she thought a poor, friendless hireling—from pain. A man eye-struck into love sees what his heart paints, his eyes being blinded.

After handing him over to Martin, Alys had bid a maidservant choose out guesting clothes of the middle sort to give to Martin for the new knight and had taken herself into her father's chamber in the southwest tower. "There is a faint stink of bad fish about Sir Raymond," she said. "I put him in the northeast tower—"

"Alys," William teased, "are you so cruel as to lead him to think you are as struck with him as he was with you? Why not a cot in the hall? And what do you mean —bad fish? He is another of that ragtail crew that follows the court, but at least he has come with the intention of doing honest service for his living."

"Honest? Are you sure?"

The laughter left William's eyes and voice. "What do you mean? The lad is poor enough—"

"Is he?" Alys interrupted. "Did you see his sword?"

William laughed, good humor restored. "Of course. Do you think I would miss a thing like that? Do not be a fool, Alys. Men often do without food and drink to buy such a weapon or, if it has been given them, would starve gladly before they would part with it. I would."

That was true. Alys frowned. Could she be seeking bad signs because she found Sir Raymond's thin, dark face with its pale eyes so attractive? She had not protested when her father said the young man was struck with her. Alys did not suffer from any mincing false modesty and knew her features to be the very image of those lauded in every romance written or sung by minstrels. They were all there—the flawless white skin, pink cheeks, strawberry lips, blue eyes, gold hair, full breast, swan's neck. . . . Say it, and she had been praised for it.

Two things had saved Alys from self-destructive vanity. One was knowledge of the dichotomy between Martin's beauty of soul and loathsomeness of body. That object lesson on the worthlessness of physical beauty alone was driven home by her constant contact with the old steward. The second was more subtle. Alys knew her father loved her and, in a way, thought she was the most beautiful and most perfect creature on earth. However, she also knew that he would have thought the same even if she had been as deformed as Martin. Papa loved his daughter. That she was fair of face and form was a happy and rather amusing accident but totally unimportant. In fact, Alys was well aware that her father was not much drawn to her kind of beauty. It was another kind of woman entirely that he desired.

Thus, although she recognized her effect upon men and did not hesitate to use it when she needed to, she was not really puffed up by her appearance. Most of the time it was a nuisance, for it was necessary to fend off unwanted attentions.

This time, however, Alys had been aware of a flicker of interest within herself when Sir Raymond's eyes fixed on her. Was it because he was more interesting to her—and she knew she should not be interested in a penniless knight who came to serve her father—that she found so many suspicious signs surrounding him?

"Perhaps you are right, papa," she said hesitantly, "but his manner—that bow—I do not know. . . . It seemed finer than it should for so simple a knight."

William frowned slightly. "Why does he have to be a simple knight? Did you see his shield—a head without a face? And it is new, nearly unmarked. He is denying his past. Many high families have been thrown down—"

"Not in Aix—you said he came from Aix."

"The king's letter said he came from Aix—yes, and so does his speech say it—or, at least, it says he comes from the south. What the devil are we talking about anyway? If Raymond is not a poor knight—simple or not—seeking a living less uneasy than the tourney route or selling his sword in a war—what is he doing here?"

"That, papa, is what I am asking you. Why should the king send *us* a knight?"

"Why should he not?" William rejoined. "It is one less mouth to eat at his table, one less suit of clothes for which he must pay. Moreover, he would be doing a kindness to both Raymond and myself. Henry *is* kind, He enjoys doing kind things. If Raymond suits me and Marlowe suits him, we will both be grateful—and Henry likes gratitude also."

Alys nodded. Her father was right. Everything he said was reasonable, and Uncle Richard might well have mentioned Sir Peter's and Harold's deaths to the king. The brothers chatted about all kinds of things. They were warm friends—when Richard was not driven wild by Henry's behavior and Henry was not enraged by Richard's criticisms. Only . . . only what? Alys sighed. There was nothing to be suspicious about. Her father might be the best and wisest man in the world, but he was not one of the great ones whom the king felt obliged to watch. The only connection he had with the power structure of England was through Uncle Richard, and Alys knew the king would not set a spy on his brother.

That drew a smile from her. The last thing King Henry wanted was someone else to tell him what Uncle Richard thought. Uncle Richard was far, far too likely to be telling him what he thought himself—at the top of his lungs and in public. Papa was *always* begging him to talk softly in private, to appeal to the king's better nature. Henry did have a better nature, and it was not impossible to lead him gently away from the silly things he sometimes wanted to do.

Uncle Richard was growing quite clever about it, although it made papa's life harder. The rage had to come out somewhere. Since he had stopped shouting at his brother, Uncle Richard shouted at papa instead or wrote him long, angry letters. Alys looked fondly down at her father, who had returned his attention to the letter he was trying to answer, frowning worriedly at a vitriolic paragraph in which the earl of Cornwall asked how reason could be applied to a man (meaning Henry) who saw no contradiction in berating the pope for filling English benefices with Italians but was using every measure, fair and unfair, to push a Savoyard into Winchester.

Leaving him to it, Alys started back toward the hall to get to the stair. Her father's low groan, "Damn the man! Why cannot he see the difference between something that will cause a growl and will be forgotten and what will stir the barons like a stick in a hive." Papa was muttering to himself, but the sound bounced off the stone wall and out into the hall where it could be heard some feet from the doorway. Alys's eyes flicked toward the northeast tower.

Most probably papa was right and there was nothing strange about the new knight besides his attractiveness. Nonetheless, Alys decided against moving him out into the hall, at least until papa's outer room could be hung with tapestries that would dull all sound. It was silly, very silly, but her mind would be much easier, and it was even sillier to make herself miserable over a thing so easily cured.

CHAPTER 3

Although he had seemed to dismiss his daughter's suspicions, William was disturbed by them. He was made no easier by Raymond's behavior during supper that night. The young man's manners were more polished than William's own—and William's, because of his training in Richard's company, were better than those of much of the high nobility of England. Raymond's knowledge of the politics of the whole European continent also seemed excessive, and he knew offense and defense in war better from the point of view of the commander than of the common knight.

It was impossible to avoid the knowledge that Raymond was *not* a simple knight, younger son to a man too poor to keep him on his own estates or find him a rich patron. Nevertheless, William also believed what he had said to Alys in defense of the king was true. There was no reason other than a wish to be useful that could have impelled Henry to send Raymond to Marlowe. This, coupled with Raymond's uneasiness when questions were asked about his family, inclined William to believe that the young man came from a good house fallen on hard times. A profligate father who had lost his lands through extravagance or, of course, a father accused of treason, executed, or disseised, was a thing a young man might well be ashamed of and wish to conceal.

The sins of the father should not be visited on the son, yet it would be hard, indeed, for the scion of such a tainted house to find a place, particularly in his own land. Tactfully, William stopped asking questions that were answered with painful care and a flushed face.

Alys, somewhat less willingly than her father, also gave up her probing.

William was reasonably satisfied with his deduction regarding Raymond's origins, but it would be interesting to confirm it. William could, of course, ask Richard, but the earl of Cornwall was not at court just now. Also, William was very wary of suggesting to Richard that there was any ulterior purpose in anything the king did. Richard was sufficiently upset just now by the problems of the see of Winchester and he had very recently been married to Sancia of Provence, Queen Eleanor's sister.

There was another possibility for information, however. Across the river at Hurley was the keep held by Mauger of Ilmer in the right of his wife. William moved restlessly in bed where, unable to sleep, he had been reconsidering Raymond's arrival and antecedents. Mauger had been William's neighbor for nearly ten years, ever since Gilbert and John of Hurley, the two young sons of the former holder, had been set upon while hunting and killed. A soft oath escaped William. Even after ten years, he was not reconciled to those deaths. Gilbert and John had been dear friends.

The killers had not been local, so they could not have murdered out of hatred. Nor could robbery have been the motive. Men do not carry purses nor go decked in jewels when they hunt on their own lands. Granted that Gilbert and John probably had come on the outlaws suddenly and been surprised. Perhaps they had threatened the band and ordered them off the land, although William would never have believed they could be so stupid if the group was large and armed.

It was a puzzle that would never be solved now, William thought, dismissing it from his mind. Mauger was at Hurley and would remain there until his son Aubery was old enough to take over the lands. William smiled. Aubery was a nice lad, in service with Humphery de Bohun, earl of Hereford, now. William sighed and shifted in bed again. Would Alys agree to marry Aubery as Mauger kept urging? It would be nice to have her so close, but she would have to wait another four or five years, and she was really ripe for marriage now. Besides Elizabeth . . . William stopped his thoughts abruptly. If he began to think about Elizabeth, he would never get to sleep at all.

In any case, Elizabeth and Aubery had nothing to do with his present problem, which was Raymond. Mauger might have the answer to that because he spent a lot of time at court and was attentive to every whisper of gossip. William found his jaw set and deliberately relaxed it. He reminded himself for the thousandth time that Mauger was a good neighbor, always pleasant and friendly. He did not encroach on William's lands, or offer hurt to his serfs, or insult, or take more than his share of the river tolls. It was none of his business if Mauger took more out of the land than he put in. Hurley was a rich property, and Aubery would be able to restore it when he took hold—Alys would see to that if she married him.

Right now it was just as well that Mauger did spend his time and money peacocking around at court instead of overseeing his property. No, William reminded himself severely, it was *not* vanity. Mauger's sycophancy and flattery might be so sickening to him that he avoided him like the plague when they happened to be at court together, but what right had he to think ill of it? He had a powerful friend from childhood and did not need to suck around the hems of the great. And Mauger's favor seeking had paid off. It had won Aubery a place in de Bohun's household—quite an elevation for a boy of no particular parentage.

It was his own fault, too, that Mauger had to crawl to find Aubery a place. He should have told Mauger he could obtain a place for the boy in Richard of Cornwall's household—he would gladly have asked that favor of Richard for Elizabeth's son. . . . But he could never bear to mention his friendship with Richard to Mauger. Besides, Mauger was not a man who liked to ask or receive favors. . . .

Nonsense! This time William grunted with irritation and turned over on his stomach. The only one in the world Mauger did not like to ask favors from was himself. Somehow his distaste must show, struggle as he would to hide it. And it was so unreasonable. Why should he dislike the man for doing what he wanted him to do? When he perceived his own thought clearly, William groaned and rolled out of bed, shuddering as the cold floor bit at his bare feet. He ignored the discomfort, pulled his night robe over his shoulders, poured a cup of watered wine, and stalked out to sit in a chair by the banked fire.

Life was such a muddle. He could not bear it that Mauger did not value his wife, yet it would have torn his heart out to see Elizabeth loving and beloved. Who would believe he could be such a fool as to love the woman all these years—twenty years? No, more. He could not remember a time when he did not love Elizabeth. He had adored her when she was four—and fat —tagging after her brothers Gilbert and John to their great disgust and his joy. She and William had sworn they would marry each other. . . .

"Oh damn!" William sighed wearily as rage and grief wrenched him again almost as painfully as it had twenty years ago when his father had told him Elizabeth was married. He had cried out in disbelief, but Sir Gilbert, her father, had confirmed the news. For a long time he had hated her for her weakness, and in the throes of that hatred he had agreed to marry the woman his father proposed to him. Poor Mary. Was she really so stupid, so ineffectual by nature, or had his inward revulsion for her destroyed her?

No. William put down the cup, shook himself, and went back to bed. Mary was Mary. He was not to blame for her. Even if he had showed his dislike, she had been more than ten years older than he. Any normally intelligent woman of twenty-seven, already married and widowed, should have been able to bend a boy of seventeen any way she liked, particularly a hurt and angry boy—and Mary had been physically beautiful, almost as beautiful as Alys. Besides, she had *not* known how she repelled him. From the beginning she had clung to him, leaned on him. No, he was not to blame for Mary. She had been as happy as it was in her nature to be. If anything had destroyed her, it was the death of all the babies.

And Elizabeth was not to blame for yielding to her father's will. What could she do, poor child? How could a girl of thirteen resist? Likely she had not even been told. Sir Gilbert was a good enough man, but he was of the old school. He would have sent Elizabeth away to Ilmer to be married without a word of warning. Sir Gilbert's wife—William wrinkled his brow—he could scarcely remember the pale shadow that had been Elizabeth's mother. She could have done nothing. Sir Gilbert was the kind who did not believe a daughter was worth the food it took to keep her alive. Suddenly William smiled and relaxed. The more fool Sir Gilbert! Alys brought him more joy and solace than a dozen sons.

He had fallen asleep on the thought and woke with it in his mind. It was true, of course, but William knew it was wrong for Alys to be his only heir. He was still young enough to breed up sons. He should have married again as soon as Mary died. Alys's children would be Ilmers—if she took Aubery, God knew what if she married elsewhere. William walked into the hall, his mind still fixed on the distasteful idea of his lineage ending with himself and came up short at the sight of Raymond standing beside Alys at the sideboard. Martin was there too, of course, but at a tactful distance. Alys was laughing at something the young knight had said and looking up at him. William strode forward quickly.

"You are late this morning, papa," Alys cried as soon as he came near.

Raymond bowed gravely. William recognized the tunic he was wearing. It had been Harold's, quite new, and made too large because Harold had still been growing. On Raymond it was a trifle short and straining over the shoulders. That meant Raymond had brought no clothing—a proper beggar. Alys was pouring wine for her father, and Raymond cut a wedge of cheese.

"I must ride over to Hurley this morning," William said.

"Is Sir Mauger at home?" Alys asked sharply.

"I hope so. He was last week and said nothing to me about leaving," William replied blandly.

It was the very devil to have so acute a minx for a daughter, William thought. No words had ever passed between them on the subject of what he felt about Elizabeth, yet Alys knew. It bred in her a strange dichotomy. Alys loved Elizabeth for herself. Even before her own mother had died, she had run to Elizabeth whenever she needed help and advice, and in the last five years Elizabeth had been as good as a mother to her.

Still, Alys was jealous. It showed in little ways. Sometimes when William reproved her, she would snap, "So I am not perfect like Lady Elizabeth. Too bad!" William had never answered that Lady Elizabeth was far from perfect because he had been afraid Alys would perceive the remnant of bitterness in him. It did not really matter if that increased Alys's jealousy. She could do far worse than strive to model herself on Elizabeth.

Then there was the additional tension produced by Alys's having guessed that Elizabeth was the cause of her father's failure to marry again. On the one hand, Alys was as proud of her name as William was. She had never regarded Marlowe as hers. When she married, her husband's property would be hers. Marlowe was where she learned how to be mistress—a practicing ground. Alys wanted there to be a brother at Marlowe. She knew it was important to her safety. If her husband should die, for example, while her children were young and after her father's death, a brother would protect her and her children, fight for her dower rights if need be. Without male relatives, she would be at the mercy of any warden set over her or at the mercy of her husband's male relations.

On the other hand, Alys probably did not relish the thought of a stepmother, a woman who would have the right to rule Marlowe. She had been too long mistress in her own right to step back into second place. From that point of view, she might be grateful to Elizabeth for holding her father's fancy so that he could not bring himself to take a second wife. And so I have thought ten thousand times before, William told himself impatiently. It is an old, old tale. He turned to Raymond.

"Until I return, do you look over the demesne farm. You will find its working much different than in your country. The people are different too, I think, although I had little time to examine such matters when I passed through the southern lands."

"Yes, sir," Raymond agreed quietly.

Alys opened her mouth, but thought better of what she had been about to say. She was wearing a slight frown, but William decided that it was not worth hurting Raymond's feelings by calling Alys aside to speak privately to her. Most likely, being suspicious, she did not want the young man riding alone around the demesne—but surely that was excessive caution. What real harm could he do? And if he attacked or mistreated the serfs—say, raped a woman—that would solve the problem. William could send him away at once as unsuitable.

When he had finished breaking his fast, William took his cloak and went out. While he was eating, he had seen Alys sign to Martin and he knew his horse would be waiting by the outside stair. He mounted the big, brown gelding, and he rode easily over the drawbridge and down toward the town, which sat on an outward bend of the river about half a mile away.

When he reached the outskirts of the town, William pulled the brown beast up and stared. What were they doing in the common field adjoining the river? Marlowe was not a walled town. It was not yet large enough to merit a wall—although it soon might come to that—and was indefensible from the river side anyway. In time of real danger, valuables were removed to the keep and the people followed their goods at the first sign of attack. Thus far Sir William and his ancestors had protected the town quite effectively by attacking first themselves. They had been burnt out only once—

nearly thirty years ago when the late Louis of France had been in England. Since then, there had been no real threat.

Riding closer to the disturbed ground, William snorted in irritation. His suspicions were correct. Those idiots were starting to erect buildings there. Commoners, free or serf, had no common sense! William touched his horse with his heel and rode forward.

"Where is the headman here?" he asked in English, but the man had already run over and was bowing.

"My lord?"

"Take it all down," William growled, gesturing at the standing framework. "You cannot build here. This is common ground."

"But my lord, it is agreed in the whole town. The cattle will not suffer. We are clearing on the north side. There will be sufficient grazing there. The merchant who needs these warehouses has purchased that land and will exchange—"

"Numbskull!" William roared, "What do I care where the cattle graze? If you build on this curve of the river, you will block my view of the town wharfs. Boats could put in here, and I would not see them."

The master builder swallowed. He had been consulted about the site and had given it his approval, but he was thinking only of how far the river might rise in time of flood and whether the ground was firm enough to support the structures required.

"It is not in my power," he pleaded. "I only—"

"It is in *my* power," William snarled. "Take it down and save your timber or I will send down my men to burn it and break a few heads also."

He set heels to his horse again and rode off, picking up his pace so that the horse was near a full gallop by the time he entered the town itself. People scattered in confusion, women screamed and snatched up small children, mules and asses were wrenched out of the way. Coming to a hall at the center of the town, near the guildhall, William reached down and grabbed a shrinking man by the hair.

"Summon me the guildmaster," he snapped.

"Wh-which gu-guildmaster?"

"The one who sits highest in the guildhall, or if he is not here, any other—so long as he be in authority."

The trembling man nodded and ran. Sir William glared around, but the green facing the guildhall was now empty. What the devil was the name of the guildmaster and to which guild did he belong? William had not even realized there was more than one. When he did business with the townsfolk, one man would usually approach him as spokesman. As long as dues and tolls were paid promptly and in full, William did not trouble himself with the town management. It had seemed to work well, but now William began to wonder whether he had been stupid.

It seemed to him, now he thought of it, that fewer and fewer cases had been brought before him when he sat in justice. That was odd because the town had grown in the past few years. Since men were men, it seemed highly unlikely that an increase in business and population could have brought a *decrease* in crime. Neglectful, William told himself. He had been sorely neglectful. In recent years, as Richard became more and more involved with public affairs, William had insensibly been drawn to think more and more about such things—even though he did not go often to court—and less of local matters.

The guildmaster—a guildmaster—was now bowing to him, introducing himself as Thomas Mercer. William told him briefly that he had ordered the building headman to tear down what he had erected and smooth over the pits he had dug. No building was ever to be constructed on that curve of the bank, he ordered.

"But my lord," the guildmaster wailed, "it is perfect dockage. The river has scoured a deep pool there, and ships can—"

"I know that," William snapped. "That is why I forbid buildings there. As the land lies, such buildings would block the view of the docks from the keep."

"My lord, my lord," Mercer cried, wringing his

hands, "we would not cheat you! Never! You may send men to watch the dockings if you will."

William could feel his jaw starting to drop with surprise, and he firmed it hastily. It had never entered his mind that the townsfolk would cheat on fees or tolls. He had been thinking solely of defense. If his guards did not have free and open land down to the river, enemies could bring boats ashore unseen. Even when the guards could not see so far, on moonless nights, for example, the open, slowly rising land was valuable, for sound traveled well along it up to the keep. It would be very hard to land enough men in a silence so profound as to fool the night watch. Buildings would block both sight and sound.

"Naturally you would not cheat me," William said quietly, with a cold threat in his voice. "It would be unsafe and unhealthy to do so, I promise you. That was not my concern. I do not choose to open so inviting a door to enemies. You may, however, build open docks on that bank if you wish."

The chagrin on Thomas Mercer's face would have made William laugh if he had not been so disgusted. The man had intended to cheat. Just a little at first, probably, then more and more if William remained indifferent and unaware. Two considerations saved Mercer from being struck down where he stood, whining about the cost of cartage from such open docks as William was willing to permit and the danger to delicate cargo from being moved in the rain or the hot sun. First, William made a nice profit from tolls and fees paid by merchants, and it would be a mistake to kill one of them in a seeming fit of bad temper over the proposed buildings. Second, Mercer was almost certainly neck-deep in some kind of dishonesty already, or he never would have conceived such an idea.

It was time for a thorough investigation into the town's government. Doubtless sufficient bad practices would be uncovered so that Thomas Mercer could be hanged; this would serve the multiple purpose of giving the man his just deserts, enriching William's purse by the forfeiture of Mercer's property, setting an example to the rest of the merchants of the results of dishonesty, and pointing out clearly that William was no longer going to allow himself to be fleeced.

The whining plea, which now included offers of money, had come to a halt. William looked down and shook his head. "I told the builder and I will tell you. If the timbers are not gone by the time I return, I will send my men down to burn the area clean." His eyes were the color of cold, muddy water behind the long, curling lashes. "Do not try my patience."

Another torrent seemed about to burst forth, but William did not wait to hear it. He urged his big gelding forward toward the river again where, a little to the west, a broad, heavy-bottomed boat lay that served as a ferry. As he did so, William was suddenly surprised at all the events of the morning. Why had he said to Alys he must *ride* to Hurley? Normally he would have taken the boat docked below the keep. Of course, that meant walking up from the village or sending someone over first to say he was on his way so that a horse would be waiting for him.

It almost seemed as if . . . Then William smiled at his own superstition. God, he was sure, did not trouble Himself with whether or not buildings were put up in the town of Marlowe. He had said he would ride because of what he had been thinking last night. When Elizabeth was alone in Hurley, he always took the boat and walked. When Mauger was there, he always rode. William had to smile wryly. He was a fine one to talk about pride. He was worse yet, not wishing either to demean himself by arriving on foot or by asking that a horse be sent to him. William could not help chuckling, despite his fury at Mercer, at his own silly pride, so that he was in a much better humor when he waved a negligent greeting to the guards at the gatehouse of Hurley and rode through.

Hurley was older than Marlowe but not so strong. Although it had both inner and outer walls, neither wall was of the height or thickness of Marlowe's. In a sense, there was no true keep, the inner wall taking its place with the dwelling portions built almost as part of that wall. It made the hall very dark because there were no windows, only arrow slits, on the outer side and the windows on the inner side seldom received the sun. Half blinded by coming in out of the bright bailey, William asked the first person who hurried up to him where Mauger was.

A pretty, tinkling giggle and a rush of scent made William recoil a step. "My lord has gone out," a little-girl voice told him.

"Where is the lady?" William asked harshly.

His clearing sight had confirmed what voice and scent hinted, that he was confronting Mauger's most recent mistress. She was an exquisite thing, fairer than Alys and far more voluptuous, her bosom almost spilling from a too-low-cut bodice and most imperfectly covered by a thin, silk tunic. The loose cotte was too thin also, showing clearly the shape of hip and waist beneath.

William had no objection to women in seductive clothing, but he did not think a married gentleman's home was the place for them. He was no saint and had never accorded even lip service to chastity. He had always been discreet in his infidelities, however. That he did not love his wife was no reason, to his mind, to affront her sensibilities or to be discourteous to her.

"Above, I suppose," the girl tittered. "I am Emma. Can I do something for you?"

William's hand half lifted to strike her for insolence, but her eyes were as empty of sense as a painted doll's. Her French was execrable. Probably she had not meant to be vulgar or insolent.

"Go and ask whether Lady Elizabeth can spare Sir William of Marlowe a few minutes of her time," he said in English.

"I am not a servant," the girl pouted, still speaking in French, which she obviously felt was a mark of status.

That time William might well have hit her, but he was distracted by an older woman's voice, exclaiming in pleasure. Lady Elizabeth's maid, Maud, curtsied, snapped her fingers at another maidservant to bid her bring wine, and led William toward a chair, saying that Elizabeth would be down in a few minutes. Throughout she acted as if Emma was an indecent and unmentionable lump of dirt on the floor that everyone must try to avoid noticing to prevent embarrassment. The blank, open-mouthed confusion with which Emma regarded Maud nearly put William back into a good humor.

This was rapidly dispelled when Elizabeth, coming from the stairway, greeted Emma gravely and pleasantly. William stood up, feeling his face flush with rage. Elizabeth looked at him and smiled slowly. His breath caught. He knew she was not beautiful. Most men would not even have given her a first glance when Emma was by. She was too tall and far too thin, her small bosom hardly lifting her cotte and the full folds of the cloth obscuring what, if any, shape she had. But William knew—her body had been well formed at thirteen—and he did not believe that twenty years or two children had changed it. She was as lean and light as a boy, but far more graceful. Her every movement was an enchantment, as now, when, still smiling, she raised a single long finger to her lips.

William set his teeth against the furious remarks he had been about to make. Elizabeth took his hand and drew him toward a wall chamber. Emma's lips pouted like a petulant child's, and after a minute hesitation, she followed them. William half turned, his free hand rising to strike. Elizabeth tightened her grip on the hand she held.

"You cannot come with us, Emma," she said gently. "Sir William is a very old friend, and he is about to say some very harsh things that will only hurt your feelings. You would not wish to hear them, I assure you." Her lips twitched, restraining laughter, as Emma paused indecisively, trying to work that out. But she did not wait for the girl's slow processes of thought to come to a conclusion; she drew William into the room she had chosen and shut the door.

"What the devil is wrong with you, Elizabeth?" William snarled when they were alone.

"There is nothing wrong with me. I am in excellent health," she replied mischievously.

This room was better lit than the hall, and William had to struggle with his breathing again. Elizabeth watched him with a twinkle in her large, misty green eyes, a strange color like shallow water over pale golden sand. Her nose was a little too long, her mouth too wide for her thin face. She looked more like a naughty elf than a fairy princess. Her complexion was of the earth also, a warm brunet, and her hair, of a nondescript brown, was very fine textured and curly. It was mostly hidden by her wimple now, but little ends had escaped here and there and curled deliciously around her face and forehead.

"Perhaps you cannot drive that creature out," William said in a constricted voice, "but there is no reason for you to treat her with courtesy nor to endure her attempts to usurp your place."

Dear William, Elizabeth thought, he always does exactly the right thing. Mauger had always had a woman or two in the keep but the others had been clever enough to keep out of the way. Emma was simply too stupid to do so. It did not mean anything; Elizabeth knew that. Nonetheless, the open exposure of the thing was painful, shameful. William's fury had turned it funny, although there was nothing funny about the emotion that fueled his rage.

"She cannot usurp my place," Elizabeth replied. "You know that is not Mauger's intention." She paused, watching William's face, and then added softly, "Why should I not be courteous to her? She does me a great service."

For a moment William stood and stared at her without answering. For ten years they had met frequently, sometimes they had been quite alone, as now, yet in all that time no single personal word had passed between them. Of course, William had never before been greeted by Mauger's whore, acting as if she were the lady of the keep, either. William understood that his rage on Elizabeth's behalf had broken through some wall of reserve she had built. It had driven her into making a clear statement of her own feelings about her husband. It was dangerous, horribly dangerous—but William did not care.

"It is disgusting," he said, his voice shaking. "He could at least keep her in the village."

Having already said too much, Elizabeth threw all caution and reason to the wind. "But Mauger likes his comfort. If it should be a chilly or wet night, he would not wish to ride out, and then . . . No! I prefer to have Emma here."

Knowing he was mad and that he would bring his world crashing down around his ears, William took a step forward and pulled Elizabeth into his arms. He almost expected her to cry out or push him away, but she did not resist, allowing her head to fall back so that he could kiss her. And her mouth was as sweet, as warm and willing as it had been twenty years ago. Completely lost, heeding now only the siren song of his long love, William devoured her face, kissing eyes, cheeks, chin, and returning to her lips between. Elizabeth was no passive partner. Her mouth opened under his, inviting the invasion of his tongue, and she clutched him with one arm while she ran her other over his neck and shoulders, down his back, as if she wanted all of him included in the caress.

After a time, William pulled his mouth free. "Come to me, Elizabeth," he begged. "I will honor you as you deserve, I will—"

She put a shaking hand gently over his mouth. "You are asking me to play Emma's role in your home."

"I have no wife," he cried.

"You have a daughter. Should I ask Alys to give countenance to such a thing? Should you?"

"I love you—"

She silenced him again. "If you love me, do not ask me what I desire to give and cannot. William . . . no! Mauger does not deserve that."

"Does not deserve—" he choked. "His behavior—"

"Is as much my fault as his," Elizabeth interrupted. "In the beginning I hated him—hated the world—and made it all too plain. I was fortunate he did no worse than turn aside from me. He is not an unreasonable husband." Then she smiled gently. "You know it is not possible, William. Mauger could not swallow such an affront. It would mean war."

He did know, but he wanted her so much it was like a physical pain. "I could take you to Bix," he said passionately.

A flame leapt in her eyes, then died. She pulled away, out of his arms completely. "We are both mad," she sighed, "to torture ourselves this way. I thought we had passed the danger point years ago. I cannot think what made me say—but you caught me at a bad time. I am so sorry I have broken your peace, William. You know it is not possible for me to leave Hurley. Even if we could keep Mauger and Alys from knowing—and I do not believe that we could—I would lose Aubery and John. I love my sons. Also, I dare not leave Mauger alone in Hurley. So far, I have kept him from despoiling the estate beyond recovery, but if I were to leave . . . You do not know what Ilmer is like—the broken, cowering people, the wasted land. . . . It is not all Mauger's fault, of course. His father ruined the place before Mauger took hold of it, but he never learned anything from the old man except how to spend and to want. He has not the slightest notion of management. William . . ."

She touched his face gently, and he closed his eyes, breathed deeply, opened them. They were blank and bitter. William knew the call of duty. He had answered it many, many times against his will.

"I have had no peace since the day I lost you," he said. "My heart is yours, my house is yours, my strength is yours. When you want any, or all, tell me, and they will be delivered."

"I will take your heart, William. I have need of it, since you have always had mine." She swayed toward him, then drew upright, away from the arms that opened to receive her. "What a fool I am. We must be more sensible, or it will be impossible for us to meet as friends. Please, William. It has meant so much to me to speak to you and to see you sometimes. If we cannot meet without behaving like idiots, I will lose even that. No, please. . . ." He dropped his arms; this time it was Elizabeth who closed her eyes and breathed deep. "What brought you here today?" she asked quietly.

He turned away and walked to the slit window that opened to the north side of the outer ward. At first he did not answer, and Elizabeth could see the muscles working in his jaw. Finally he turned back and told her about Raymond's arrival and Alys's suspicions.

"I thought I would ask Mauger whether he had heard any rumor of other such placements or whether he heard anything about young Raymond himself."

By the time he had got that far, William had calmed down and Elizabeth was also well under control. The flush had died from her cheeks and she was now paler than usual, but her eyes were quiet.

"He said nothing to me," she remarked, "but there was no reason to mention a thing like that. He should be back soon, if you would like to wait."

Struggle as she would, Elizabeth's voice held a faint quiver. William swallowed, torn by emotions he was sure she shared. He could not bear to leave, but he could not bear to stay either. It would do no good to ask Elizabeth which she wanted him to do. To send him away would hurt; to keep him would hurt. Life hurt.

"I . . . are you on easy terms with Mauger just now?" William did not want to push Elizabeth into approaching her husband if the advent of Emma had caused a coolness between them.

"We are always on easy terms," she replied. "Why not?"

William had started to move toward the door, but he stopped. Elizabeth bit her lip in chagrin. She had forgotten how much more perceptive William was than her husband. William had "heard" far more than the words she said. He had "heard" the reiteration of the fact that she did not care enough for Mauger to care when he brought a mistress home. Mauger would never have noticed the fact under the simple remark. Elizabeth, who knew her husband thought she was docile and stupid, took great pleasure in saying things with quite outrageous double meanings to him, knowing he would never catch them.

Before William could speak, Elizabeth shook her head and opened the door. On the threshold of the hall, she stopped so suddenly that William bumped into her. She stepped aside and gestured courteously for him to go forward, but her eyes warned. The boiling ferment inside William congealed. Sitting near the fireplace drinking from a handsome goblet, was Mauger.

Standing back, Elizabeth looked at both men with new eyes. In looks there was no comparison. Handsome, William was not—except for those ridiculous eyelashes. On the other hand, Mauger was handsome, definitely so; his hair was true gold, his mouth well formed, his nose straight, his eyes a lovely blue, innocent and guileless. Was there something in Mauger that repelled her? No, it could not be that. It was simply that she loved William; love was not a matter of face or form.

"I am glad you are back," William said.

To himself, his voice sounded peculiar, but Mauger did not seem to notice anything. Perhaps he would put the stiffness down to William's displeasure at finding Emma putting herself forward so much. If so, all to the good. Mauger said something civil in reply, invited William to sit and offered wine. He did not mention Emma, but asked with more than usual eagerness what he could do for William, as if he were aware of being caught in something disgraceful and were trying to re-win William's esteem. William obliged with a second recital of Raymond's arrival. He was somewhat surprised by the intensity with which Mauger listened.

"No," Mauger said, when he had heard the tale out. "I have not heard of any similar thing nor was the young man at court when I left, so I cannot tell you anything on that score either, but—but I do not like it, William."

"Do not like it? What do you mean?"

"The king is growing more and more suspicious of everyone and everything," Mauger said with great excitement.

"What set him off? I know he was fulminating about Winchester, but when Walter Raleigh went to France—"

"No," Mauger interrupted, "it is the Welsh business. When Llewelyn ap Iowerth decided that David, his son in wedlock from King John's daughter Joan, should rule the whole land, his bastard Gruffydd would not accept it. This Gruffydd claims half his father's estate —on what right I cannot guess."

William nodded. He knew the story much better than Mauger because his old lord, Rannulf of Chester, had been a friend and neighbor of Llewelyn ap Iowerth. He knew why Gruffydd could claim half the estate and find supporters for that claim. It was the Welsh custom that "the son of the handmaid should be heir with the son of the free." To William it seemed quite mad that not only legitimate younger sons were entitled to a share with the eldest but that illegitimate sons had the same right.

Llewelyn had decided to break with custom. Although legitimacy meant little to him, he recognized that David, who was King Henry's cousin, was more fit to rule than Gruffydd, and he had bound his vassals by oaths to obey the younger, but legitimate, son.

William knew the rest of the story too, but he had no intention of interrupting Mauger. He was always careful not to mention his own close contact with high-level policy lest he should be thought to be boasting. Thus, he listened quietly while Mauger explained how Gruffydd, not unnaturally, took exception to this arrangement and how his half-brother David, hearing of his rebellious attitude, had made him a prisoner. But David's power had gone to his head, and in 1241 he contended the ownership of the border fortress of Mold with Henry. David had agreed to submit the matter to arbitration, but he never appeared before the arbitrators, among whom had been Richard.

Mauger noticed William's expression and hurried on, skipping the charges and countercharges that followed, the brief war, in which Henry had an easy triumph because the Welsh princes who were supposed to be subject to David supported Henry instead, and came to the terms of the peace. Before he thought, William sighed and shook his head.

"You did not think them just?" Mauger asked.

Too cautious to fall into the trap of saying the king was an idiot, Mauger replied, "Just or unjust has little meaning in dealing with the Welsh, I fear. I thought the terms would make trouble, and King Henry thought better of certain things himself. The king forgot that all brothers are not Richard of Cornwall. He realized what he planned would never work and took Gruffydd into his own hands."

"Yes, and his captivity was light in the beginning, for he gave his parole, but last spring he violated that oath and tried to escape and, since then, the king has kept him prisoned in the Tower of London."

William knew that too. He and Richard had visited Gruffydd several times. Personally, he did not like the man and had never liked him. Nonetheless, he could not help but be sorry for him. Gruffydd was suffering no hardship, his confinement being eased with every luxury he requested and even the presence of his wife— but it was still confinement.

"So what has changed?" he asked Mauger. "The king has held Gruffydd thus since last June."

"It is said," Mauger replied, a faint note of triumph at his superior knowledge in his voice, "that David has written letters to the pope complaining that the terms of the treaty of 1241 were extorted from him by fear and force, and he has also sent rich bribes to incline the Holy Father to give him permission to set aside those oaths."

William mouthed an obscenity. This, if it was true, was news, and most unpleasant news.

"There is more," Mauger continued with satisfaction. He was delighted with oversetting his neighbor's normal calm. "I have heard rumors that there is a plot to free Gruffydd—and if I have heard, the king has certainly heard also—"

"Free Gruffydd! Who would wish to do that?"

Mauger shrugged. "That I cannot say, but the king is furious. If it were to happen, David could say Gruffydd was loosed apurpose to torment him, and take it as a cause to violate the treaty. In any case, these rumors have set the king to looking about him on all sides for any man who has any connection with the Welsh. You were squire to Rannulf of Chester and served many years near Wales."

"But so long ago—"

"Likely I am wrong," Mauger agreed smoothly, "but it can do no harm for you to mind your tongue in front of this Raymond and keep as much business private from him as you can. The most innocent things can be twisted awry by someone who comes to find wrongdoing or looks at things with a poisoned eye."

CHAPTER 4

Shortly after William left Marlowe, Alys and Raymond followed him. What Alys had started to point out to her father at breakfast, and then thought better of, was that Raymond could not go around the farms on his own. He spoke not one single word of English, and the serfs and villeins spoke no word of French—nor understood it either. Within the keep, most servants, like their masters, were completely bilingual. On the farms, however, only English was used. Thus, the opportunity for misunderstanding between a young man of high estate—Alys was more and more convinced that Raymond was no simple knight—and serfs who were accustomed to being protected from interlopers was too great to be ignored.

There was, of course, no need for Alys herself to accompany Raymond. She could have told Diccon, the master-at-arms, to have gone with him. However, it seemed to her an excellent opportunity to discover more about Raymond. Unfortunately, the expedition started on the wrong foot. Raymond's surprise when Alys said she would go with him made her bristle.

"I know the land and the people best," she said coldly. "As my father is much away, the management of the estate falls to me. What is there in that to make you lift your brows?"

"But a woman—" Raymond protested unwisely.

"I have never noticed that a bull is wiser than a cow or a stallion than a mare—quite the contrary. Led by their noses toward a female's rump, they will fall into any stupidity. So a woman is no less clever than a man, even though she cannot swing a sword—and she is less easily distracted by pretty wives and

58

daughters. Thus, my father trusts me better than a bailiff. You should know, if you intend to serve my father, that most matters of the farms are left to me."

Poor Raymond simply gaped. First, he had never been spoken to like that by a "lady" in his life. Second, his mother and sisters were far too great ladies to trouble themselves with running the house itself, and, as for managing any estate, they would have fainted away with disgust if one of the common serfs approached them.

He heard Alys ordering the saddling of a palfrey for him. "Do you think I am unable to ride a horse?" Raymond gasped, undecided whether he should be outraged or worried that his destrier was being appropriated.

Alys looked at him as if he were a total idiot. "I have no idea," she snapped, "but if your seat is as lacking as your wits, I cannot guess how you won your spurs. What do you think you will learn if your whole attention must be on keeping your stallion in hand? Papa is not too proud to ride a palfrey. Are you better than he?"

"Why should I need to keep my horse in hand?" Raymond asked.

"It is plain you know nothing of overseeing a demesne," Alys said, looking him up and down. "Is it not the habit in your land to ride about the farms? Do not the serfs come running to you, more especially the children? No, I see by your face that you are astonished by what I say. Well, it is so here, and I do not choose to have your destrier trampling papa's people."

Raymond opened his mouth to say sharply that it would be their own faults if they did not know enough to stand clear of a war-horse, but he recalled in time that he was a stranger. He remembered Sir William saying he would find not only the crops but the people different here. He thought ill of a difference that inconvenienced the lord to protect the serf, but he had taken warning from Alys's tone. For some reason, she did not accept his pose, and Raymond thought it would be well not to increase her suspicions. However, once he had gotten over the embarrassment of finding himself astride a docile, old creature that could not, he judged, work up more than a trot without dropping dead, he found what Alys told him of great interest. In no time he was blessing the idly ambling palfrey, which was equally undisturbed by the farm dogs that snapped at his heels, the children who rushed out from the hedges that lined the road to run beside him, and the husbandmen who dashed suddenly from a gate to wave agricultural implements in his face while they screamed gibberish at Alys.

The first time the latter happened, Raymond reached for his sword—which he was not wearing because Alys had asked him caustically which of her servants he was planning to hew down.

"A son has been born in their house," she said to Raymond. "Wulf wants me to look at the babe."

When they reached the mud and wattle hovel, he asked, "You are going in there?"

"Yes, of course. Do you expect a two-day babe to walk out to me? The woman has not been churched yet and cannot come out. I will not be long."

She was not and came out smiling, although she breathed deep to get the stink of the place out of her nose. "A very likely babe," she said approvingly, as Raymond cupped his hands for her to step in to mount. "I hope it lives. The poor woman lost two children this past winter, although one was only a daughter."

"They are very free with you," Raymond said stiffly.

"How so free?" Alys looked surprised. "All creatures wish to show their young to their masters. Does not my bitch pull me by the skirt to admire her pups? Why should Wulf be more shy? Both serve papa well, and both need a pat now and again to show we notice them."

That seemed quite logical. Raymond nodded, suddenly realizing that he had lost a level of society. As he and his father would occasionally stop at the manor of a very minor vassal for a special event—a wedding or the knighting of a son—so Alys, daughter to a minor vassal, visited a hut to do honor to her servants. Once he recognized the situation, it lost its repugnance. Raymond began to ask questions about the tenure of the land, how rents were paid, how many serfs compared to how many villein freeholders there were. Alys answered readily, all the information at the tip of her tongue.

By the time they turned homeward, they were arguing freely on the relative merits of rents in money or in kind and whether it was more economical to take labor service from serfs or higher rentals from free men and then pay for labor. From time to time Raymond lost the thread of the argument when he contemplated the sweet, rosy lips from which the words came.

Alys did not lose the thread of her conversation, because she knew her subject so well, but scarcely half her mind was given to the argument. The rest of her thoughts considered Raymond himself. There could no longer be any doubt that he was the scion of a really great house. Rentals in terms of marks, rather than pennies, and labor in terms of knight service, rather than sowing and reaping, could only be the business of the son of a high noble.

Alys, however, was no nearer knowing what Raymond's purpose was. He showed no contempt or indifference to what she was telling him. And she did not think the interest was spurious. He was clearly giving his mind to the subject, except for a momentary distraction now and again. The cause of that was obvious because of the way his eyes rested on her face—and it made him all the more attractive to Alys. Admiration was written large in Raymond's eyes, but not one word of praise or entreaty passed his lips. The self-restraint was admirable. The lively intelligence was refreshing. All in all, Alys found Raymond the most attractive young man she had ever met.

If only she had been able to guess what his purpose was—what the king's purpose was. If it were evil, she could settle her mind to dislike and distrust Raymond, in which case he would soon be gone. But Alys wished very much that Raymond's purpose were innocent. She was lonely for the company of someone young of her own class. She missed Harold, with whom she had gone hawking and played games. It would be so nice if . . .

To curb her treacherous feelings, Alys went to report her findings to her father as soon as she was back in the keep. He was where she wanted him to be, engaged in finishing his letter to Richard of Cornwall.

"Raymond is no simple knight, papa," she said as soon as she closed the door.

William looked up at her. "No, I thought not myself. Has he told you—"

"He told me nothing of himself, but I took him over the demesne as you—"

"*You* took him!" William exploded, laying down his quill and pushing the parchment out of his way. "I thought you had more sense than to go riding alone with a man we know nothing about. What the devil—"

"Oh, papa, do not be so silly. What do you think he could do to me astride a horse? Besides, I am not such a fool. I was riding Vitesse and I had him atop old Bonté."

That made William laugh, although he was still annoyed with Alys. He had to admit she had not been in any danger. The old gelding had never had much of a turn for speed. On her fleet mare, Alys had not been likely to be captured. Yet . . .

"What made you go with him? Surely he is old enough to ride around the farms without getting lost."

He did not like the interest Alys was showing in this young knight. Perhaps he should put aside the idea of her marriage to Aubery. It was selfish to make her wait just so that he could have her near him. There had not seemed to be any hurry because he had never perceived in Alys the slightest interest in any of the men, young or old, who passed through Marlowe. However, if her heart was ready to love, he had better ask Richard about a suitable man for her. Besides, Aubery and Alys might not suit. They were very friendly, but always competing for who should lead, and Elizabeth said . . . William's heart lurched at her name.

"What is the matter, papa?" Alys cried, reaching toward him across the table. "Did Sir Mauger say that Raymond was a danger to us?"

"No, not at all," William replied, furious with himself for showing a distress he could not explain. "It has nothing to do with him. Why are you so concerned —and why 'Raymond' rather than 'Sir Raymond'? I want to know why you chose to ride out with him?"

"Because he does not speak a word of English, papa. What *is* wrong? Why should I say 'Sir Raymond' to someone who is little more than a servant in our house? I went rather than sending Diccon or one of the other men because I wanted to find out what I could about him. And—and he is *not* what he says he is. He does not know the things that Harold knew, and he knows things he should not. Shall I drive him out, papa? I can do it by—"

"No," William interrupted, much calmed by Alys's willingness to be rid of Raymond. "There is nothing in what Mauger had to say that reflects on Raymond, although Mauger thought there might be. I will tell you about that presently. As for Raymond's past condition, I judge the same as you. He has a style and a way that shows high breeding."

"Then what is he doing here? Why did he lie to us?"

"I do not believe he did lie to us," William replied consideringly. "He said nothing other than that he hoped I would give him a place in my household— and I believe that to be true. I think his family has fallen upon bad times. Perhaps they were ruined by ambition or vice or, even more likely, fell afoul of the king of France."

"I see. Of course, he would be ashamed of that and not wish to tell us—or anyone. And it is reason enough to leave his own country where he would be known and might be suspected or pitied. Yes. That is quite reasonable, papa. But what did Sir Mauger say?"

"Oh, he knew nothing of Raymond. Apparently Raymond did not arrive at court until after Mauger had gone. What Mauger did not like was that the king had sent him at all—because, he says, Henry is growing more suspicious of everyone and everything."

Alys gasped. "Then he may be a spy. He—"

William guffawed. "A spy on what? How many lambs are being born? Alys, have a little sense. You know I have no influence on the doings in the see of Winchester and no connection any longer in Wales."

"Wales? What—"

A scratch at the door interrupted her, and William called, "Enter." Raymond stood in the opened doorway.

"I am sorry to interrupt, sir. The messenger you asked for is waiting, and Martin was not in the hall, so I—"

"Good," William said, and then, impatiently, "well, call the messenger in and come in yourself. In fact, sit down for a minute. You, too, Alys. Just let me add two words to this letter and seal it."

He picked up his quill, dipped it, glanced over his retelling of what Mauger had said about David and Gruffydd, and wrote, "Most likely you know all this already, but, if it has not come to your notice, that would be particularly interesting because it would mark a special effort to keep you in ignorance. Sir Mauger might be wrong about any or all of the facts, but he is skillful at picking up rumor and has a son in Hereford's household. Both David's appeal to the pope and this rumor of freeing Gruffydd smell of trouble to me—if true. I hope Mauger is mistaken as to the facts, but, if so, why are these tales flying about? It can do no harm to lay your ear to the ground. In haste, with love from myself to you and respect to Lady Sancia, William."

He rolled the parchment, sealed it with string and wax, then handed it to the messenger. "To Earl Richard with what haste you may make. I think he is still at Wallingford. Put it into his hands only."

The man bowed and left. Raymond felt like weeping. He had hoped so hard that the king's suspicions would be groundless, and then this—a letter to be put into the Earl of Cornwall's hands only. That meant that the content was dangerous if read by someone else, but what could a simple knight have to say to an earl that could be dangerous?

"I have just had some news from Sir Mauger," William said, almost as if he were answering the question in Raymond's mind, "that concerns your service with me, Raymond."

"Who is Sir Mauger?" Raymond asked in surprise. "I have never heard of the man before."

"No, you would not. He is my neighbor, across the river, and spends a good part of his time at court." William went on to tell again the tale he had written to Richard. "You see," he finished, "if either is true, it is likely to mean war with Wales."

Alys drew in her breath sharply, and Raymond gritted his teeth, expecting a wail of protest followed by hysterics. William, however, did not glance apprehensively in her direction, as Raymond's father would have done. In fact, Raymond could not imagine his father making such an announcement in the presence of his wife or daughters. William's eyes remained fixed on Raymond, and he went on speaking quite calmly.

"If there is war, it is very likely that you will have to fight in it if you take service with me. By my tenure of Marlowe and Bix, I am required to furnish two knights and seventy footmen to Richard of Cornwall, who is my overlord. It is near certain that the king will call on his brother to support him, and if Richard goes, I go. Now, war in Wales is a very nasty business."

"War is always a nasty business," Alys said bitterly.

William laughed. "You are prejudiced, my dear. I do not blame you. You have the bitter of it without the better. For men, war has its good points when fought in a normal manner, but as I was saying, war in Wales often does not go by the usual rules and can become very dirty work. I can see no reason why you should be mixed into such a business, Raymond."

"Do you have some reason, sir, to impugn my courage?" Raymond asked tightly.

"Good God, no!" William exclaimed, fighting a desire to grin and add injury to insult—all unintended. "Nor did I mean to cast the slightest shadow on it. If I had heard that Richard was going to Normandy or Gascony, I would not have given it a second thought. But there is nothing to be won in Wales, except hard blows. If we take a Welsh keep, it will be bare bones of stone; if we take an English one overrun by the Welsh, what would be left in it—if anything—will already belong to the king or one of the Marcher lords. It just seemed unfair to me that you should fight so hard without even a hope of booty or ransom."

Raymond blinked, then bit his lip. He had almost asked haughtily what need William thought he had for booty or ransom. That would have been a prime piece of stupidity and totally foreign to the part he was playing. "I did not come to take service with you in the expectation of booty or ransom," he said.

The remark had the merit of being true, but Raymond was very much troubled. Was this an attempt on the part of Sir William to be rid of him? If so, what had made the man suspicious? On the other hand, Raymond thought, his heart lightening, if he had not given cause for suspicion—and he could think of nothing unusual he had done or said—it was just as likely that Sir William meant no more than he had said. It would be the most natural thing in the world for a considerate man to warn one he thought in need that a campaign would not be profitable.

Alys had grimaced with disgust when Raymond spoke what she felt to be a peculiarly male idiocy. She had learned, however, that it was useless to protest against the lust of men to fight. Her mother had wept and wailed, pleading with papa to hire a knight to fight in his place and sending him tragic letters with all the bad news in the hopes that it would bring him home. All she succeeded in doing was making papa hide things from her.

"But it is not certain," Alys said hopefully. "How could Sir Mauger know what Prince David did or did not do?"

"I did not say he did know," William rejoined. "It is a rumor spread in the court."

"By whom? Perhaps this is William of Savoy's way to divert attention from Walter Raleigh's woes?"

"Alys!" William exclaimed. "That is ridiculous! And for God's sake, do not dare say it to Richard if he should come here."

"Is Uncle Richard coming?" Alys asked joyfully, momentarily diverted even from the question of war.

"He might, if he is still at Wallingford and if he has not already heard what I told you."

"Oh, goodness," Alys gasped, "will he bring Countess Sancia?"

"Now how can I tell you that?" William asked, smiling indulgently. "I do not even know whether Richard will come. If he wishes to spend the night, he will send ahead and let us know. But Alys, I am serious. Not one word of such a stupid idea about William of Savoy."

Raymond had barely restrained himself from gasping when Alys did. The one thing the king had not considered was that Richard of Cornwall might bring his bride—who was also Raymond's aunt—to his friend's keep. Naturally, if Sancia laid eyes on Raymond, there would be no question of maintaining his pose. Internally, Raymond writhed with embarrassment at the thought of explaining himself. It was fortunate, he thought, that Sir William's attention was wholly on Alys and hers on him, or both might have wondered what there could be about Countess Sancia to make their hireling knight red as fire.

In this, Raymond underestimated William, whose quick eye had caught both the stiffening when Sancia's name was first mentioned and the blush that followed. It seemed a confirmation of his deductions that the young man should be so affected. Very possibly Sancia knew him from the days before his family had been ruined. William was annoyed with himself for forgetting to mention such a possibility to Richard so that he could warn his wife to pretend ignorance. But he had not wanted to mention Raymond or how he arrived at Marlowe at all. So far, between his interest in his new lady and years of experience, Richard had behaved with great circumspection in his opposition to the king's persecution of Walter Raleigh. However, the tone of this last letter indicated that the Angevin temper was rapidly pushing its way through both preoccupation and experience.

Recently, Raleigh had been hounded like a felon. The gates of Winchester had been closed against him by order of the king. His goods had been confiscated, his friends forbidden to give him food and shelter. Richard could not tolerate this injustice and, in addition, could see that the other prelates and the nobility were growing resentful of Raleigh's treatment. Thus, Richard had changed his stand and began to try to induce Henry to drop the matter. His approach was delicate at first. Nevertheless, although William of Savoy had himself begun to express doubts, Henry remained adamant, and Richard was beginning to lose patience.

Because he was distracted by his concern for Raymond from the primary object, which was to keep Richard from boiling over, William unwisely brought William of Savoy back into his daughter's mind. He could have kicked himself for it. Had he just kept his mouth shut, Alys would have concentrated on the possible visit of Sancia and busied herself with household matters.

Now her eyes sparkled, and she said, "Why is it stupid?"

"William of Savoy is a good and clever man," her father replied sourly. "He would never think there could be any ultimate benefit in stirring up a war. Besides, even if he has lost his mind and becomes possessed of devils and *has* done such a thing, it would be far better for everyone if Richard did not know it."

"How can you say that?" Alys cried. "How can it be better for a false rumor to start a war—"

"Do not talk like a fool," William snapped. "If it is a false rumor, it will not start a war, and Richard's patience is already much strained by the difference of opinion between himself and the king on the treatment of the bishop-elect of Winchester. I will not have anything said—no matter how silly and no matter that it comes from the mouth of a chit who should know better—that could further inflame Richard against his brother. Are you an idiot, Alys, to think of such a thing?"

Her eyes dropped. "I am sorry, papa. I do not want a war."

Raymond had forgotten completely his concern over his aunt's possible discovery of him. What he had just heard virtually proved his uncle-by-marriage was wrong about Sir William. Far from inciting Richard against the king, Sir William seemed intent on keeping the earl of Cornwall and his brother on good terms. But there must be substance to the rumor William described. Raymond remembered that Henry had said to him that there was trouble in Wales.

"Sir—" he began, then hesitated, realizing he probably should not know of such things. But William was looking at him questioningly, and he had to say something. "Do you mean that the Earl of Cornwall would rise against his brother?" It was a question a stranger might safely ask, and the answer might well amplify or confirm the opinion he had of Sir William's innocence.

"Of course not," William replied smiling. "I do not believe anything could make Richard into a rebel, but certainly not a difference of opinion about the disposition of the see of Winchester. However, there is much bad feeling about it, and it would be better for all concerned if the king yielded and found some other see for William of Savoy. The thing is, if Richard loses his temper, he will shout and rant—as likely as not in public—and tell Henry a few home truths about being stupid and stubborn."

"But that is no way to bring the king to reason," Raymond protested.

William laughed. "You know it, and I know it—and Richard knows it too. But the Angevins have tempers. It is said that the king's grandfather rolled on the floor and chewed rugs and pillows when his rage became ungovernable. Thus far Richard has spoken the king most fair, entreating him gently to reconsider and seek a new solution that will content everyone. I would not for the world have a word said—true or untrue—that would overset him."

That seemed to settle the matter. Raymond could not believe this scene was set up to deceive him. It had come about too naturally. Besides, there had not been the smallest sign that Sir William or Alys was trying to hide anything. There was no need for Sir William to have given his letter and instructions to the messenger in Raymond's presence. If he had not been bidden to sit down, he would have left the room; he would never have known a letter had been sent to Richard or that it was to be delivered into his hands only. Thus, Sir William had no cause to hide those facts.

There was then only the question of how Sir William felt about the war in Wales. He had said already that if Richard went, he would go also, but would he try to prevent Richard from going? "You say there is no profit in fighting the Welsh. Will you urge Earl Richard to try to divert the king from that also?"

"No. I doubt he will speak against it, and I certainly will not. If David ap Llewelyn is trying to break the agreement he made, he needs a lessoning. For myself, I do not at all mind a campaign in Wales. I only thought I should warn you that you will get no more out of it than your shilling a day."

Alys uttered a frustrated sob, and Raymond stiffened and turned toward her, but William only said warningly, "Now, Alys!" and her face composed itself. Raymond could hardly believe such a marvel of self-command in a woman. He made some suitable remark about it being a poor kind of service that was only content with extra reward, and William smiled at him warmly. The young were always generous of their strength, being so sure they had enough and to spare of it—and of time also—to win a fortune.

Then he said gently, "Alys, will we eat today or not?" and she started out of the unhappy thoughts masked behind her quiet features and jumped up to see whether the tables were laid for dinner. Raymond rose also, and William nodded dismissal at him pleasantly.

When they were gone, he covered his eyes with his hands and let out a long breath. He hoped he would be able to eat enough so that Alys did not notice he was out of sorts. Welcome a war in Wales? He would welcome a cataclysm that shook the earth! Anything that would take him away from Marlowe would be welcome. How the hell was he going to sit here, two miles away from Elizabeth? . . . He could feel the muscles in his legs tense with the desire to get up and go to her.

Ridiculous! For ten years they had lived two miles apart. But he had not known how much contempt and dislike she felt for her husband. He had not held her in his arms, nor tasted her lips, nor realized that she had loved him as quietly and hopelessly as he loved her all those years. If Mauger should die . . . William removed his hands from his eyes and they made fists. No. Mauger had done nothing in himself to merit hatred. He had his faults—he was vain and ambitious and a bad landlord and he cared nothing for his wife's comfort and self-respect—but he was not cruel or brutal or even dishonest.

There was no way out of this coil—none. Why had Elizabeth not stood fast? When his father had first announced to him that he was to marry the heiress of Bix, he had said no flatly. He would have Elizabeth of Hurley or no one. For days his father had reasoned and pleaded; then he descended to more direct methods of persuasion. William had been beaten, confined to a dank wall chamber, threatened with everything old Sir William could think of. He would have endured forever, or died, but Elizabeth had yielded. Why? Why?

Stop being a fool, William told himself. She was thirteen, a frightened child in a strange keep with no one to turn to. She did not betray you. She could not help it.

CHAPTER 5

Lady Elizabeth had sat quietly as her husband and the man she had loved all her life discussed the knight who had come to William's keep and the pending trouble in Wales. She did not really hear what they said, although her body seemed to throb in response to William's voice. Why had he yielded, Elizabeth asked herself bitterly. He was older than she, stronger than she. If she had been able to resist being beaten, locked up, fed nothing but bread and water—and not much of that—why had William broken the oath they had sworn to each other?

She rose when the men did, but did not accompany them out of the keep. Like a sleepwalker she said a formal farewell and issued a formal invitation to her guest to return. Then she went up the stairs to her own chamber and closed the door. There she sat in a chair beside the banked embers of the morning's fire. She tried to free her mind of old grief, but the feeling of being betrayed had been renewed, almost as fresh and bitter as when her father had first told her that William was married. Perhaps she would not have believed him if he had not enjoyed telling her so much. They had been through the familiar pattern. . . .

"You will go to Ilmer and marry Sir Mauger."

"I will not. I will escape on the road and take sanctuary. If I am watched too close, I will refuse at the altar. If I am made unconscious and answers given for me, I will escape from Ilmer and take sanctuary and seek annulment by right of forced unwillingness. I will marry no man except William of Marlowe."

She had waited, braced for the beating that would come, eyes full of tears, trembling and wincing away

73

from the pain of blows on her already bruised body—
but no blow had fallen. Her father had laughed.

"You will not marry William, for he is wed already
to Lady Mary of Bix."

And while she was still stunned, he had led her out
to confront William's father, who had confirmed the
news. Seeing her battered countenance, old Sir William
had looked distressed. "You must understand,
Elizabeth, that marriage is not a matter of childish
dreams. With your brother Gilbert already contracted
to my daughter Alys, there is no reason for another
blood bond between Hurley and Marlowe. Your
brother John must be provided for. Your daughter's
portion is simply not enough for my heir. William has
accepted Lady Mary. She brings a most comfortable
estate, plus the keep at Bix, into our family."

What galled her worst of all was that "has accepted."
The words rang in her head for months so that all
through the trip to Ilmer and her marriage, she was like
a lackwit. She thought of how she had suffered, the pain
and fear and hunger and thirst—and William "had accepted"
a better offer. She hated herself for being a
fool, hated William for having made a fool of her, hated
Mauger simply for existing. But life rolls on.

The shock of her husband's blatant infidelities as
soon as she was with child had, oddly enough, restored
Elizabeth's balance and her sense of humor. It was
when she heard herself muttering, "I will kill him,"
that she began to think rationally. Kill him for what?
she asked herself. Do I want him abed with me? The
answer was no. She had made it clear that she found
her husband loathsome. Was it so unnatural that he
should salve his pride by bedding a mistress openly?

Aubery's and John's births had given her someone
to love, and then all her father's plans had come undone.
First William's sister Alys had died in childbirth
and the child with her; then Gilbert and John. . . . That
memory hurt. Such a senseless, inexplicable way they
had died—and Elizabeth had loved her brothers, who
had always tried to shelter her from their father. So

they had come back to Hurley, she and Mauger, for her father had been broken when his sons were killed and he had not outlived them long.

By then Elizabeth no longer hated William. She herself had made expedient adjustments to life for the sake of her own comfort and she understood such expediencies better. Was she not already thinking in terms of advantageous marriages for her boys? It was just as well she had adjusted because Mauger, casting his eyes over the lands of Marlowe, insisted that they be good neighbors and dear friends with those so close to them. He had ridden over to visit, had seen five-year-old Alys, and had come back full of a proposed union of the estates. How he induced William to come to Hurley, Elizabeth did not know, but the instant their eyes met she knew William had not forgotten. And as soon as she saw him with Mary, another pain had been salved. William was no happier with his wife than she was with Mauger.

He had been stiff at first, formal and awkward, but time had smoothed their meetings until the easy exchange of thought and laughter between them had become a pleasure once more. Then Mary died. For months misery and jealousy tortured Elizabeth again. This time William would choose a wife for himself and, naturally, he would choose a girl that he could love. But William did not marry. Years passed and Elizabeth grew happy, even though she often lay awake at night tortured by unfulfilled desire. She mothered his daughter, teaching her the women's skills that Martin did not know.

And now . . . Mauger had had many mistresses, but none of them had been so incredibly stupid as Emma. In the presence of a noble visitor, the preceding whores had the sense to make themselves scarce. William's rage had undone her. It had showed her that he had never shamed his wife in the same way, no matter how little he cared for her, and the rage had also salved a hurt she did not know she had borne. The passion she had hidden so long broke its bounds. She would have given herself to him with joy, if only he had not said those words.

I will honor you as you deserve. How dared he! He had betrayed her once. When it became convenient, would he not betray her again? Even as the bitter thought passed through her mind, Elizabeth knew it was unfair. William had loved his father. It is a hard choice between love and love, and William was only seventeen, his best friend the richest earl in the kingdom. The need for a greater estate must have been very clear to him, even if she, who had never been to court nor mixed with those far richer than herself, did not then understand. She understood now. Mauger never ceased to cry of his poverty, of his need to make a show to impress those who could advance his sons' positions.

Because life had taught her tolerance, Elizabeth did not wound William by speaking her bitterness aloud. Besides, she loved him. That he had given her up for profit was a weakness she could never forget nor completely forgive, but it had no effect on her love. And he had been steadfast for five years. He could have married and married very well. Yet—he did not marry. Surely that was for her.

The bitterness faded. Elizabeth's green eyes glowed as she recalled instead the heat of William's mouth, the blessed strength of his arms around her. She wanted him . . . wanted him! Yet all the things she had said were true. She loved her sons. Was it right to burden them with a mother who could rightfully be called "whore"? It would bring war. William's hope of concealing her at Bix was foolish. It would certainly be the end of any hope that Alys would wed Aubery.

That, at least, would be no disadvantage, Elizabeth thought, temporarily diverted from her own troubles. It had been some years since she had thought that that marriage could possibly be happy. At first, when Aubery and Alys were children and played pleasantly together, Elizabeth had been as enchanted with the idea as Mauger had been, and supported it warmly. In recent years, however, she realized that Alys had been mothering Aubery, that she was far older than he in emotions and outlook, and that as Aubery matured and noticed this, he strove constantly to dominate Alys. This, Elizabeth knew, would be disastrous to a marriage between them. Both Alys and Aubery had much good in them, but Alys needed a man who would appreciate her strength and Aubery needed a woman who would appreciate his.

She had already mentioned this problem to William. He agreed that it was something to consider but felt that it was too soon to reject the relationship out of hand. Elizabeth understood that the attraction of having his daughter so near him, of not losing her entirely, made William unwilling to face the facts. That had annoyed Elizabeth at the time, but now when she thought of it her throat tightened with unshed tears. Poor William. He was lonely.

She was lonely also. Perhaps she and William . . . No. It was best not even to think of it. She was still young enough to get with child, and that was surely a way to come home by Weeping Cross. Mauger had not been in her bed for many years. Tears filled her eyes. She had said she needed William's friendship, but could they be friends now?

She heard a shod horse clattering over the planks of the drawbridge over the inner ditch. It seemed to her that Mauger and William had stood talking a very long time after they had left her. Had Mauger noticed anything different in her manner? William's voice had been as usual—or had it? Elizabeth had not dared look at him. Had Mauger noticed that? She was of so little interest to him—except that she saved him the cost of a steward—that he had never noticed previously how much she looked at William.

But, Elizabeth was totally mistaken. Although it was generally true that Mauger, who was by no means stupid, did not pick up the sly double entendres his wife used to relieve her feelings about him and that he did regard her as a dull and docile domestic animal, he was enormously proud and possessive. He had no intention that any other man should be able to use his property or cuckold him and was always alert to signs of incipient betrayal.

Elizabeth's rejection of him and lack of interest in any other man during the first five years of their marriage had nearly convinced Mauger that she was a sexless creature only capable of breeding. Then William of Marlowe had come to Hurley and could not, no matter how he struggled, keep his eyes for long from her. That had set up a train of thought in Mauger's mind.

Marlowe was a rich holding, richer than Hurley partly because the town of Marlowe held the docks for the river traffic. The tolls were shared, since Hurley commanded the river also and could stop the traffic if the demands of its holder were not satisfied. Yet the profit from the town itself, from the merchants and artisans who sold to the boatmen and repaired the boats, went to Marlowe alone. It would be very nice, Mauger thought, if he owned Marlowe too. And the hot spark in Sir William's hazel eyes held out a hope of how that could be arranged.

Within the year the families visited back and forth frequently and the children were fast friends. Mauger proposed that Alys and his son be contracted in marriage. William, his eyes on the happy children and his memory full of how Elizabeth and he had played and loved, young as they were, was ready to agree. There was no thought in William's mind that Mauger desired Marlowe. Mary was alive and, in fact, breeding when the proposal was first made. Although many babes had died, Alys lived, and the next to live might be a son.

It was Mary, limp, colorless Mary, who objected. She did not wish her daughter to be contracted until she had a son alive and likely to live to maturity. There would be plenty of time for a formal contract. Let it go for now as a hopeful possibility. If she had no son, she pointed out to William when they were alone, Alys, heiress of two rich holdings, could look far higher than Aubery for a husband.

William had explained to Mauger, saying frankly that

he did not care for a greater marriage but that Mary asked very little of him, ever, and he would not go against her will in this, especially at this time. Mauger was annoyed, but he concealed it well, comforting himself with the fact that the longing in William's eyes when he looked at Elizabeth grew and grew. It would do no harm to let the man heat up a little more. Then, when the children were betrothed, he would thrust William and his wife together. Doubtless the man would try to take her. He would hear of it, spy on them, rush in on them—an offended husband—and kill the insulter of his wife. By right of the betrothal of the heiress to his son, Mauger would then hold Marlowe. Mary could go back to Bix. He would arrange for her to die there after a decent interval so she could not marry again and complicate the inheritance.

The plan was excellent—only it had not worked. As Mauger came back into the hall, a flash of irritation ran through him. Without ever seeming to object, William had managed to avoid a formal betrothal or even a formal promise. Mauger had never really dared to press too hard. He disliked William intensely. Under the smooth and courteous exterior, William was rock hard —and he had a sickening sense of honor. For all the heat of his looks and in spite of being insinuated into various private and even intimate situations with Elizabeth, he had never said a word or made a gesture to which the most jealous husband could take exception.

As he sat down by the hearth again, Mauger actually licked his lips. That was over. Something had happened between William and Elizabeth. He was not sure what or how far it had gone, but the easy rapport between them had been destroyed. Where previously their eyes had met often, even when their remarks were addressed to others, this time neither had looked at the other. Mauger was sorry now that he had given Emma such a beating for her presumption. She had done him a good turn.

All his plans were working now. Mauger was so excited that he could not sit still and had to get up and pace the hall. The tale he had paid Theobald of Hurley to tell the king had had far more direct results than he expected. The abbey at Hurley, to which Mauger owed knight service, was corrupt and rotten all through; that was all to the good. It made the abbot very willing to do Mauger a good turn whenever he could so that Mauger would be disinclined to complain about the behavior of the monks among his serf women and in other ways. Thus, when one of their number had been selected to serve the king, the abbot had sent him to Mauger to ask if there was any little service he could do.

Mauger was aware that William was vassal to Richard of Cornwall and that he was often in service with his lord. He was not aware of how close the bond between them was because William never mentioned it. Since it would never have entered Mauger's mind to be so restrained—if he had an earl for a friend, he would have screamed it aloud every moment—Mauger assumed the relationship between William and his overlord was formal. All he had expected Theobald's story to do was to raise suspicions against William's character that would reduce any sense of surprise or outrage in his overlord when he was murdered for tampering with another man's wife.

It had never occurred to Mauger that the king would take Theobald's story so seriously, but then, he did not know exactly what tale Theobald had told—aside from the fact that it must show William as treacherous and dishonorable. Actually, most of the details had been owing to Henry himself, who had, by his questions, directed Theobald's quick mind into the suggestions that would most disturb and infuriate the king. All Mauger knew was that the knight in William's household must be a spy, and he chortled with joy. There would be plenty of material to gather—plenty. Probably William would follow his advice and try to keep the most innocent things secret from the spy—that would make the fellow suspicious. Then, too, William was not by nature secretive or mealymouthed. Surely he would forget himself and say something to criticize the king.

Mauger's pacing stopped suddenly. Had his warning to William been strong enough? He went back to his seat beside the fire to consider the various ramifications of William's behavior. Mauger wanted the spy to report that William was disloyal in intention, but he did not want the king to be so convinced that he would disseisen William. That way Alys would not inherit and Mauger could not hold the lands through her. It would be useful to have the betrothal made formal—Mauger intended, now that matters had changed between William and Elizabeth, to make another effort in that direction—but it was not essential. After William was dead he could simply seize the girl. No one would care, and he had witnesses enough that the marriage had been discussed and even approved by the girl's father.

What was necessary was to keep a close eye on what was taking place at Marlowe. In a day or two he would ride over. Perhaps he would take Elizabeth and try to judge from her reaction and William's exactly what had happened between them. Mauger sighed with satisfaction. Yes, he was sorry he had beaten Emma so hard. Perhaps he would find some trinket of Elizabeth's to give her.

The rays of the sun had pierced Elizabeth's window. From where she sat, the light struck directly into her eyes. After a moment this assault broke into her painful/wonderful waking dream. She shook herself angrily and rose to take up the ordinary tasks of her daily life. When she opened the door of her chamber, however, she heard the heavy shuddering sobs of a woman who had been crying for a long time.

Elizabeth went to discover what was wrong and found Emma, bruised and terrified. The previous day, Elizabeth might have simply walked away or even felt some satisfaction. She did not want Mauger but, being human, could not help resenting the women he took to his bed. Also, Emma had given herself airs, which the others, seeing that Mauger was on good terms with his wife, had been clever enough to avoid. Now, however, Elizabeth felt differently. The passionate pleasure she had experienced in William's arms, and the knowledge that it was Emma's indiscretion that had furnished that pleasure, were still fresh in her mind. She bent over the disconsolate, sobbing heap.

"Poor child," she murmured, "you should have been more thoughtful, but he should not have beaten you so hard. Come with me. I will put some salve on your bruises so they will not hurt so much."

Having soothed Emma's physical hurts, Elizabeth also calmed her terror by assuring her that she would not be cruel to her if Mauger was so angry that he did not want her as a mistress any longer. It was an easy enough promise to give. Elizabeth knew that Mauger would never leave such a beauty to be a maid in the keep. If he became bored or disgusted, he would sell Emma for a round price to some other man. He had always done so with his women in the past, and Emma was so exquisite that she should bring a nice profit.

There was no point in telling this to Emma, because it would add to her fear, Elizabeth thought, but Mauger probably was not yet ready to part with the girl. He would not have bothered to beat her if he did not wish to teach her a lesson. One of Mauger's good points was that he was never cruel or even harsh without a purpose. Most of the dreadful things he did were the result of neglect or necessity. With this in mind, Elizabeth even went so far as to tell Emma that, if she behaved properly, Mauger would probably keep her for the present.

These assurances stilled Emma's weeping, but left her nervous. "How will I know?" she wailed.

Elizabeth tried to hide her laughter. The situation really was funny. It was not every household in which the mistress ran to the wife for help and advice. Still, it might have its advantages. "If you are puzzled, come and ask me, Emma. I will do my best to tell you what Mauger will expect."

Emma was stupid but not completely an idiot. She looked at Elizabeth with suspicion. "Why should you?"

There could be no harm in telling her part of the

truth, Elizabeth thought. "Because I do not desire that my husband share my bed. If he puts you aside, he will come to me or take one of my maids—and that would make trouble in my household. As you have learned," Elizabeth pointed out, "you are no danger to my place. You do me a service in occupying Mauger. Why should I not help you?"

To Emma it made sense. She was not clever enough to look for layers of meaning. She knew deceit, but only the direct kind—stealing or lying for an immediate purpose. She knew nothing of laying out a path to be followed in the future. Thus, she was not suspicious and accepted Elizabeth's kindness as it was meant. Having given the girl a soporific draught in warmed wine, Elizabeth went to see that dinner was properly served.

Skinny, homely bitch, her husband thought as she entered the hall, but a good housekeeper. She was stupid, too, but that was useful. Talking to her was like talking to a wall. Sometimes something echoed back from it that made sense, but it did not volunteer anything. That was just as well. At least Elizabeth had never given any trouble. It was too bad he would probably have to kill her as well as William if he used their liaison as an excuse. Perhaps some other way of being rid of William would turn up. Elizabeth was useful in managing the estate.

Alys was no great trencherwoman, but this dinner she ate more than either of the men who sat beside her. The fact that her father's appetite was small did not surprise Alys. He usually ate very little—if he came home at all instead of spending the night with a whore in town—after a visit to Hurley. But she was surprised and somewhat worried by Raymond's picking and feeding half of what he put on his trencher to the dogs. It was not in the least unusual for a young man seated beside her to lose his appetite, but Raymond did not display any of the symptoms Alys knew as characteristic of being smitten by love.

That, however, was just Raymond's trouble—although he had not yet admitted it to himself. He only admitted that, instead of being overjoyed when he discovered Sir William to be totally guiltless of anything the king suspected, his heart had sunk like a stone. First he tried to deny he was depressed; then he tried to dismiss the feeling. Finally, he told himself that it was because his mother would hear of his whereabouts sooner if he went back to court. That reason for his depression was so rational that he seized hard on it, only too willing to allow it to cover a deeper and far more dangerous reason for his distress.

Put in terms of his mother, Raymond was able to examine the problem more calmly. His first thought when he realized Sir William was innocent was to rush back to court and tell Henry so. But what was the need for haste after all? An odd fluttering in his chest when Alys asked him a brief question, which he answered as briefly, strove to warn him that there *was* need for haste, that there was a desperate danger for him in this keep, but he would not heed the warning.

In fact, Raymond told himself, it would be stupid to rush back to Henry and assure him Sir William was faithful. What evidence did he have? Only his own interpretation of a single conversation.

To recount such a thing convincingly was another matter entirely. More likely the king would think he was a silly, inexperienced boy befooled apurpose by a clever older man. Then his defense would do Sir William more harm than good. What he needed, Raymond told himself, was better evidence. He should wait at least until Sir William was called to serve in the Welsh war, if there was one. Then it would be real proof to say: He called up his men at once and went and fought bravely. Yes, that would be best.

"I fear my cooks are less skilled than those you are accustomed to," Alys remarked snippily.

Raymond turned blank eyes to her, then followed the direction of her gaze to the untouched food before him. It was true enough that English tables were furnished with far more plain roasts and fewer "made" dishes.

Raymond did miss the highly spiced and seasoned ragouts of his home.

"The food is different," he admitted, "but just as good. My mind has been so full—so full of what you showed me today that I have forgotten to eat. I did not mean to offend you. I beg you to forgive me. New things, like new foods, take time to be digested."

All very smoothly spoken, but Alys was quite sure it was not how the serfs of Marlowe tilled their land that had glazed Raymond's eyes. She was ashamed of herself for picking at him. To sit with herself and her father and be served so simple a meal—a soup, a baked swan, a boiled carp, a roast of venison, and a suckling pig, plus two stews of veal and beef—must indeed be a bitter reminder of his losses. How cruel of her to make it worse by stabbing him with words that named the difference aloud.

"You must forgive me," she said remorsefully. "I am out of temper because of this stupid Welsh business."

Raymond smiled. What a delightful way to be out of temper. No red eyes and nose; no lugubrious sobbing. "Oh, I imagine it will come to nothing," he said mendaciously, accustomed to lying to women to comfort them.

Alys would have been furious had she known he was lying, but she merely thought him ignorant of the true facts of the case. "I think it will come to war," she said. "Papa thinks so too, I fear. I know he thought the terms imposed on David too hard, and Uncle Richard did also. When the king took Gruffydd prisoner instead of making David share the lands with him, he grew more hopeful, but even then he said he feared the treaty would not hold very long."

"Your uncle—pardon me—Earl Richard talks of these matters to you?" Raymond asked in a slightly stunned voice.

"If I ask him—of course. I do not mean he tells me secrets of state. That would not be right, and neither does papa tell me such things—not that I would ask—

but he is very good about explaining public matters to me."

Alys glanced at her father, but he was chewing slowly, his eyes blind. He would hear nothing, she decided. And, if Uncle Richard was coming, it might be well to warn Raymond, who clearly did not think much of women.

"Papa likes me to ask Uncle Richard questions," Alys went on with a little giggle. "It not only improves my mind, but it helps Uncle Richard. You see, while he is explaining to me, there is no harm in his shouting and stamping about and calling great men idiots, which, if he did it to their faces, would cause infinite trouble. I would never betray him, of course, but it is doubly sure I will not because I do not come among such men."

"You are fit for it, certainly," Raymond said, ridiculously angry at the notion that Alys should not be considered the equal of any woman, even his aunt, the queen.

"I do not know about that, although papa has taught me court usage as well as he can. But it is not my manners anyway. The thing is that I am not rich enough to marry so high and one of Uncle Richard's friends made—made papa an offer for me, to have me out of wedlock—"

"Who?" Raymond roared, his hand falling to where his sword hilt should be.

"Hush!" Alys hissed, casting a glance at her father.

"Who what?" William asked, starting out of his private thoughts.

"Who is my Uncle Richard," Alys replied hastily, kicking Raymond good and hard under the table.

"What do you mean, 'Who is your Uncle Richard,' and why in that voice?" William insisted.

Alys giggled. "Because Raymond is annoyed with me. I have been teasing him."

"Teasing Raymond? What the devil is making you act the fool today, Alys? If you cannot act as befits your age and station, go and sit among the children of the maidservants as you deserve."

"I am very sorry, papa." Alys lowered her head under the rebuke. It was the correct gesture, but it also hid the fact that her eyes were dancing. Perhaps papa should have stopped to couple a whore in the town. He was out of measure cross. Never having been afflicted either by love or desire, Alys found such torments rather funny. Still, it would be better to appease papa before he really lost his temper. "I miss Harold," she said quite truthfully. "Harold did not get angry when I teased him. I forgot."

Raymond had listened to this exchange in silence because he had not been able to command his voice. His sense of outrage at the insult offered to the most perfect woman he had ever met was so great that, had she named a name, he would have ridden out to challenge the man. He knew it was ridiculous. Plainly Alys had come to no harm, and between her father and the earl of Cornwall, she had sufficient protection.

It was all the more painful in that, instead of protecting her, his stupidity had brought trouble on her. The violent blow on his shin had pointed out to him most sharply that to remind her father of such an incident would be a dreadful solecism. And then, instead of saying that she did not know why he had fallen into a rage or tried to pass it off some other way—as his sisters would have done—Alys took all the blame upon herself.

"I am at fault, sir," Raymond put in, finding his voice. "I had no right to speak in such a tone to your daughter. I beg your pardon."

Alys's apology had made William ashamed of his outburst, which he knew was caused by his own unhappiness. He smiled at the crimson-faced young man. "I am glad you were so moderate. Alys's teasing has made older and calmer people wish to strangle her." He turned his eyes to his daughter. "Have a care," he warned. "Harold grew up with you from a child and knew your ways." Then he looked back at Raymond. "I imagine you wanted to know why Alys calls so great a man as Richard of Cornwall uncle. It is true that there is no blood bond. Simply, we have been friends from boyhood, Richard and I. He dandled her on his knees when she was a babe, and he did not wish that she should grow in awe of him." William paused and his lips twisted wryly. "He should have known her better. Alys is not overgiven to awe. However, he bade her call him uncle and so she does."

"I see," Raymond said. "Thank you."

Alys was still looking down, but her father noticed a faint wrinkle between her brows, as if she were considering some puzzling question. He could only hope that his warning had taken hold and she was thinking about how unsafe it was to be playful with a young man who had not grown up regarding her as a sister. Alys was too kind to wish to inflict needless pain on anyone. She was, indeed, but it was not her father's warning that had given her food for thought. She was considering, with a strong mixture of concern, doubt, and pleasure, Raymond's reaction to her mention of a proposition being made for her. Alys was quite familiar with the characteristic male response to deep insult— and Raymond had reacted like a man whose own wife had been offended.

CHAPTER 6

A week later Richard of Cornwall accompanied only by two squires rode into Marlowe just in time for dinner. He was travel stained and weary, for he had ridden from London the previous afternoon. Raymond had heard much of the close friendship between Richard and Sir William, but it was still a surprise to him to see the familiarity with the earl and all the residents of the keep.

He not only embraced Martin but asked anxiously about his health, referring to an illness the steward had suffered late in the preceding year. There was no mistaking the earl's real concern nor his fondness for the elderly, ugly cripple. By the time he had been reassured, Alys had flung herself into his arms in joyous welcome.

"I'm so glad you have come. I have not seen you for so long," she cried.

He hugged and kissed her warmly. "And I to see you, dearling, but you will soon wish me at the devil's door, because I bring bad news."

"Never," Alys exclaimed, although Raymond could see that her joy had been dampened. "Wales?" she asked.

"Yes, but where is your papa? There is no sense telling bad news twice."

The question went unanswered as Sir William came in from the outer door and strode quickly across the hall. The two men embraced each other, but William drew back with concern in his eyes.

"Come into my chamber, Richard, and rid yourself of this armor. You look tired to death. Is something wrong?"

"A very good question," Richard replied, smiling

wryly. "I do not know whether to answer yes or no or only a little. I have a long tale to tell and you will think I am making some of it up, William, but I swear—"

"Come and get comfortable first," William interrupted. "Alys, make ready a bath—"

"No," Richard interrupted in turn. "I will not stay the night, and it is too cold to ride out again after bathing." He smiled again, a little shyly this time. "I wish to sleep at Wallingford."

"Sleep?" William teased, drawing Richard toward his rooms. "Perhaps you wish to lie abed there, but sleep?"

"Do not be so crude, papa," Alys said reprovingly, but her dimples quivered in her cheeks, betraying hidden laughter.

"Shocking!" Richard rejoined, laughing openly. "You shock me, Alys. You should not have the faintest idea what your father is talking about. And, even if you do, it is very—very unmaidenly to show it, not to mention improper to be remarking on your papa's gross vulgarity."

"It was not gross," William said blandly. "I thought I had wrapped the whole thing up very neatly."

The three of them were so obviously enjoying themselves that Raymond, who really had been shocked, began to reconsider. It really was rather pleasant that Alys did not turn red or grow angry or simper and run away. Perhaps it was because the serfs always seemed to be consulting her on which cows should be sent to the bull to be serviced and which mares offered to which stallion. He was starting to wonder whether there was not something good to be said for a less sheltered life than his sisters had led.

"The boys must be exhausted," William remarked, waving away Richard's squires, who had started to follow their master to be made comfortable by Alys and Martin. "Besides, I would like you to meet Sir Raymond, who is new in service with me. Let him disarm you."

Richard nodded acceptance and the three men went together into William's chamber. Politely, Richard

asked how Raymond had found his way from the south
—which so plainly marked his speech—to England.

"He is from Aix," William put in hastily. "Henry was
so kind as to send him to me. I suppose you must have
told him of Harold's death and that I needed someone.
It was good of Henry to remember so small a matter
among all his other concerns."

"He *would* remember and be glad to do you a kindness, but . . . it is very odd, William. I do not recall
saying anything. . . ."

He stared attentively at Raymond, whose color rose
and who wished the floor would open and swallow him.
Raymond knew he had never met Richard, but he also
knew that he looked something like his grandfather, as
did Queen Eleanor and Richard's wife, Sancia. He was
also worried sick that Richard would guess his brother's
purpose. A week in Sir William's service had taught
Raymond much about the quality of the man and had
confirmed everything Martin had said. Raymond could
not bear to lie openly to Sir William, and yet it would
be monstrous to expose the king's stratagem, not to
mention Raymond's own embarrassment at confessing
the part he had consented to play.

"You must have spoken to Henry about it," William
insisted. "Raymond brought a letter from him. How
else could Henry know I needed a knight? Mine is not
a large household where any number may be employed,
so it must be that you spoke of it."

"I suppose I must have," Richard agreed slowly. "I
was just trying to think. . . . Well, it does not matter.
You are right, William. I must have mentioned it to
Henry." But Richard's eyes had never left Raymond's
face as the young man removed his armor. Finally, he
said, "Sir Raymond, and from Aix. Do I not know
you? Or, perhaps, your father?"

"Not me, certainly, my lord," Raymond faltered.
"As—as to my father—I—I think not. . . ."

At which point, William kicked Richard hard enough
to make him wince and also to get across to him that
he wanted him to drop that line of questioning. Richard

promptly did so, remarking blandly that so many fair complexions in England made one think all dark-skinned people were kin. William then asked a question about one of Richard's favorite horses that had been giving trouble and the reply kept them busy until Richard had changed into one of his friend's gowns.

It was natural enough for Raymond to take leave then, which gave William time to explain his theory of Raymond's background. Richard did not argue. The situation certainly would explain Raymond's embarrassment and even the fact that his face was vaguely familiar. Still the earl felt it was odd that he could not remember discussing William's need of a retainer with his brother. He could not, in fact, remember thinking about it at all.

Richard never thought about what he could do to help William. One firm rule in his life was that he must not offer William *any* kind of assistance. That had been settled when they were still children, respectively ten and twelve years of age. William had admired a handsome, richly jeweled eating knife Richard had received as a New Year's gift, and Richard had handed it to him, saying, "It is yours if you like it. I have so many." Instead of taking the knife, William had flushed and said bitterly, "You fool!" and stalked away. Naturally enough, Richard had been furious that what he had meant as a kindness should be rejected with insult.

For two days the boys had not exchanged a word. On the third night, Richard had been found by the earl of Chester crying himself to sleep. The old earl had already been alerted to trouble because earlier in the day William had asked to speak to him and then had asked for leave to go home. William would not say why, but Rannulf of Chester had the story out of Richard, who was terribly hurt and still did not understand what had happened.

It was easy enough to explain to Richard once Chester knew the facts. Richard was well aware of his position as the king's second son and heir apparent to the throne. He simply had not associated his wealth and position with William, who was in those days almost an other self. Once it was made clear to him that William could not be his friend, truly a friend, if he received material benefits from that friendship, Richard had been very careful.

It had worked well, and by now was a habit so long established that Richard did not need to be careful. He simply did not think about being helpful to William. He thought about what *he* wanted from William sometimes, and this made him uneasy with the idea that he had discussed William's need with his brother. Still, there did not seem to be any other answer, and Richard put the matter out of his mind. There were a great many more pressing things to worry about than how Raymond had obtained an introduction from the king.

"Usually," Richard said, when they were seated to eat, "one gives the bad news first, but the bad is so complicated that I think I will start with the good. The matter of the see of Winchester is settled."

"Which way?" William asked.

"Henry will soon invite Walter Raleigh to come home and will assure him of a good welcome and that Winchester will be open to him."

"Thank God for that," William said heartily, then grinned. "I told you so. I told you that if you reasoned softly, only in private, and did not cross the king's will with the whole council gaping at you both and, moreover, did not throw insults at him, which you and I both know are false but you always say in anger—"

"Papa, it is very rude, unwise too, to tell people 'I told you so.' You have told *me* so a hundred times or more." Alys was teasing, her eyes and voice merry, her dimples showing distinctly.

"And so it would be," Richard chuckled, "if I had had the slightest part in Henry's decision—but I did not."

"So much the better," William exclaimed.

Richard's smile grew a little awry. "You mean because he would resent it later? Well, I do not mind that. Better he should be angry with me than meddle with

the Church further. You remember that Neville, bishop
of Chichester, died in the beginning of February?
Well—"

"But Chichester is no see fit for William of Savoy,"
William interrupted.

"No, of course not. I am sorry for it, but I do not
think Savoy would stay now even if Henry could offer
him Canterbury. He was hurt, much hurt by the behavior of the nobles and the clergy. I blame myself in
part. I tried to explain, but perhaps my own feelings
showed and I may have made matters worse instead of
better."

"There is no blame to you, and I am not sure I *am*
sorry the queen's uncle goes," William remarked. "In
himself, Savoy is a good man, but there is so much
murmuring against 'this horde of foreigners'—even at
Wallingford I heard it. No, do not shake your head,
Richard. These are the lesser men, men like me, some
of them your own vassals, others in the retinues of the
other earls. They would not speak to you, but to me
they do."

"What the devil do they mean—foreigners? I am
Angevin and Poitevin and Angoulême. You are Norman—"

"Mostly, with a few other strains, but that is not what
I meant. We were both born here in England and our
main interest and heritage is here in this land. Even in
little things. . . . Do you not speak English, Richard?"

"Of course. These people are so stubborn about
learning French one cannot deal with an artisan or stop
in an inn without using a translator—and that is so
awkward. Besides my English servants—"

"I speak French to you, Richard, but Alys and I
often fall into English when we are alone or in company with our neighbors because we use that language
so much every day. Perhaps it is a little thing, but it is
one of the things at the heart of the ill feeling over
these Italian priests the pope sends in ever-increasing
numbers to English benefices."

"Now that is perfectly reasonable," Richard said

firmly. "A priest must minister to a flock, and if the flock cannot understand one word the priest says, what kind of ministry can there be? But in the higher offices of the clergy, the language cannot mean much."

"Why not?" Alys asked. "The canons and monks are mostly native born and many not even from the nobility. For most, English is the only unlearned tongue they speak. To Latin they grow accustomed, but French comes slowly and awkwardly to them. I think in their hearts there is anger when they are made to feel stupid by slow understanding."

Richard opened his eyes wide. "You may be right, my love. I think you are. Whatever put it into your pretty head?"

Alys giggled. "Raymond."

Both men turned to look at Raymond, where he sat at William's left, but he looked even more dumbfounded than they did. "I never said a word about the canons of Winchester," he protested. "I never spoke to one of them and know nothing about them."

"It is by example you taught me," Alys laughed. "You grow irritable when the people on the estate or the castle speak to me in English, and it is even worse when they speak in their broken French that you cannot follow easily. But that was not all." She grinned at him merrily. "I would have put that down to plain bad temper, if I did not myself feel like telling you to take the pebbles out of your mouth when you speak to me. Moreover, I often feel like saying something much worse when I ask you to repeat, and you look down your nose at me as if I were deaf or a lackwit." She turned to Richard. "And it is not all a matter of temper. Do you not think there must have been misunderstandings from time to time that brought blame or even punishment and that would linger most hatefully in the mind?"

"It might," Richard agreed thoughtfully, and William nodded his approval.

The two older men looked at each other, thinking only of a new facet on an old problem. Raymond looked at Alys, marveling at her ability to enlarge on a personal irritation in an impersonal way. His sisters never did so. Offended by an equal or a superior, they merely scolded or wept. Alys had considered the reason behind what had happened. When his attention returned to the men's conversation, it had moved from the general to the particular, William having recalled Richard to his initial statement about the see of Chichester.

The earl sighed. "Yes, well, Henry suggested Robert Passelewe to the canons, and between a judicious gift here and there and their memory of the misery of Winchester, they elected him without argument."

"Passelewe, eh?" William shrugged. "He is a good servant and did right well, if a little too harshly and suddenly, on the matter of the king's forests. Of course, he is no scholar. However—"

"You need not go any further. It may not matter to you or to the canons that he is no scholar, but it does to Boniface. He gathered a group of bishops and 'examined' Passelewe, found him wanting—and annulled the appointment."

"No! What the devil got into them? To begin another brangle with the king, and when this damned Master Martin is just waiting to swallow the revenues of any vacant see for the pope's purposes, is plain idiocy. Boniface of all men—"

"Yes, he should be grateful when my brother fought so hard for his appointment as archbishop of Canterbury. I spoke to him. He said there is a higher good. . . . Damn! I think he even believes it and is convinced he is doing his duty to God this way. You remember that old story about my grandfather and St. Thomas à Becket. However, Boniface is not a fool with regard to the pope's greed. He has already appointed Richard de Wiche as bishop and seen that all the revenues were distributed to the proper persons."

William made no reply to that other than a low whistle. Richard nodded and continued. "That settled the matter of Winchester. Henry knew it was a lost cause anyway, and I think Savoy had told him he no longer desired it. Henry was hanging on out of stubbornness, but he saw quickly enough that yielding on Winchester—which the pope has been urging so strongly—would gain much sympathy for his point of view about Chichester."

"So be it," William remarked. "Chichester is not important enough to worry about, and since Passelewe and de Wiche are both 'English,' the barons will not care much, although there are many who hate Passelewe because of his exactions after the forest inquisition. Still, this is not the tinderbox thing that Winchester was. If that is all of your bad news, we are most fortunate."

"No," Richard said grimly, and had anyone been there who had known King John, he would have shuddered, so strong was the look of the old king on the son at that moment. "Gruffydd ap Llewelyn is dead."

"Dead?" William's voice scaled upward.

"The day I had your letter, I had also one from Henry on the same matters. I had known about David's appeal to the pope. If I did not mention it to you—"

"Never mind," William put in, smiling. "You were in no mood for business when I last spoke to you and the matter was scarcely urgent."

"Then it was not, but this matter of Gruffydd makes it much worse."

"Was there something suspicious in how he died?" William asked.

Richard shrugged. "No. . . . Yes. . . . I do not know. William, you know what the Welsh are. He tried to escape. He made a rope of cloth—sheets, tablecloths, tapestries—and tried to climb down. The knots did not hold. He was a big, heavy man. He fell to his death."

There was an appalled silence out of which Alys said softly, "Everyone says they are like wild beasts, and I suppose it is true in that they cannot bear to be caged."

William shuddered, but he did not take his eyes from Richard's. "There was no other way to hold him," he assured his friend. "His parole was worthless. No one will blame Henry for this. He was permitted his wife's company—and others—and provided with every luxury—"

"Except freedom," Richard broke in bitterly.

"Be reasonable," William urged. "He would have raised war when Henry had promised David peace. And, if he had been taken by David, his fate—I mean while he lived—would have been worse."

"You never liked him," Richard said.

"No, I did not, and I do not like David any better. I wish old Llewelyn had been less farsighted and abided by Welsh custom. If he had divided the lands between them, they would have been enough occupied with fighting each other to leave us in peace."

"Oh no," Richard remarked angrily, "it would have been the same. One or the other would have appealed to Henry, and he would have let himself be dragged in—"

"It is his duty and his right," William stated. "He is overlord of Wales. He must settle quarrels between his vassals."

"Everyone except the Welsh is in agreement," Richard snapped, and then sighed. "Well, it does not matter. They are in arms again."

"What? Over Gruffydd's death? How did they hear so soon?"

"How can you ask that, William? You yourself wrote to me about the rumors that everyone had heard. What did you think Gruffydd intended to do when he reached the ground—walk or swim to Wales? This was not one man's doing. How could it be that the guards did not notice tablecloths and tapestries missing? Do you think it takes a minute to cut such things and tie so long a rope? I do not doubt someone rode off to Wales less than an hour after it happened. All that I cannot guess is who was involved and whether it was intended that Gruffydd escape or die."

"One would depend upon the other, I should think," Raymond said, then stopped and flushed when both older men looked hard at him.

"Yes? Well?" William urged.

"I beg your pardon," Raymond said. "I should not have thrust myself forward."

"Oh, no," Richard remarked, "you cannot whet our appetites with a statement like that and then withdraw. Let us hear the rest."

William also smiled encouragingly, and Raymond realized his sharpness had been interest not irritation because a young man intruded his thoughts on his elders—a frequent problem Raymond met at home. Still, he continued a little less certainly than he had begun.

"It seems to me that there must be two, or rather three, possibilities. The first is simplest—those who love Gruffydd and simply could not bear to think of him caged."

"A small and unlikely group," William muttered under his breath. Richard shook his head at his friend, but did not speak.

"Then there are those who either do not desire a war in Wales or, rather, wish to see King Henry's influence reestablished by the desire of the Welsh rather than by force of English arms. Last, there must be a group that urgently desires to have all impediment to free action by David ap Llewelyn removed."

William shifted uneasily in his seat, but Richard cast him a warning glance and he held his tongue.

"I see where you lead," Richard commented, "but say it for me. Those who loved Gruffydd, of course, desired him alive and free for his own sake. Go on from there."

"From what I have heard," Raymond continued, so intent on what he was saying that he missed the byplay between Richard and William, "if Gruffydd had come to Wales alive his first act would be to gather those faithful to him and attack his brother. The immediate result would be that David would have to use the force he has raised to resist Gruffydd rather than to attack the English. The second result must be that either David or Gruffydd, or both, would appeal to King

Henry for help and reestablish the treaty as the king desires."

"Are you suggesting that the king urged or was party to the escape attempt?" Richard asked quietly.

"Sacred Heaven, no!" Raymond exclaimed, with every evidence of sincerity. "I never thought at all," he added with a guilty look in William's direction. "I was only reasoning it out like a puzzle."

As he spoke, a last nail was hammered into the coffin holding his suspicions of Sir William. The clerk could have heard a conversation very like this one, Raymond thought, where innocent speculation had taken on an ugly implication. Certainly Raymond had no intention of turning Richard's mind against his brother, yet that implication could very easily be read into his words—and he had spoken them even after William had warned Alys against just this sort of thing.

"I am sure," William said dryly, "that if the king was in any way interested in Gruffydd's escape it would have been accomplished safely. What need for sheets and tablecloths? If no tale of bribery—so that Gruffydd could walk out the door—would work, surely a decent rope could have been provided. It is far, far more likely that David wished to be free of the millstone around his neck."

"It is more likely that one brother would seek to destroy the other?" Richard remarked with distaste.

"Oh, Richard, you know it is a family tradition among the Welsh. Do you want me to give you instances? There was never any love between David and Gruffydd. David himself imprisoned Gruffydd and, I heard, not so kindly as Henry did."

"He imprisoned him. He did not kill him or even arrange his death," Richard said softly.

"While David held Gruffydd himself, he did not need to do so," William snapped. "What could those who favored Gruffydd do with their lord in David's hands? It was a very different matter while Henry held him. For David it was better that Gruffydd should run free than that he should be available for your brother's use."

"It is indeed very curious and significant that Gruffydd should die just when David was seeking to throw off King Henry's yoke," Raymond added, trying to redeem the damage he had done. "If he had not, the king would have had an alternate ruler to offer the Welsh. That was the third case—and the most likely of all, I believe. I agree with Sir William that a better type of escape could have been arranged had it ever been intended that Gruffydd should come alive out of the Tower. None could benefit from his death except David ap Llewelyn—or those attached to his cause."

Richard sighed and nodded. He had been playing devil's advocate because he had a dreadful fear that Henry had been somehow involved. It was a relief to him that someone who, he believed, could not have any partiality absolved his brother from considerations of pure reason. Alys neither agreed nor disagreed, but her eyes were admiring as they rested on Raymond. No other young man had spoken with such freedom before her father and Richard of Cornwall—and had made good enough sense that they hung on his words with deep interest. Competent herself, Alys had a strong taste for competency.

"Then it will be war," William said, smiling slightly. "When should I be ready?"

Raymond heard the hiss of Alys's indrawn breath and looked up the table at her, but her face was still, her eyes fixed now on the remains of the meal. Richard's squires moved around with well-trained quiet efficiency, refilling wine cups. The earl had also heard, and he looked down at the girl beside him and patted her hand. But, even while he offered wordless comfort, his attention was really on William.

"You have not heard it all yet," he said wryly. "I told you it was a long tale. The king of Scotland, moved by that devil of a father-by-marriage of his, has sent a repudiation of his homage to my brother. He claims he holds no lands in Scotland of Henry—and to make this true he has spread the border of Scotland south to cover all the territory he did homage for when he was last here."

"Do you think this was concerted between David and Alexander?"

"God knows, but it is hard to believe that so close a coincidence is completely an accident."

William growled softly, then shrugged. "There is no difference whether it is planned or not. Both challenges must be met. We will be spread a little thin, but we are big enough for them both. Just tell me which we are to fight."

"You will go to Wales," Richard said, a dissatisfied frown on his face.

"I will go to Wales?" William echoed, frowning also. "I will do as you bid me, of course, but to speak plain truth, Richard, I had rather go with you."

"I had rather also," Richard said, "but I have little choice in the matter. The Welsh war is to be managed by de Bohun and Clare."

"Clare?" William gasped. "But the earl of Gloucester is not much older than Raymond here, and de Bohun—"

"Yes," Richard interrupted, "that is why I said I had little choice. You must go, and if it seems that those two hotheads are about to do something particularly stupid—"

"Now what attention would de Bohun or Clare pay to me?" William asked, smiling.

"Little, but you will not be afraid to open your mouth, which is important, and my men and others who know how dear you are to me will be willing to support you once you speak, although they would not be willing to step forward on their own."

"So much is true, Richard, but you give me too much credit. I have fought in Wales before, but only as squire to Chester or in your tail. How do you expect me to know what is brave lunacy and what is daring practicality?"

"You have this comfort," Richard responded, "that

few will know better than you. The great old Marcher lords are all dead. We are all novices—David ap Llewelyn no less than we. And you have this advantage: the lesser men, who have long lived and fought in Wales, will be willing to tell you of their doubts where they would not be willing to broach such ideas to Clare or de Bohun."

William scratched his head and sighed. "Very well, Richard, I will do my best. Do you want me to call up extra men and buy stores?"

"No extra men; de Bohun has a grant of money for that—I think. As to the stores, I will send you a list from Wallingford of those stewards who are to furnish stores from my keeps and towns."

"Oh, damn you, Richard, are you going to make me quartermaster for your men?"

Eyes alight with laughter, Richard replied, "Yes."

William groaned dismally. "Richard, have mercy. I have not kept accounts for years, and I was no dab hand at it when I did."

The earl now laughed aloud and cried shame on his vassal for putting the burden of accounts on his young daughter. But, when William protested, in self-defense, that Alys liked to do them, Richard relented and promised a clerk would come with the list who would do the actual labor of recording what was received and disbursed. William would only be responsible for checking the records and for making sure that they were honest. He spoke gaily, but there was a warning in his eyes, and William did not ask why Richard could not check his own accounts. Later, when they were embracing before Richard mounted up to ride away, the earl explained that he was not going to Wales at all. He was off to obtain mercenary forces from Flanders for the Scottish war.

"It must be kept secret lest the French intervene," he said softly, "so do not speak of it. And I go tomorrow so I will have no time to talk further with you. William, you have hidden it well, but I have seen that something lies heavy on your heart. Can I help?"

"No one can help."

"A curse on this need to fly away," Richard said passionately. "Could I stay, I could at least draw it out and share the burden."

William smiled. "Not this burden. It will pass, Richard. It has passed before and will pass again."

CHAPTER 7

It was not the truth. William had never completely shed the burden of his love, but there had been many years when it was barely perceptible. After the first few months of his marriage, when he felt he could not live, William had been back in service with Richard and sufficiently interested in acquiring the skills necessary to knight and landholder that the worst misery had passed. Although Mary was like a limp wet cloth abed, she never refused him, so that there was an outlet for his physical needs when he was at Marlowe. Away from the keep—and he was there as little as possible in those years—on campaign or at court with Richard, he forgot he was married. There were plenty of women who were glad to entertain William, both for his own sake and as the favorite of the earl of Cornwall.

When Elizabeth had returned to Hurley, there had been another peak of misery. In some ways it had been worse. She was there, close by; he saw her often. It was like a sore tooth that one cannot resist touching and biting on. William spent much more time at Marlowe then, unable to tear himself away from the siren lure of her nearness and the pain/pleasure of her company. However, with time a sort of ease had come, and the pleasure had outweighed the pain.

This time, William thought, was worst of all. He could not hate Elizabeth as he had the first time, nor feel she was unreachable, even unapproachable, as she had been when she returned to Hurley, a wife with two sons and, for all he knew, another babe under her belt. Now he knew she loved him still, desired him as much as he desired her. He could find no peace. He could not rid himself of the feeling that, if he were only clever

105

enough to see it, there was a way to have her, although he admitted that what she had said to him was true.

He had one piece of luck—bad or good William would not define. Mauger had come the previous week, bringing Elizabeth. William had been at Wallingford to meet and bring back to Marlowe the clerk Richard assigned to do the accounts. It hurt to have missed Elizabeth, yet it would have been worse to see her. Alys said she had dealt with Mauger, and William thought no more of it. Alys knew William preferred his relationship with Richard to be kept quiet. William guessed Mauger had come to have a look at Raymond, but why bring Elizabeth? How awful to have missed her. Perhaps . . . No. He would *not* think about Elizabeth.

Richard's visit had been a major blessing. Although he groaned and complained, William knew himself quite capable of handling the burden Richard had laid on him. Richard had tried to induce him to take on far greater burdens, in fact had begged him more than once to be marshal of his lands. In the past William had always refused, partly because he was not ambitious and really did not care for the hectic striving in the world of the great men but far more because, if he accepted, he would have been away from Marlowe— no, from Elizabeth—all the time.

Suddenly William groaned aloud. He had completely forgotten that Richard's last marshal had died just before his marriage to Sancia. This business in Wales must be the toe in the door, the "you see it is not so bad, come, take the place" introduction to another offer of the marshal's position. Perhaps he would take it this time, William told himself. It was impossible to go on living with this desire burning in his gut. He must either have Elizabeth or leave her. Leave her? He could not!

Damn! He would *not* think about Elizabeth. But he would not have thought about her on campaign any-way—not much, at least. Why had Richard chosen to push this on him now, he asked himself petulantly, then laughed. Campaigns had always been a time for merry roistering. Not this time. William did not at all like the look of the fat, smooth clerk who had come with Richard's lists and letters. Nor did he like the way his questions about suppliers had been answered—or half answered and that much only after hard prodding.

A frown grew between William's brows. A dishonest clerk could not prove a task easy, but might be a device on Richard's part to show how ill served he was and how badly he needed an honest marshal. Richard was the best and sweetest man in the world, but not above a stratagem when he felt it would be the best for everyone. If the clerk was dishonest, there might not even be time properly to oversee his own men, William thought. That problem had never troubled William before. The castellan of Bix had seen to such things if Richard was making heavy demands on William's time.

Raymond would have to pick up that burden now, William decided. Even without roaring around drunk one night out of three and thereby losing the following day also, he would have no time for his own troop; specially not if he was to discover the unniceties of fighting in Wales from the older vassals of the Marcher lords. William sighed and swung his legs out of bed. There was plenty to do already.

Diccon, the master-at-arms, and most of the experienced men-at-arms would have to remain behind in Marlowe—and some at Bix. Alys could manage the estate fairly well, but she could not protect it. There was not much danger of any attack on the keep; William was on good terms with his neighbors. However, there were bands of marauders about, and Marlowe was rich. There was no sense in leaving an open invitation for the lands to be raided by outlaws—and that was what it would amount to if it became known that the master was gone and the keep was manned only by raw recruits.

The only way to leave enough experienced men at Marlowe and Bix was to hire or train new ones. William considered his finances as he dressed. He was not behindhand, but he did not like the idea of needing to spend money on mercenaries. There would be the costs of Alys's marriage soon. He would not need a money dower, of course, because Bix was hers and would be her portion, but the clothing and feasting would be very costly—and his income would be decreased by a third when the revenues of Bix went to Alys's husband.

Besides, it was a good idea to have some of the men on the estate trained to arms. There were some likely boys on the demesne farms and the outlying freehold lands beholden to Marlowe as well as in the town itself. All together, there should be a good crop of sons eager to learn to wield a sword.

Many of William's peers did not approve of training the serfs and villeins and putting weapons in their hands, but he did not agree. He never turned the trained serfs back to the land, of course. He kept them on at the castle, or passed them into Richard's forces if they took well to the life. Several had found advancement and were now free men, masters-at-arms themselves. They were grateful to their old master.

The villeins were different. They were free men to begin with. After a campaign, they could do as they liked. Some elected to stay on in William's small army; a few younger sons joined a mercenary band or sold their swords as individuals; most went back to their farms or businesses, proud of their extra abilities and serving as a nucleus of a large defending force if Marlowe should ever be attacked.

Dressed and washed, William came out into the hall to break his fast. Alys and Raymond were at table already, talking and laughing eagerly. William hesitated, struck by a special light in the two young faces. Damn! He had been too wrapped in his own troubles these past two weeks. He had not noticed that the liking between Alys and Raymond was growing out of bounds. Raymond was a fool to let his heart get the better of his common sense, but the real fault was with Alys, who should know her worth better. She could easily have discouraged the young knight. That would not stop him from loving, perhaps, but it would have kept him from being hurt by hope.

Fortunately there was an immediate, if partial, remedy at hand. Raymond could go out with Diccon to pick the men for training and after that could stay at Bix training them until it was time to leave for the muster at Hereford. Once Raymond was gone, William could remind Alys that a penniless adventurer knight, no matter how attractive, was not a suitable husband for a girl with a good estate.

Even as he thought it, a doubt flicked at William. Why not? If the young people loved each other—why not? He liked Raymond. Working closely with him over these past weeks, he had come to respect the young man's quickness of mind, his willingness to work hard, his earnest attempts to learn to understand the language and customs of the people with whom he now lived. It was true that Alys's beauty and dower could take her up a step in the social scale. Even if she married Aubery, she would end as the mistress of four keeps, a state approaching real wealth. Of course, if her affections were unalterably fixed on Raymond . . . No. He would give her no encouragement to throw herself away. When they returned from Wales, if . . .

"Papa! Why are you standing like a stock staring at us?" Alys asked.

"I was just thinking," William replied, coming forward and taking the cup of wine Alys held out.

She frowned. "You have been 'thinking' a great deal recently, and it appears your thoughts are not as pleasant as they could be."

"No," he answered, and allowed his eyes to move to the door where Richard's clerk lodged and through which he had not yet come. Late and lazy the creature was, but William had not yet caught any evidence of dishonesty.

Alys accepted her father's unspoken reason for thoughtfulness, although she had her own ideas. William did not read those in her face nor, though he watched her covertly, could he find any sign of guilt when he told Raymond the duty he would begin that day. Alys did look disappointed, perhaps somewhat more disappointed than when Harold was sent away, but that small thing was swept away in her concern when she understood her father's decision.

"You will not go with untrained men," she cried. "Oh, papa, please do not. I will manage well enough. And Sir Mauger would come to my aid if I sent to him. Even if he was away, Elizabeth would send out her men to help us."

"Do not be silly, Alys. By the time we go to Wales the men *will* be trained. That is why I am sending Raymond and Diccon to choose them now and begin training. The march across country will harden them, and the little, early skirmishes will blood them and finish them finely. Besides, I will take some of the veteran men-at-arms to stiffen my force."

"But papa—"

"Alys, do not make me tell you to mind your needle. I am no hotheaded young fool to court danger unnecessarily. I assure you I will take good care that the men are ready."

She subsided obediently. William was well pleased with his plan. It seemed to him that, although Alys was only a little regretful at losing her companion, Raymond had been sore stricken. William had caught the way he looked at Alys when he first heard they must part. It was time, and past time, William thought regretfully, that Raymond be sent away.

Mauger had been exactly opposite to William in his perception of the growing attachment between Alys and Raymond. He had noticed too much for his own comfort the preceding week and had been so enraged by what he saw that he almost forgot his initial reason for coming to Marlowe. When he saw the way Raymond backed up every word Alys said, Mauger suddenly realized it would do no good to get rid of William if the girl was not formally betrothed to Aubery or had a protector she preferred to Aubery.

Mauger had heard some things about Richard of Cornwall that worried him. The earl was known to have supported several women who had said they were unwilling to marry, and Alys would have a strong case if the slightest suspicion concerning William's death fell on Mauger. It was not unreasonable for Alys to object to marrying the son of the man who was suspected of killing her father, no matter how justifiable the act was. Moreover, Richard might wish to keep Alys unmarried and collect the revenues of Marlowe and Bix, or he might have a pet henchman for whom he wanted to find a good livelihood.

All the way home, Mauger had ranted and raved to Elizabeth about William's carelessness in permitting the close association of so young a hireling knight with his daughter. Elizabeth did not answer, but her heart swelled with tenderness. She did not think it was carelessness. She read Alys better than her husband and could see the girl was not yet deeply touched. Doubtless William would set Raymond a task that would separate them before any damage was done. Meanwhile he would have weaned Alys away from the notion of marrying Aubery, which Elizabeth was convinced would end in misery for both her son and his daughter. Poor William. It was very unselfish of him. When Alys married and went away, he would be all alone.

As if the thought had passed to her husband, Mauger said, "I must talk to William about this. He must get rid of that fellow at once. I did not like him at all. I am sure he is a spy in the king's pay. Did Alys say to you how long her father would be away?"

"No, Mauger," Elizabeth answered, "but I am sure it would not be more than a week. She would have said something, I believe, if William was to be away longer than that."

"Well, you had better think of something you need from her or want to tell her," Mauger ordered. "I need an excuse to go back there next week. I am going to write to de Bohun to send Aubery home for a while. He had better exert himself to get that girl to agree to a marriage, or . . ."

He stopped, aware of Elizabeth stiffening beside him. She was crazy about those two idiots she had borne him. He had better not admit what little use he had for either of them—sniveling fools, mouthing chivalry and honesty and service at him when he asked them to get a favor from their lords or squeeze a tenant or a merchant on the sly for money. Why the devil did they think he had placed them with such powerful men if not to make a profit from their positions? But Elizabeth need know nothing about that. The only time she had ever defied him had been over those sons of hers. He glanced at her expressionless face, remembering suddenly how she had looked then. He had been almost frightened of her, but he had dropped the idea and it had passed.

The truth was that Mauger was much braver in his own mind than in actuality in dealing with his son's powerful patron. His letter was not, therefore, a bold command but a mild request filled with "if it please your lordship" and "if it will be no inconvenience to your lordship." It did *not* please Humphery de Bohun however, to part with a squire who had become a favorite because he was quick, clever, and aggressive; he wrote a brusque refusal, stating his own need of Aubery's services.

This did not improve Mauger's temper and made him all the more frantic to do something, yet he could not think of an excuse to go to Marlowe and fell back on the idea of "accompanying" Elizabeth. She acceded docilely to his demand and searched out a length of fabric of a color that did not suit her but would suit Alys. Mauger applauded the idea of making Alys this gift, thinking it would butter up the girl. The next day they set out for Marlowe right after breakfast. Elizabeth's heart fluttered. She did not know whether she hoped or feared that William would be at home.

William was at home. There was no reason for him to ride out with Raymond and Diccon recruiting. He had plenty to do around the keep. He was, in fact, coming from the stables when Mauger and Elizabeth rode in. The look on both faces was sufficient confirmation of Mauger's belief that something had happened between them. Elizabeth grew ashy pale, and William stopped dead in his tracks and stared at her for one long moment. This gave Mauger less satisfaction than it would have given him a week earlier. He had decided definitely that his original plan would not work. If he killed William as an outraged husband, he probably could not marry Alys to Aubery. William's death would have to come about less directly.

Another pack of "outlaws" such as those who had killed Elizabeth's brothers? Not easy. William was a convivial soul and invited all his neighbors to join him when he went hunting. A knifing in the town would be best. Mauger knew that William frequented several of the whores in the town. The trouble was that probably no one who lived in the town would dare, not even the whores themselves or their men. They all liked William.

The thoughts milled around in Mauger's brain while he greeted William and Elizabeth presented her excuse for coming to see Alys. William swallowed as if there were something stuck in his throat and finally got out, "She is within. Shall I take you?"

"Let her go herself," Mauger said. "She knows the way, and I would like a word with you about Alys."

He watched William take a hesitant step forward, knowing the man was dying to lift Elizabeth down from her horse but was also afraid that touching her would cause him to betray himself. Mauger bent down to fiddle with a stirrup to give William his chance. Maybe the idiot would be so muddled by touching the dross he desired that he would agree to Mauger's importunity this time.

Unaware that Mauger was acting deliberately, William moved very fast when he saw his neighbor occupied. He had Elizabeth off her horse—on the far side from Mauger—in one swift motion. Their eyes met and Elizabeth walked away smoothly. William grabbed her palfrey's rein and led it toward the stable, thus hiding from Mauger the fact that sweat was beading his forehead, even though it was a nasty cold day. By the time Mauger dismounted and followed him, William could speak again.

"Sorry to make you lead in your horse," William said. "The grooms are busy with my young destriers. I was trying their paces to see if one would serve Raymond—the young knight who is with me now, you remember, the one the king sent—in this Welsh business."

Mauger had opened his mouth to say he had met Raymond and been unfavorably impressed, but instead he asked, "What Welsh business?"

"You were the one who told me about David trying to creep out of his agreement with the king," William replied.

"Assuredly, but what has that to do with horses for Raymond?"

"Had you not heard that Gruffydd ap Llewelyn is dead?"

"No, I had not!" Mauger exclaimed. "But I still do not see—oh yes I do. Now Gruffydd is dead, Henry has no alternate prince to offer the Welsh and raise civil war so David thinks it safe to repudiate his agreement. Has it come to war already?"

"Not yet, but the king is sufficiently sure it will that he has warned my overlord and Ri—the earl has courteously warned me. So far no levy is called, but it is certain."

"Will Henry call out the whole kingdom?" Mauger asked.

"I would not think it," William replied cautiously. He did not wish to confess his knowledge of the Scottish troubles because he thought that was not generally known yet. "I cannot believe a very large army will be necessary to depress this upstart's wild ideas, but I am certain to be called because Henry will naturally summon his brother."

Mauger looked furious, which at first surprised William. Then he associated the anger with Mauger's opening remark that he wanted to talk about Alys. However, when he glanced at Mauger again, after handing Elizabeth's palfrey to a boy, the man was smiling broadly. William could only assume he had misread the earlier expressions. He had not. Mauger had been furious, but only briefly. All his problems had flown away. Nothing was easier than disposing of a man during war service. The enemy might do it quite legitimately, and if enemies did not, there were dozens of ways to commit murder and blame it on someone else.

Moreover, from what William said about the second destrier, it was clear that Raymond was going to Wales also. Mauger could have kissed William for solving all his problems for him. Alys would be completely alone in Marlowe. Nothing could be more natural than that a close friend and neighbor should bring the news of her father's death and offer comfort and consolation.

Now Mauger understood why de Bohun had refused to send Aubery home. Thank God he had refused. It would be far better if Aubery came after the Welsh action while Alys was still desolate at the loss of her father and the young knight she had set her eyes on. Doubtless Aubery's offer of affection and companionship would be very welcome then. There would be no problems in controlling the girl or preventing her from communicating with her father's overlord. How fortunate that Elizabeth had brought that cloth as a present. It was a good beginning. Now he would have to talk to Alys himself.

"Probably I will be called too," Mauger remarked, having managed to remember what William said to him last. "I am glad to have this early warning."

There was no probability about it. Mauger intended to have a clerk write to de Bohun as soon as he returned to Hurley and volunteer his services. The fact that Aubery was with the earl would be excuse enough. The fact that he and William were longtime neighbors and "friends" would provide sufficient reason that they should serve in the same actions. For the first time in years, Mauger saw his object actually within reach.

William should have realized that something was very wrong with Mauger's statement. Hurley Abbey seldom sent out the knights who owed it service. The abbey preferred to compound for a fine, which it could get back—with considerable profit—by collecting recompense from the knights. William was not thinking about the usual behavior of Hurley Abbey, however. His mind was not capable of grasping anything beyond the fact that Elizabeth was probably up in his women's quarters. He managed to agree with what Mauger had said, hardly having heard what it was. When he managed to wrench his mind away from the fact of Elizabeth's presence, he began to wonder why Mauger had accompanied her. Alys . . . Mauger had said something about Alys.

"Did you say you wished to speak to me about Alys?" William asked.

"Yes. Frankly I did not like the way this new knight of yours looked at her. He is very young to be trusted—"

"I do not distrust him," William interrupted, leaping to Raymond's defense. Although he had never thought about it, the truth was that William liked Raymond much better than he liked Mauger. "However, I agree with you that he might be hurt. I have sent him off to Bix to train the troops I will take."

"There would be no problem," Mauger suggested, "if Alys were formally promised. She is a good girl, and once her mind was settled on Aubery she would discourage any other advances." Mauger did not, in fact, think Alys was a good girl. He thought her a willful bitch but was wise enough never to permit a hint of such a thought to come across to her doting father.

"But her mind is not settled, Mauger," William pointed out. "I know you think me doting in that I do not simply tell her that Aubery is to be her husband. Perhaps I am doting, but I cannot do it. I will speak 'plain to you. Mary was a good wife to me. Still, I was unhappy in my marriage for there was no love in it for me." William stopped suddenly and his color rose. He had nearly said he loved another woman—to that woman's husband. "I would not bring such dissatisfaction on my daughter—nor upon Aubery, whom I love also—for any benefit in the world."

"But you have no objection to Aubery, do you?" Mauger asked.

"You know I have not. Aubery is a good boy and will make a fine man, I think. If Alys will agree to have him, nothing could gladden my heart more. But it is Alys who must live her life with Aubery, not I."

"Would you object if I talked to Alys alone? I have some messages for her from Aubery." Mauger hesitated, then said, "I am a fool! Aubery sent word that he wished to come home but could not. I should have known then that trouble was stirring in Wales and de Bohun did not wish to give him leave. He entrusted me with some words for Alys. I wondered why, but if he believes there will be a war . . . Yes. Aubery has always taken it as final that he is betrothed to Alys, you know."

"No, I did not know," William said.

It would be horrible beyond belief to inflict on Aubery what he himself had suffered all these years. Now William tried to think of any sign at all that Aubery had felt about Alys as he felt about Elizabeth when they were children. He was almost ready to swear it was not so—but not absolutely ready. Part of his unsureness, he knew, was owing to the fact that he could not really concentrate. Elizabeth was in the keep. Elizabeth. . . . Suddenly it came to William's mind that if Mauger took Alys away to talk privately about Aubery, he and Elizabeth would also be alone.

"I may talk to Alys? Would you permit her to ride out with me? It is very hard to transmit tender messages with servants coming and going or a father listening and—"

"Yes, certainly," William said, his mouth going dry with desire. "If Alys is willing, I have no objections."

Mauger's plan was excellent, and it might have worked had he been even slightly acquainted with his wife's character and thus kept her apart from Alys. The girl was not yet in love with Raymond, but his suppressed emotion had communicated itself to her and something in her was coming awake in response. A clear declaration of passion from almost any desirable young man might have toppled her. Mauger's second-hand relations of Aubery's love would not have been as effective, but Alys might have been sufficiently moved by the false words to agree to a formal betrothal.

Elizabeth, who had seen what was happening to Alys, was equally determined that Alys and Aubery not be precipitated into something they would both regret. She was not certain of exactly what moves Mauger would make, but she knew William would never force Alys into a betrothal. Therefore, her path was clear; she had to make sure Alys would continue to resist. She smiled at the polite, pleased, but puzzled thanks Alys gave for the length of cloth.

"It will suit you better than me, love," Elizabeth said, laughing, "but you know it was never bought for me. It was meant for Aubery. Mauger wanted an excuse to come here, and this was it."

"Oh," Alys said, and laughed also. "Would you like me to make a gown for Aubery from it?"

"No!" Elizabeth exclaimed. "Alys, do you have any love for Aubery?"

"Of course," Alys replied, shocked. "How could I not? I have known him forever."

"That is not what I mean at all," Elizabeth said. "Do you want to marry him?"

Alys looked uncertain and rather embarrassed. A dark, thin face with bright, intense eyes flickered through her mind. But how could she say to Aubery's mother that her son was not desirable?

"You have misunderstood me," Elizabeth continued hastily, reading Alys's expression correctly. "I do not wish to urge you to marry my son. To tell you the truth, I do not think you would suit each other at all."

"Well," Alys temporized, "I do love Aubery, but—but I have known him so long that he is like a brother. I—I am not certain. If papa wants me to marry him . . ."

"Your father only wants you to be happy," Elizabeth said very firmly. "Believe me, Alys, there is no hell like an unhappy marriage. I know! Do not allow anyone, even your father, to convince you that you feel what you do not feel. I think my husband has come here to press for a betrothal. Do not agree unless you are very sure that you wish to spend your life with Aubery."

"I am not sure of that," Alys replied promptly. "How can I be sure? And what about Aubery?"

"Aubery?" Elizabeth smiled again. "It is true Aubery is a few months older than you, but in many ways he is much younger. I assure you Aubery does not wish to marry anyone—not yet." She hesitated, and a thoughtful expression came into her eyes. "Alys," she said slowly, "do not believe what Mauger may say about Aubery's feelings. I—I do not like to criticize my husband, but—but he is not overcareful to speak the truth when he thinks a lie will serve his purpose better."

"Are you saying that Aubery does not love me?" Alys asked.

There was a hint of pique in her voice. Elizabeth thought swiftly. Was she doing her son harm? Was she depriving him of a rich marriage with a beautiful, intelligent woman? She thought of the last time they had been together. No. Aubery already seemed to lean toward gentle girls who desired protection. Alys infuriated him, although he was very fond of her.

"If you want the truth, he does not," Elizabeth answered. "Oh, like a sister, to quarrel with—as you love him, yes. But he is young, and you know your father has filled his head with the need to be dutiful. Mauger could doubtless convince him it was his duty to mouth words of love, but . . . Alys, you will know love when it comes to you. You are fortunate in having a father who cares more for you than for wealth or pride. Do not permit yourself to be rushed into any avowal. There is plenty of time to take Aubery if you want him, but once you are betrothed it will be too late to change your mind."

Alys nodded. That was an argument her father would accept without being hurt, but she felt dissatisfied. "Why do you suddenly speak to me of this, Elizabeth?"

"Because Mauger has been speaking of it to me and says he wants it settled in writing. He even sent to ask Aubery to come home, but he did not come."

"He did not? Did he send a message?"

Elizabeth's face softened. She did not realize that what she said implied Aubery knew his father's reason for asking him to come home. Her mind was on the fact that de Bohun's messenger had sought her out after he had delivered his master's letter to Mauger. He told her softly that Aubery sent his love and wanted to assure her that he was well and very happy. Also her son wished to know if all was well with her. If his father's message was on her account, the messenger said, Aubery would beg his lord to allow him to come home—which he had not done—and he was sure the indulgence would be granted.

"Only his love to me," Elizabeth said softly.

"Then it is certainly true he is not dying for love of me," Alys snapped.

The tart tone made Elizabeth realize the mistaken impression she had given Alys. "No, he is not," she agreed, laughing, "but he did not refuse to come. The earl of Hereford would not give him leave."

"Oh." Alys's face cleared and she laughed also. Then she sobered. "I did not think. Of course de Bohun could not let his squire go now. He will be needed in this Welsh war."

"Welsh war?" Elizabeth repeated, growing pale.

"Did you not know?" Alys cried softly. "I am so sorry. I should not have told you, but I thought . . . Papa goes too."

"Your father also?" Elizabeth's voice shook and her eyes were enormous.

"No harm will come to Aubery," Alys comforted,

although her voice was not very steady either, "and you will not need to worry about him because papa will write to me often, you know he does so, and he will look to Aubery and send news of him."

"Yes," Elizabeth faltered, "yes, of course. Alys, you will send me word if you cannot come yourself of how —how your father does—even if he does not mention Aubery. I—I can judge from that, you know, what action is taking place."

A flicker of reluctance touched Alys, who guessed that Elizabeth's uneven breath and pallor owed only a little to fear for her son. She was almost inclined to temporize so that she could keep knowledge of her father jealously to herself, but a maidservant came in to ask that she and Elizabeth come down to the hall.

CHAPTER 8

When they entered the hall, Elizabeth sheltered behind Alys and the maid so that her pallor and trembling were not perceived. She heard her husband's voice and tried desperately to understand so that she could answer sensibly, but no one seemed to expect any answer from her. She was so shaken by terror that she could not attempt to understand it. It was nothing new for William to ride to war in Richard of Cornwall's tail, and although she had always feared for him, it had been nothing like this.

The exchange of voices in which, surprisingly, Alys had taken a major part ended. Alys and Mauger were going off somewhere together. That seemed peculiar, but Elizabeth had no fear that Mauger would insult Alys, and she only felt relief. She would be able to rest for a few minutes and absorb the shock so that she could face Mauger when he returned. She had taken a single faltering step toward a chair when she was seized in a strong hold.

"Elizabeth!" William's voice held fear. "What ails you?"

"Nothing," she whispered, "a slight faintness. Let me sit down a moment."

"You are so cold," he said. "You are shaking."

His touch made it worse. Such a violent mixture of fear and desire roiled in Elizabeth that the room dimmed and her knees buckled. She was aware of being lifted and carried and clung instinctively. Then, as she was set down on a bed, the world steadied and cleared. She felt William reach up to unlock her arms from around his neck so that he could cover her, but she whispered, "No, do not let me go. I am afraid."

He sat down on the bed beside her. "Of what? In my house, what could you fear, Elizabeth?"

The supine position had restored her. Fear still ate her, but the physical effects of it were gone. Her hands had slipped down from William's neck, but she still held tightly to his arms.

"I am better already," she assured him. "You have done all that was necessary in letting me lie down. Let me rest a moment."

"But what overset you?" William asked anxiously, and then a horrible notion came into his mind. Elizabeth had been with Alys. "Did Alys say something unkind to you?" he snarled.

"Alys? Have you told Alys what—what . . ."

"I have told Alys nothing, but one does not need to tell Alys things. She is very clever. Elizabeth, if that pert devil said something to hurt you after all the kindness you have shown her, I will lift her hide with my belt."

"No!" Elizabeth drew a deep breath. Color came back into her face. "I had no idea she knew about—about us."

"Knew is too strong a word, perhaps, but a guess so certain . . ." She still held him, and heat coursed up his arms from where her hands lay, running over his body. Desperate to say something, anything, he went on, "But something happened, something was said to distress you."

"Alys told me you were going to war in Wales."

She had her eyes fixed on his slightly averted face and all of a sudden the dear, familiar features were startlingly clear, as if she were seeing him for the first time. He was not handsome in terms of a hero of romance—like Mauger. In particular those ridiculous, long, curling lashes that now hid his eyes made her want to laugh at the same time that she could barely prevent herself from pulling him down and kissing them. The thought of kissing brought Elizabeth's eyes to William's mouth and she began to tremble. He looked back at her when he felt her shaking, his own eyes dark with passion. He did not dare make any direct advance. He had asked her that time at Hurley and she had refused. But he could see the desire as plain in her face as he knew it must be in his own.

"Yes, I go to Wales." His voice was thick.

"When?"

"A few weeks. I must train some more men. I cannot leave Alys defenseless."

They were staring at each other, only partly aware of what was being said. Elizabeth's hands slid down from William's arms and lay above his hands, not clutching but stroking them gently. He did not move, but his breathing grew uneven and finally he closed his eyes altogether. The long lashes had. an unusually bright sheen. Tears? It was more than Elizabeth could bear. She drew his head down and their mouths came together.

Almost at once, William pulled free. "I cannot bear it," he said. "I cannot give you up and I cannot have you. I am a man, not a mouthing ape who sighs for a glance from his lady's eyes or a glove from her hand. I am a man! I want you! I wish I were dead!"

"William!" Elizabeth cried.

He turned away. "Thank God I am going to Wales. Thank God for it. Perhaps—"

"William!"

He was only going to say that perhaps he would be able to sleep a night through when he was a hundred miles from her, but Elizabeth had put together the wish for death with the Welsh enterprise. William might try to get himself killed in battle. It was a notion that would never have entered his mind—not because his cry of misery was false but because he would betray his men and Richard and his duty to his daughter if he deliberately permitted himself to be killed. It would never occur to William to ease his own pain at the cost of his duty. But Elizabeth, who was not thinking clearly at the moment, did not realize that.

The sense of doom, of looming disaster, which had gripped her when Alys first spoke of the Welsh war, returned. She felt driven to act, to do something to avert the disaster. There was no sense in begging William not to go; both his duty and the fervor with which he had spoken of leaving proved to Elizabeth that any plea in that direction would be useless. All she could think was that she had to give him a reason, provide him with a hope that would bring him back. She followed the few steps he had moved away and gripped his arm.

"William, I love you."

"Do you think that makes it easier for me to bear?" he muttered.

He did not pull away, but his arm was rigid under her fingers and his face was averted. Elizabeth's eyes took in the fair stubble of beard, the downturned corner of his sensitive mouth, the broad cheekbone, the bleached, lighter tip on the curling lashes.

"Close the door, William," she said softly.

For a moment he stood still. Then he turned his head to look fully at her, his eyes wide open.

"Elizabeth?"

She did not answer, only let go of his arm and put her hand up to the fastening of her wimple. It was crazy, she thought, to endanger William's life, to torture him and herself for the sake of a man who would take no hurt except in his pride. No, not even that, for he would never know. No harm would be done to any living creature in the entire world, and to her and William it would be more precious than the hope of salvation—and if it was a sin in God's eyes, He who was Goodness itself and She who was Mercy would pity and forgive.

Even after he spoke his question in her name, William did not move until Elizabeth's hair fell free. Then, with an intake of breath that was near a sob, he strode through the outer chamber and closed the door. After a brief hesitation, he dropped the bar across.

Returning, William was struck immobile again as he entered the bedchamber. Elizabeth had made excellent progress. Not only her wimple was gone but her cotte and tunic also. The lines of her slender body showed very plainly under the thin shift. Committed now, Elizabeth was not such a fool as to blemish her brief joy with guilt or fear. She laughed softly, well aware from the avid eyes that ate her what had stopped William in his tracks.

"Come now," she teased, "you knew I was a skinny wench. Surely I have not become so ugly as to turn you to stone like a Medusa."

Gold glittered in William's eyes. He closed the distance between them in a few long strides and pressed her against him. "Perhaps not all," he chuckled, "but you have certainly turned one part of me hard as stone." Then he buried his face in her hair. "I do not know what you are in other eyes, Elizabeth, but to me you are the most beautiful being in the world. You are perfect. To look at you is heaven and hell together, for I joy and I burn."

Elizabeth found she could not draw breath properly. Even William had never said such things to her before. They had been too young, too sure of a long life together to need such words. On the other hand, she was not totally unacquainted with sexual arousal. She and William had done considerable experimenting before they had been parted. All her pleasure in sex had stopped at that point, however. Mauger thought her ugly and made no bones about it. His perfunctory attempts to ready her for coupling had produced nothing but distaste, and the act itself became a thing to be endured with stoicism, like a beating.

In one thing Elizabeth was fortunate. She never transferred her revulsion for coupling with Mauger toward coupling in general. Thus, William's praise—more than that, the proof of his violent arousal—worked on her like an aphrodisiac. "Oh, William," she sighed, kissing his neck and ear.

He said something she could not hear, and his hands began to roam caressingly over her body. Soon he plucked impatiently at the shift, which prevented him from touching her skin directly. Elizabeth was willing, even eager, to take it off, but once she did she gasped in William's renewed embrace. The harsh wool of his common outerwear rasped on the tender skin of her breasts and belly like a hair shirt.

That brought them enough to themselves to permit William to undress. Elizabeth watched, growing more and more excited as his strong body was bared. She did not think how ridiculous the sensation was, how many naked male bodies she had seen without the smallest reaction. She did not think at all, only fed his lust and her own by touching and kissing. When his shoes and chausses were off, he grabbed her close again, and she thrust her hips forward instinctively. William gasped and pulled away, lifted her to carry her to the bed, but midway there fell to kissing her breasts and sucking her nipples.

Elizabeth had to bite her lips to keep from screaming with excitement. She moaned and twitched in his arms, bit at his neck, tried to reach his genitals but could not. She gasped his name and the word "please," feeling she would die if she did not soon have some relief from the intolerable pressure of pleasure that was building in her.

William's state was no better than Elizabeth's. His wife had been a passive partner, never refusing but never showing any sign of delight, although after he had got over his initial rage he had dutifully tried to give her pleasure. Beyond Mary's dull acquiescence, William had known only the practiced caresses of whores. Thus, to him, Elizabeth's response was new and so exciting that he was nearly beside himself. He knew she was ready; he wanted to put her on the bed and take her, but he could not stop what he was doing. Every time he sucked, Elizabeth squirmed and moaned. Every time she squirmed, her back just barely touched the tip of his upstanding shaft and a hot throb of pleasure racked his whole body.

Finally William began to shake so much he thought he would drop her, and that drove him forward to deposit his burden on the bed and fling himself atop her. She cried out when he entered, and he stopped his thrust, fearing he had hurt her, but she heaved against him and he lodged himself, sighing with satisfaction.

"Wait!" Elizabeth cried, straining against him, thinking the sigh was the end for him. "Wait for me. Wait."

"Hush," he soothed, kissing her. "I am not a green boy. There is no hurry. Trust me."

She did, and he was as good as his word, although she put little strain on him in the keeping of his promise. In a very few minutes, he was muffling her cries and his own groans by locking their mouths together. Finished, he could not bear to withdraw, knowing there might never be another time. He braced himself on his elbows, trying to relieve Elizabeth of most of his weight and still cover her body to give her warmth.

Her hair was in the wildest disorder, but her eyes were like still water, luminous and full of peace. "I never knew," she sighed. "I never knew."

William was astounded. He lifted his head higher. "You mean in all these years . . ."

"Not so many years. He never came to me after he got John upon me—and you may be sure I did not invite him. He thinks I am ugly—"

"Ugly? What a fool!"

Elizabeth smiled at the passion in William's voice. "Each to his own taste," she said. "I assure you I did not mind what he thought of me, so long as he left me in peace."

"Thank God for that," William muttered.

"You need not fear, beloved. There is only you. I could never bear his touch, never!"

It did not occur to Elizabeth to doubt her own words. As far as she knew, she was telling the truth. However, if she had been as precious, as beautiful, in Mauger's eyes as she was in William's, it was not likely she would long have clung to the memory of her childhood sweetheart—except as a pleasant memory. She could read what William thought of her in his face, and she grew radiant, seeing herself with his eyes. There was a new value to her slender limbs, her smooth

brown skin, her small breasts, as high and firm as those
of a girl just entering puberty.

William did not doubt what she said either. Her response to him was evidence enough, and the new
knowledge that he had been the first—the only man—
to bring Elizabeth to climax was another iron fetter to
bind him to her. There was also the bitter knowledge
that he must lose her as soon as they parted. The joy
and pain drove William into renewing his caresses.

"No, William. We have no time."

"We have nothing," he said harshly.

Her eyes filled with tears. "Was it nothing to you?
It was everything to me. Let me up, William."

"In God's name, do not be angry, Elizabeth. You
know I did not mean that—only that I cannot bear to
part with you, that it is not enough for me to lie with
you and then go our separate ways."

"Let me up," she repeated, but her voice was softer
and she stroked his cheek. "If I do not get up, I will
soil the bed. I do not need to give your servants and
your daughter evidence that I am a whore."

"Never say that!"

William got off her hastily and she rose also, appalled at the pain in his eyes. "William—"

"Is that what you feel?" he asked, his voice shaking.
"Is that what I have done to you?"

"No!" She embraced him, kissed him. "William, look
at me. Do I look ashamed? You have given me a precious jewel that I can hold in my heart, a joy that will
light the dark hours of my life. Forgive me, love. It is
not what I feel but what others will say."

"Why should you care what others say?" he muttered. "Do you think I cannot protect you?"

Elizabeth shuddered. He could have protected her
from twenty years as Mauger's wife, have saved them
all the agony, if only he had stood firm against his
father's will. But she did not say it. It was twenty years
too late, and bitter words would only destroy the joy
they had without mending anything. She kissed William

gently again and began to dress in the clothes she had so hastily discarded.

He watched her sullenly for a while, but her grace of movement was such a joy that the anger slipped away. It was her only fault, that she cared too much what "others would say." Elizabeth did not lack physical courage, and "what others would say" was doubtless one of the weapons used to get her married once she was at Ilmer. "Think what others will say if you are sent home unwed," the women must have told her.

Elizabeth was as swift as she was graceful and was buttoning the sleeves of her cotte when William reached for his own clothing.

He put on the gown but, resentfully, did not move. "If you care as little for Mauger as you say, why are you so fearful? Let him discover us. He can do you no harm in my house, except to repudiate you. And do not sing me any sad songs about your sons. I will tell you plain that they do not love their father, and they do love you—and me, a little. They would soon—"

"They would not soon learn to take pleasure in having their mother called a whore. William, stop! In any case, how can you protect me when you are in Wales?"

"Wal—"

The broken word, the startled look, told Elizabeth he had forgotten the coming war, forgotten everything in his concentration on her. She felt a thrill of satisfaction that was damped by a wave of fear. William put his arm around her and drew her into the antechamber where he seated her by the fire. After that, he unbarred the door, opened it silently and carefully a little way. If no one had tried it previously, it might seem that he had never shut it completely, only drew it partly closed so that the chill would not come in from the hall. His face was grim when he came back to stand in front of Elizabeth.

"I am a fool," he said bitterly. "I forgot! I completely forgot about this stupid business in Wales. Oh, God! Elizabeth, believe me, I just did not think. . . . Now what are we to do?"

"Nothing. You may have forgotten, but I did not. I—I was frightened. I did not wish to let you go without having something. What I did, I did in full knowledge of what might come of it. You are not responsible for me, William. I am a grown woman."

"Not responsible! Are you mad? Of course I am responsible for any trouble that comes of this. I will—Oh, my God! I cannot even write to Richard and tell him to find another man to take the duty he set on me. He is in Flanders—" He gasped, clenched his jaws too late over what was supposed to be kept secret. *"Jesu Christus,"* he groaned, "be deaf, Elizabeth. Where Richard is was meant for no ears but mine."

"It is forgotten," Elizabeth said calmly. "Do I understand you aright? You have some special duty in Wales?"

"Yes. That is no secret, but—but I would prefer if you did not speak of it to Mauger."

"I never speak about you or of anything you tell me to him." Elizabeth raised her brows. "How could you think you needed to warn me?"

"I do not seem to be able to think at all," William sighed. "It is a harmless enough thing that Richard and I are friends, but I have found when it is known it brings envy and—and enemies. People ask for favors from him I know he would not be willing to grant of himself. He would do it for love of me, but I cannot ask things of him—I cannot. So I cannot accommodate them. You understand, do you not? Richard and I could not be friends if I used that friendship."

"Yes, I understand." Tears stung her eyes. That was the difference between friendship and marriage—a marriage was meant for giving and taking. But that was lost forever for her and William.

"What is it, beloved?" William asked, down on a knee beside her. "Do you want me to take you to Bix? No, that would be worse than Marlowe once I was gone—to Wallingford? Richard's man would keep you safe for me until I came home again. You would not be alone there. I believe the countess—no, perhaps she will go to her sister. The countess! Elizabeth, I can put you in Sancia's keeping—"

Laughing through her tears, Elizabeth leaned forward and stopped his lips with hers. She had certainly accomplished her purpose. William had every intention now of coming home alive and well from the Welsh war. What was more, the boy who had failed her was a man now. He thought first of protecting her, and a long way second of everyone else. He had said he would not "use" his friendship with Richard of Cornwall, but in the next moment he was willing to saddle the earl's young wife with his mistress or leave her in Wallingford. That would precipitate Cornwall into the unsavory position of being a party to the seduction and conspiring with a favorite to deprive an innocent gentleman of his wife.

"Do not be so foolish, William," Elizabeth murmured, breaking their kiss reluctantly. "Everything I said to you in Hurley is still true. I do not love Mauger, but he does not deserve that I abandon him and shame him. And even if you are right and the boys could some day bring themselves to forgive me for—"

"Do not say that word again!" William exclaimed, getting to his feet. His eyes were unnaturally bright.

"What word? Oh. . . . No, but—"

"A divorce," William said forcefully. "We will find some innocent reason. It need not be very compelling. Richard will ask Boniface—the archbishop of Canterbury—to grant it, and—"

"William." Elizabeth rose and took his hands in hers. "Mauger would never agree unless I left Hurley in his hands. I love you—with all my soul and all my body— but I could not do that to my people. He would destroy them and the estate."

That was an argument William could not counter, and he stood, biting his lips, trying to think his way around the obstacle. "I could make it worth his while," he said finally. "I have not much ready money, but Richard would lend me whatever I asked for. I could—"

Again Elizabeth stopped his speech with a kiss. Internally she shuddered at the load of debt William was ready to shoulder to obtain her. Pride mixed with horror. It was sweet to be so precious.

"You can do nothing now," she pointed out, as soon as she released his lips. "When you come home from Wales, we will consider this again."

Her voice was calm, but a shudder of fear passed through her at the mention of Wales, and her eyes grew blind-looking for a moment. William pressed her back into the chair, bending over her protectively.

"You are afraid," he murmured. "I cannot leave you to Mauger alone and afraid. Shall I—shall I write to Richard and . . . and . . ."

He could not even bring himself to say that he would refuse to do the duty laid upon him and thereby betray his overlord's trust. For one moment joy leapt in Elizabeth's heart while she thought she could keep him safe out of the battles to come. In the next, she realized that he would be as good as dead, worse than dead, if she destroyed his pride in himself.

"I am not afraid of Mauger," Elizabeth said. "It is the war I fear. It is nothing new, William, that I should fear war."

"Well, go in." Alys's voice came sharply through the opening of the door.

"I do not wish to intrude on such old friends," Mauger replied, completely without inflection.

"Do not be so silly," Alys snapped. "Oh, I beg your pardon, Sir Mauger, but if papa wanted privacy he would lock the door. He often closes it to keep in the warmth."

Elizabeth laughed aloud at the stunned expression on William's face. Plainly Alys had told a barefaced lie in the smoothest and most natural manner—and her father had never before caught her at such a thing. The sound, as well as Alys's warning guaranteed that Mauger would neither hear nor see anything improper whether he waited or burst in at once, so he opened the door fully. He found his wife still smiling, her face turned toward the door, and William wearing an expression of surprised affront that was scarcely loverlike—

"I heard you had been taken ill just after I left, Elizabeth," Mauger said. "I am glad to see you so quickly recovered."

"I was not ill," Elizabeth answered colorlessly. "I had a shock and felt faint for a few minutes. Sir William brought me in here because he also thought I was ill and cold."

It was the exact truth. Elizabeth, who had to live with Mauger, did her best not to lie to him because she would have to remember her lies or be caught in them.

"But what could have shocked you here?" Mauger asked.

His voice was smooth, but Elizabeth knew he was in a violent rage. Suddenly she realized that he had almost certainly gone off with Alys to try to talk her into becoming betrothed to Aubery. If Alys had been careless and Mauger guessed that Elizabeth had warned her . . . He would kill her! She paled and did not answer; she had forgotten the question. She did not see William's color rise as hers fell or the way he tensed, but Alys saw.

"It was my fault," she said, her voice sharp and spiteful. "I forgot it was the custom in your family, Sir Mauger, to keep your women in ignorance like Moslem slaves. I told Lady Elizabeth about the war in Wales."

"Alys!" William snapped, shocked at the tone and disrespect.

"I am truly sorry," Alys then said, having given a good reason for her father's flush and tenseness. Her voice softened. "I had forgotten also that Aubery was with the earl of Hereford and would be in some danger."

"I had no intention of keeping my wife in ignorance," Mauger growled, goaded away from Elizabeth's doings by his fury with the spoiled bitch of Marlowe. "I did not know myself."

The exchange had given Elizabeth time to think. Alys, she realized, would never betray her to Mauger, whom she had never liked. She had better get Mauger and William apart before something happened to put them at each other's throats. Elizabeth stood up.

"I would like to go home now, please," she said. "I would like to write—I mean, have a letter written to Aubery."

Numbly, William responded to the flat statement by going into the hall and telling one of the menservants to have Sir Mauger's horses brought from the stables. Aubery! But Elizabeth had not once mentioned the boy in connection with the Welsh war, only when they had been talking about . . . He sought wildly for an excuse to keep her, but there was none except the truth and it was unthinkable to expose her when he must soon leave.

But he could not go back to the old relationship with Elizabeth. He had tasted her. What if Mauger— no, Elizabeth said he had not touched her in years and there was that woman—Emma. William sighed. Thank God for Emma. Besides, now he remembered Mauger had said something about being called up for Wales himself. That was odd. . . .

He had no time to think it through, however, for Mauger was beside him, saying a formal farewell. William had to give his attention to it lest he do something stupid, and by the time he turned to help Elizabeth to mount, she was up already. She was pale, very pale, but that did not surprise him. He felt as if his own heart was being torn out.

CHAPTER 9

William shifted on his cot and thought wearily that a hundred miles or a thousand separating him from Elizabeth would not procure him a full night's sleep. Distance did not mute the siren's song. He was in no physical need—there were drabs enough in the camp, and he had no taste for anything better than a vessel to empty himself into as he would use a chamberpot. It was most fortunate that Richard was not with this army. William did not believe he would have been able to fulfill his usual part in the jollifications Richard made so much a part of camp life. He was actually glad to be able to say he was too busy when the other vassals wished to make merry in the town.

He need not have been "too busy." Raymond could have checked that clerk's accounts. It was obvious that large-scale supplies for war were things with which Raymond was very familiar. Raymond. . . . William shifted uneasily again. Raymond was not happy. Oh, he was enjoying the war. He had been delighted with the two small engagements they had fought. Perhaps he was a trifle too daring, but he was a very strong fighter and he had held his place well, not indulging in *dangerous* heroics.

Raymond was carrying a burden around with him, however, just as William himself was. They were sharing a tent for convenience and economy, and too often when William lay awake he could hear that Raymond was also sleepless. Another symptom of the young man's unease was a recent spate of looking unhappily at William and saying, "Sir—" and then letting his voice drift away. Or, if William was so unkind or lacking in thoughtfulness as to ask, "Yes, what?" flushing up and

136

shaking his head with an awkward, "Nothing. Sorry, sir."

William's sore heart ached for him also. It seemed so hard that, having lost so much already, he could not have the sweet compensation of a woman he could love. The hunger in his eyes when a messenger rode in from Marlowe with a letter from Alys was pathetic. Why should Raymond not have Alys, William asked himself again. Alys seemed somewhat inclined in that direction, and she had certainly decided against Aubery for good, although she confessed to her father that she had not been as definite with Sir Mauger, because it was really her father's business to refuse the match.

That knowledge sent William off to Hereford two days ahead of his troop so that he could speak privately and at length with Aubery. The talk was one bright spot in the muddle of unhappiness. Shamefaced but honest, Aubery had confessed he had no more desire for Alys than she had for him.

"I do not know why, sir," the boy said, blushing hotly, "for she is the most beautiful girl I have ever seen, but—but . . ."

"Never mind, Aubery," William had replied, sighing with relief that Elizabeth's son, whom he loved for his own sake also, would not be hurt. "I am only glad that you and Alys are agreed. I would have liked you for a son, but I hope I have not lost much. I hope you will love me even if there is no blood bond between us."

The answer to that had been completely satisfactory, but, three days later, Aubery had come, whitefaced, to beg William not to tell his father he had admitted he did not love Alys. William reassured him, saying that the admission had really had no effect on the question of the marriage. He would have grieved, if he knew Aubery had been hurt, but he would not have forced the marriage on Alys in any case. Aubery need not worry. It was William's business to settle with Mauger, and he could easily do it from Alys's point of view without ever mentioning Aubery.

Although that was true, William found he could not approach Mauger with a rejection he knew would hurt and disappoint him. It just seemed too much first to refuse his son—for that was how it would seem if Aubery could not bring himself to say he did not want Alys—and then to take his wife. As his thoughts came back to Elizabeth, William groaned aloud.

"Are you ill, sir?" Raymond's voice came anxiously from the other cot.

William barely suppressed another groan. "No," he said. "Go to sleep, for Mary's sweet sake." There was no reply, but William knew Raymond was watching him in the dark, and he added, "I have eaten and drunk nothing but from our own supplies. I am not sick or in pain. Go to sleep."

That was another puzzle. Two weeks past, when they were still mustered at Hereford, William had returned from a hunt with the earl and some cronies to find a roast and garnished goose in his tent. The gift had not surprised him. When men with loving wives received special tidbits from home, they often shared them with friends. He had not eaten of it because he was bid to dinner in the keep and, because he was hurried, he forgot to leave a message that Raymond should eat it. Then, either he or Raymond had left a flap of the tent undone, and one of the dogs that roamed the camp had found his way in. When William had returned he had tripped over the sprawled body of the dog—dead.

Anything might have killed the animal. It was a stray, mangy and scrawny, but it was a suspicious thing that no one would come forward and say he had sent the goose. William had not inquired about any of these matters—but Raymond had gone about the camp to offer thanks for the gift—and no one would accept the thanks. That roused Raymond's suspicions, and he had voiced them to William, who had laughed at him, asking who in the world could want him dead.

Neither of them could answer that question, and the dog's body and the half-eaten goose were already disposed of. It was a suspicious circumstance, but there was no one to suspect except Richard's clerk. William like him no better than he had at first, but there was no sign of dishonesty in his records. It was ridiculous to suspect him anyway because he could not have had anything to do with the other two incidents. But they *must* be accidents of camp life, William told himself.

Private quarrels did break out in an army, and the men involved were sometimes so infuriated that, instead of quieting when ordered to do so, they turned on the authority that tried to constrain them. It was fortunate that he and Raymond had been armed, being on their way to practice jousting. Even so, it had been a near thing. There had been only four men when they dismounted to settle the fight, but several more had rushed over. The noise had carried, and rescue had arrived before he or Raymond had been hurt. The men had scattered, except the few Raymond and he had killed or wounded—so that was the end of it.

But then there had been the arrow that had skinned his left arm. That was a little harder to explain. It was a Welsh arrow, but many Englishmen used the Welsh bow now because it was easier to aim and much quicker to use than the crossbow—and it really was not likely that one single Welsh bowman would be so near the English camp. A few inches to the right, and William knew he would have been dead. Raymond had insisted that it was done apurpose, an attempt at murder, but William could not believe it. There simply was no reason for anyone to murder him—except Mauger.

William nearly groaned again, but remembered Raymond in time and kept his feelings to himself. It could not be Mauger. Mauger did not yet know that he had a reason to hate his neighbor. He could not know. His manner to William was exactly the same as it had always been. In fact, Mauger had very good reason to want to keep William alive. Since he had not yet rejected the marriage between Alys and Aubery, Mauger must believe he still favored it. His death would end all hope of that union. Richard would doubtless find a much better match for Alys.

The whole thing was ridiculous anyway, William thought exasperatedly. No one wanted him dead. God knew what the dog died of—maybe too full a stomach; the fight in the camp was an everyday occurrence; the arrow had doubtless been loosed by a thoughtless idiot who was scared out of his wits by his near miss and had hidden himself away. William would never have given any of the matters a second thought if it had not been for the way Raymond reacted. Suspicion not being enough, the young knight now dogged his master's steps with the watchfulness of the nurse of a precious heir.

It was embarrassing and yet so good and kind that he had not the heart really to scold Raymond. The anxious care would have been completely comical, except for one thing. William knew Raymond liked him —it was mutual—but he was sure such devotion was owing to Raymond's terror of needing to tell Alys that harm had come to her father and he had not been there to prevent it. Raymond and Alys. . . . Raymond had no lands, no home, and he loved Alys. If Raymond was there to protect Marlowe and Bix and Alys, he could take Elizabeth. . . . William's eyes closed and at last he slept.

Just at dawn, he woke with a start, listening, but whatever sound had dragged him from his delightful dreams—if it had been a sound—was gone. He lay, thinking about those dreams, acknowledging with pain that Elizabeth was not bound to Mauge but to Hurley and, even if he was free of the responsibility of Alys and his lands, she would not be similarly freed. He sat up suddenly, and then looked guiltily toward Raymond, sorry if he had wakened him. He realized at once that Raymond had not been asleep. His glance had been so close to his quick movement, that he caught Raymond's unguarded expression. William's heart was wrenched. He knew that look too well. His own face had worn it too often for him to mistake the misery it betrayed.

William said nothing. Raymond had already turned his back. In any case, what could he say? If Alys could be happy with the man Richard had in mind for her, should he deprive her of luxury because he wanted her with him or because he wanted to ease Raymond's suffering? Then it occurred to William that, although Richard loved Alys dearly, he had no idea what it was to want a woman he could not have. Richard had married twice for duty and both times had been fortunate. His first marriage had been happy, if not wildly passionate; his second looked to be even more successful.

Without doubt, Richard would expect Alys to do the same. William had never thought about the matter before. He knew Richard would do no more than suggest as long as he was alive, and he had always rather counted on the marriage to Aubery. Richard knew about that plan. He had not been enthusiastic, saying Alys was worth much better, but agreed that if she wanted Aubery the union would make a nice block of power and land in a rich area.

Things had changed, however. The plan concerning Aubery was ended, and William thought suddenly, I am about to go into battle today. I am not immortal.

He had not even been scratched in the two skirmishes thus far, but accidents did happen. If that arrow had been a few inches more to the right . . . They were about to set a trap for the Welsh in a small village this very afternoon. By some crazy mischance it might happen that he could be killed. Richard was far away—still in Flanders or marching toward Scotland. Alys would be left naked. He used to count on Mauger to protect her, but Mauger would be in the same action this afternoon, and even if Mauger came out unscathed, he was no safe protector for Alys. He would force her into an unwanted marriage.

No. No more forced marriages. William drew on a bedrobe and got his writing desk. Setting it across his knees, he explained the whole situation in great detail to Richard, including his wish that Alys be permitted to marry Raymond if that was what she desired.

When William looked up from sealing the letter, he found Raymond's eyes on him. "Sometimes," he said with a smile, "I think I am a fool. All the times I have gone to war before, it was in the earl of Cornwall's tail. Thus, I have never had to think what would befall if I were hurt or killed. Richard, as you know, would care for Alys as if she were his own. This time, however, he is far away—too far away, if . . ." William hesitated, then told Raymond of the plan for marriage with Aubery that had been aborted.

"Does Sir Mauger know you are opposed to it now?" Raymond asked, suspicion rising in his eyes.

"No. I did not think this a good time to tell him. He is not—not easy with his sons. I was a little afraid he would be harsh with Aubery, blaming him for not fixing Alys's affection. There is another reason too," William said slowly, "which is private to me. However, you need not suspect Sir Mauger of wishing me ill. My death could not profit him because Richard, who is my overlord, has no reason to favor a marriage with Aubery, except to oblige me."

Raymond nodded, but his face was frozen. The talk of Alys's marriage was tearing him apart. It was impossible for him to offer for her, impossible from every way he looked at it. His father would have a fit, would probably disown him for taking a wife who brought no fortune and no alliance. On the other side, he would do Sir William, whom he loved dearly, great harm if he married Alys. She would need to live with him in Aix, and Marlowe would have no master. Worse would befall the estate than what William was now saying he feared for it.

Raymond already understood that Sir William, who was well young enough to father and raise a male heir, would not marry again. The subject had come up in an early talk with Alys. She had only shaken her head and said, "There is a woman he cannot have. He will take no other." In the beginning, Raymond had thought that attitude lunatic. Now, when he thought of marrying some woman other than Alys for lands or power, he felt sick. Sir William thought he would leave the estate to

Alys and her sons. Could Raymond take even that away from him?

Reason was all on one side. Reason told him that when this war was over and he had proof to give King Henry that Sir William was a loyal man, he should not return to Marlowe. As he thought of it, such a pang of longing tore at him that, involuntarily, his breath hissed in. Surprisingly, Sir William did not ask about it, did not even look at him, but went on explaining how dear Marlowe was to him and that he hoped Alys's husband would be willing to make it his home.

Reason flew right out the tent door flap when Raymond realized Sir William was subtly encouraging him, whom he thought to be a penniless and homeless hireling, to try for Alys. "Sir—" he gasped.

But Sir William shook his head firmly. "There is no need to consider such matters now. Only if I should die, you must go at once to Marlowe to make sure that no one tries to seize Alys or to influence her against her will until Richard should be free of his duties and able to take her into his care. Here is a letter for him, explaining all I have said to you."

"You think that there is great danger in this raid that is planned?" Raymond asked, rather surprised.

William smiled. "No. More than in the two previous ones, yes. From what the scouts have told us, the village might be a trap, but it is a trap we wish to spring and precautions are being taken to avoid excessive danger."

"I did not think you were deliberately leading me to my death," Raymond said, grinning. "You would not do that without telling me in the fairest manner—as you told me, most truthfully, that there would be no loot in Wales."

"Puppy!" William exclaimed, looking fondly at the young man and laughing at his teasing. "However, I have not told you all. Go get us something with which to break our fast and I will confess everything I learned in council. It is time for you to know."

It was true that William knew a great deal more than

he told Raymond or anyone else, for he was deep in the council of the earl of Hereford. De Bohun, despite his youth and Richard's fears, was no fool at all. He had guessed why Richard always knew what the lesser men were thinking. Hereford was a good leader and went out among his men, but he knew there was always some restraint in what they said to him. Probably they would warn him if what he intended would cause a disaster, but they were chary of offering too much advice lest they offend someone much mightier than themselves. Sir William, childhood friend and close companion of Earl Richard, had no such reservations. So Hereford had invited William to come to the war councils which were ordinarily reserved for the great vassals that held directly from the king.

Thus, William had all the news and a much wider view of the planning than the other minor knights. Now, only hours before the action was to begin, William felt free to describe the situation fully to Raymond.

"You have heard, I imagine, that the king was faced with a war from Scotland as well as this little business here in Wales," William began, after a servant had brought them bowls of some cereal mush flavored with bits of salt meat and cheese.

"It was rumored about, yes," Raymond answered. "Some of the men say it was agreed between David ap Llewelyn and King Alexander."

"Perhaps, although I think 'agreed' is too strong a word. Having married the daughter of Ingelram de Coucy, Alexander was too swayed by his father-by-marriage's proud talk and his offers of support. He cried defiance to Henry. David, most reasonably, chose to use Henry's preoccupation with Scotland to accomplish his own ends without waiting for the slow and uncertain deliberations of the pope."

"Does the war with the Scots go ill?" Raymond asked.

William shook his head. "Far to the contrary. Richard obtained the count of Flanders's support. With this and the levy and other mercenaries, the king marched north. Meanwhile, Ingelram had died in a most peculiar fashion. His son John upheld his father's promise but the barons of the Cinque Ports were warned, ships were out, and the French were turned back."

"I suppose that cooled Alexander's ardor," Raymond said.

"Yes, it did, more especially because John de Coucy made it plain that he had honored his father's promise but did not agree with him and would do no more."

"Then Henry had a clear victory?"

"You might call it that," William said, laughing, "but no one did a lick for it, except my poor Richard, who rode back and forth between the parties until terms were agreed."

"Then they did not fight."

William laughed again at the disappointment in Raymond's voice. "No, they did not."

Raymond frowned. "But the king has been at considerable cost, I guess, to bring the count of Flanders and his men here. What kind of victory can be won without a fight?"

"I do not know the terms of the peace," William replied. "I can only guess that we are back where we were before Alexander cried defiance. Possibly Alexander will pay Henry's costs. I do not know, but, with the Scots, this peace will last a little longer—I hope—than one gained by force of arms. That is some advantage."

The look of doubt on Raymond's face, which must have mirrored his own, made William laugh aloud. "In any case," he went on, "the peace with the Scots does not concern us—except that, when the Welsh hear of it they will doubtless believe that Henry will bring the great army he has gathered here to use against them. Thus, they will divide into small parties and flee up into the mountains so that it is impossible to bring them to battle. No, do not shake your head. This is their practice."

"But that will leave their lands defenseless," Raymond began, and then started to laugh himself. "Where there is nothing to defend, I suppose it does not matter if the land be defenseless."

William shrugged. "The older men tell me that large armies have repeatedly been driven out of Wales this way. A large army soon starves in this wilderness, and its spirit can be broken by harassment. There has been considerable surprise that we have been so little troubled by raids on the camp and arrows on the march. They think that David is not so skillful as his father and might be fooled. Thus, Hereford and Clare are agreed that we should spring this trap and see what comes of it. Indeed, if we wish to inflict any real hurt on them it must be within the next few days, before they hear about the peace with Alexander."

"We are to be bait?" Raymond asked.

"Yes, exactly. The men who know Welsh ways think there is a large force nearby. If we go into the village and seem intent on looting, we hope it will bring the large force down on us. They like to wipe out small detachments and then fade away into the woods. We must seem like a renegade group—carrying skins of wine, spread out over the village to loot, and seeming half drunk. Hopefully we will be too tempting a target to resist."

Raymond's brows shot up. "You say well. In such disorder, we *will* be slaughtered."

"I hope not. As soon as they attack, you will fire the largest barn, which we will have soaked with oil—that is what will be in our 'wineskins.' When the smoke from that is visible, and it should rise in minutes, Sir Mauger will bring his troops to our aid if we are engaged with a small group. If the main army should take the bait, Mauger will send signals to Hereford, who will be ready with the full army."

"I am not accustomed to such actions," Raymond said, but his eyes were bright with interest.

"Nor I," William admitted. "I fought in Wales in my youth as Chester's squire, but we were defending keeps in the usual way or sometimes raiding a village in retaliation. Still, the men who fought against old Prince

Llewelyn think this is the best hope to draw the Welsh into battle."

"I hope so," Raymond replied, "but I cannot understand the need. They are brave men. I could see that when we engaged with them. Why then must they be 'tricked' into battle. Why do they not attack us and drive us out?"

"There is sense in what they do," William responded judiciously. "Wales has fewer people and they are not as well armed as we. They have few horses and are not trained to fighting on horseback. This mountainous country gives them easy shelter from which they can fall upon us and retreat to safety. Why should they risk losing all? I understand their practice worked well in the past. Why should they change? We must hope they are grown a little rusty. Otherwise, we will be till winter chasing will-o'-the-wisps and gain nothing."

"Well, I certainly do not desire that," Raymond said, laughing, "so I had better get about preparing our surprise."

William watched Raymond stride off purposefully and smiled. A real fire-eater that one, but sensible with it. It was a pleasure to see a young man enjoy a war so much. William's smile broadened as he realized he was feeling much better himself. Nothing could assuage the pangs of love like the prospect of a good fight. His eyes grew thoughtful. He had a clear report on the village and felt he knew just where to make a stand safely until Mauger could bring up reinforcements and, if necessary, the main army could arrive. Now all that remained to do was confirm where Mauger would lie hidden and from what direction he would approach the village. They had discussed it already, but a last-minute review of plans never hurt.

The truth was that the matter had not been as fully discussed as it should have been. Ridiculous as it was, William felt embarrassed to accept Mauger's support when he was Mauger's wife's lover. Yet he could not object when de Bohun had suggested Mauger. It was a most logical choice that longtime neighbors and friends support each other. Moreover, de Bohun wished to give his favorite squire's father a chance to distinguish himself. William gritted his teeth over his distaste and began to walk toward Mauger's encampment. He had stolen enough from the man. He would see that Mauger got all possible credit for the action if it was successful.

CHAPTER 10

Somewhat earlier than he had intended to start, William watched the men he would lead form up. He was still chewing over the peculiar fact that Mauger had already been gone when he went to discuss the disposition of the troops with him. Mauger had not forgotten or become confused about the action—that was sure. A man had been left in the encampment with a message for William, confirming all the plans that had been made—only the man was sick and, William feared, not too clever either.

"I do not like it," Raymond said, as William gave him some last-minute instructions. "Why should he go off like that?"

"Eagerness," William replied. "You know, Raymond, Mauger has very little experience of war because the abbey usually pays a fine instead of sending men. You saw that he was wild with joy when Hereford proposed this action to him."

It was true, and Raymond said no more as he signaled the troop to start, but he disliked Mauger even while he realized the cause was ridiculous. There would have been more sense in disliking Aubery, but Raymond did not dislike Aubery—quite the contrary. In any case, he did not care whether this trick worked on the Welsh or not. He would prefer the war to continue. When it was over, he would have to decide about Alys —but there was plenty of good fighting weather left.

Mauger, sitting comfortably with his back to a tree, was contemplating the same fact with great pleasure. There was plenty of time to accomplish his purpose even if this trap did not work. It would certainly reduce the number of men in William's troop, and that would increase William's vulnerability. If not this action, then another—but William would die.

With the end so clearly in sight, Mauger was content to wait. He would be sweetly revenged, not only on William but on those two women. Imagine that slut of a girl saying she did not think it proper for her to marry Aubery because she did not love him as a woman should love a husband. And that ugly, sexless bitch of a wife—she would be well served.

Thinking about the women always made Mauger so angry that impatience stabbed him again. That man had too much luck—too much. Imagine a dog getting the goose. Then Mauger sighed. It was not William's luck that had saved him but his own. That goose had been a stupid move. Someone would surely have whispered "poison," and questions would have been asked. And that loose-tongued idiot of a son might have . . . Well, the question would never arise now.

Still, William had been lucky to get out of that brawl. No, that was not so much luck as the stupidity of the mercenaries—or of Egbert. He had given his fool of a man a good knock for not telling them specifically that they should not act unless William was unarmed—but they should have known that themselves. It was the mail that had saved him—and who would expect men to be "practicing" at arms in the middle of a war? That last escape from the arrow was plain luck though —but the luck must be growing a little thin. The arrow had caught him in the arm.

There was no use regretting it, Mauger told himself. It was a good idea, but this way was really much better. This time should do it. All that was necessary was to come too late, and he had set himself up as a sitting duck for attack. He was pretty sure that the Welsh knew the whole plan—the prisoner he had allowed to escape spoke French pretty well. And if William was only wounded, it would be most natural for his friend and neighbor to carry him off the field to safety. One more wound would never be noticed, and William would be dead before any leech saw him.

William's troop approached the village with care, as a raiding party should, but the truth was that their eyes and ears were more attuned to the woodland beyond the small fields than to the village itself. Their personal experience and the hearsay evidence of men who had fought the Welsh in the past was that the ambushing party would come from the woods after having ascertained that the troop was not too large to attack safely. What was more, the signs of recent habitation gave, to their suspicious minds, the implication that an attempt was being made to fix their attention on the village itself.

Inside the huts of the outermost ring the men found skins lying on the floor as if thrown off a sleeper, stones and ashes still warm from where a fire had died. William nodded at this information. Obviously a few men must have been at the village watching to see if the bait would be taken. Unfortunately the signs could also easily mean the trap had been abandoned when news of Mauger's movement was received. William signed for the worn and filthy skins and a few dented and cracked drinking vessels and bowls to be collected. It was scarcely the kind of loot worth taking, but it was all they were likely to get.

They moved in toward the center of the village. There was one house finer than the others and the large barn they intended to fire as their signal that they were under attack. Near the house were storage sheds and a few neater huts, probably the homes of upper servants. William had kept the troop well together up to this point, sending small groups with Raymond to investigate each hut while the others waited. Now, however, he had to allow the men to act as if a fever for loot had seized him and them.

It made William very uneasy to relax control over the men, but he knew it was necessary if he wanted to draw out the ambushers. Reluctantly he gave the order to disperse. Raymond led about one-half the troop to the main house; the others broke up and ran toward the huts. Within minutes a cry rang from one of the nearest. William's hand flew to his sword hilt, but there was no sound of a fight and the man, made honest by surprise, rushed out to display a ring he had found. It was a cheap, brass thing, but it was worth a few mils. It was amazing that such a thing should be left behind.

Before William could comment, two more shouts of success rang out, one from the house and another from a hut at the far end. One thing he had not considered was that the Welsh might be clever enough to leave a few things of value. It did not need to be much. After the long period in which the men had no extra reward at all for the fighting beyond their pay, any trinket would be likely to raise a feverish hope of more valuable loot, which would make them reluctant to stop searching and thus slow to obey orders. And the devil was in it that he dared not call them to order now, before the trap was sprung. Any indication of special wariness on his part might well cause those lying in wait to melt away into the woods without attacking.

A man had run out of the house now and was speaking excitedly to Raymond. He gave an order William could not hear and then looked uneasily toward the barn, which was to the northeast of the house.

Another few minutes passed. William swept the perimeter of the woods with his eyes. By rights the trap should be sprung now. The men were all dispersed and intent upon their search. There was another yell of joy from the huts. William looked around as far as he could see. Still nothing, but the barn blocked his view. He touched Lion with his heel and moved toward the barn. His eyes flicked over it, but not with a very searching scrutiny. The doors stood wide, as they had been left when the stock was driven out. The upper doors, through which hay was loaded, also were open.

William's eyes were already moving past the barn toward the new strip of woodland border he could now see when that second set of doors stuck in his mind.

He turned his head for another look. Open? For what? There were no sheaves lying ready to be raised. The first haying was in ricks; the second growth of hay was still standing uncut in the fields. He could see it. Why should the loading doors be open when there was nothing to put in or take out?

"Arnald!" William bellowed, turning his head toward the huts.

Simultaneously, he lifted his shield away from his body to draw his sword with more ease. Everything happened in that moment. There was a thrumming. Lion screamed and reared. William screamed also, as pain lanced into his left shoulder and his right side. He struggled to control his destrier, to bring him down, but it was too late. More arrows flew from the treacherously open doors. Caught in the throat, Lion plunged to his knees, blood pouring from his pierced jugular. Instinctively William pushed his legs forward to counteract the angle, and both stirrups broke, pitching him over the horse's head before the animal toppled over on its side.

The peculiar accident saved William's life. Rather than being pinned under Lion, he was able to roll free. Then it was possible to crouch behind the horse's body with his shield over him. This kept him from being finished by another shower of arrows. William realized that he was a dead man if he could not rid himself of the long arrow shafts. One would prevent him from swinging his sword, the other from holding his shield close enough to protect him.

Balancing his sword on his knees, he gripped the shaft of the arrow in his shoulder and pulled. Tears burst from his eyes and he bit a bloody gash in his lip. Worse than the pain was the knowledge that the effort had been useless. He had felt his collarbone give with the pull. The arrow was lodged. Even as his mind accepted this his hand had pulled down sharply. That time he screamed again, but the shaft broke short.

There were other voices now. War whoops from the Welsh, shouts of consternation and warning further away. Sobbing with pain, William gripped his sword again, bent his head lower to keep it under the shield, let go the handgrip, and grasped the second arrow shaft. There was no reason in what he did. If he could have thought beyond his own agony, his mind would have told him he was going to die anyway and it was irrational to inflict further pain on himself.

Habit ruled, however; the long years of training had imprinted patterns on him, patterns that taught him to ignore pain, to continue fighting as long as he was capable of moving at all. Without much conscious volition, William's left hand pulled sharply on the shaft. Black swirled before his eyes as the flesh tore, and his head dropped still lower. A yell of triumph sounded somewhere above him. He released the loose shaft of the arrow to fumble blindly for the handgrip of his shield. He knew it was too late to lift the shield and ward off the blow, but he hardly regretted the coming stroke that would sever his head from his body and cure all ills.

Bent over as he was, William did not see the Welshmen pouring out of the barn, racing around toward the troop, which was occupied with looting. Those in the buildings had not heard his shout, but a few who were running from one hut to another did hear—and Raymond had heard. Thus, the victorious yell of the man who paused to finish William turned into a shriek of pain. Dimly William heard the nervous snort of a warhorse, the thud of hooves as the animal was curbed down from a rear. Then a strong, young voice was roaring, "A Marlowe! A Marlowe!"

William found his handgrip. The blackness that had been threatening to engulf him receded as the piercing agony in his side dwindled to an ache. William was not deceived. He could feel the blood running down under his already-soaked shirt and tunic. He did not have much time. Then a shield hit his. A hand grasped the mail on his shoulder ungently.

"Mount, my lord! Mount!" Raymond urged.

"No," William gasped. "I cannot."

He levered himself to his feet with Raymond's help,

and the young man cried out when he saw the broken shaft still protruding from his shoulder and the flood of blood on his right side. The arrow he had torn out of his flesh was still caught in his mail, the shaft banging against him as he moved. Before he could speak again, two more of the Welsh were at them. He thrust Raymond's shield away, grunting with pain but pleased that he could still protect himself. One man, unwary because William had seemed half dead a moment before, was killed with his first swing. The other fell to Raymond's stroke while still watching William.

Raymond had the reins of the horse clutched with the handgrip of his shield and he pulled the animal forward to afford a rough shelter for William, but William shook his head impatiently.

"I can still stand," he muttered, "but not for long. Burn the barn. Burn it!"

"No need, sir," Raymond replied, shoving William forward with his shoulder.

William turned his head to stare, stumbled, recovered. "Mauger is come?" he asked, his voice slurring.

"No. I set the roof of the house alight as soon as I heard you cry out. It will make as good a smoke. The men will soak the walls with the other skins of oil if they can." Suddenly he pushed William harder. "Put your back to the wall, sir."

Wall? William wondered what wall? Where was the wall? He felt the pressure against him relax, heard the clang of metal and a shout. Dimly he realized Raymond was engaged again. He began to turn toward the sound but had sense enough left to understand that he would be more a danger than a help to the young knight. It was dark ahead. Sight fading? Perhaps, but . . . The wall! He lunged forward, felt a glancing blow on his right shoulder and swung his sword blindly in that direction as hard as he could. There was a thwack that should have been satisfactory, but it nearly jarred his sword from his weakening grip.

"Ware! Guard!" an anguished voice bellowed.

It was too late. William made a convulsive effort to

lift his shield, but it was too heavy, too heavy. He plunged forward into a most welcome darkness in which there was no pain and no duty.

To Raymond it seemed as if the blow launched by the Welshman had struck William's unprotected head with full force. With a roar of fury, he whirled away from his own opponent and slashed at the man who had struck William down and was still off balance. The edge of his blade bit deep, severing the leather corselet and breaking the bone. He shoved the screaming man off with one foot and swung around, not bothering to lift his sword but using the force of his whole turning body to drive it.

He barely missed the legs of his own stallion, but did not miss the man who had leapt forward hoping to catch him from behind while he was engaged with the one who had struck William. His sword hit just above the knee, sheared through the unarmored leg, and bit into the other. The wail of agony was soon cut off. As the man toppled, lowering his shield, Raymond's second blow nearly severed his head from his neck completely.

In the relative silence that followed, Raymond could hear a hoarse panting. He looked down at William hopefully, but his body did not seem to be moving. The sobbing breaths were those of the other man who was not yet dead. Raymond was suddenly filled with grief and hatred. He took half a step forward to finish the work he had begun, but shouts and sounds of battling men made him aware of his responsibility.

It was only then that he realized he had let go of his horse's rein in the few past wild minutes. The destrier was young, not completely trained, and was totally confused by a lack of weight in the saddle and a loose rein. It was rearing and fighting, but too far away for Raymond to reach without abandoning William. Raymond cursed the luck that had strained the foreleg of his own horse, but he did not waste time. He dragged William the few feet to the barn wall, pushed him against it, and took up his stand. At least he would bring her father's body home to Alys, he thought, not realizing he was crying until the salt tears wet his lips.

Soon, however, he was too busy to cry. He fought and bellowed "Marlowe! Marlowe!" One man of the troop found him, then another. All raised their voices together, and little by little the remains of the troop rallied around William's still body. Fortunately there were enough of them to make a turtle because, after several rushes had left more Welsh dead and wounded than English, the wily fighters withdrew and strung their bows again.

Seeing their intention, Raymond considered ordering the men to take shelter in the barn. In the next instant he realized that could easily lead to disaster. With the house burning already, they would not need to look for ideas on getting their enemies into the open again. Then, thinking of the house afire, he realized it was long, very long, too long since he had set that blaze. Mauger should have come long ago. In the heat of fighting and the cold of grief he had forgotten that they were bait, a force deliberately too small for the odds they faced.

Guilt grasped at him with poisoned claws. He had been too hurried. His firing of the thatched roof had failed. With the thought his eyes rose—and his breath caught with fear. He had not been too hurried. The house was in flames, plumes of smoke being swept up and out by the wind—up and out over the barn!

It came to Raymond then that he would not have the grief of bringing William home to Alys. How fortunate he had covered her father's letter with his own addressed to the king. Raymond heard his own voice giving orders to the men—some to kneel with their shields before them, others to stand to guard the heads and middle, still others to hold shields above their heads so that a near-invulnerable surface would be presented to the Welsh archers.

Useless, all useless, his mind cried, simultaneously surprised at the firmness of his voice, at the cheerful way he was urging the men to be steady, promising that they would not be abandoned, that even if Sir Mauger was by some cause delayed, the earl of Hereford himself would soon be on his way with the whole army. That might be true, Raymond thought, but it would make little difference to them. Soon the barn would be in flames and they would have to move. And he would not leave Sir William to burn. He would not!

They withstood that volley and another. Now, however, some of the men were craning their necks to look above. Raymond urged them sharply to look to their shield wall. "The fire is on the other side," he assured them. "It will be long before it eats through the beams."

But he knew he could not hold them still much longer. They were fighting men and feared the fire far more than they feared the weapons of the Welshmen. He feared it himself and knew the fear was muddling his mind, making him slow to think of expedients that might save them.

William had fallen forward on his shield, his arm sliding out of the hold as he went down. His right hand, still clenched on the pommel of his sword, had been jammed against his right side, pressing the torn shirt and tunic under the mail directly against the wound. The pressure had stopped most of the bleeding and the heat of his body with the group of men crowded together for the defense had dried blood and cloth together into a hard plug. This held tight, even when the feet of the men backing tight together pushed him so that he rolled to the left. The broken shaft of the arrow was pressed into the ground, driving the head deeper under his collarbone.

Pain lanced redly into the pleasant black nothingness that had enveloped William. He moaned, his left hand scrabbling weakly on the ground in an effort to lift himself away from what was stabbing into his shoulder. His fingers found a purchase—clutched. Raymond, who had been standing above him, bent down with a cry of joy. He had been so sure William was dead, having seen the stroke on his head and blood running down his neck, that he had never bothered to confirm it.

"Sir William is alive," he cried.

Momentarily, all spirits were lightened. Those of the troop who had survived were the more experienced men William had taken from Marlowe and Bix to strengthen his force of recruits. They were used to thinking that Sir William would get them out of any trouble he led them into. He always had in the past. They were willing to fight for Raymond, who was brave and steady. They liked him and trusted him—but they *believed* in Sir William.

The lines of the turtle, which had been wavering as one man and then another inched forward away from the sounds of fire above and behind, firmed. Raymond knelt, lifting and turning William so that he was face up, propped against his knee. The whole side of his face was plastered with mud and blood, but the eyes blinked as light hit them. Before Raymond could speak, another volley of arrows came, but the men had pulled together just in time. The chinks that had been in the shield wall seconds before, which had induced the Welsh to shoot, were closed.

The men knew it, recognized their escape, and their spirits rose still further. Taunts and catcalls came from behind the shields. Volleys of abuse flew in answer to the volley of arrows that had failed its purpose. The sound of their own voices launching insults for want of better weapons was cheering also. It made them feel less helpless, less trapped, even though the situation had not changed.

"We are trapped," Raymond was saying urgently to William. "Sir Mauger has not come, and the barn behind us is afire."

William's hazel eyes lifted to Raymond's face. They were dazed, but William's lips moved. Raymond bent closer, struggling to understand the indistinguishable mumble. "South," he made out and then, "to Hereford."

Revelation came to Raymond. What a fool he was to

keep the men standing here. Softly he began to give orders. The men were to close the turtle further so that four of them could load William on his shield. Then they were to move down along the barn—that was south, as Sir William said. This would take them much closer to the huts.

The change in position, Raymond realized, would provide a number of advantages. First and most important, it would give the men something to think about, a feeling that they were doing something to save themselves rather than simply waiting to be burnt or slaughtered. Perhaps they actually could do something—make a dash for the huts when the barn became too dangerous. Among the huts it would be far more difficult to shoot at them and almost impossible for a large group to rush them.

A real roar came from the roof of the barn. Instinctively Raymond looked up. He was aware, even while he stared, frozen, at the pillar of fire that had shot up, that the voices of the men had fallen into silence, the taunts and laughter dwindling away. It was time to move, to give them a second dose of hope. Raymond brought his eyes down to gauge what the Welsh would do, and his voice froze in his throat. He stared every bit as blankly as the men around him. There were no Welsh. The area they had occupied was empty. Even the old cow and the few sick sheep that had been left in the field to the north of the barn had disappeared.

CHAPTER 11

❖•❖

The comfortable dark would not enfold William properly. Little red flickers and flashes of pain kept piercing it. From time to time there were sounds, most of them were distant, but a few times his name was called loudly and persistently. He tried to answer. There were tears in the voice, so it was important. However, when his eyes opened, a whole pitch barrel of agony burst in his head and he slipped back into the dark with relief.

Then, suddenly, fire blazed in his shoulder, and it did not die but burned fiercer and fiercer until he struggled against it, crying out, trying to quench it with his hands. But he was bound. Torture? The Welsh? But why? Who? He forced open eyelids weighted with stones, but the blur beyond them was meaningless. At last, as suddenly as it had flared up, the flame of pain diminished. The blur congealed into a face—old, concerned, with a rim of gray hair.

"What . . ." William whispered.

"You will be easier now." The voice was also old, very gentle. "The arrow was lodged under the bone and it was needful to cut deep, but it is out now, my son. Sleep."

"Water," William pleaded.

"Yes, of course."

His head was raised and a cup held to his lips. He drank thirstily, drank again, and lay back. His eyes closed; he forced them open once more. But the man had already turned away, and William caught only a glimpse of a gray robe belted with a rough cord. Not the Welsh, he thought muzzily. That was the robe of

161

one of the new orders of friars. He must be in the infirmary of a holy house.

Later—William knew it was later because when he was awakened he was aware of a raging thirst. Since the last thing he remembered was drinking, he knew time had passed. However, it was not the thirst that woke him now, it was voices and one of them was familiar. Somehow, he did not wish to answer that voice, and he lay limp.

"Are you sure he will live?"

"My son, all things are in God's hands, but there is no reason why he should die. He is strong, and no vital organ was touched, no inner part of the body. The wounds are large, but they are of the flesh and are clean. God willing, yes, he will live."

"I am glad of that. He is a longtime friend and my close neighbor."

Mauger, William thought, and was flooded with a double and triple guilt. He was ashamed of disliking the man, knowing that he disliked him because of the many injuries he had done him. Worse yet, he was aware that he had not wanted to recognize the voice or answer because he did not want it to be Mauger. Quicker than thought, he had hoped that Mauger had also been caught in the trap and was dead. Now William would have spoken out of shame, but guilt intensified his weakness, and he could not find his voice.

"I do not like this place you have laid him," Mauger was saying.

"We are crowded, my son," the friar answered. "There are many wounded."

"I know, but you could take away that table under the window and turn the two other pallets. Then he could lie near the window where there is better air. If you will do that, I will make an offering to the church."

William felt even worse, but he could do nothing. He could not bear to be beholden to a man he had cuckolded, whose fond hope of alliance he must oppose.

"Well, there can be no harm in that," the gentle old voice said. "When he wakes, we will move him."

William fought his burning thirst. He was hot and his whole body throbbed, with peaks of pain centered in his right side above the waist, his left shoulder, and his head behind the right ear. He thought longingly of the place by the window where there would be a cool breeze, but he could not accept a favor from Mauger. He could not. *Water.* The word rang in his body, but he set his teeth over it, refusing to admit he was awake. He thought he would die of longing, but, instead, worn out by the struggle with himself, he slipped into darkness again.

The next time it was the thirst that awakened him. Before he remembered it was important not to wake, he croaked the precious word. At once his head was lifted. After the first few swallows, the cup was withdrawn. William opened his eyes the better to say he was still thirsty and saw it was Raymond bending over him.

"Raymond. . . ." Then it all came back, quite clear in his mind. "Thank God, you are alive," he sighed, and then, petulantly, "I am hungry. When is this?"

"Dawn, sir."

"Dawn when? How long since that damn raid?" Then William groaned. "What a fool I was. How many men did we lose?"

"Not so many," Raymond soothed. "And you were not a fool, sir. We would have all been dead if you had not called a warning. How did you guess they were in the barn?"

"The loading doors were open."

Despite pain and remorse, William could not help smiling at the puzzled expression on Raymond's face. That too-well-brought-up young man had never in his life given a thought to loading doors in a barn. Well, if he was going to marry Alys, he would have to learn such things. There was little doubt in William's mind now that Raymond would be his son. Alys was halfway in love with him. William had only to tell her he was willing and she would yield her heart completely. One thing was sure. William knew he owed his life to Raymond. Watching him rise and put the cup away, he saw the young man was moving stiffly.

"Are you much hurt?"

"No. A few cuts. Nothing of account. They have been tended. Ah, here is your broth."

This time William was propped on pillows. He wanted to feed himself, but the acolyte would not permit that. By the time half the bowl was finished, William was grateful. He was surprised at how tired the simple act of swallowing made him. He had been hungry, but he could not even finish what was in the bowl, and he slept again. However, he could not have slept long when voices woke him. Raymond's was immediately identifiable, but William paused before he opened his eyes. Shame or no shame, he did not feel well enough to speak to Mauger.

Then the friar said, "We were going to move him to the window, but—" His voice was submissive.

"Nonsense! He is to be lodged in a private chamber. The earl of Cornwall will use my guts for garters if the smallest attention is lacking. You must put him in the abbot's guest house, and a man to watch by him."

Now that he was fully awake, William recognized the impetuous tones of the earl of Hereford. He opened his eyes and smiled. "I am quite comfortable where I am," he said.

"Oh, so you are with us again. How do you feel—no, that was a stupid question. I know how you feel. Can I do anything to help you?"

"Thank you, my lord, I think not. Raymond will see to the men—"

"No he will not," de Bohun said forcefully, with a peculiar expression on his face. "He has a nasty cut on his sword arm and a hole in one leg. He will stay here. Sir Mauger has offered to take your men into his care, and they seemed willing also. He may not know much about war, but I have looked at his encampment. It seems well enough ordered, and his men are not sullen. I would judge him to be a fair master."

Unable to object without doing Mauger still more harm, William nodded. He felt as if he would choke on unwelcome favors, and his head was ringing with pain and fever. Hereford, who was familiar with wounds, cocked an eye at him and then looked over his shoulder. The friar was coming back with four strong acolytes.

"I see you are about to be moved," Hereford said. "I will leave you in peace. No, one protest for form is quite enough. Do not waste your strength on more. Richard will not be pleased about this whole thing. Probably I should not have—"

"Please, my lord," William said, laughing in spite of his physical discomfort, "I am not a feeble old woman who needs to be cosseted. I have been hurt as badly in Richard's own service. Both of us know the chances of war. And I beg you not to write to him. I will do so myself in a day or two."

"Perhaps," Hereford remarked with patent disbelief. He could see the glaze of fever in William's eyes and suspected it would be a good while longer than a day or two before he wrote to anyone. "Nonetheless," he continued, "Richard would rightly blame me for allowing his friend to lie in the common room with the men-at-arms."

That was true enough, and in any case, accepting de Bohun's favor would save him from accepting Mauger's. William smiled and said, "Thank you." Hereford made an *It is nothing* gesture and walked away.

There was no need, de Bohun thought, to add to William's difficulties the necessity of putting a brave front on his pain while he was being moved. That was a good man, but why the devil anyone should want to kill him was inexplicable. He did not seem to be the type that made enemies. He had nothing worth killing for. Nonetheless, the stirrups of his saddle had been cut nearly through. Someone intended that William of Marlowe should fall from his horse in the middle of a battle and be killed.

The young hireling knight had discovered the cut stirrups when he went to take his master's saddle from the dead horse. He had come to de Bohun nearly frantic because he had to see to William's troop and William was alone and helpless with his hurts. At first de Bohun had wondered whether Raymond had been hit on the head during the fighting. But, when he heard of the goose, the fight in camp, the arrow, and looked at the knife marks on the stirrup leathers, he changed his mind.

It must be something to do with Richard of Cornwall, de Bohun decided as he walked out of the abbey to ride back to camp. There was nothing about William himself that was important enough to kill for. Thus it behooved him to put William where it would be somewhat more difficult to get at him. It also would be a good idea to keep the whole matter quiet; Richard was too near the throne to take attacks on his favorites lightly. Having done what he could for the moment, Hereford put William out of his mind and wondered whether there was any other device he could use to bring David ap Llewelyn to battle.

If Mauger could have aided the earl of Hereford on that score, he would have done so; he would have done anything he could to redeem himself. Everything had gone wrong. The plan had worked perfectly—and *still* William was alive. Worse, Hereford had blasted him for being a fool.

How could he have known there would not be another month or so of fighting? Had he known about the Scottish peace, he would never have sent those messengers off to summon de Bohun when he was attacked. Deep inside Mauger there was a quiver of doubt. He had had no idea how difficult it was to fight a group of men who seemed to appear and disappear in and out of the wooded glades. Their archers shooting from the shelter of the trees had done more damage than Mauger expected. It had taken them so long to win free from their own attackers, he had never dreamed that William's troop could hold out—especially with their leader dead.

Only William had not been dead. That accursed hireling of his had saved him. Who would have expected the young fool to show such devotion? If he had had a brain in his head, he would have gathered what was left of the troop and run for his life. But no! He had to be a hero—offer his horse, just like one of those puling knights in the romances, and stand over what he must have believed was a corpse to protect it from being robbed or mutilated. It was because he had hopes of the girl, Mauger thought, and ground his teeth.

Neither of them must be allowed to live. They must both die here in Wales. It was out of the question for Mauger to leave now. He did not dare do anything that would further irritate Hereford. Therefore, neither Raymond nor William must leave Wales either. At least it had been easy enough to have William moved to the window. That would mark the position of the bed clearly. Mauger wished he had not needed to approach the friar personally to make that arrangement, but none of the tools he had used to carry the goose or start the fight or slit the stirrups was the kind of person to make such a request. The friar would surely have wondered why such a wretch should seek William's comfort. Not only that, no one would move a pin for the amount of offering such a person could make.

It should not matter—Mauger looked up as Egbert— body servant, tool, faithful henchman—entered the tent. "Well?" he asked.

"It is well," Egbert replied. "I did not go in because I did not wish to make an excuse that might lead someone to remember me, but I saw a bed moved under the window and a man therein. I could not see his face though. It was turned away, and I did not dare stand and watch."

Egbert had been with Mauger since they were boys. He never thought about the things his master asked of him, only performed them as well as he could. This was not owing to any lack of intelligence on Egbert's part. Usually he knew quite well why Mauger did the things he did without being told. He was totally devoted, although he did not love his master, because his comfort, his well-being, even his life was Mauger's to dispose of as he liked.

With all of that, Mauger was a good master, never cruel or unreasonable, although he could lose his temper and land a sharp buffet. Egbert certainly did not hate or really fear Mauger, but there was no warmth in their relationship either. Never had Mauger asked after his health or considered whether he was warm or cold, fed or hungry. He was rewarded with money—and the comfort and status that would buy—but never with a word of heartfelt praise.

He also knew he was by no means indispensible. If he claimed sickness, he was excused from duty and indifferently replaced with another. Thus, Egbert understood that he was only of value while he performed and performed well. If he failed, he would be cast aside to sink into the poverty and total deprivation from which he had risen when he had been chosen to be Mauger's servant. That was what he feared—not Mauger himself —and that was what kept him faithful and close-mouthed and efficient.

"Then the friar has done as I asked," Mauger responded. "Very well, but remember it must not seem as if Sir William was sought out especially."

"No, I remember. I will steal some things—I saw several worth taking. It will appear that he woke and saw me stealing and I silenced him. Otherwise, if you prefer, I could slit three or four throats as well as his."

"No. You had better stick to the thief idea. They will not search as hard or long for a frightened thief as for a madman who goes about slitting throats for no reason." Mauger reached into his purse and drew out a gold coin. "There will be more when I am richer, as I will be when I hold Marlowe and Bix. Now, have you heard anything said among Sir William's men about how he was hurt?"

"None saw it happen, but he was hit by arrows."

"I know that. I wondered if anything was said about those stirrups. I thought they would both be dead and I could get the saddle, but that interfering bastard was before me."

"The stirrup leathers were gone from the saddle when the troop came back to camp—that is all I can tell you. But no outcry has been made. I would say the young knight took them off and threw them away for fear he would be blamed."

It was a pleasant relief to come innocently up to the abbey the following day with the offering he had promised and find the place in turmoil. It was the most natural thing in the world to ask what had happened. It was a pure delight to be told that a thief had somehow gotten into the infirmary, struck the acolyte on watch unconscious, stolen several fine eating knives and purses, and had killed one man who must have wakened and been about to cry an alarm. Mauger had not the slightest difficulty in making his voice tremble as he said his friend was in the infirmary and expressed a desire to see him and be sure all was well with him.

When Mauger entered the infirmary and saw the empty bed under the window, he felt for a moment that he would faint with joy and relief. He stared at the empty bed, transfixed, not really believing in the midst of his joy that the planning of years had at last come to fruition.

"What is it, my son?" the infirmarian's voice asked at his elbow.

"My friend," Mauger stammered, "the man I asked to be moved to the window—where is he? I heard . . ."

"No, no, it was not he, not Sir William," the friar comforted, patting Mauger's arm. "By the earl's desire, he is in a private chamber in the abbot's guest house." Mauger's face, which had been pale, blazed red with rage. The brother took it to be a flush of joy and smiled happily. "He is safe, quite safe."

"May I see him?" Mauger asked.

The infirmarian's smile faded. "See, yes—speak to, no. He is greatly fevered and would not know you, likely. We try," he added apologetically, "when such high fever comes to keep all excitement, all stimulus away."

"Greatly fevered?" Mauger's voice was shaking with hope again. Perhaps all the failures had been to save him the trouble of committing murder. Perhaps William was fated to die of his wounds. "Is he then in danger of his life? Yesterday you said he would live."

"God willing, he will." The voice of the infirmarian was troubled. "But the fever is worse than I expected, and the wounds, specially that in the shoulder which had to be cut to remove the arrow, are greatly inflamed."

"Will you take me to him?" Mauger asked.

"Yes, of course," the brother said. He summoned an acolyte and told him where to take Mauger, warning him again not to go into the room or, at least, not to speak to William. "They have such strength in their fever," he remarked, walking to the door with Mauger, "that they can do what weakness would prevent otherwise. If seeing you should remind him of some duty he thought left undone or some slight unavenged, he might rise from his bed and open his wound or take a chill. That would be a disaster."

"No, no," Mauger assured him. "I will not speak to him."

It was unfortunate for Mauger that the acolyte had heard the brother's instructions. Although William was alone, tossing and muttering incoherently, Mauger did not dare try to send his guide away or step into the room while he watched. As he rode back to camp he cursed the earl of Hereford bitterly for an overactive conscience. Just because he had agreed that William should lead the raid was no reason for all this special attention. In a way it was all to the good, however. He had noticed William's gear in the room. This time there would be no mistake. He would see to it himself that the fevered man fell on his own knife while fighting dreams.

Mauger ate a leisurely dinner, mulling over various plans for seeing that Raymond followed William into the grave. Afterward, he disported himself with one of the better whores in the camp and, just before dark, rode off with Egbert, with whom he had had a few words on the subject of stabbing the wrong man. The words had not been too sharp. Mauger realized that Egbert had to work fast and in the dark. Besides, his hatred of William had grown with each check and now he was looking forward with real enjoyment to plunging a knife into him.

No one raised any question when Mauger passed through the abbey gates. So many men from the camp came to visit comrades or to collect belongings of those who had died to send to relatives that the gateman paid no heed to single incomers. Egbert rode around to the small postern in the west wall that led to the abbot's residence and tethered his horse out of sight. He drew his hood over his head so that his face was shadowed and rang the bell. This gate was always kept locked, but a brother who worked in the abbot's house was assigned to answer the bell. He was annoyed when Egbert stated the cause of his visit and told him he should have gone round by the main gate. When Egbert begged pardon humbly and said that he had walked far and was afraid the gates would be shut before he could get around to them, the brother admitted him. Having relocked the gate behind Egbert, he pointed the direction to the guest house and went back to his own work.

A shadow followed him out of a patch of darkness in the direction he had pointed. Egbert watched, then lifted the key from the hook where it hung, unlocked the gate, replaced the key. That was all of Egbert's task this time, but he did not slip out. Of late, he had failed too often. Mauger had been unusually pleasant about it, but he did not intend to take any chances this time. He found a shadowed nook in the abbot's garden from which he could see the gate and sat down to wait. It might be several hours until Mauger could finish Sir William. If by some chance a late visitor should arrive, the gate might be discovered to be unlocked and the "oversight" remedied. Then Egbert would have to unlock it again.

Although Sir William had been alone when Mauger looked in on him, he was not alone long. Raymond's absence had been brief. The killing in the infirmary, about which he had heard when food was brought for him to break his fast, had brought his suspicion to fever pitch and sent him off to Hereford. Both remembered the infirmarian saying he had planned to move William to the window. That was not proof that someone had died in William's place—it could have been a coincidence. A man bent on murder seldom stops to steal knives and purses. Still, it was a strange coincidence.

Raymond's first reaction had been to move William again, at once, but Hereford objected. Such desperate efforts to be rid of William could not be stopped by moving him. They would merely continue as soon as his new position was discovered. It would be far better, the earl insisted, to catch whoever was trying to kill him.

It was, of course, impossible to move a whole troop into the abbey. Even if Hereford could have overborne the abbot's objections, such an action would almost certainly warn the intended murderer, who would put off his attempt. In the end, it was decided that Raymond should watch by Sir William's bed and four men would hide in each adjoining room and the rooms opposite ready to rush to Raymond's aid should he cry for help.

The first hitch in this plan occurred ten minutes after full dark when Raymond lit a candle. William had been lying quietly, but minutes after the faint light appeared he began to toss and mutter. Raymond bathed his face and gave him a drink, but he could not quiet him. William's eyes roamed from side to side, watching the shadows cast by the flickering candle. Suddenly he began to scream warnings of an attack from dark doorways.

The shouts brought Hereford's guards rushing into the room, weapons drawn, which excited William so much that Raymond had considerable difficulty holding him in the bed. After some confusion, he explained what had happened to the guards and begged them not to come in again unless he himself called them with certain agreed-upon words. Having got them out and William relatively quiet, he put out the candle which seemed to have caused the trouble.

Although William remained on the bed, he continued to mutter and even strike out from time to time, so that Raymond did not dare light the candle again. He did not dare to do anything else either. As soon as he moved in his chair, William reacted. The sick man's hearing seemed preternaturally acute.

The enforced stillness was making it very difficult for Raymond to stay awake. He had carried more burdens, both physical and emotional, in the past two days than in his entire life before. As the slow minutes passed, his head began to nod. Three times he caught himself and forced his eyes open; eventually, however, his head sank forward on his breast and he slept.

Not quite an hour later, the latch of the door clicked softly. Raymond twitched uneasily and then sank back into sleep. William's eyes opened, glittering with fever. The moon had not yet risen, but a luminance from the starlit sky cast a faint shadow from the window onto the wall opposite. William's muscles tensed. He was vaguely aware of pain, but all his senses concentrated on the shadow. Somewhere outside of his direct focus of vision he was aware of movement. He shifted his eyes, but his fever-sharpened senses were also distorted and unreliable, and he was caught in a nightmare in which arrows flew out of a high darkness. He looked higher while Mauger silently opened the door.

Mauger's footsteps were soft enough not to disturb Raymond. William heard, but the sound did not fit with his fever dream and caused a whirling confusion. He lowered his eyes and saw the darker shadow advancing on him. This did not fit with any hallucination in his mind, and he watched it advance with puzzlement. He did not move or protest when Mauger pulled off the light blanket that Raymond had laid over him. There was a familiarity in that action, which, even fevered as he was, he associated with his own good. The brothers uncovered him when they cleaned him and rebandaged his hurts.

It was when Mauger bent low to clap a hand across William's mouth so that he should not cry out that William saw his neighbor's face. William jerked his head away, not because he suspected Mauger wished to harm him but for the contrary reason. Mauger had taken care of his men; Mauger had done his best to procure extra comfort for him; now, he assumed, Mauger had come to nurse him. He could not bear it.

With the strength of madness, William pushed Mauger away. The suddenness of his action, coupled with the abnormal strength of the shove, sent Mauger staggering backward. A chest against the wall caught him just behind the knees so that he sat down with a thump. This sound wakened Raymond, but he was so dazed with sleep that he could not account for what he had heard and he stared wildly around the room, missing Mauger, who, immobile with surprise, was no more than a slightly darker darkness in the dark room.

Meanwhile, William had struggled upright. "No," he cried, "no! I am quite well, quite well."

Raymond leapt to his feet and grabbed for William, but William had gotten out of the bed and stood up. Still befuddled, Raymond leaned too far so that he fell forward on the bed, and then, instead of jumping up and running around the end to grab William—he still had no idea that Mauger was in the room—he began to crawl across the bed, thinking it the quickest way. William, however, had not stood still. Somehow his fever-moiled brain had come to the conclusion that courtesy required him to walk to the door with Mauger and that that act would serve the double purpose of proving he was well enough to dispense with Mauger's nursing.

"See you out," he mumbled, staggering forward. "My thanks. No need. See you out."

Mauger could believe neither his ears nor his eyes. After fighting him off as if he knew what was intended, William was coming toward him with hands outstretched. Mauger's own guilt made him interpret William's delusion as suspicion. A trap! his mind shrieked. He knew all along what you were trying to do and set a trap. Mute with terror, Mauger leapt to his feet, made one violent thrust at William with the knife he held, and dropped the weapon. He burst past William, flung open the door, and ran out.

At that moment, Raymond swung off the bed behind William. He saw the violent gesture, realized for the first time that there was someone in the room beside himself and William, and leapt to attack. But William, who had been stabbed in the left arm, staggered back into his arms, bellowing with rage, pain, and surprise. Thus, Raymond's first call for help was drowned in William's outraged cry. What was worse, the blow catapulted William into an entirely different hallucinatory sequence and he began to fight Raymond.

Twice more Raymond shouted to Hereford's guards that the assassin was escaping. Unfortunately, the first time William landed such a blow in the young knight's midsection that the warning was choked off into a howl of anguish. The next time Raymond called, he received instant response, but it was too late. Although the men needed no more than a word to send them hunting through the rooms and corridors and into the garden, Mauger was already out of the postern. Egbert had smiled grimly when he realized his master had also failed. He was very glad he would not be in the camp when Mauger returned to it. Silently he slipped around to the front of the main building and then into the stables where he settled down beside his master's horse, which he would dutifully bring to camp the next morning.

CHAPTER 12

Alys chose a tally stick from the bundle she had been translating into written accounts. This was not because she distrusted Martin's honesty or accuracy. Each stick was clearly marked with the nicks and scratches that identified the merchant or farmer to whom it pertained and the amounts were clearly incised in large and small notches. She chose to make a written record for several reasons: One leaf of parchment took much less space than a bundle of sticks. Moreover, written records produced awe and suppressed arguments. The villeins and serfs, at least, seemed to regard them as magic—as if the fact of writing a thing down on parchment made it true or inevitable.

She was sufficiently absorbed in her work that Martin had to clear his throat to draw her attention. She finished inscribing the line and looked up.

"There is a messenger from Wales," Martin said.

Alys smiled and said, "Well, send him in. Papa is a most faithful correspondent. I had a letter from him only five or six days ago."

She spoke before she thought, before she saw the unnatural glitter in Martin's eyes. The fact that the steward's eyes were full of tears came to her simultaneously with his words.

"The letter he carries is not from the master."

"Dead?" Alys shrieked, leaping to her feet. "Papa is dead?"

"No!" Martin exclaimed, scuttling around the table to take hold of her. "But he was hurt, sore hurt."

"You lie! You wish to make it easy. He is dead," she whimpered.

"No, lady, no," Martin assured her, stroking the

177

hand he held. "He was alive when the messenger left. The letter is from Sir Raymond."

The panic that had closed Alys's throat and made her heart pound until she thought her breast would burst receded a little. There was a comfort in hearing Raymond's name. She did not think about that but ran eagerly out into the hall to question the messenger. She tore the folded parchment from his hands, ripped off the seals, and began to read.

The haste undid her. At first she could not make out more than a few words. Although the hand was clear and firm and she could distinguish each letter, they combined all wrong and made nonsense words, full of z's, that she could not understand. Weeping with frustration, she sounded out a sentence to Martin, crying, "What does it mean? What does he say? Has he writ in Latin?"

"Not Latin," Martin replied. He could not read or write himself, but he had heard enough Latin in his years at the monastery that he understood it a little. What Alys had spoken was not Latin. The sounds were harsher, like— "Lady! He has writ as he speaks, not as we speak," Martin exclaimed.

Alys wiped her eyes and tried again. She found she had to read the letter aloud and to think of the sounds in Raymond's voice, but Martin was right. In those terms the words were intelligible, and hearing in her mind Raymond's pleasant baritone saying them calmed her. Somehow it was more possible to believe he was telling the truth, that her father was badly hurt but not dying. I will go to him, Alys thought. I will make him well. But the next sentence caught her eye just as she was about to lay the letter down and stopped her.

"For certain reasons that I will tell you when we arrive, the earl of Hereford has thought it best that I bring your father home to Marlowe."

Alys read it aloud twice to Martin. "Am I right in what he says? Is he bringing papa home? But if he is hurt, will it not be very dangerous to jolt him in a cart so many miles?"

"I do not know, my lady," Martin replied. "I did not nurse the sick and know nothing of such matters, but I am sure Sir Raymond does what is best for our lord."

Only he was not sure. A horrible fear had come into his mind. Raymond desired Alys. If her father were dead . . . Martin pushed the idea away, telling himself that Raymond was a decent, honorable man.

"But why?" Alys was crying. "I could be with papa in a few days. I could ride faster to Wales than he can be brought here."

"Sir Raymond must know that, and the earl of Hereford also," Martin replied, trying to hide his worry. "They must feel that the danger of the journey is less than the danger of remaining."

There was no older woman of authority in the keep. Alys's nurse-companion had died years in the past, and now Alys sensed Martin's concealed fear. She needed comfort and support, and for all his soothing words, this time she could not obtain it from Martin. Clutching the letter nervously, she stood up.

"Lady Elizabeth will know," she said breathlessly. "She is a good physician."

She would have run to the boat just as she was, but Martin clung to her hand crying that it was getting cool and begging her to wait until a maid could fetch her cloak and Diccon could warn two men-at-arms to accompany her. Alys could have pulled away, but the long habit of years prevented her from using any physical force on Martin—even as a child she could hurt him —and the little delay of making ready was in its own way soothing. It was what had always been done when she went to Hurley.

The normalcy implied normalcy, implied that all was as usual, that the pattern of life was *not* broken. Papa had set the pattern of being accompanied to Hurley by two men-at-arms when she was a little child, and Alys had never gone without them, even though, as she grew up, she thought it was silly. There was no person in Hurley that did not know her almost as well as her own servants in Marlowe. She could not come to harm in Hurley. Peculiarly, relief flooded her at this check to her headlong flight, and she thanked Martin passionately for making her wait. Hope can breed on nothing when it must do so to avoid despair. Because she was still obeying her father, Alys was suddenly convinced that he would live. She did not think how silly it was. She hugged the comfort to her and did not even urge the boatmen to paddle faster.

Only when she was hurrying up the short road to the keep did Alys begin to fear that Elizabeth might be out. She nearly burst into tears when Emma minced up to greet her. She guessed as quickly as her father who the stunning creature was, but she had no emotion to spare for outrage. All she could do was ask where Lady Elizabeth was.

The answer came from the lady herself, who had been warned by a servant of Alys's arrival and came running down from the women's quarters just a minute too late to shield Alys from Emma's greeting. She drew the girl quickly into the stairwell.

"I am so sorry, my love," Elizabeth murmured. "If I had known you were coming, I would have sent her away. She is the simplest creature, really silly, and likes to pretend she is mistress. Do not tell your papa—"

Elizabeth's voice checked suddenly as Alys winced. It was so dark in the hall and stairwell that Elizabeth had not noticed the girl's pallor and too-wide eyes. She swallowed and stood still, clutching the rough stone and fighting a sudden overwhelming fear.

"William?" she breathed. "Alys, is something wrong with your father?" She tried to stiffen her knees, which were threatening to buckle and pitch her over the unguarded edge of the uneven stair. "Dead?" she whispered.

"No, thank God," Alys got out, and then began to cry.

It was impossible for Elizabeth to take Alys in her arms. The stairs were too narrow and precipitous. She patted her and urged her upward, following close behind, one hand on the wall to steady herself. In her own chamber, she finally held Alys close until the girl could control her choking sobs.

"Not dead," she kept assuring herself, "not dead. He is not dead."

The murmured repetition penetrated to Alys, who began to shudder even harder and wailed, "But he is sore wounded and Raymond says he is bringing him home. Oh, Elizabeth, is that right? Can it be right? Will it not do him harm if he is hurt to drag him hundreds of miles in a jolting cart?"

"Not in a cart, love," Elizabeth said, scarcely knowing her own voice. "You told me when your father's last letter came that they were west of Shrewsbury. Most likely they will carry him in a litter so far and then take him by water down the Severn to Gloucester. From there it is only fifty miles to Oxford—and that road is a good one. From Oxford they can come by boat again down the Thames right to Marlowe."

Alys stopped sobbing and looked hopefully at Elizabeth. "But the horses and the men . . ."

"Does not the letter say, sweetheart?" Elizabeth asked tenderly, struggling to hold back her own tears. "Who wrote to you?"

"Raymond wrote." Alys took a deep, shaken breath and produced the letter. "I do not know. I did not read the whole letter. It is so hard to read. I was so afraid. I came here."

"You did just right, love, just right," Elizabeth soothed. She looked at the sheet of parchment Alys was holding. "Come, read it now, while I sit with you."

"It is so hard to read," Alys sighed. "He writes in his own tongue."

"The *langue d'oc?*" Elizabeth asked.

Alys blinked at her. "What?"

"Does Raymond say *oc* for *oui?*" Elizabeth asked.

"Yes, he does. Do you know Raymond?"

"They all say *oc* in his part of the country. I know from the poetry."

"Poetry?"

Practical from the top of her highest curl to the tip

of her longest toe, Alys would never have thought of
wasting so useful a skill as reading on poetry. If Alys
herself was to take the time from her work to read, it
had better be a treatise on how to make better crops or
get more milk from a cow or remove stains from silk.

"Do you read poetry?" Alys asked in a puzzled tone.

"Yes, and much of it is in the *langue d'oc*," Elizabeth said. Her voice shook. Over the years, that had
been William's gift to her—books and scrolls of tales
and poetry—a gift that would be safe from her illiterate
husband. She looked hungrily at the letter in Alys's
hand, but Alys was already extending it toward her.

"Read it to me," she cried eagerly.

Elizabeth stumbled over the first few words, but that
was more because of the choking sensation in her throat
when she read Raymond's description of William's hurts
and illness than any trouble with the language. Alys was
crying softly but Elizabeth did not stop reading until she
finished that part. There was no need after that. The
tears were more of relief than of fear now. The poor
child had not really been able to make out what Raymond said and had thought the case was worse than it
seemed. Unless Raymond was lying . . . No, he could
not be such a fool as that.

"It is not so bad, love," Elizabeth said. "Your papa
is very strong and—and he has a great desire to live."

She then read the sentence that reported Raymond
would bring William home and went on, translating into Norman French as she went along. "It is thought
here that the war is over for this time and that the
earls of Hereford and Gloucester will soon dismiss the
levies. Until that time Sir Mauger, your neighbor at
Hurley, will care for your father's men. Arnald remains
as master-at-arms so there should be no trouble. Sir
Mauger will also bring home Le Bête, Gros Choc, and
the young destrier. Lion, I am sorry to tell you, is dead.
He did not suffer, as his throat was pierced by arrows
in the same instant that your father was wounded."

"Poor Lion," Alys sighed, "papa will grieve for him."

There was then a description of the rescue which

ended: "I should have stayed close by my lord, but the village seemed completely empty, and I fell neatly into the trap. I pray that you will try to forgive me, for I will never forgive myself."

Elizabeth stopped and looked at Alys, who had made a soft, inarticulate sound. The struggle in her face was very revealing, and after a moment, she asked, "Could he have saved papa from being hurt?"

"I doubt it very much," Elizabeth replied. "It was not hand-to-hand combat but a flight of arrows. How could Raymond possibly stop that?"

"Then why does he blame himself and ask my forgiveness?"

In spite of her anxiety, Elizabeth could not help smiling. "I think he is just overwrought, love. He does not say, but it is possible he was lightly hurt himself, and he has doubtless been tending your father—and he knows how frightened and worried you would be when you had this news. He sounds like a very nice young man, just the kind to blame himself for what was not his fault."

"Do you really think he was hurt also?"

There was a breathless quality to Alys's question that confirmed Elizabeth's suspicion. Alys either already loved the hireling knight or was on the thin edge of it. It was most unsuitable. She watched the girl with troubled eyes as she said, "Very likely not. I was just trying to make a reason for what he says. Alys, you should not think about this Raymond. He is only a hireling, without—without even a shirt to his back but what you have given him."

"It was you who said I must marry for love," Alys snapped.

"Oh, Alys," Elizabeth sighed, "there are so many fine young men. Do not permit yourself to love the wrong man—please do not, dearling. It hurts. It hurts so much."

"I do not love anyone," Alys said hastily, appalled by her sudden perception of Elizabeth's long agony.

She had never understood. Papa had concealed his

misery behind silence, business, and bad temper. Elizabeth had always presented a facade of placidity and gentle humor—except that last time she and papa had been together. Alys had almost forgotten that. In fact, she realized, she had wanted to forget it. Now, however, Elizabeth was concealing nothing. It was all she could do—the best warning she could give—to the girl she loved as a daughter.

It was the wrong thing to do entirely. Elizabeth was steadfast rather than daring. Alys could be steadfast, but she was far more inclined to rush forward to meet trouble halfway. Although she cringed from the knowledge of Elizabeth's pain, that was for Elizabeth's sake. From her own point of view the depth of Elizabeth's agony only made love more interesting. Anything to which one would cling in spite of such suffering must be precious indeed.

But Elizabeth's eyes had already returned to Raymond's letter which held news of William. He went back to describing the battle and Elizabeth could not help thinking that the poor young man must be far deeper in love than Alys. He must know it was not necessary to spend all this time and effort to tell her things he could tell her in person. Most likely he wrote because he could not stop, because writing made him feel closer to her. Oh dear! As soon as William was well enough, she must warn him of what was going on.

"Your father is much beloved by the earl of Hereford, who has provided us with every care and luxury this place affords. Do not fear for your father's comfort while we travel. We come by water nearly all the way, as this will be swifter and easier for a man who cannot ride, and I hope will be in Marlowe by the end of the month."

"There," Elizabeth said, looking up from what she was reading and sighing with relief. She had told Alys they would come by river, but it was good to have her guess confirmed.

"The end of the month," Alys exclaimed. "Today is the twenty-eighth. The messenger was very slow. They may be here the day after tomorrow." But it was not relief Elizabeth saw in Alys's face when she spoke.

"My love, what is wrong?" Elizabeth cried.

"I am afraid," Alys whimpered. "I will not know what to do for him. I will do something wrong and hurt him—make him worse."

"No," Elizabeth began in an automatic reflex of comforting, and then drew in her breath sharply. This was her opportunity, her excuse. "Alys, do you want me to come to Marlowe to nurse your father?"

There was a long silence. Elizabeth scarcely dared to breathe while Alys stared at her own hands, knotting and unknotting in her lap. Both women knew exactly what was at stake. If Alys conceded Elizabeth the right to care for William, she would also withdraw her right to object to the relationship between them. Fear struggled with jealousy, but a third force entered the field. Raymond d'Aix would be coming home also.

"Yes," Alys sighed. "Yes, please come, Elizabeth."

It was fortunate that the boat bearing William and Raymond arrived in the late afternoon of the second day. Had the voyage been slower than expected, Alys might well have changed her mind. Although Elizabeth did not deliberately put herself forward, it was very strange to Alys to have another woman of authority in the house. Having heard, "But Lady Elizabeth says it must be done thus and so," from Alys for years, the maids simply came to Elizabeth for directions and advice if Alys did not happen to be there. And Elizabeth gave the order or advice without thinking. She was very proud of Alys's management, feeling quite correctly that it was largely owing to her teaching, but she also felt as if Alys were a little girl playing at keeping house.

A faint resentment flickered in Alys that might have grown, but it was completely drowned when her father was carried ashore. She and Elizabeth were waiting at the dock, and they heard William raving before the boat was warped in. Alys burst into tears and rushed forward as the stretcher was lifted out of the boat. Raymond had climbed up just ahead of it, and he was bare-

ly able to pull Alys out of the way as William struck
out at her.

"Careful," Raymond cried, "let me—"

But Elizabeth had already stepped forward and she
said, "William, stop that!" not loudly, but in a clear,
compelling tone. At the same time she laid one hand
on his forehead. His glazed eyes turned toward her,
and his struggling body went limp.

"Why did you bring him when he was so sick?" Alys
cried, turning on Raymond.

"I had no choice, I swear it," Raymond replied. "If
I had not—"

"Later," Elizabeth said firmly. "First we must get
Sir William into his bed." She turned to the four large
serfs that had come with them and directed them in
English to take the stretcher and not to jostle it. "Will
you be so good," she said to Raymond, having switched
to French again, "as to ride my horse back to the keep.
I wish to walk beside Sir William."

Elizabeth's face was calm and her voice steady, but
she was sick with terror. William seemed a ghost of
himself. All she could think of was getting him where
she could examine him carefully and do something for
him. Had she been less frightened, she would have
waited for Alys to say whether she wished to walk with
her father also. Had Alys not already had another preoccupation, she would have been furious with Elizabeth. However, when Alys made her protest to Raymond and received his answer, she had been looking
full into his face. He was hollow eyed and haggard.

"You are not well yourself," Alys said.

"I am only tired and—and very, very worried."

His voice faltered. Raymond had remembered Alys
was beautiful, but his memory had been pale in comparison with her reality. The blue eyes that could glitter with anger or twinkle with humor were misty with
concern for him now.

"Were you hurt also in that battle?"

"It was only a raid," Raymond murmured idiotically.
Ever since Alys had budded breasts and her body

had formed, men had been looking at her with the bemused longing that showed in Raymond's face now.
Mostly she had found it very funny, because it followed
or preceded sessions of boasting and strutting that reminded her sharply of cocks strutting before the hens
in the poultry yard. Once or twice she had been frightened or disgusted, because there was an ugly rapacity
mixed into the longing. A few times she had felt pity.

This time, Alys did not even remember that she had
ever before seen men look at her thus. She was suffused
with tenderness, with the desire to put her arms around
this man and tell him not to worry, that she would
bring him peace, fulfill his longing. She had moved a
step forward and put out her hand, which he took, before she remembered that he was only a hireling, totally unsuitable for her. It would be a dreadful cruelty to
lead him to believe she could be his. A sharp pang of
loss made her push the ugly thought away. There were
more immediate problems than her relationship with
Raymond.

"Are you hurt, Raymond?" she repeated sharply,
squeezing his hand and giving it a little shake to wake
him from whatever dream held him.

"Hurt? Oh, not to speak of."

"Idiot!" Alys exclaimed, but somehow the tenderness
she felt crept into the word and turned it into a caress.
Raymond caught his breath. Alys hurried on. "If I did
not wish you to speak of it, I would not have asked.
Where are you hurt?"

"A cut on the arm and another on the leg. Nothing."
His voice was not steady.

"Are they healed?"

"Not—not quite."

"Come then, I will see to you."

She turned from him to give orders about bringing
what little baggage Raymond had carried along up to
the keep and then gestured the man holding the horses
forward. Raymond moved to lift her to the saddle, but
she shook her head, telling him that he looked as if he
would have enough to do to mount himself. As they

turned toward the keep, Alys saw the group carrying her father and guilt smote her. She had forgotten him! Then while she watched, Elizabeth bent over the litter, either speaking to or touching William. Guilt and jealousy dwindled together. Elizabeth would care better for her father than she could herself, and she would be free to . . . No, she would not think of that now. When she had time and quiet would be soon enough to reexamine things in her life that she had considered basic principles.

"Why did you bring papa home?" Alys asked again, when they were moving slowly in the wake of the walking party.

Raymond looked at the beautiful face turned to him, at the firm chin and steady eyes, and could have wept with relief. Had his mother or sisters asked that question, he would have had to lie, to continue to carry the burden all alone—and he was so tired! Alys would not fall into hysterics. Alys would help him.

"Someone is trying to murder him. I—and the earl of Hereford also—felt he would be safer at Marlowe than anywhere else."

Alys's eyes opened wide with astonishment, but she did not, as Raymond expected, give any sign of fear. "That is ridiculous," she said. "I do not believe there is anyone in the world who hates papa."

"You must believe me!" Raymond exclaimed. Hastily he related what had happened in the camp and the abbey. Alys listened, belief and confusion growing together.

"I do believe you," she said at last, "but it is quite mad. Who could possibly wish—"

She stopped. Her eyes were fixed on Elizabeth, who now seemed to be holding her father's hand while she walked beside him. If Sir Mauger knew . . . Alys remembered him standing outside her father's closed door, listening. What if he had heard something that made him suspicious. She had come as quickly as possible, but she had been lagging behind, making herself busy with something. She had had quite enough of Sir

Mauger on the little ride they had taken. Like a fool, he had been sighing over Aubery's passion for her. Did he think her an idiot? Alys remembered Aubery's attitude on his last visit—it had only been a few months earlier—and, to say the least, it had not been one of deep passion. Elizabeth had warned her, too, that Aubery had not changed.

"That is what Hereford and I could not imagine. Your father is well liked everywhere. The earl and I came to believe it must be something to do with Richard of Cornwall."

Alys had been about to voice her suspicion of Mauger, but that stopped her. Hereford's idea was far more reasonable, really. After all, Elizabeth and her father had loved each other for many years. Sir Mauger had done nothing in all those years. Why should he burst into violence all of a sudden? On the other hand, it was not at all impossible that someone wished to separate papa permanently from Uncle Richard. No one had ever tried to kill him before, but other attempts of all kinds had been made to destroy Uncle Richard's love for papa. And at war it might have seemed that it would be easy.

"That is possible. I had not thought of it before." Alys's eyes narrowed. "While papa is sick, there is no need to worry. It will be easy to tell the servants that no one is to enter his apartment but you, me, Martin, and Elizabeth. Once he is on his feet again—" Her voice quivered. "He will get well, will he not?"

"I am sure he will," Raymond said as heartily as he could.

At that moment they caught up with the litter party. Alys bent to look at her father. He was quiet now, although his lips moved as if he were talking in his dreams, but his right hand was free again and it clung to Elizabeth's. Elizabeth turned to Raymond. Her lips trembled. There was something she was afraid to ask, but she had to know the answer.

"Has he been out of his head the whole time?" she asked.

"No, my lady. Yesterday for a few minutes he knew me, and this morning." Raymond's voice thickened, and he cleared his throat. "This morning I thought he was better. He woke and spoke to me quite sensibly, asked me about the men and such, and he slept quite easy, not trying to toss about or muttering. I thought . . . but then he seemed to grow worse again."

"Oh, excellent!" Elizabeth exclaimed, and then smiled at Raymond's expression. "No, I did not mean it excellent that he grew worse. One does not put off a fever like this in a single day. But if he knew you in the morning, he is growing better. When he is washed and cooled, he will be easier, and still better tomorrow morning, I hope."

In the keep, after the bustle of getting William settled was over, Alys came out of her father's chamber into the hall and found Raymond sitting limply in one of the chairs near the great hearth. He began to struggle to his feet when he saw her.

"Sit," she said, and then, "no, get up." She came forward and lent a surprisingly strong hand to pull him out of the chair. "Come into your own chamber and let me see to you. I think you would be better in bed yourself."

"Should I speak to Diccon about—"

"There is no reason for you to speak to Diccon now," Alys said, pushing him gently toward the northeast tower. "I cannot believe anyone will send an army against us. In any case, the guards will give warning. That would be soon enough to speak to Diccon."

It was obvious Alys was not taking that possibility seriously. Raymond said, "But . . ." and then fell silent. He did not really expect any attack. What had happened in Wales was beginning to seem like a bad dream. Inside the strong walls of Marlowe, surrounded by devoted servants, it seemed impossible that any harm could come to William. Raymond sighed as the load of responsibility, which had become nearly intolerable, slipped away. He was so tired. The bed in the dim inner room beckoned invitingly, but his progress toward it was stopped abruptly.

"Stand still," Alys said.

Dull with fatigue, Raymond tried to think what he had forgotten to do. While he wondered, his surcoat was whipped off and, before he could marshal his wits to protest, his tunic followed.

"Sit down now," Alys directed, pushing him toward a chair.

Alys then untied his shirt. Raymond put up his hand to stop her, but she grasped his wrist and looked at the sleeve, which was stained with pus and dried blood and stuck to the wound under it. At once her eyes went to his legs. Above the right knee was another similar mess.

"Sit still," she said. "I must get cloths and water to soak your shirt and chausses free of that muck."

Raymond gaped at her back as she walked away. When he tried to stop her from removing his shirt, it had been because he wished to save her from seeing the ugly wounds. He could not even imagine his mother's reaction to such a sight. One of his sisters had become faint from seeing a nearly healed scar. His fatigue was so great, however, that he was reacting to everything in slow motion. By the time he had formulated the ideas clearly, two maids had come in. One woman wet his arm and knee with warm water and oil shaken together. The other carried a small table near and began to lay salves on it.

Raymond closed his eyes and leaned back, dozing in spite of the increased ache in arm and knee. He had slept only in few-minute snatches for almost two weeks. Eventually, he was wakened by a sharper pain as the shirt was pulled away and removed, but he did not bother to open his eyes until Alys's voice said, "Lift your hips a little, Raymond, so we can get these chausses off you."

That snapped him nearly awake. "What?"

"I have cleaned and bound your arm. Now I want to do your knee. Then you can go to bed and sleep yourself out. Come, Raymond, just stand a little."

"No."

"No, what?" she asked, smiling at him tenderly.

He was dazed with insufficient sleep and his brow was furrowed with anxiety. He looked like an overtired little boy with a problem.

"You cannot . . ." he faltered, and shook his head to clear it.

In an eyeblink Alys thought she understood. He did not wish to be naked before her. Alys flushed slightly. She had not thought about it at all. Naked men had no particular meaning for her. She bathed her father and Earl Richard, as her mother had done before her, and had salved hurts on Harold, John, and Aubery that necessitated their being bare. But now she felt shy, all of a sudden, not at all inclined to say, *Do not be ridiculous,* as she would have to Harold or Aubery.

"Fetch a clean shirt for Sir Raymond," Alys said to a maid, "and bring me a—a drying cloth."

The maid looked surprised but trotted away obediently. Raymond did not notice. He had just made sense of what Alys said three remarks back—that she had cleaned his arm. He looked down at it, neatly bandaged in clean linen. His mind then grasped the fact that Alys, not the maids, had tended his hurt and that she intended to do the same for the wound on his leg. He stared at her, but she looked just as usual, not pale nor faint nor nauseated.

"The wounds are very ugly," he said apologetically, knowing the truth but not quite believing it.

Alys patted his shoulder comfortingly. "That is only the spoiled blood and the evil humors coming out as they heal. Do not fret yourself. It will heal all smooth and do your fighting skill no hurt at all."

"Do you know of these things?"

It was strange enough that Alys could force herself to wash and bandage; it was stranger still that she spoke as if it was an everyday thing—more, as if it was one of her skills, like embroidery.

She smiled at him. "You need not think I offer false comfort. I cannot say I have set as many stitches in flesh as I have in cloth, but I am no novice at it. Lady Elizabeth taught me, and she is a fine physician. I know what will heal well and what will not. You may trust me."

Before he could answer, most fervently, that he did, the maid returned. Alys slid the shirt over his head and laid the drying cloth across his lap. Then, under this concealment, she grasped his chausses, which she had untied before she first told him to raise himself. "Hold the cloth and lift," she said. Her eyes were on what she was doing and she did not see Raymond's expression, which would have surprised her greatly. It was an unlikely moment for a man's face to set into iron-hard determination.

The delicate thought of shirt and cloth to save him embarrassment was the final stone in the structure of Raymond's love. He would have this woman, he decided, whatever the cost. There could be no other, he believed, with Alys's combination of beauty, courage, and good sense. He had seen her in every circumstance likely to try a woman, and she had never failed. She had met every test, surpassing even hopes he did not know he had.

Raymond thought of his father's life with his mother. She was sweet and loving and had brought great estates, but in her presence there was always constraint, always a need to watch each word and gesture lest something offend her sensibilities or frighten her. Then Raymond thought of the three weeks he had spent in Marlowe keep, of the ease and the laughter, of the talk that covered everything from low jests to high politics—and Alys in the midst of all. Not once had she disturbed her menfolk with tears or offended silence or haughty withdrawal.

Humanly perfect—those words described her best. She was no saint, whose perfectness shamed all about them and brought discomfort. She had a quick temper, a sharp tongue, and a low sense of humor. Alys would twitch a cow's ear to see it kick a man into a dung heap. She was willful as the devil, and far too prone to do things on her own without asking the advice or consent of her menfolk. But all of those things made her a woman rather than an angel, made her the woman he intended to marry.

CHAPTER 13

‡·‡

As the late afternoon waned into evening, William's sleep became easier and less restless. He was cooler, too, Elizabeth thought, although she was not sure whether that was owing to the fact that she had been wiping him with wet cloths. Her worst anxiety had been relieved, however. The wounds were not mortified nor were they so bad as she had feared. He was terribly thin. Raymond had mumbled something about his unwillingness to eat.

Alys stole softly into the room. She did not speak but looked questioningly at Elizabeth, who nodded and came toward her. Together they went out into the antechamber where torches and candles had been lit.

"He seems better," Elizabeth said at once. "There is no mortification. I think—oh, I am sure—he will recover."

There she stopped. When the case had seemed desperate, Alys had been willing to cede her right to care for her father so that he should have the best care she could furnish for him. Now that there was no need to consider a last-ditch battle with death, it was possible she would want her right to him back. Elizabeth would have gone down on her knees to plead for permission to stay, but she feared that would worsen rather than improve her chances by exacerbating Alys's jealousy.

She need not have worried. Alys loved her father, but she had found a new focus for her attention. She would never have abandoned William to the care of the servants; she would have sat with him and nursed him herself, knowing that Raymond's need was far less. Nonetheless, since she knew Elizabeth's nursing was

195

more skilled and would be equally, if not more, devoted, she was glad to relinquish the harder, less precious task, for the easier, more delightful one.

"Thank God for that," Alys said softly. "Will our voices disturb him? I must tell you why Raymond brought papa home. And I have brought something for us to eat."

"Oh, thank you, love," Elizabeth sighed, lowering her eyes to hide her tears as she realized Alys had not come to wrest the joy of tending William from her.

Alys drew a small table between two chairs, set the tray on it, and uncovered the food. They ate hungrily, as Alys retold Raymond's story. Before she was half finished, Elizabeth was ashen again.

"Mauger!" she whispered.

Alys stared at her. "I thought so too," she burst out, "but Hereford believes it must be someone who wishes to destroy papa's influence with Uncle Richard. And there is no reason, Elizabeth, after all these years—" She broke off abruptly and covered her lips with her hand, blushing.

Elizabeth swallowed and color came into her face also. "I am sorry, Alys," she said at last. "I hope you know that we—we did nothing, ever, that could have been an insult to your mother. It was an old, old thing that began when we were children. We expected to marry and swore to each other, but your grandfather felt that my portion was not enough for his eldest son —my brothers were alive then. And my father agreed. He preferred to accept your grandfather's offer of your Aunt Alys—she died the year you were born, I believe —to be betrothed to my brother. That way he had the blood bond and he could use me to make another bargain."

There was a long silence. Elizabeth looked at her hands, folded quietly in her lap. Alys stared into the distance. A few months ago, before she met Raymond, she might have been jealous or might have regretted the marriage had not taken place. If it had, she would have been Elizabeth's daughter. Today the simple story struck her in a most painful spot—her conscience. Her father, she feared, would be no better pleased with her choice than her grandfather had been with his heir's. Papa had warned her twice not to give Raymond hopes that could not be fulfilled.

Could she resist papa? That would be very wrong. To hurt him, who had always placed her good, her joy, ahead of his own was terribly ungrateful. It was a sin in the eyes of the Church and in the eyes of all men to disobey one's parents. But to lose Raymond? . . .

"Did you not even try to tell your father that you loved—"

"Try to tell him!" Elizabeth interrupted harshly. "I defied him outright! He beat me and starved me, but I would not yield."

"But then—"

"Your father 'accepted' the better bargain," Elizabeth hissed. Then she covered her face with her hands, murmuring through them, "No, do not listen to me. That was my old bitterness speaking."

"You mean papa gave you his word—and broke it?"

Elizabeth uncovered her face and sighed. "You do not understand, my love. It was easy for me. I never loved my father. He never cared for me. I was a waste, being a woman. But your papa loved his father, and—"

"No," Alys said. "I do not believe it. If papa gave his word, he would not break it—not for love or hate or anything."

"He was young then," Elizabeth suggested, but there was an uncertainty in her voice.

"No," Alys repeated. "People do not change that way. Have you changed?"

"But your father's papa came and told me that William had—had accepted Lady Mary." Elizabeth's voice roughened on the hated word.

Stubbornly Alys shook her head. "Papa would not break his word. Are you so certain your father and my grandfather did not lie to you? They might not have thought it a lie because you were only children, and if they told it, then it would become true."

Elizabeth stared at Alys, dumbfounded. A pall that had clouded her whole life seemed to be lifting. Could it be true? If it were so—if only it were so. . . .

"Ask papa," Alys said.

With that, Elizabeth turned her head to listen, but all was still quiet in William's bedchamber. When she looked back, there were tears in Alys's eyes. "He will be well soon," Elizabeth soothed, thinking her gesture had worried the girl, but Alys did not respond, merely bit her lip and stared at the wall. "What is it, my love?" Elizabeth asked then.

"I have done what you warned me against," Alys said. "I have fallen in love with Raymond."

"Oh dear," Elizabeth sighed, "oh dear. Oh, it was very wrong of him to—"

"He has done nothing—except to look at me. And he tries not to do that," Alys interrupted defensively. "I did not really know it until he came ashore with papa. I saw him—and I forgot about papa." Her voice was stricken.

Another woman would have brought out a host of platitudes. Alys would have been told she was very young, that she would soon forget the hireling knight when she was the mistress of a fine estate, that she should consider how she would be robbing her own future children if she married a man with nothing. And all the platitudes would have been true.

Elizabeth could say none of those things. They were contrary to her own experience. And, for Alys, there was already Marlowe and Bix. If William did not marry again, Alys's children would be well provided for—and Richard of Cornwall could be depended upon to find good places for any extra sons. Besides, a little evil voice said, if Alys married Raymond, William would have no reason to marry. His daughter would remain with him, and there would be children.

"My pet," Elizabeth said, "it is natural for a woman to place the man she loves above her father. Do not blame yourself for that. But . . ." Elizabeth's conscience pricked her painfully. William had such hopes for his daughter, "Oh, dear! Do try to curb this feeling in yourself, especially while your father is so sick. When he is better, if—if you feel the same—but you must promise me you will try to change your heart—I—I will plead with him for you."

"Will you?" Alys cried, and then clapped a hand to her mouth.

Elizabeth jumped up and went swiftly into the other room. Although he was not awake, William was stirring. Alys was waiting in the doorway and stepped back as it became clear Elizabeth would come out again. However, she did not sit down or go back to the subject uppermost in Alys's mind.

"Love, will you tell the cooks to send up some clear broth and also some with finely minced meat in it. I am not sure what he is able to take, but I think he will soon wake enough to eat a little."

Alys agreed and went out immediately, although she felt a bit aggrieved that her discussion with Elizabeth had been cut short at such a point. Then she felt guilty for thinking such a thing when her father's need was so much more important. Last she laughed at herself, remembering that Elizabeth had said it was natural she should think first of Raymond. It was such a comfort to have Elizabeth there. If only Elizabeth could stay, papa would think first of her and not care—much— whom Alys married.

Raymond and I could go to Bix, which is really mine, Alys thought. The idea was so lovely—it would make everything so perfect, just like heaven. Papa happy and well, never lonely, never worried because he did not have a son and Marlowe might be neglected. She thought of herself and Raymond at Bix, so near to Marlowe that she could see papa anytime and yet far enough that she would be, as she had been for so long, a lady in her own keep.

She gave the necessary order, dimly aware of the eagerness of the servants to hear and their relief when they understood that Sir William would eat. That was one order that would be fulfilled without watching. The broth for her father would reach his chamber probably before he woke. Her mind reverted at once to her dream. Its bright colors had dimmed. Elizabeth would not be at Marlowe. As soon as Mauger came home . . . Mauger. If Mauger had been the one who tried to murder papa and that could be proved . . . No, Alys thought, I am growing into a monster! Think of the shame for Aubery and John. I must not seek my happiness out of the pain of others or it will turn bitter in my mouth.

It was bitter already, but Martin came up to her to tell her that the servants had been told that no one must enter Sir William's apartment. He would sleep in the antechamber himself, on a pallet, so that he could fetch anything Lady Elizabeth might want during the night. He had ready a cot to be set up in Sir William's bedchamber for Lady Elizabeth. Alys sighed. Martin never could see that his service was enough. He always wanted to do more. One of the cook's assistants was by her elbow when she finished speaking to Martin, and she took the pots from him and went to the door of the bedchamber. The room was dark, except for what light came through the door. Lady Elizabeth saw Alys's shadow and came toward her.

"He is not awake yet," she reported. "You look tired, my love. Perhaps you should lie down for a while."

It was true Alys looked tired. There were mauve shadows around her eyes, the result of two wakeful, fearful nights. Elizabeth's concern was largely selfish, however. She was well aware that fatigue would do Alys, who was very strong, little harm. What Elizabeth wanted was to be alone with William when he woke. The cheerfulness with which Alys accepted this stricture and the lightness with which she tripped away alerted Elizabeth to what she had done. Doubtless the girl would go to young Raymond. Well . . . would it not be best after all?

The bed creaked as William moved restlessly and he began to groan. Elizabeth hurried toward him, fearful that he had wakened to some false reality of delirium in which he might do himself some harm. Her heart sank when she came through the door and his voice snapped a harsh, "Who is that?"

"Elizabeth," she replied. He had responded to her voice each time he had been restless, but this time the silence after she spoke was so profound that she grew frightened. She bent over. William's eyes were open, the whites gleaming faintly in the dimness.

"Light some candles," he said, "I think I must be still dreaming."

His voice was softer, hesitant, and the reply was perfectly sensible. Elizabeth sighed with relief and ran to bring a branch of candles from the antechamber. She heard the bed creak again and William utter an oath.

"Lie still," she cried, prevented from moving quickly by the guttering flames. "You will open something."

He could see her face now, lit as it was by the candles she carried. "I know I have been wandering. Am I still? What are you doing here at this hour of the night?"

"Alys asked me to come care for you. She was afraid her skill would not be sufficient."

That produced another profound silence, but shorter this time. "Either I have been more desperately sick than I thought," he said at last, "or I have been wrong about my daughter's perceptions—and I thought I knew her."

"Neither," Elizabeth answered, smiling. "As to the first, it was Raymond's fear to which Alys responded. He wrote a letter wherein it really sounded as if he was bringing a dying man home as a last hope. He is a good young man, William. His anxiety for you is most touching—but it frightened Alys out of her wits, so she begged me to come. As to the other—you read her aright, but she would never risk harm to you, no matter how small, just because of jealousy. Besides, I do not think she is very jealous any more."

"What does that mean?"

William sounded puzzled rather than angry or apprehensive, but Elizabeth knew this spurt of strength would not last long. She had no intention, moreover, of telling him more until he had thought over the hints she had already give him.

"Not now," she said, lighting two more sets of candles. "Does the light bother your eyes?"

"No. I have a little headache, but not much."

"Then I will bring you the pot, and then something to eat."

By the time he had relieved his bladder and bowels and had eaten the clear broth—he would not take the stronger one with meat in it—William's eyes were glazing with tiredness. Nonetheless, he asked, "What is it, Elizabeth? There is something different about you. It is something good, I am sure, and could do me no harm. Tell me."

Elizabeth's lips parted, but all she said was, "You are too tired. Sleep now."

The flicker of relief on William's face as his eyes closed was Elizabeth's reward for self-denial. Deep inside, there was also a suppressed sense of panic averted. When Alys first said, "Ask papa," Elizabeth had been so sure of William's answer that she could barely wait for him to wake. By the time his necessities had been attended to, however, she was remembering that Alys had only known her father as a mature man. She had said that people did not change—but that was not completely true.

Thus, Elizabeth kept putting off her question. The light inside her dimmed with her doubt. Sensitive to her most vagrant mood, William felt the change in her. With proper food and rest plus the treatment of his hurts William was improving rapidly. Nonetheless he still felt ill enough that he could not bear to look for trouble. He did not ask Elizabeth for an explanation of the change, hoping the deep, vibrant joy would come back, not wanting to hear what had spoiled it.

There was also not much time alone. Elizabeth took the night watches and Alys sat with her father during the day while the older woman rested. By the fourth day at home the scab was hard on the cut in his arm and was forming well over the edges of the wound in his side. The draining had almost stopped from the shoulder wound; its edges were less raised and the angry red was paling. That day, for the first time in the afternoon, William's head and body remained cool. On the fifth day, William ate his breakfast with real appetite and demanded to see Raymond. Elizabeth looked at him, shrugged, and summoned the young knight from the antechamber.

"Sit," William said, pointing to a stool. "How bad is that leg wound? I see you are still limping."

"It is nothing," Raymond assured him. "I am only favoring it because it is near the knee and pulls when I bend it."

"So? You should exercise it a little at a time. Do not favor it too long or it will heal tight. Now, tell me why you dragged me home without my men or my horses or, for all I know, even asking leave of Lord Hereford and Lord Gloucester."

"Not that. It was the earl of Hereford who said I must take you all the way to Marlowe." Raymond looked doubtfully at Elizabeth. He was not sure a sick man should be told someone was trying to kill him.

"I am not a child or a fool," William snapped. "Did you run to Hereford with that crazy tale that someone was trying to kill me?"

"Crazy tale!" Raymond exclaimed. "It was true enough. How do you think you got that cut in your arm? Someone entered your chamber at the abbey and tried to stab you."

Seeing that William was about to protest that no one *could* want to kill him, Raymond described the cut stirrups and detailed the incidents at the abbey and then told him Hereford's theory that the attempts were somehow related to Richard of Cornwall. That stopped William's argument, and he thought it over.

"Perhaps," he said at last, "although I cannot think of a person or a cause. I had not even caught that accursed lazy clerk in any dishonesty—but my head is still thick. In any case, it is nothing to worry about now that I am home. Let it go. You had better start riding out again and see if you can glean some more men to train. I have a feeling that this business in Wales may not be over. If the king brings the army he gathered to oppose the Scots to Wales, that will end it—if I know Henry aright, he will not do that. When that army is disbanded, David will come down out of the hills again."

"But you will not—"

"I will be healed in a month," William said firmly. "If Richard goes, I will go too."

"That is enough for now," Elizabeth said, and Raymond rose at once, shaking his head at William's protest. "If you wish to be healed in a month," Elizabeth went on sharply, "you must not do yourself a hurt now."

William subsided. He was not tired yet, and Elizabeth must know it. Therefore, she wanted to be rid of Raymond for a reason. When he was out the door, she drew her chair even closer to the bed and said softly, "It is Mauger."

What she meant was perfectly clear to William. He hesitated a moment, wanting to believe it. If it was Mauger who had tried to kill him, his oppressive sense of guilt would be assuaged. Of course, Mauger had a right to kill him—but not on the sly. It would have been just and reasonable for Mauger to challenge him to judicial combat. William would have fought him, although he was by no means sure he would have survived. Probably he was the stronger, more experienced fighter—but William believed in the power of God. He was not sure that the chaste Almighty would understand or approve his hunger for another man's wife.

The strong temptation William felt to believe Mauger guilty convinced him that Elizabeth was seeking the same balm for her guilt. "It cannot be Mauger," he said reluctantly. "He cannot want me dead." He told her of his talk with Aubery and confessed his inability to tell Mauger that any hope of a union was over. Then he went on. "Mauger must know that Richard would be her warden, and he must know also that Richard would not favor his suit—why should he? Even if Mauger does not realize how much Richard loves Alys, he does understand that an overlord seeks to marry his wards where it will best profit himself. There could be no advantage to Richard in giving Alys to Aubery."

Stubbornly, Elizabeth shook her head. "That all may be true, but—but I am sure it is his doing. I think your hurts are his doing also. That he did not come to you in time apurpose."

For answer, William took her hand and kissed it. He did not wish to say he believed her conviction to be a result of a desire to assuage guilt. Thus, his kiss was no formal gesture. He put his lips to the palm, not the upper surface of her hand, and then nibbled the fingers, caressing the balls with the tip of his tongue. Elizabeth drew in her breath sharply and then, very gently, withdrew her hand.

"For shame," she murmured, "to make such an invitation when you cannot furnish a feast."

"Who says I cannot?" William rejoined.

Elizabeth was startled by the eagerness of his expression, and she could feel her color rise. William saw that too, and reached out as if to take her in his arms. She caught his hands and held them. "Raymond," she mouthed, almost silently, and gestured toward the door with her head.

"Call him," William whispered. "I will send him on an errand. What the devil is he doing there anyway?"

Elizabeth blushed even more, but shook her head. "He guards you," she murmured. Then, ignoring William's astonished expression, added, "It is better that he be there. If you yielded to your desire, you would be sorry for it, and so would I."

"I would not be sorry, whatever the cost," William urged, forgetting his surprise at being told Raymond was guarding him.

"Nor would I, for my cost," Elizabeth said, smiling ruefully, "but when you must pay for all, William, I cannot be so careless."

He turned his hands to seize hers and grinned at her.

"I promise the cost would be little. I know many ways. You can do all the work, Elizabeth, while I lie at my ease."

He laughed at her startled look. For all of her two children, she was nearly as innocent as a young girl. Silently, William blessed the high-born whores who were always seeking novelty and thus greatly enlarged his knowledge of the many positions—some weird enough —in which one could make love. What a delight it would be to teach Elizabeth. William did not fear she would be shocked or refuse. Her face, now that the surprise was gone, showed curiosity and eagerness.

In the next moment, however, that look was replaced by one William could not read. Elizabeth dropped her eyes to their linked hands and her color faded. She said, "Not now, William. When you are stronger," but it was not the act of love she was thinking of. It was the doubt that had dimmed her joy that turned her cold. It could be put off no longer. William raised Elizabeth's hands and kissed them, this time with a tenderness that was not touched by sensuality.

"Tell me," he said.

Elizabeth knew at once he had read her change of mood right. Often there was no need for words between them. They had communicated quite well over and around Mauger by occasional glances. Panic rose in her, and she tried to disengage her hands. Somehow it would be worse now to learn that she had been told the truth, that William had "accepted" his marriage. The brightness of the hope she had had would make what was only a small, dingy failure in an uncertain boy seem like a black sin.

No longer very much weakened by illness, William's grip was firm. It would have taken real violence for Elizabeth to pull away. She made a single abortive move for freedom.

"Tell me," he insisted.

"Why did you marry Mary?" Elizabeth asked.

Of all the responses in the world, William was more surprised by this than any other Elizabeth could have made. He released her hands and stared at her. It was ridiculous! She must know the answer. Bitterness lashed him. If she had stood fast, the guilt that soured their joy in each other would never have cursed them.

"What was left for me after you yielded? What did it matter whom I married, since you were wed already and beyond my reach?"

Such rage and hurt were in his voice that William was appalled. He had not meant to flay Elizabeth with the anger he had carried all the years. But his surprise at her question was nothing compared with his amazement at her reaction to his cruel answer. She glowed with joy. What had been leashed in by doubt at first and then had nearly died from being smothered burst all bounds.

"William," she cried, "they lied to us! They lied to us both!" The loudness of her voice startled her, and she went on more softly but just as intensely. "I did not yield, I swear it—not until I was told you had already accepted Mary. I thought you had broken your oath first, and I, too, felt it did not matter whom I married if you were lost to me."

"You mean my father lied to me?"

To William, this revelation was almost as painful as his original belief. He had loved his father and trusted him. Moreover, it was not as important to William that Elizabeth be strong. To her, the fact that he had not betrayed his oath knowingly was of paramount importance. It permitted her to trust implicitly, to place her fate, her life, in her lover's hands, to believe he would protect her no matter what the consequences. To William, the discovery of Elizabeth's steadfastness besmirched a dear memory. Fortunately his question exposed that hurt nakedly enough for Elizabeth to perceive it.

She cared for nothing except William's peace. It did not matter to her whether old Sir William had lied or not. "Be reasonable, William," she urged. "Think how often you have held back something from Alys or told her a half-truth because you believed it was for her good."

"I do not—" he began and then fell silent because, like any parent, of course he did.

"Probably by the time your father told you, it was true that I was married—or, at least, sent away." She leaned forward and kissed him. "William, they could not have known. I am sure even my father did not wish us ill, and yours was doing what he thought would end in the greatest happiness for you, even if there was a little pain in the beginning."

"God forbid I ever wish Alys well the same way," William sighed. "But you are right. My father was a great believer in raising his hand to me lightly when I was young so that he would not need to use a whip when I was older. It worked too—in everything but this. You were my siren, and I always heard your song."

CHAPTER 14

✠·✠

When Elizabeth cried sharply, "They lied to us. They lied to us both," Raymond jumped to his feet and stood watching the door. Although he knew it to be impossible, he could not help expecting Alys's outraged and infuriated father to burst out on him demanding an explanation of his improper behavior. He had not been listening to the sounds from the bedchamber previously, being immersed in his own not-too-pleasant thoughts. But the voices again dropped to an indistinguishable murmur, and his tension eased.

Once the shock was over, it was obvious Lady Elizabeth and Sir William could not be talking about Alys and him. Certainly he had not lied, for he had been asked no questions. As for Alys—Raymond swallowed uneasily—did she care enough to need to lie about him? She did not display any of the symptoms of love familiar to him. She neither sighed nor blushed when he spoke to her about ordinary everyday topics—and he did not dare speak of anything else—nor was she haughty and cold in the tradition of *amour courtois*.

On the other hand, her voice did seem softer when she spoke to him, and her eyes—he would swear her eyes lingered on him when they were in the hall together but not close. Still, there was nothing that could give him any real assurance of her love.

Nonetheless, Raymond could not help wondering whether the order to ride out and recruit was a deliberate effort on Sir William's part to separate him from Alys. He was very much afraid he was not as good at hiding what he felt as Alys was—if she felt anything. The order was kindly meant, he was sure. Sir William, not Alys, was the crux of his problem. If Alys did not yet love him, she did not love anyone else either and he could win her love. It would be far more difficult to win Sir William's approval.

How, Raymond wondered, had he ever allowed himself to be thrust into so disgusting a position? Damn King Henry and his sweet smile and airy request for a "little" service that needed a trustworthy man. Raymond had taken William's full measure by now. He loved the man for his directness and honesty. But how would such a man judge the "little service"? How would he judge the man who had blithely accepted the task and the deceptions that went with it? How, Raymond wondered, would he ever be able to explain what he had done to Sir William?

With many men, Raymond knew that his wealth and position would more than compensate for the omission in mentioning them. Unfortunately that was not true for Sir William. Alys had said enough the last few days for Raymond to understand that her father was more interested in keeping her near him and ensuring continued good management for Marlowe than he was in having his daughter make a great marriage. That had been the final blow to Raymond's confidence. He leaned his head against the rough stone surrounding the window he had been staring out of sightlessly and closed his eyes in misery.

Alys glanced at him when she entered the room, but he did not stir and her lips tightened.

"Do you feel ill?" she asked. "Is your head hot?"

He jerked upright and turned to face her. "No. I was thinking."

"The thoughts cannot have been very pleasant."

Alys was having the most frustrating experience of her life. She was having her first taste of rejection—not complete rejection, for that would have raised her pride and she would have been able to strangle the newborn love in her. She thought she was meeting the kind of honorable rejection that counts no cost in pain so long as right is done. It was easy to recognize. She could see the longing in Raymond's eyes when he looked at her, but not even the broadest hints that her father did not specially desire a rich son-by-marriage could wring a word out of him. In fact, he looked more despairing each time Alys proffered that comfort.

There could be several causes for that. Raymond could believe she was not telling the truth—or telling it as she wanted it to be rather than as it was. This fear had considerable weight. She was sure her father would not force her into an unwelcome marriage, but that he would willingly forgo a rich and influential match in favor of a penniless young man was much more doubtful. Probably he would want to send Raymond away, and Uncle Richard would provide a dozen suitors in the hope that Alys would change her mind.

Doubtless if she held firm, she could have Raymond in the long run, but how long? Years, perhaps. Alys did not want to wait years, and she knew quite well how to get around that. All she had to do was swear to Raymond and have him swear to her also. Papa would yield if she told him that. He might be angry, but how angry could he be when he had done the same himself?

When she first thought of the idea, it had seemed so simple. But it had not worked out that way at all. She expected Raymond to leap on the suggestion that her father would accept him and instantly avow his love. Instead he looked frightened and—yes—hopeless. This left the possibility of confessing her own love first, but Alys could not do that. It was not strictly a matter of pride, although pride did add to the problem.

Alys realized that many of the things she did surprised Raymond. She was not "a lady" in the style to which he was accustomed. Some of the things that surprised him also gave him pleasure; others shocked him still, but he accepted them as part of her different way of life. For a woman openly to pursue a man, however, would not only shock but disgust him. Even Alys's forthright nature quailed at the thought. Decent women did not do such things. They waited until their fathers

or guardians told them whom to love. To propose love
uninvited was to proclaim a lewd nature, to brand oneself a whore.

There was another reason for Raymond to reject the
careful overtures she had made. He might agree that
Uncle Richard was right and that her father was doting.
He might feel that it was his duty, because he loved her,
to save her from her father's foolish fondness—expressed
in the willingness to accept any man Alys chose—and
see that she married a rich and powerful husband.
When she thought of that, Alys felt like grabbing Raymond by the ears and banging his head against the wall.

Now irritation swept her again as Raymond dropped
his pale, clear eyes and said softly, "No. They were
not pleasant thoughts."

"You are doing yourself no good by chewing them
over alone," Alys remarked dulcetly.

"It is not a matter of choice for me," Raymond said
miserably. "I—I have—I have not *told* a lie but allowed one to be believed. . . ."

Alys's eyes widened. The one thing she had not
thought was that Raymond might think himself unac-
ceptable because of the stain on his family—whatever it
was—that had sent him into exile. She had forgotten
about that. No wonder the poor thing looked even more
unhappy when she said papa did not care about wealth
and position. But papa would never blame the son for
the father's fault.

She came across the room and took his hand. "Tell
me," she urged. "You know papa and I think differently than you on many subjects. Perhaps because of the
mists of your unhappiness, what you believe is a moun-
tain will turn out a molehill in our clear vision."

Raymond raised his eyes from the hand she was
holding and they were caught in the perfection of her
face. He wet his lips. It was over anyway, he told himself. As soon as Sir William was strong enough to defend his own land, he must go back to the king. The
sooner Alys knew the better.

"I am not a poor hireling knight," he said harshly. "I

am the eldest son of Alphonse d'Aix, comte d'Aix, and nephew to Queen Eleanor."

For a long moment Alys stared at him. Then she let go of his hand and wiped her own on her skirt as if she suddenly realized she had been grasping some slimy, revolting object.

"I hope you have had sufficient amusement from your experiences of living among the common herd," she said icily. "But I am sure the jest has gone on too long for your taste. You are free to go, my lord. We will manage quite well without your support."

"Alys!" Raymond exclaimed, but softly, remembering William and Elizabeth in the bedchamber beyond.

She did not hesitate but turned away, and he leapt after her and grasped her arm. "Let go," she spat.

"No jest. It was not a jest!" Raymond pleaded.

Angry as she was, it was not possible to believe Raymond was insincere now. Perhaps he had meant to have an amusing few weeks laughing to himself over the coarse and common ways of a simple knight and then —Alys knew she was beautiful—he had come to desire her. No wonder he had been distressed when she said her father would be willing to permit their marriage. He did not intend *marriage*.

"I am not of your kind," she snarled. "We stupid, common, simple people do not lightly play at games of love. You will gain nothing here."

"Games of love? No!" His voice shook. "There is no price I would not pay—"

Alys hit him so hard he swayed, but he did not release his hold on her. "I am not for sale! Let me go, or I will call the men. You may be a great man elsewhere, but here—"

In her fury she had miscalculated. Raymond had a hand across her mouth in seconds. She pulled back her lips, but before she could bite him, he said, "To have you to wife! Alys, in God's name, what I have done is disgusting enough. Do not believe it worse!" Her eyes blazed at him, but he let her go. "You can put me out. I will go if you bid me, but do not believe me so foul as that."

The mark of her hand was deep red on his cheek. Alys stepped backward toward the door, but Raymond only watched her go without protest, his eyes too bright. If he had tried to stop her or excuse himself further, she would have shrieked for help. She did nothing because his eyes were full of tears, because he did not speak or move, because he said he wished to marry her—but that was easy enough for a man to say when there were no witnesses. He knew she would not demean her pride by trying to hold him to his word—still, he had said it.

She stopped and stared at him. If his coming to them was not some kind of drunken jest or wager and he had not stayed in hopes of seducing her, what had he done that was—in his own words—disgusting? Why was he in Marlowe?

"Papa always says I am too hasty, that I must not judge without listening," she said more calmly. "Why are you here?"

He flushed so darkly that the mark of the blow she had dealt him was swallowed, and his eyes, which had been pleading, dropped. "The king heard ill said of your father. I came to see if it was true."

Again Alys stared at him without speaking for a moment. Then she shook her head. "I could not, no matter how hard I tried, think you more foul than you are. It must have irked you sadly that papa is so good a man that you had to linger so long to find a lie to tell about him. Go then, and tell what tale you like."

"I did not come to find a lie, but to unravel one. I have unraveled it. I can truly say that your father's friendship with the earl of Cornwall can do only good to the earl, to the realm at large, and to the king himself. Oh, God, it was you who trapped me into this folly —you and the stupid desire for a little freedom."

"What has Uncle Richard to do with this," Alys snapped. That he should blame her was natural and she ignored it. The remark about his freedom was inexplicable, but Alys was in no mood to concern herself with his problems. She stuck to what had meaning to her.

"Of himself, nothing. Will you let me tell you the whole?"

"I have no doubt it will be as pretty and fanciful as a romance, but why not?"

Raymond was near tears at the scorpion lash of her voice. Had he been older, wiser, or what Alys was trying to force herself to believe he was, he would have been overjoyed instead. Her youth and her love both spoke in the sentence. If she had been more experienced, she would have bespoken him gently, pretended to be willing to believe, cozening him into a good opinion. If she had not loved him, she would not have listened at all.

Shamed and distraught as he was, Raymond made short work of his story, telling it without embellishment and without excuses, painting himself in his despair blacker than he was. In fact, he did himself much good. Ungarnished, the tale sounded what it was—the truth. Besides, Alys knew more about the king than he did. Before he was done, Alys had moved to a chair to sit and gestured him to another.

"After Earl Richard came," he finished, "I should have gone back to the king and told him the clerk heard amiss, but I—I wanted to go to war in Wales and—and I could not bear to be parted from you. So I stayed. I told myself I would have more evidence to offer to the king after the Welsh war, but I only wanted to see you again."

"It was not right," Alys said, but her voice was sad rather than angry. "You know your father would never agree to such a marriage—and I will agree to nothing else."

The last words were said harshly, but Raymond looked up at last, his expression tense with hope. "Would you take me for a husband after what you have heard?"

This time Alys's eyes dropped. "It is nothing to do with me," she answered. "Your father—"

"My father has no bond on me," Raymond said, getting to his feet. "I do not care whether he agrees or not. Alys, answer me from your heart—do not think of fathers or anyone else. Of yourself, would you be willing to marry me?"

"It is not possible," she said faintly.

"I will make it possible, if you are willing," Raymond exclaimed. He knelt by her chair and took her hand.

"I would be willing to *marry* you," she said, and withdrew her hand.

He understood, rose, and backed away a few steps. "You need not fear, I swear. Alys, I beg you, do not think me a liar. I am not that. I withheld the truth, but never spoke a lie. I will tell your father as soon as he wakes, and—"

"No. Papa will not like this. He will not like it at all. He must not be upset until he is stronger."

"I know he will not like it," Raymond sighed, "but I will agree to any condition, anything at all, so long as he will let us marry. Something can be worked out. My love—"

"Do not call me that," Alys said. "I was very willing to be your wife when you had nothing. Now, I am less sure. I am not lost for love, and the more I think of this the less easy I grow. I must value myself, and what value can I have in the high world in which you live?"

"You are a pearl without price, and will be in any world," Raymond exclaimed passionately.

"Is that your mind speaking or your shaft, Raymond?" Alys asked, deliberately crude. "I am beautiful, but close your eyes and think what I am under my face and my body."

"It is that I desire," Raymond assured her. "I have seen beautiful women before, and never once did it cross my mind to defy my father's will and ask for one of them to be my wife—not even when it would have been a match to please him. Your beauty did catch my eye. It must blind the eye of any man who sees you, but it was not until I learned what you were that I thought of marriage."

If that were true . . . Perhaps it was, but there were still insuperable problems. Alys sighed. "It would be easier and best for us both to turn our backs on this thing. If you will go, Raymond, I promise I will explain to my father in such a way that he will remain your friend. Go home. You will soon enough forget me."

"I will go if you order me gone, Alys, but on my life and honor I swear I will have no other woman to wife. I have seen pure gold, and I will not have dross instead. I swear—"

"No, do not!" Alys exclaimed, putting out a hand to stop him but knowing it was too late.

"To my mind and heart you are my wife. To marry elsewhere would be a sin. I am no Turk."

Alys stared at him, wide eyed with distress, torn between joy and fear. She did want Raymond but thought she could have buried that desire in time. Apparently, however, he had gone further than she. All Alys knew of men, really, was her father. He had sworn to love Elizabeth, and for twenty miserable years he had done so. Alys did not understand the peculiar circumstances that had riveted William's attention and affection on his childhood sweetheart. She knew all men were not like her father, of course; she had heard of love betrayed. Nevertheless, she believed that all *good* men were fixed in their affections.

Then it was too late. Whatever difficulties Raymond had to face to win her would be better than the utterly hopeless misery of living as her father had lived. If Raymond could have felt as she did—that time would cure his trouble—the brief unhappiness might have been worth enduring. But Alys could not inflict a lifetime of regret on him—besides, she did not want to. She was a little afraid of stepping into a style of life that was unfamiliar to her, but the more she looked at Raymond the more she forgot those fears.

"If you have sworn to me already," Alys said slowly, "it is too late for me to bid you look elsewhere—and—and I love you also." Raymond took a step toward her, but Alys shook her head firmly. "No, do not come closer. And do not be so foolish as to cry, 'Why will you not trust me?' It is myself I do not trust. Until we are publicly sworn, I will not even touch your hand nor permit you to touch mine."

Raymond was not hurt. He had meant only to kiss her hand in formal thanks for her acceptance of him. However, he acknowledged her wisdom and was proud of her self-control. Despite her beauty, which would draw a gaggle of besotted ganders to woo her, he felt he would never need to doubt her. Alys was not one to yield her honor to her passion.

"Then bend your mind to how I may come to that public swearing as quick as may be," Raymond urged. "I have been half mad, thinking you would have nothing to say to me when I confessed my stupidity—yet I cannot regret it," he admitted, smiling, "for had I not fallen into the king's stratagem, I would not have met you."

Alys smiled back, her eyes sparkling. Now that the matter was settled, she felt very happy and her doubts dropped away. Somehow they would manage. "Papa will give in," she said, "not because he is doting but for—for reasons of his own. However, as I said, he will not like it, and he will be hurt and—and so lonely, Raymond."

"He may not need to be lonely," Raymond pointed out. 'I have a younger brother. If my father disowns me, I will truly be a penniless hireling, so—"

"Raymond," Alys interrupted, eyes wide with horror, "would he do that?"

"I do not know," Raymond answered honestly. "He is a kind man—too kind sometimes—and most loving to us all, but he has strict notions also and will not yield on those. It is very hard to read him, Alys. He will yield and yield and then, on some point, stick fast so that neither reason nor pleading will move him."

"Take back your oath, Raymond. I absolve you of it gladly. If you lose so much, you will come to hate me. I could bear to lose you, but I could not bear that."

He came forward impetuously, then stopped short when Alys shrank back into the chair. "My love—you said not to call you that, but I cannot help it—nothing could make me hate you. On this point, however, you need fear the least. For myself—I have never been happier than in these months of service with your father. And that, though you may think it unloverlike in me, had naught to do with you."

"But you come from a great house, where—"

"Where I had no more to do than to be a doll, a pretty popinjay for my mother's dressing. I will grieve if I am cast out, for I love my father and my mother, too, although she drives me mad, and my brother and sisters, but that is all I will grieve for. Besides, Alys, I am sure my mother would write to Queen Eleanor and beg her intervention in my favor with the king. I know what is felt about 'foreigners,' but I am learning English—"

Alys looked doubtful, but she was not worried about Raymond needing a livelihood. If her father agreed to the marriage, he would give them Bix. She was more concerned that so powerful a family could find a way to hurt them all.

"It is more likely that your mother would ask the king to prevent the marriage than that she would ask that help be given you."

"If she did," Raymond said, his eyes blazing and his lips thinned, "she would be soon sorry for it. I am not a doll that she can play with at her will. In any case, Alys, that will be my problem and in the future. For now, it is more immediate to tell me how to present my case to your father so that he will not try to kill me before I finish asking for you."

"I am not sure. Perhaps Lady Elizabeth—"

"Lady Elizabeth? I should think she would be the last person to help us." Raymond suddenly wondered whether it was possible that Alys did not know about the marriage planned with Aubery.

"She and my father are—they are very old friends," Alys said, her color rising as she realized what she had nearly said. "And—and Elizabeth has been like a mother to me."

"I think she *intends* to be a mother to you," Raymond pointed out dryly. "It is her son who—"

"Oh no. She does not wish me to marry Aubery," Alys interrupted. "She thinks we would not suit. Of course, I love Aubery—"

"Do you?"

Alys was startled by the voice, low, but hard and sharp. She had never heard Raymond use that voice. "How—" she began, meaning to say, *How dare you speak like that to me,* and then she realized Raymond was jealous. "Silly," she said, smiling. "I was not angry when you told me you loved your sisters. Believe me, I feel no differently about Aubery."

"He is not your brother, however," Raymond snapped.

"It does not make any difference," Alys giggled. "And you may be as angry as you like, but I cannot change the fact that I do love Aubery, and John also, and always will. However—"

Raymond's lips tightened when Alys laughed at him. Then he grew really angry. He was not accustomed to being told by "his" woman that a thing was so and—by implication—he must swallow it if he did not like it. He had been told things by Alys before—but she had been his "overlord's" daughter then. Now she was, to his mind, his wife.

"Alys!" he roared—and then clapped a hand to his mouth, but it was too late.

"What is it?" William called from the bedchamber. And Elizabeth's voice followed, "Lie still. It is nothing."

Alys shot out of her chair and into the bedchamber. "Forgive me, papa. I forgot. It was a jest, and Raymond—"

"Alys," William sighed, passing a hand over his face

to rub the sleep out of it, "while I am still so sore, I wish you would tease Raymond elsewhere than my apartment."

"It was my fault, sir," Raymond said, edging into the room.

"I doubt it," William remarked, and smiled wryly.

He lifted himself on an elbow, and Elizabeth bent over him to raise his pillow higher. Her wimple brushed his cheek and the scent of her filled his nostrils. The emotional shock of discovering that they had not betrayed each other had temporarily quenched William's sexual impulse, but sleep had refreshed him. At that moment he had all he could do to keep himself from pulling her down to be kissed and caressed despite the witnesses. He had to get rid of them. He shifted his eyes to Alys and laughed softly.

"And I do not wish to hear anything you have to say, mistress mischief. Go away and take Raymond with you. You should be ashamed of yourselves, to insult my servants by setting a guard over me as if they wished me harm."

"But sir—" Raymond protested.

"If you are worried, you may tell Diccon to close the gates to strangers for a day or two or to set a guard at the hall door and permit none but the servingmen and women to enter, but I do not want anyone in the outer chamber. That is an order."

"Very well, papa," Alys agreed hastily, seeing that her father's color had risen and not wishing to excite him. It made no difference, after all. Raymond or Diccon could sit in the hall right outside the door. The safety would be the same and her father would know nothing about it. "I will sit with you now—"

"No. I slept through the night and did not disturb Elizabeth. I have the headache a little. Let Elizabeth stay. You must be behindhand with everything. Why do you not ride out with Raymond, if he can sit a horse, and see how the crops are coming and what is to be first harvested."

Alys was about to protest that she would trouble

him no more than Elizabeth, but the words froze in her throat. William's face was still deeply flushed, although he plainly was not angry now. Another fearful glance showed her that his eyes looked funny and his expression had an odd rigidity. She swallowed nervously and glanced at Elizabeth, but there was no comfort to be found there. Elizabeth had gone white.

The stiffening sickness? Usually the dreaded condition that locked a man's jaws and arched his body like a strung bow began within a week of the wound being taken, but sometimes much longer passed. Sometimes even after the wounds were healed, a man would complain of a difficulty in chewing or speaking. Then his fever would rise; his neck would stiffen. Soon after, he would die, screaming in agony through his locked jaws.

Alys dared not ask, dared not put that fear into her father's mind. And she did not want to know! Terrified, she backed out of the room, unconsciously seizing Raymond's hand and drawing him with her. Without a word, she pulled him across the hall and into his own room, where she turned and pressed her face against his breast and began to cry.

"What is it, love? What is wrong?" Raymond whispered, longing and fearing to embrace her.

"Hold me," she sobbed, "hold me. I am afraid."

He complied with alacrity, begging her to tell him what she feared and promising to protect her. Trembling, Alys named her terror. For a moment, Raymond clutched her tighter, also terrified, but then he loosened his grip.

"It cannot be, beloved," he soothed. "The wounds were wide and clean and bled freely. It cannot be." But his voice shook. "Listen, beloved," he urged, "you are building a whole keep out of a handful of pebbles, and I know less than you. It will be many hours before he grows better or worse. Your father set us a task. Let us do it. No matter what befalls, he would not like us to disobey him."

Alys shuddered, but she lifted her head and nodded agreement. She did not think Raymond unfeeling. She could hear the concern in his voice. What he had offered her was the only thing she herself knew to be efficacious in time of fear or sorrow—work. Following her mute nod, she made a tiny gesture of withdrawal. Immediately his arms dropped away. Alys touched his hand gently in silent thanks as she stepped back. Under the fear for her father was a masked joy for she now knew she could trust Raymond better than herself. In her fear she had offered him the opportunity to make love to her—and he had not taken that unfair advantage.

CHAPTER 15

‡‡‡‡‡‡‡‡‡‡‡‡‡‡‡‡‡‡‡‡‡‡‡‡‡‡‡‡‡‡‡‡‡

In William's chamber Elizabeth had waited, frozen, until she was sure Alys and Raymond were gone. Then she bent over the bed. "When did your head start to ache?" she whispered. "Where does it hurt? Is your neck stiff?"

William's right arm encircled her, pulling her off balance so that she nearly fell on top of him. "No," he answered. "I have no pain and my neck is not stiff—but something else is! Do not be such an idiot, Elizabeth. I had to say *something* to be rid of that pair."

Elizabeth was too close to see him properly, but there could be no doubt what he meant because he pulled her lower still and fastened his mouth to hers. His lips were warm, full with passion, but soft, his tongue quick and flexible as it sought a haven in her mouth. Slowly, she disengaged her lips from his. Now that her fear was gone, she read his expression correctly. The heavy eyes and rigid features were owing to desire not illness.

"You will hurt yourself, William," she sighed, but without conviction. Ever since June, she had relived and dreamed of the exquisite experience of his lovemaking.

"I will do nothing," he murmured. "Take off that stupid headdress. I want to see you." Still she hesitated, flushed and wide eyed. "Must I get up and undress you myself, Elizabeth?" he asked, his voice harder and commanding.

With an intake of breath like a sob, she shook her head and began to remove her clothing. All the while she felt William's eyes on her and she could hear his breathing, harsher and quicker than usual, broken once or twice by a long, shaken sigh.

She ached with desire but felt it was wrong and she

224

fought herself, but William said, "Come here," again a harsh command, and she came, her eyes on her own bare feet until the edge of the bed appeared. A heartbeat longer she hesitated, heard William's breath draw in, and quickly lay down beside him, knowing he had thrown back the light blanket. She thought he would seize her immediately, as he had the last time they were in bed together, and she closed her eyes, not to see the healing flesh torn open again with his violence. However he only touched her arm, his fingers gentle, hesitant.

"Elizabeth?" The tone of command was gone, replaced by uncertainty and anxiety. "Beloved? Are you not willing?"

A dark blush dyed her cheeks dusky rose. She opened her eyes. "Not willing! I am much too willing. I should not let you. You will hurt yourself. But I cannot help it. I want you!"

He laughed softly. "You are a most innocent elf, Elizabeth. I will not hurt myself. I will lie still if it kills me. I assure you that I will not unseat a stitch nor loosen a scab. Come, sit up, love, and bend over me so that I may love you with my mouth."

She still did not understand how he would manage, but she could not bear to worry any longer. Eagerly she leaned over so that he could kiss her throat and breasts. She found that one arm was enough to support her. The other stretched downward. William was whole below the waist and she knew she could touch him there without hurting him. Her hand went down his thigh, slipped between his legs investigating what, although long married, she had never before been willing to touch.

His legs spread at her touch, and where her wrist lay across his thigh, Elizabeth could feel the tension and faint trembling in it. She ran her hand up, then down. It was immediately apparent that her curiosity was having a violent effect on her lover. His lips and hands grew more urgent, and he began to moan deep in his throat. William's excitement fed Elizabeth's so that the pain caused by his too-hard sucking and biting turned to an exquisite pleasure. Then he tore his mouth loose.

"Mount me," he gasped. "I am your stallion. Mount me. Ride me."

Elizabeth's eyes opened wide with surprise. How simple! What a fool she was never to have thought of it. Hastily she came upright, straddled him.

"Take—" he began, and choked on his eagerness.

But it was not necessary to give further instructions. Elizabeth's own need taught her. Heaven! She was, for the first time, mistress of her own pleasure. Unfettered by her partner's weight, she could twist, grind, move fast or slow, apply pressure where she wanted it. Beneath her William panted and groaned, but he lay still as he had promised, only running his hands up and down her body, playing with her breasts and belly, fingering her navel and buttocks.

The heaven Elizabeth had found was too deliriously exciting to last. She fell forward, catching herself just before her full weight came upon her lover, thrusting quicker, quicker. Her mouth opened, a shriek of agonized joy rising in her throat, but William was ready. He pulled her head down so that her cry was muffled into his mouth. Again! Again! Again! And then she was still.

"Move," William groaned. "For God's sake, move— or I must!"

His hands gripped her hips, lifted her a little. Elizabeth drew a trembling breath, pulled away, thrust forward again when William's hands drew her down. She was dazed with reaction, almost unwilling, but in seconds she understood the demand being made of her. There was no discomfort in obeying. Opening her eyes, which had closed as her own orgasm came upon her, she watched William's response to her movement with interest and delight, taking, at last, almost as much pleasure in his climax as she had had from her own.

When his breath came evenly again, she eased herself off him and lay by his side. He moved his arm to take her head upon his shoulder, having forgotten for a moment his hurt, but winced and desisted. They lay quietly, just touching, holding hands. There was no need for words. Contentment enfolded them both. William slipped asleep, and Elizabeth's mind wandered here and there idly for quite some time until, while admiring William's cleverness in obtaining privacy for them, she remembered that the last thing he should have done was sent Alys and Raymond out together.

That worry brought a flood of others, the most pressing being what they were to do when Mauger returned. Nothing had really changed. Elizabeth's responsibility to her sons and to Hurley still lay upon her. She lifted herself carefully away from William, got out of the bed, and began to dress. Before she was finished, William reached out to where she had been lying, muttered, and then opened his eyes.

"Come back," he sighed.

Elizabeth shook her head. "Go back to sleep."

The long lashes drooped, then lifted again. "I cannot bear it," he said.

"Do not be so silly." Elizabeth forced herself to smile. "Even a wedded wife would flee your bed at such a time. For shame! In the middle of the forenoon, and you still abed with your hurts. Such wantonness!"

That made him smile too, but the trouble did not clear from his eyes. "I have waited long enough," he said, "more than half my life."

"Let it be, William," Elizabeth sighed.

"You mean I must go on waiting—forever? That when Mauger returns we are to be no more to each other than we ever were?"

"What can I do?" she cried. "Must I brand myself publicly as a—as an adulteress? Do you find that word prettier than whore?"

"Nonsense! There are reasons enough to annul a marriage if we are all agreed. I have Richard's ear, and through him the ear of Boniface, the archbishop."

"Mauger will never agree."

"Why not?" William asked sharply. "Does he hold you so dear?"

"He holds Hurley dear!"

"I have thought of an answer to that," William said, lifting himself on his elbow.

Automatically Elizabeth pushed the pillows so that he could sit, but then she stepped back and folded her hands. "Be reasonable, William. No woman is worth what Mauger will demand for spite. I cannot bear to think of you struggling, as I have struggled, to pay debts that only grow larger and larger with each year. Besides, even if he wished to agree, his pride would not permit him to do it. Can you imagine what would be said if it became known that his wife was now the wife of his neighbor?"

"I have thought of an answer to that also," William interrupted. "I have had much time to think these past days, and I have thought of nothing else. Listen to me. I will not offer your husband money but an equivalent estate—perhaps one that carries with it a minor title."

When he said that, Elizabeth's eyes brightened. "A title? Oh, William, do you think it is possible to arrange such a thing? To be called 'lord' Mauger might release me, even if the estate were not so rich as Hurley." Then her enthusiasm dimmed. "But there remains the problem of our marriage—if it were known I was your neighbor—"

"That problem would not arise if you and I did not live at Marlowe."

"Not live at Marlowe?" Tears came to Elizabeth's eyes and she knelt by the bed to kiss William's hands. To be so precious that William would give up Marlowe for her! "I cannot let you do it," she sighed. "You would come to hate me."

He drew her up to sit beside him. "Not for that, surely, if I never came to hate you over the years when I thought you had betrayed me—like a siren you drew me to destruction with the song of your grace and your beauty."

Elizabeth laughed and kissed him. "William, William, my beauty is in your eyes."

He stared at her, almost as if he were trying to see if what she said were true, but after a moment he smiled and shrugged. "In any case, dear heart, it would not be forever. I have been gone for a few years at a time before—"

"But Alys was here, and Sir Peter. William, what are you thinking of? Alys must marry, and soon. You cannot expect her to wait—"

"I do not expect it. Did you not see the way she seized on Raymond when I bid her go? I admit my attention was somewhat divided, but it seemed to me—"

"You are willing for her to marry Raymond? But he has nothing!"

William shrugged, winced, and uttered a soft oath at his carelessness. As he grew better, he continually forgot his half-healed wounds and hurt himself. "None of us will be rich," he said. "Bix must go to Alys when she marries anyway, but she and Raymond may remain here and manage both places. And we are not so young, Elizabeth, that you are likely to give me a large brood for which I will have to provide. As for me, Richard has been after me for years to be marshal for him."

"You will not get poor doing that!" Elizabeth exclaimed. She was breathing quick with excitement. "It might work, William. Alys does love Raymond—but will the king be willing to bestow a title on Mauger?"

"Probably yes. And just now, when all is sweetness and light between Richard and his brother, Henry will enjoy doing any favor asked of him."

"William, where is Earl Richard?"

"There is the one rub, my love. He is in Scotland, and I cannot ask him to come home just to do this for me."

His expression was perfectly serious, and Elizabeth burst out laughing. "Oh, William, how silly you are. How can you say such a thing in all seriousness—as if our little problem was of such import that the earl of Cornwall must abandon negotiations that concern the whole realm to attend to us."

William grinned at her. "It is ridiculous," he admitted, "but it *is* important to me—and do not think Richard will be indifferent. He has used every device, short of an absolute command, which he knows I would have to obey, to induce me into his service. Nonetheless, I will say nothing to him when I write. We will have to wait until he returns—but it cannot be very long, beloved. A few weeks or a month."

"No . . . only . . . William, you must say nothing to Mauger until everything else is settled. Every minute he has to think will raise his price."

"But that would mean—"

"I will have to go back to him until everything is ready—yes. Oh, William, do not look like that! You know there is nothing between us nor has been for fourteen years. Besides, Emma is there. Who could want me when Emma was available."

"I!" William replied dryly.

"Well, you are a little mad." She leaned forward and kissed him long and tenderly. "I—I must ask you to say nothing about Alys and Raymond either. I know you do not believe Mauger was involved in the attempts on you, but—"

"I do not like to deceive him further, Elizabeth. And perhaps if he knows the estates can never be joined, he will be better content to take another."

"Then add that to the whole." Elizabeth paused and looked down at her hands, then raised her eyes. "It is for my own sake that I ask this, William Mauger is not cruel to me usually, but he will kill me for coming here and leaving Alys free to fall in love with Raymond. It does not matter what *you* will say to him, that is how he will think of it. And I cannot claim I could not know it would happen because he warned me of it that time he brought me over in June."

"If he lays a hand on you, I will kill him," William said softly. "If he ever in the past—"

"No! William! Do not throw away our chance for happiness. I assure you Mauger does not mistreat me and never has. It is only that this thing is so important to him That is why I cannot help feeling he had something to do with your troubles in Wales. The joining of

Ilmer, Hurley, Marlowe, and Bix has become an obsession with him."

That was possible. William frowned as he thought about it. It was possible, but he wanted to believe it enough to make him suspect his own judgment. "Very well. I will say nothing, but that means I must also say nothing to Raymond or Alys. That makes it harder. It is cruel to leave them in doubt. And what am I to do if Raymond makes a formal proposal to me? He is a most honorable young man. If he suspects Alys favors him, he will either ask for her hand or ask leave to go away—and I cannot spare him, not for a few weeks until I am sufficiently healed to bear arms."

"I can manage that for you," Elizabeth said, and began to explain how Alys had confessed her love and she had not had strength enough to deny her.

William listened, but his mind was not completely on what she was saying. He pulled her toward him and kissed her lingeringly. Martin, who had come to bring his master a meal, stopped dead in the doorway and then backed silently out of sight. He had not been particularly quiet in entering, but William and Elizabeth were too wrapped up in each other to hear.

"My love, my love," William murmured, "did you think I would count the cost if Alys's heart was set?"

"No, but—oh, William, we are not being very wise. Alys is *so* beautiful. Are we letting her waste herself? Are we being selfish?"

"I tell you Raymond is a fine man, loyal and honorable and not one to put his pleasure above his duty. He will be a good husband. If Mauger had been as rich as Richard, Elizabeth, would you have been happier with him?"

"No!"

"Do you think Alys of a flighty, changeable nature?"

"No—no, she is not. You are right, I suppose. It is better to be poor and happy. Well, then, what I will do is tell her I have hinted the matter to you and that you did not fly into a rage or forbid it out of hand. That will give her a good hope that you will agree. I will also tell her not to speak of it to you—and to forbid Raymond to speak of it —until you are able to bear arms."

"Why? Are you going to tell my daughter that I am so delicate that a shock would throw me into a decline? She will never believe you."

"Do not be ridiculous," Elizabeth giggled. "You are not the declining sort, William. You glower. No, it is most reasonable. Alys will understand that if Raymond speaks and you do not approve or even feel you need time to think, you will have to send him away. Then, if there should be trouble of any kind, you would naturally feel obliged to put on your armor and settle it, even if you were not sound."

"I see that you prefer me as an idiot to a decliner. What the hell good would I be to anyone if I was not well enough to wield my weapons?"

Elizabeth raised a brow. "What you consider well enough and what Alys and I consider well enough will be sufficiently different to keep her—and Raymond—silent for some weeks."

In the antechamber the tray Martin was carrying began to tremble in his hands. He was an old man and had never been strong. Normally Raymond or Alys would have brought the tray, but they were both out. Now, of course, Martin saw that decision as Divine intervention. It would have been beyond measure horrible if anyone else had seen the master and Lady Elizabeth kissing. It was not the kind of kiss that could be explained away; they were clearly lovers. Martin had recoiled instinctively from the sight. It was a sin, a dreadful sin. Lust was one of the seven deadly sins. But, as he stood rooted with shock, he could not help hearing what they were saying. There was no lust in their voices or words. There was a tender love for each other, and for Alys, and even for Raymond. Could such love be a sin?

Martin did not feel guilty about overhearing the conversation. There was no harm in his hearing. He might even be able to help. So, when the weight of the tray became too much for him, he coughed and shuffled forward as slowly and noisily as he could.

"Oh. it is you!" William exclaimed with relief. "Elizabeth, take that tray from Martin before he drops it. Dear man, whatever made you carry that load?"

Elizabeth had taken the tray and put it on a table. Now she tried to tuck her hair under her wimple.

"Take it off and redo it," William advised, laughing at her. "You have it all rucked up on a side, and you look like a drunken elf."

He spoke quite uninhibitedly, as if Martin were not there—and in a strange way that was true. Over the years, William had begun to think of Martin almost as a part of himself—an extra hand, pair of eyes, brain. It no more occurred to William that Martin would betray him than that his own right hand would suddenly seize a knife and cut his throat.

In that sense, William was right. Martin would no more hurt him or Alys than their own bodies would. The old cripple had purpose and volition, however. He thought for himself and thought well. What made him responsive as an extra limb was love, and, unconsciously, William fed that love continually. His eyes did not slide away from Martin's deformed body and ugly face. He called him "dear man" and meant it.

The careless exposure of his master's darkest secret—his relationship with Elizabeth—was to Martin a greater and surer symbol of affection and trust. Martin was still aware that their love was a sin, but, naked now, the sin was no more revolting to him than his deformity was revolting to his master. Somewhere deep inside he wished there was a way to take that sin upon himself, but he knew it to be impossible. To love unwisely was a sin of the strong and beautiful.

"Sit down, a minute, Martin," William said, while Elizabeth spread a cloth over the covers to protect them from crumbs and spills and moved the tray to his knees. "Lady Elizabeth and I believe that there is a fondness between Lady Alys and Raymond. Is this your opinion also?"

"Indeed, my lord, it is," Martin confirmed, nodding his too-large head. "I was greatly troubled in my mind over it, and wished to speak to you—not that either child has done a thing or said a word that could be blamed—but I feared their hurt from so unsuitable an affection. I was afraid to tell you also, while you were so weak. My lord, I must confess, I overheard what you said to Lady Elizabeth."

"How much?" William asked calmly.

"That you did not oppose the marriage but for some reason do not wish to give permission at this time."

"You might as well hear the whole," William said and explained the situation with regard to himself, Elizabeth, and Mauger, finishing, "I do not want the children to suffer, Martin. If there is any way for you to ease their minds without giving them the notion that they may act as a betrothed couple, you may do what you think wise for them."

"I understand," Martin said, "but I do not think you need to worry about their suffering. I know Raymond has already been much distressed—probably he wished to speak to you and feared, as I did, to worsen your health. I can take that need away by warning him that he must on no account confess his own sins before you can bear arms—just as my lady said. This will ease his conscience, and he will cast off all worry for a time. And if he is happy, my lord, Lady Alys will be happy."

CHAPTER 16

It was not long before William had proof that his advisers had judged correctly. Alys and Raymond came home for dinner, and Alys, trembling with renewed terror, crept to her father's door. She heard an oath, followed by a hearty burst of laughter and flew through the antechamber to the bedroom doorway. There her relief and joy were confirmed. Her father and Lady Elizabeth were playing chess, and from the look of the board, he was being soundly beaten.

"Papa," she cried, "you are all right."

"Of course I am all right, you silly chit. Do you really expect me to be murdered by my own servants if you and Raymond are out of the keep for a few hours?"

"No, but—but you said your head ached, and you looked so strange—and Elizabeth got all pale. . . . I thought—I thought . . ."

"I am so sorry, dearling," William said contritely, realizing for the first time that he had frightened his daughter when he sent her away. "I had been wakened suddenly and I was—er—cross and—er—" He glanced at Elizabeth, but her face was wooden with suppressed laughter, which did not help in the least. "I was just stupid with sleep, Alys. I am fine. I will get out of bed tomorrow for a while."

William thought that the announcement would distract Alys, and it did, but it did not produce quite the enthusiasm he expected. Alys said she was glad, but there was a shade of reserve in her voice that William did not think had anything to do with fear that he was not well enough to get up. Hastily, to forestall a confession he did not want to hear, he asked what she had seen on the demesne.

"The hay is nearly all in," she replied, "and the crops are very good. Next week the men will begin to harvest the south slope. There was something though—" Her eyes sought Elizabeth.

"Something about the farm, love?" Elizabeth asked brightly, her eyes warning.

"The town—" Alys said hesitantly.

William slapped a hand on the chess board, sending the pieces flying. "Sorry," he said to Elizabeth, "I concede," and looked back at Alys. "Do not tell me that they have put up buildings at the near curve of the river. I—"

"No, papa, no," Alys soothed.

"Something is wrong in Marlowe?" Elizabeth asked, the warning gone from her voice.

The question was clearly permission to discuss that subject. Alys now understood that Elizabeth had been warning her away from mentioning any personal matters that might distress her father, and she was relieved. Raymond's anodyne for fear had been most efficacious. Once out of the keep, with her attention fixed on the fields and the serfs, her terror had become muted. Raymond had suggested that they ride through the town and look about there also. Here, he was more cognizant than Alys. He was well accustomed to dealing with tolls and fees from towns and commerce. Although much of his experience was with larger places, the principles were the same.

The busy wharfs had gained Raymond's approval, but he had begun to frown a trifle when an obsequious merchant hurried up and began to explain the activity as most unusual. When the merchant also made obvious efforts to lure them away from the area, the frown disappeared and Raymond began to look so bland and guileless that Alys had some difficulty in restraining herself from laughing. She took her cue from him, however, and agreed to everything the merchant said, like a perfect fool.

They had ridden home after that, but Alys had no chance to be afraid because Raymond had pressed her with questions about Sir William's arrangement with the town. Was it chartered? Was it Sir William's land? Was it a "farm" with a stated fee? If so, was the farm "at pleasure"? Was it contracted for so many years?

For once Alys had to confess herself at a loss. She knew the town was not chartered and that the land was in her father's fife—but little more than that. One of the guildmasters had come with money, and she had entered the sums in the account books. Her father had never complained, but then, he was not a greedy man. Raymond's questions reminded her of her own doubts. Alys was not greedy either, but she objected violently—as would Sir William—to being cheated.

Thus, she was glad Elizabeth thought her father well enough to answer such questions—and even gladder that she had been wordlessly forbidden to mention more personal subjects. The hours she had spent with Raymond had increased her desire to be his wife. There was an ease, a meeting of minds, a fitting together of knowledge and experience—one complementing the other—that gave great promise for a rich life together. The better that life seemed, the more nervous Alys became about her father's reaction to Raymond's true status and reason for being with them.

"Is it really all right to talk business with papa?" she asked outright. "He may get angry."

"That is a damned stupid thing to say, Alys," William remarked, laughing. "First of all, I will be angry before you start if you introduce a subject like that. Secondly, you now *must* tell me because I will be even angrier if you do not. Very well, out with it. What is wrong in Marlowe?"

"I think Raymond can explain better than I, papa. May I call him in?"

"Certainly," William said, but he cast one glance at Elizabeth.

She smiled reassuringly at him as soon as Alys was out of the room. "She will warn him to say nothing. She understands that business is not so heating to the blood—for you, at least—as love."

"How true that is," William responded with a leer.

"Shameless!" Elizabeth reproved sternly, but William nodded with such enthusiasm that she burst out laughing.

Alys found Raymond coming out of Martin's chamber. "Oh, there you are," she exclaimed, "papa wishes to speak to you."

"Now?" Raymond asked apprehensively. "But I was just talking to Martin, who said I must, on no account, ask your father—"

"Not about us. Do not dare even hint at that." Her smile was brilliant. "I was wrong. Papa is quite well. He wants to know what is going on in Marlowe. Lady Elizabeth thinks it is quite all right to talk business, even if it makes him angry, but I could not explain clearly enough."

"Yes," Raymond said, his jaw hardening, "that needs explaining."

He marched firmly into William's bedchamber, sufficiently intent on the business in hand to be rid, temporarily, of his feeling of guilt. Moreover, he knew this was a subject about which he probably understood more than his "master." It eased his conscience somewhat to know that he could do Sir William a good turn. In a few minutes he had the basic facts concerning the town's obligations to its overlord clear.

"Then you are being badly cheated," Raymond said angrily, adding hastily, "I beg you not to lose your temper, sir."

"No, I will not," William remarked calmly, although there was a grim tightness in his lips. "It is mostly owing to my own neglect and is almost as much my fault as theirs. One should not set temptation in the way of common men. They have no sense of honor. To them, what will make a profit is good."

And William did manage to keep his temper as they discussed the matter thoroughly, deciding that the first step was to set a guard on the docks and determine what was shipped in and out. Raymond's only doubts were as to the value of the goods here in England.

"Martin will know that," William said, "but I do not like to send him into the town. I know you will not let anyone hurt him, Raymond, but getting him there will be a problem and he feels it so much when people make signs at him to ward off evil—"

"I know also, papa," Alys put in brightly.

"It will not be necessary for anyone to be with me," Raymond said stiffly. He realized that Alys was trying to push her father into a tacit acknowledgment of her right to be with him. "I can write down how many bolts of cloth, bushels of grain, and so on, and—"

"And we will need an interpreter to understand what you write," Alys laughed. "I could hardly read a word of your letter. Perhaps I should go as your clerk."

William bit his lip, torn between anger and laughter. He understood quite well what Alys was doing, and if he had not been almost as eager to get her out of the keep as she was to be with Raymond, so that he and Elizabeth could have some privacy, he would have been furious. As it was, he was amused and tempted—all the more because Raymond seemed more reluctant than eager for her company.

"You do spell most vilely, Raymond," William admitted.

"He does not spell vilely," Elizabeth protested, before Raymond could decide whether Sir William was using this excuse to give Alys the permission she desired or had spoken the simple truth as he saw it without realizing where it would lead. "He writes a fair hand of the French of the south. Anyway, it does not matter how he spells, since he will be here to read his own writing."

Elizabeth was aware of William's motives. Part of her was in sympathy with them, but she knew that Alys would not be free to leave the keep. Once William rose from his bed, she had no excuse to remain at Marlowe. Until then, he might be considered seriously ill enough to require more experienced nursing than Alys could give him. After that the true reason for her lingering must become obvious. Elizabeth did not fear that Wil-

liam's servants would censure her or dare to be dis-
repectful, but anything they knew was transmitted with
startling rapidity to the servants at Hurley.

The same reasoning applied to allowing Alys to be
seen too often in Raymond's company. Thus, Elizabeth
turned a blind eye to the reproachful glance William
cast at her. "If you do not like the records Raymond
makes, Alys can transcribe them when he comes back
from the town." She had to restrain herself from laughing after she spoke; the word "traitor" was so clear in
two pairs of eyes. Later she would explain to Alys, and
Alys would understand. William—she would apply a
balm to William's feelings at night that would soothe
away all hurt.

Elizabeth's precautions were for the most part in vain.
Mauger had long known that she and William loved
each other and had planned for years on what profit
would salve his pride. In fact, profit was no longer his
sole aim. Frustration was not good for a character like
Mauger's. It turned him vicious. And frustration was all
he had had from the beginning of the Welsh campaign.

All his plans had gone awry. Every device to kill
William had failed, and the last two failures were his
own. Unable to find someone else to blame for the
debacles, Mauger tried to put William out of his mind
completely. But this was not possible either. It seemed
to Mauger as if everyone in the entire army came to
his encampment day and night to enquire about William's health. The first day after Mauger's attack on
William these innocent inquiries gave him some relief,
indicating that no one suspected him of that attempt.
Once that fear was gone, however, any mention of
William was like rough cloth on a rash.

There were peaks to Mauger's irritation. The earl of
Hereford had called him in and given him an icy
tongue-lashing for disobeying William's orders. "I love
Aubery too well to do his father a despite," Hereford
concluded, "and Aubery tells me you have not previously fought in this kind of war, but a man your age

should have sense enough to take advice from those, like Sir William, with greater experience. In the future—be careful."

Wisely, Mauger did not try to justify himself. Dismissed, he went back to his own area, growling at Aubery to come to him as soon as he was free. That message led to more rage and frustration, for the first words out of Aubery's mouth were of his anxiety about William.

"My lord says someone tried to kill him again last night, and that Sir Raymond is taking him home to Marlowe."

"Never mind William," Mauger snarled. "What the hell do you mean by making me out a sniveling idiot to de Bohun? How dared you tell him I was an inexperienced fool."

"To be inexperienced and overeager for battle is not to be a fool," Aubery snapped, leaving his father open mouthed with surprise. "I did my best for you. What could I say? Would you have preferred that I say you are so envious of Sir William that if he said you were riding a horse you would contend it was a cow?"

Mauger struck out at his son, and Aubery jerked himself out of the way. It was an efficient gesture, the mark of a keen-honed eye for attack and defense—a far better eye than his father's. Then the boy dropped his eyes.

"I am sorry," he said. "You may beat me if you like. That is your right, and what I said to you was disrespectful—but I did do my best to excuse you to my lord. He was furious! I had to tell him the truth."

Something in the way Aubery had moved, the controlled power that pulled him barely an inch clear of the blow and left him close enough to strike back gave Mauger some very sour food for thought. There was a change in Aubery's expression also. Mauger suddenly realized that he was not dealing with a little boy who could be overawed but with a young man who was dangerous. Aubery might bow to his father's will or even take a beating because both were his father's "right" in dealing with him; however, it was clear that if he desired he could defend himself, possibly even win any contest between them. Mauger dropped the hand that he had half raised.

"What smirches me, smirches you," he spat. "Do not forget it. There is something far more important to me, however, than this stupid business. That idiot hireling was made to move William. Likely he will die on the road."

At that point Mauger got another unpleasant shock. Aubery turned ashen pale and tears rushed to his eyes. "No!" he exclaimed. "I cannot believe it."

Then his voice choked and he could say no more. Thus, Mauger never learned that de Bohun, Raymond, and the friar in charge of the infirmary had had a long, anxious conference about the subject in the small hours after the attack on William. The infirmarian's opinion had been the deciding factor. With many references to the "will of God," the infirmarian had admitted that he was reasonably sure the journey would not kill William. It would set him back—he warned them of prolonged fever and weakness—but if the wounds did not mortify, a factor the journey would not affect, he should live.

"Who cares what you believe," Mauger snarled.

What a fool he had been to let his sons spend so much time at Marlowe. Now he understood where they had gotten their idiotic ideas about honor. Honor was for those who could afford it, not for a poor man who had to make his way upward by tooth and claw and cleverness. Blast William! Mouthing inane platitudes and stealing his sons' affections. He had not cared when they were little boys—nuisances they were, always wanting to show him something. Now that they were nearly men they should know better. They should see for themselves that his way was the path of wisdom and profit. William's stupid ideals would leave them in the mud. Well, if that was what they wanted, let them have it. He was through with them—except . . .

"You must arrange a leave of absence with the earl of Hereford as soon as this action is over," Mauger went on. "You must be married to Alys at once, before William's overlord can take her."

"No," Aubery said firmly, although he was whiter.

He had been boy enough when his father first raised the subject with him to wish to slough off the responsibility of refusal. Aubery knew William would do it and save him from needing to oppose his father openly. It was natural for Aubery to ask William's help. From the time Aubery was six years old, William had been his bulwark in any trouble his mother could not solve.

Mauger had been away too much or "too busy" to listen to his little problems. It was William who gave him his first metal sword, who gave him his lessons in swordplay. It was to William he managed to send a message when he was a page, miserably homesick and, as the newcomer to the group, teased and taunted. William had responded with advice; better yet, he had come himself, all the way from Marlowe to Hereford, to be sure Aubery's trouble was only homesickness and teasing. The assurance of support had been really all Aubery needed. After William's visit he had been more sure of himself, more able to assert himself, and he was soon very happy in his new life.

"What do you mean, no?" Mauger gasped.

Aubery wet his lips nervously. William had always emphasized the need to be obedient to his father—within the limits of honor—and he knew he had met a limit here. "Sir William says that Alys does not wish to marry me, and it is his will that she have free choice. To speak the truth, I do not wish to marry her either. I would have done it at your will and Sir William's, but he has the right of disposal of his daughter. I will crave leave, if you desire it. I will do my uttermost to protect Alys, as a sister, if—if Sir William—" His voice trembled and he had to stop.

"You idiot! The best way to protect her is to marry her."

"I will not oppose Sir William's will, sir. He has been too good to me all my life."

"Get out," Mauger snarled. "Get out!"

Gratefully, Aubery fled. Mauger stood staring at the quivering tent flap, unaware that his abrupt dismissal of his son had kept him from learning another, essential piece of information—that Alys needed no protection from Sir William's overlord. Mauger's mind had been busy while Aubery explained his refusal. His remark that the best way to protect Alys was to marry her had been automatic, but it had come from his train of thought.

There was no need, Mauger realized, for Aubery to marry Alys. It was stupid anyway to put Marlowe and Bix into Aubery's hands. Aubery might think he really had a right to the properties and contest his father's will concerning them—particularly this new Aubery. Thank goodness he had seen the change soon enough. All he needed to do was dispose of Elizabeth, which would be no trouble at all. Then he could marry Alys himself.

Now Mauger was eager to get home and discover whether William had died on the road, as he hoped, or whether he would need to find a way to dispose of him. In this, too, he was frustrated. For more than a week the earl of Hereford made feints at Welsh keeps and tried various devices to draw David ap Llewelyn into battle. Mauger remained part of this useless attempt, unwilling to stay but more unwilling to draw Hereford's unfavorable attention by asking leave to go.

At last de Bohun was convinced that David's forces were temporarily dispersed. He sent messengers to the king with this information and told Henry he was releasing the levies under his command, as their term of service was nearly finished and it was pointless to pay them day wages to wander around the Welsh forests. He urged the king to bring the army gathered to fight the Scots to Wales after the treaty with Alexander was signed.

Two days after William arrived home, Mauger received his release and began to march his troop and the remnants of William's toward Marlowe. So eager was he for news—so passionate his hope that William was dead and he could convince Alys to come home with him to be comforted by Elizabeth—that he came to Marlowe with William's troops, leaving his own to find their way to Hurley by themselves. The casual greeting he had from Diccon should have warned him that all was well with William, but Mauger cared nothing for his own subordinates and could not imagine that they could care for him. Thus he was able to blind himself to the truth for a few minutes longer.

Unfortunately that made his shock all the greater when he came to the entryway of the great hall. The servants were just finishing clearing away the tables after dinner, but their activity did not hold Mauger's attention or block his view. William was sitting in his usual chair by the hearth. Mauger stopped dead, livid with rage. Since he had waved away Diccon's offer to send a man to announce him—a common enough thing for a long-time neighbor and friend to do—no one noticed his arrival. Instinctively, Mauger took a step back into the passageway through the wall. From where he stood, he could not hear what was said, but what he saw was appalling. William was staring into the embers in the fireplace while Raymond and Alys had drawn two chairs very close together and were reading something. Raymond's finger moved down the page, apparently he was reading aloud, and Alys was in fits of laughter.

Had Mauger's courage been equal to his rage, he would have charged out and killed them all. However, achieving exalted status had always been the strongest drive Mauger had, and public murder could scarcely bring him that. Thus, he went quietly back down the stairs, retrieved his horse from the groom, and rode out toward Hurley, leaving both Diccon and the groom open mouthed in surprise at the expression on his face.

He had calmed himself sufficiently by the time he reached the ferry in Marlowe to notice the heavy concentration of men-at-arms at the dock. This was so unusual that Mauger stopped one of the men and asked what had happened. The answer, which led to other questions and answers, somewhat assuaged Mauger's bad temper. Here was obviously a new and very hopeful method of killing both William and Raymond.

Although Mauger did not really think the merchants of Marlowe would have enough spirit to attack their overlord or his agent, the blame would certainly fall upon them if Raymond was set upon in the town and killed. Raymond's death would almost certainly bring William out of the keep and into the town to investigate. His death would be harder to accomplish. Mauger snarled over that, but it did not disturb him long. William would surely pick up his duties once Raymond was dead. He would then be out and around the estate—fool that he was, constantly meddling with the serfs and mouthing stupidities about protecting the lord's share. Lord's share came first. If there was not sufficient left over, the animals could do without.

Nonetheless, it was a convenient idiocy. Sooner or later William would ride out alone. He always did so, saying he had nothing to fear from his own people. Perhaps not, but there were lonely stretches between the farms. Something could be arranged, and doubtless it would be blamed on the townsfolk, who were known to bear a grudge. After all, it would have been proved that they did away with Raymond. What could be more likely than that they finished the master as well as the hireling.

That would leave Alys completely in his power—if that little bitch did not close Marlowe against him. She might think he wanted to force her to marry Aubery. How to get her to Hurley? That question made Mauger reconsider his plans for Elizabeth. He had intended a simple accident to overtake her—like falling into the waste shaft or down the stairs. He realized, however, that Alys would never come to Hurley if Elizabeth were not there. Therefore Elizabeth must live long enough . . .

Suddenly Mauger began to laugh. If Elizabeth was sick, it would bring not only Alys but William in all haste to Hurley—and that would solve all his problems at once. Alys could be imprisoned and William killed. Then Egbert could put on William's clothing and ride his horse back onto Marlowe lands to a spot where he had originally concealed the body, reclothe the body, set the horse free. . . . Yes, that would work.

Mauger had all the plans made by the time he rode into Hurley keep. Unlike the times he had planned in Wales, however, he was not filled with sunny optimism. Hope permitted him to keep his angry, frustrated resentment chained, but it was there, seething under the surface. This would not be sweet and easy as it would have been in Wales. Two murders and his too-quick marriage to Alys so soon after his wife's and her father's death would be bound to raise questions. Still, he would wait no longer.

In Hurley, Mauger dismounted, threw his reins to a groom and made for the inner bailey and the great hall. Raymond would have to be dealt with first, of course. He shouted for wine and Egbert. The servant was at his elbow, even as the sound of his voice died away.

"William did not die," Mauger snarled.

Egbert bobbed his head. "I know. Your lady returned only yesterday from Marlowe where she nursed him during the worst of his sickness."

Mauger stared at his man, speechless with rage for a minute. So Elizabeth had helped foul his plans! So much the better. He need not regret her loss. Bitch! Whore—in mind if not in body. He showed his teeth and Egbert stiffened. His master had been very strange since that night at the abbey, but Mauger's eyes were not on his man and the servant relaxed. He did not, however, fail to pay strict attention to the instructions Mauger was giving him. They were interrupted briefly when Emma came tripping up carrying a cup of wine. He snatched it from her and snarled that she should go tell Elizabeth to await him in her chamber. Emma made the mistake of pouting. Often Mauger called it adorable, and kissed her pursed lips; this time he hit her in the face so hard he knocked her down. He did not even turn his head to watch her pick herself up, but continued to tell Egbert how to arrange Raymond's murder.

The voice was low and Emma did not hear much, but she heard enough to deepen her fear of the man who owned her. Emma burned with resentment, the helpless, bitter resentment of a child. Here she felt alone and imprisoned. In a city Emma would know well enough how to find a new protector, but she had no idea where the nearest city was or how to get there. Emma gave Mauger's message to Elizabeth. She did not dare hint at what she had heard, but because of her sense of outrage she did find the courage to warn Elizabeth that Mauger was in a foul temper.

The warning was scarcely necessary as the mark of his hand showed plainly on Emma's fair skin. Elizabeth knew that Mauger's men had come in well ahead of their master and guessed that he had stopped at Marlowe on his way. There were so many things that could have enraged him. Elizabeth could not guess which was the particular cause. All she desired at the moment was to be able to master her own fear sufficiently to be able to think clearly.

As a first step, she fixed her attention on Emma, exclaiming softly at the bruise on her cheek and offering to put some salve on it. Emma looked over her shoulder fearfully and Elizabeth realized she was afraid Mauger would come. Swallowing nervously, she went to her chest of medicinals and brought the pot of salve, which she put in Emma's hand.

"You are right," she murmured. "Take it and go. Have one of the maids put it on for you if you wish. There is no need for you to see him again until he calls for you. Perhaps then he will not be angry any longer."

Emma fled at once to find a corner in which to hide herself. She did not even ask a maid to help her but smoothed the salve on her aching cheek by touch, shuddering at the thought that Mauger might soon want to use her. Never before had Emma felt revulsion for her sexual duties. She had always been delighted at the pleasure she gave. She was totally undiscriminating and, until now, had liked all men, regardless of age or appearance. Now there was an exception—Mauger, who had hurt her and rejected her.

CHAPTER 17

When Mauger struck Emma, she had been a substitute for Elizabeth. He had, in fact, intended to beat his wife soundly. However, by the time he had finished planning Raymond's murder, he had reconsidered that. There must be no evidence that he had been on bad terms with Elizabeth so soon before her death and his remarriage. In fact, there should be evidence of his loving concern for her. Thus, Mauger walked quietly up the stairs and into Elizabeth's chamber, not quite closing the door behind him. She rose from her chair, concealing her trembling as well as she could.

"Stand there," Mauger said softly. "Do not turn to look at me. Just stand still."

It was so peculiar a thing for him to say, the soft voice so wildly different from what she expected, that Elizabeth did exactly what she was told She stood perfectly still, her eyes wide with surprise but staring directly ahead of her. Mauger smiled as he stepped around her and hit her hard on the back of the head just behind the left ear. She crumpled forward without a sound, but it would have made no difference if she had cried out because Mauger let out a bellow designed to cover any cry she uttered.

"Elizabeth!" he shouted. "What ails you?" Then he rushed to the door and flung it wide open, noting with satisfaction that several of the maids were already running toward the room. "Come to your mistress," he called, then knelt beside Elizabeth and lifted her in his arms. "You stupid sluts," he snarled, "did you not see that your mistress was not well? She rose from her chair and fell fainting right at my feet."

"Tell Egbert to fetch a physician from Marlowe,"

Mauger ordered as he carried Elizabeth to her bed. "Where is her chief woman?" he asked, and when Maud came forward he bade her undress her mistress.

"My poor lady," Maud muttered, sniffing back tears as she stripped off Elizabeth's clothes, "my poor lady. I saw all was not well with her when she came home. She was worn white, so thin and trembling. Oh, my poor lady, my poor lady——but she would not go to bed. She said she was well. Dearling, speak to me. Speak to Maud, lovey."

"Stop that hen-witted grizzling," Mauger snapped, although he could have kissed the woman. Not only had she accepted Elizabeth's collapse but she had provided a logical reason for it. Nonetheless, he had to get rid of her before Elizabeth revived. "You are enough to make a healthy person sick. Get out! I will watch by my wife."

Maud was surprised by this mark of attention, but only slightly. Although Elizabeth had never confided in her maid, as many women did, Maud could not help knowing that Mauger did not seek his wife's bed. On the other hand, there had never been anything to indicate that they were on bad terms. They never quarreled, and Mauger seemed content to leave the management of the estate in Elizabeth's hands. He might prefer that stupid slut Emma abed, but he knew he would be lost without the lady's care. Perhaps, Maud thought, as she withdrew, it was Elizabeth's will that Mauger did not act as a husband. She glanced back over her shoulder as she went out and saw a worried frown on his face.

"Close the door," he called after her. "I do not want Elizabeth to be disturbed by the noise you make."

Maud was greatly relieved. The lord would see the lady cared for. He was wrong to send her out; the lady was used to her ways, but all would be well.

Mauger's worried frown had been owing to his concern that Maud would not shut the door before Elizabeth recovered her senses. It was a near thing. As the latch snicked, Elizabeth lifted a wavering hand to her head and moaned. He let her moan and toss herself into full consciousness, smiling down at her nastily when recognition came into her face.

"Mauger," she whispered.

"Did you expect William?" he asked. "You stupid slut. Did you think I did not know?"

Elizabeth did not answer. She did not remember anything after Emma's warning, but she realized Mauger must have hit her because of the pain in her head. It was a terrible shock to hear how badly she had underestimated Mauger. Still, dizzy and confused as she was, she knew that she dared not throw aside her cover. Whatever could be salvaged from this disaster lay in sustaining Mauger's belief that she was stupid.

Irritated by her blank stare, Mauger slapped her.

"Idiot!" he raged—but softly so that no sound should pass the locked door. "Did I not tell you that Alys and that hireling must be kept apart? You have ruined everything. You knew I would forbid you to nurse that sanctimonious fool—"

"But Mauger," Elizabeth gasped, "you have always urged me to be a good neighbor. When Mary was sick, you sent me to nurse her. How could I guess—"

The protest earned her another slap. "You are stupid, but not that stupid. I wanted Mary alive so that William could not marry a woman who would give him a living son. You knew I intended to have Marlowe—and for that purpose William must be dead."

"No!"

Mauger laughed. "You are that stupid! You really thought I intended to wait until he died of old age." Then he laughed harder. "Do you mean you never guessed that your brothers' untimely deaths were—"

With a gasp of horror, Elizabeth tried to launch herself at her husband, but he pushed her back and held her, a hand over her nose and mouth so that she could neither scream nor breathe. Red-splashed blackness swam before her eyes; her struggles became feebler and feebler. At last, Mauger slipped his hand away from her nose.

"Lie still," he snarled, "or I will put a pillow over

your face and weep because you died before my eyes and I could do nothing."

He would do it. For herself, at the moment, Elizabeth would not have cared. The idea that she had served and coupled with the monster who had arranged her brothers' deaths and had, for years, planned William's death was incredibly revolting. She would have died willingly to blot out the knowledge of her own deliberate blindness and arrogance. All those years when she had laughed inside herself at Mauger's dullness he had been laughing at her. What kept her quiet and willing to obey was the knowledge that Mauger had not given up. Perhaps if she were alive she could send some warning to Marlowe.

"Now listen and listen closely, Elizabeth. Your women—and therefore the whole keep—believe that you suddenly fainted and I have sent for a physician from Marlowe town. He will say you have a disease that could run through the whole keep. I will permit your chief woman in here and you will tell her this yourself. You will tell her that no one in the keep must come near you, not she nor any other servant. I will 'nurse' you myself with Emma's help. Now, if you do not say exactly what I have told you, I will kill the woman and tell the other women that she decided to sacrifice herself and nurse you. Do you understand?"

Elizabeth closed her eyes and nodded as well as she could. There was no doubt in her mind that Mauger would do exactly as he said. Tears trickled out under her closed lids. Mauger watched her suspiciously, then removed his hand from her mouth. Elizabeth lay still, eyes closed. Very softly Mauger stepped back, watching her. He did not care, really, if she cried out; he had the ready excuse that she was out of her senses. His attention was mainly to gauge her submissiveness.

Hours passed. Both Mauger and Elizabeth were completely silent except for an infrequent soft sob of pain and fear from Elizabeth. Neither was bored, however. Both minds were well occupied until Egbert returned with the "physician." The man wore the long, sober gown and furred cap of his profession, but his face belied the grave robes. It was hard and seamed with vice. the look in his eyes an insult to any woman they fixed upon. Elizabeth shuddered with horror. There was no hope to be found in this man.

"Do you desire a 'potion' to rid yourself of her?" the "physician" asked.

Mauger began to shake his head, and then stopped and nodded instead. His negative response had been owing to an initial unwillingness to put himself into the creature's power by buying poison. Then he realized it was too late to worry about that. The "physician" would have to die as soon as Elizabeth did. That would raise no problems, and the poison might be useful. He could have Emma administer it, perhaps. Everyone in the keep already disliked the little whore. Should there be an investigation of Elizabeth's death, it would seem that a jealous mistress had poisoned her lover's wife.

"And which disease do you desire she die of?" the man asked.

"Any complaint that would begin with a fainting fit— but I do not intend that the lady should die," Mauger said pointedly. "I only want to keep her quiet for a little while. She will die only if she is not properly obedient."

"I see." The brightness in the nasty eyes dimmed somewhat. What had seemed a ripe case for blackmail now was much less promising. Dissatisfaction made the cruel mouth even harder. "I will need to examine the lady. Her form will tell me what disorders are most likely to attack her."

"No!" Elizabeth cried.

Mauger laughed and pulled the cover off her, grabbing her flailing arms. "Whore," he hissed, "your modesty is a little late."

Wild-eyed and gasping, Elizabeth lay still until the "physician" bent over her. Then she struck out with her feet, catching him in the chest and face with such force that he tottered backward and fell heavily. Her satisfaction was short lived. Mauger struck her in the temple so hard that blackness enveloped her again. This time she was not unconscious long, but when her vision cleared only Mauger was in the room. Although her senses spun, she clutched to her the remembrance that she had deprived Mauger of enjoying her shame.

Seeing the flickering of her eyelids, Mauger came closer "I will call your woman now. If you do not tell her exactly what I told you to say, you will both die. If you convince her, and do not again anger me, perhaps you will live."

Elizabeth knew that to be a lie, but she had to pretend to believe it. She could not guess why Mauger wanted to keep her alive for a time, but obviously he did. Nonetheless, she realized he would kill her at once if he had to and certainly he would kill Maud without the smallest hesitation. Time. If she had a little time . . . Mauger brought Maud to the bedside. The maid tried to come closer, her hand extended to brush Elizabeth's hair from her face. Mauger held her back, his eyes on Elizabeth, coldly threatening.

"Do not touch me," Elizabeth whispered. "You will take my illness."

"I am not afraid," Maud cried. "I am strong. I will care for you, my lady."

"No," Elizabeth replied, "no. I cannot spare you, Maud. You must see to the women. There is no one else. You must see that the keep does not fall into disorder."

"But who will tend to you?" Maud wailed. "I have always attended you, my lady."

"Emma can do what I need," Elizabeth said breathlessly, seeing Mauger's hand poised to clamp over the maid's mouth. "Truly it is nothing but to carry the pot and wash me, which is more fitting for her than for you. And she is the most useless creature. She can best be spared of all the women."

The slow smile that came to Maud's face relieved Elizabeth. She had said the first thing that came into her mind and struck lucky. Maud now believed that Elizabeth was using her illness to take revenge on her husband's mistress, to demean her by making her do the things that only the coarsest, untrained women would do. Maud herself never emptied a chamber pot nor carried washing water.

"Go now and let your mistress rest," Mauger growled at the woman.

Maud went away willingly enough. Elizabeth did not look very sick to her. She was also pleased by the fact that Emma was pale as a ghost and most subdued in manner when she was sent to Elizabeth's chamber. All the petty, flaunting arrogance was gone. The girl crept in like a mouse, tearful and trembling. In fact, when Mauger dropped the bar to lock the door behind her she nearly fainted. Mauger's sharp slap—not hard enough this time to knock her down but quite hard enough to hurt—and his snarl warning her not to indulge herself or he would give her a real reason to faint forced her to hold onto consciousness.

"My wife has greatly offended me," Mauger said. "She is unfaithful, and I have decided to punish her. You will be her warden. You will remain in this room with her and you will not allow any of the castlefolk in—no one except myself. Do you understand me? The door is to be barred at all times when I am not in the room. I do not want that nosy bitch, Maud, or anyone else sneaking in and bringing my whore of a wife comfort."

Unable to speak, Emma stared. She was shivering with terror. Mauger did not doubt she would mean to do as she was told, but still he did not trust her.

"Go and look through the chests," he ordered. "Bring me some sashes or some thin scarves. You are such a stupid slut that I dare not leave anything to chance."

When Emma supplied what he asked for, Mauger bound Elizabeth's hands and feet and gagged her. Then he looked from one woman to the other and an idea came to him that tickled his fancy. He lifted Elizabeth from the bed and dumped her on the floor.

"Take off your clothes," he said to Emma.

The girl gaped at him, her eyes flying to Elizabeth. He struck her once more, lightly, just enough to sting her cheek and remind her who was her master. Tears overflowed her eyes, but she began to obey. Never had anything like this happened before. Emma had been assiduously shielded from priests who would tell her the profession for which she was destined was "bad." Thus she knew only vaguely that what she did—coupling with men to whom she was not married—was a sin. Actually, she had never felt sinful or ashamed. Now, for the first time, she was sickened, horrified by the idea of the sexual act.

"Now undress me," Mauger ordered.

Weeping and trembling, Emma obeyed. Although he usually liked complaisant women, Mauger was enjoying Emma's distress. Her plainly unwilling obedience soothed the frustration that had eaten him for months. While she drew off his clothing, he pinched her nipples and stroked her, murmuring the crudest obscenities. When she knelt to take off his shoes and cross garters, he bent over and nibbled her neck and ears.

He found the situation so exciting—his naked wife bound and gagged a few feet away; his naked mistress kneeling at his feet—that he was suddenly unwilling to wait any longer. "Take me in your mouth," he panted, pulling Emma up by the hair. "Suck me."

The climax he achieved nearly brought Mauger down on top of Emma. He was thoroughly delighted, recognizing that the intense pleasure was partly owing to Elizabeth's helpless presence. Emma was nothing; any woman could play her part. It was Elizabeth's degradation that had pushed him above his normal sexual response. He turned to her and laughed when he saw her eyes were shut tight.

"Skinny, ugly bitch. You cannot close your ears." As he said it, another idea came to him, but he was too played out at this moment to enjoy it properly. He looked back at Emma, doubled over, trying to control her heaving body. "Get up and get my clothes back on and be quick about it," he ordered.

After he was dressed, he noticed that Elizabeth was shivering violently from the cold. He turned to go, then realized he did not want Elizabeth to be sick. He wanted her to be an unwilling witness to his sexual pleasure. If she was fevered she would not notice. He scooped her up and dumped her back into the bed. Last, he ordered Emma to bar the door behind him and not to dare to speak to Elizabeth or touch her. Then, sated and somewhat relieved of the gnawing sense of powerlessness that had afflicted him recently, Mauger went down to demand a supper of roast pasty as well as bread and cheese, and to listen to Egbert's report on the final arrangements for Raymond's assassination.

It was unfortunate that Mauger had not arrived at Marlowe fifteen minutes later. Very soon after he went down the stairs, the tableau that had so infuriated him broke up. Raymond came to the end of his list of cargoes and Alys stopped giggling at the way he pronounced the names of the goods, rolled the sheet of parchment, and rose to her feet. In moving, her glance fell on her father. The laughter went out of her eyes. She was no longer amused by the dumb misery that masked itself as thoughtfulness.

"You should go back to bed, papa," she said softly.

William did not move. Alys touched his arm. He started, looked up at her, and smiled. "Sorry, I was thinking. Did you say something to me, my love?"

"I said you have been up and about long enough and you should go back to bed."

Back to bed—where the scent Elizabeth used lingered very faintly in the sheets and covers. How long would it be before that odor was fresh in his nostrils again? How long before he could bury his face in her wild hair and feel the warmth of her body through it on his lips? He had lowered his eyes slightly so that Alys could not see them. For a second they were blind, but the roll of parchment she held soon took on meaning. He turned his head toward Raymond.

"I will go in a minute. What was your count today, Raymond?"

It was Alys who answered because she was quicker at summing a total, and they were soon plunged deep in a discussion of the cheating merchants of Marlowe.

"Now do not lose your temper, papa," Alys warned when it became apparent that the merchants must have cheated on tolls as well as on fees. She was not entirely serious, however. She preferred her father to be angry rather than sad.

He cast her an irritated glance, saw she was teasing him, and laughed. "You have been down there three mornings—right?" he asked Raymond.

"Yes, sir. And I think—"

"I will lay you a gold mark against a copper mil," William interrupted, "that the traffic is already less than it first was. There has been time enough now to send messages up river and down that an agent for me watches the docks every morning. We will try a small deviation from our pattern. Tomorrow you will go down after dinner instead of in the morning, and the day after also. Then you will miss a few days—we still need to get the recruiting done and I do not like to send Diccon alone. He picks more by size and shape than by willingness. Then you can pay visits on odd days— or I will. I should be well enough to ride next week."

Alys shook her head at him. "You should be, but you will not if you sit here and tell Raymond what he knows perfectly well already instead of going to rest."

"Very well, I am going," William said, and laughed at the alacrity with which Raymond hurried forward to help him from his chair and give him the support of his arm into his bedchamber.

Hardly had Raymond disappeared with him than Diccon came up to report on the condition of the men who had returned with Mauger. Alys slumped and sighed with relief, realizing she had got her father out of the way just in time. Had he heard this news, he would have become frantic to have word of what had happened in Hurley now that Mauger was home. He had been most unwilling to let Elizabeth go; they had quarreled bitterly over her insistence on leaving, Alys knew.

Alys was afraid her father would insist on going to Hurley to make sure Elizabeth was safe. She could not see why there should be any danger to Elizabeth, and she did not know of Mauger's peculiar behavior. Diccon, assuming that Mauger had spoken to William, did not mention him at all to Alys. If she mentioned to her father that Mauger was back, he would not sleep all night.

I will not tell papa, Alys thought, settling more firmly into her chair. If he is angry, I will say the truth—that it was too late to visit and ask for news of the campaign—which would be the only excuse possible for a visit from her father—and also that it would not look decent. It must be assumed—even if we know better—that a man returning from a two-month absence would wish to be alone with his wife. Yes, Alys thought, that would do quite well to excuse her for today, but how could she prevent her father from going tomorrow?

The answer came swiftly—by going herself. And again she could speak the absolute truth. She could confess she had concealed the knowledge of Mauger's arrival to prevent her father from going to Hurley. Not even an idiot—and Mauger was no idiot—could believe a man with half-healed wounds would rush out of his sickbed to hear news that his second master-at-arms could give him in his own keep. However, Alys could go without raising doubts in anyone. It would be most natural for her to want to consult Elizabeth about her father's recovery—and while she was doing so she could find out whether it would be wise to ask Mauger to come to Marlowe to give her father the news. She might even ask him to bring Elizabeth so that she could assure Alys all was going well with William's healing.

The next morning, William finally wrote a letter to Richard. It was little more than a note in which he stated what had happened to him and that he was well on the way to recovery, told Richard when his surveillance of the clerk had ended, and asked for news of the Scottish negotiations. William could only hope Richard would not think he had been hurt worse than he said, but he dared not write more than the simple facts for fear that his sense of need would permeate the letter.

The small effort tired him so much that he ate his meal alone and went back to bed. Alys could hardly believe her luck. She had been dreading the morning, not knowing whether she would be able to conceal her guilty knowledge from her father or whether a servant would inadvertently mention the arrival of the men from Wales. In fact, everything conspired to suit her purpose. Because she was so pleased with her father's behavior, Alys began to fear that she was blinding herself to some evil symptom he was displaying. She fussed around him—touching him to see if he was fevered, asking how he felt, why he was so tired, finally demanding to change his bandages to make sure healing was advancing properly. At that point, William was driven to bellow at her to get out and leave him alone so he could sleep.

The volume and ferocity of the order did much to convince Alys that there was nothing much wrong with her father. With the conviction came the realization that she could have done nothing more efficacious. She could now avoid William without his having the faintest suspicion that she wished to avoid him. Moreover, she could even go to Hurley without telling him before she left that Mauger had returned. If she left a message that she had gone to see Elizabeth, papa would certainly assume that she had gone because she was worried about him!

She and Raymond had a very early and light dinner. Raymond could eat again at any time in the town and Alys intended to have an extra meal with her father when she returned, at which time she could confess and tell him—she hoped—that Mauger would bring Elizabeth to visit him soon. Both she and Raymond were preoccupied with their own coming activities and Raymond found this singularly pleasant. At home, no matter how busy his mind was, he was required to make conversation suitable to ladies at dinner. Alys was surely the most delightful woman alive, for she was as comfortable to live with as she was beautiful to look at.

He rode off into the town in a rosy haze. Probably Sir William would be furious when he heard Raymond's full story, but Raymond did not fear he would refuse permission for Alys to marry him. The past two days, although nothing had been said, implied the matter was settled. Raymond's conscience was much easier. When Sir William was ready—presumably when he had a chance to inform Earl Richard of his intentions—he would broach the subject. Raymond hoped the letter that had gone out to Richard of Cornwall this morning carried the news.

CHAPTER 18

When Raymond arrived at the dock, he dismounted and listened to the reports of the men-at-arms stationed there. Sir William had been right; traffic had been much lower in the morning. However there was already a ship coming from downriver. Raymond went back to the shed he had commandeered as a headquarters so that he would be out of the rain, which had been spattering about on and off all day, and sat down to wait until the vessel came in. His mind drifted back to a pleasant contemplation of his forthcoming betrothal.

The thoughts were interrupted by the docking, by the now-familiar arguments of the merchant and the men-at-arms who went to inspect the cargo. Some yielded readily; some required the authority of Raymond's manner, his gold-decked sword, before they would permit an examination of their goods. This was a particularly stubborn case, the merchant protesting that he had been robbed in the past with just such an excuse and ordering his crew to cast off the lines that held them to the dock. It took Raymond some time to calm him. In the end, he had to promise to stand by and oversee the entire operation himself.

The boat was well laden. As about half the cargo was for Marlowe and it had to be separated from what was to remain, several hours passed before Raymond's count was complete. He was soaked to the skin by the time he got back to the shed. Although it was not time for sunset, the clouds were so heavy that it was almost dark. Raymond called out to one of the men-at-arms to obtain a dry cloak for him. Before that man returned, he had to call another and ask for torches or a lamp. The clouds were more and more threatening of a real downpour to follow the off-and-on drizzle that had plagued them all week. Finally his cloak arrived.

The man who had gone for the torches had not yet returned. Despite the cloak, Raymond shivered again and wondered whether it was worthwhile waiting any longer. Dark as it was, most boats would do as the one that had just come in and tie up wherever they could. With the wind high, there was a danger of running into low water. The channel of the river was easy enough to follow in daylight, wind or no wind, but the curving course made travel in the dark dangerous. Once more Raymond walked to the edge of the shed to examine the sky. As he did so, a shadow slipped around the end nearest him.

"My lord, my master would wish to speak with you —in private."

The whisper was coarse, a broken French. The man's face was a pale glimmer in the dim light. All Raymond could really make out was that he smelled worse than the men-at-arms, wore a short tunic and baggy chausses bound with ill-tied cross garters. But he did speak some French, which implied that his master spoke it better. Almost certainly, then, his master was a merchant. No one else in Marlowe would need to speak French. In the dark, Raymond smiled. It looked as if his investigation had shaken up the merchant community. Probably one of them had become nervous enough to try to get into Sir William's good graces.

"Very well." Raymond looked toward his horse at the other end of the shed, but the man plucked his sleeve.

"It is not far, lord. Do not call your men or ride. My master will be in deep trouble if it becomes known that he spoke to you."

Better and better, Raymond thought. From what the man hinted it was likely his master was prepared to confess the other merchants' sins as well as his own. Concealing his eagerness, Raymond nodded curtly. He wondered whether he should tell the nearest man-at-arms that he would be gone for a while, but the merchant's servant was already sidling away around the side of the shed.

Raymond hurried out, relieved to find the man just at the end of the shed. He started ahead as soon as he saw Raymond and kept far enough in advance that the young knight's whole attention was given to keeping him in sight—a task made no easier by the dark, intensified as it was in the narrow twisting alleys they threaded.

Raymond was a brave man and his courage was bolstered by the unconscious arrogance that assured him no common churl would dare attack a nobleman. Nonetheless, he was somewhat surprised at the area into which he was being led. It was reasonable that a merchant about to betray his fellow guildsmen would avoid his own house and his usual haunts, but it was not at all likely he would choose to meet his overlord's agent in a sty a pig would scorn. Perhaps the person who wished to speak to him was not a merchant. One of the criminals who haunted every waterfront might have information he believed would buy him a pardon for his crimes and a little silver.

Although he still did not fear for himself, Raymond loosened his sword in its scabbard. The guide stopped at the door of the most miserable inn Raymond had ever seen and waved him forward. Raymond shook his head firmly. He did not want to give the man a chance to disappear before he was questioned. It was the man's slight hesitation that warned Raymond all was not as it seemed. There should have been no difference which one of them preceded the other. The next move was even more peculiar. The man knocked on the door and said, "Egbert, it is Rolf," as he entered. One did not knock on inn doors nor announce oneself, particularly if the "guest" you were bringing was supposed to be a secret.

At that point, Raymond should have turned and run. Already his brain was shrieking, *trap*. His pride, his training and tradition, betrayed his good sense. A knight does not flee from trouble before he even finds it; a nobleman does not flee from a gaggle of churls. As the door opened to admit the guide, Raymond launched himself forward, pushing the man ahead of him so hard that he fell, and leaping over him. The suddenness of what he had done saved him from being dispatched by a violent blow from a man who had been waiting beside the door.

That assassin leapt forward, as did half a dozen others, expecting that Raymond would continue his rush or that he would stand at bay. Instead, he turned and ran back, twisting aside just enough to avoid the man coming toward him. Foolhardily brave Raymond might be, but he was not suicidal. The inn was dim, lit only by a few rushlights, but Raymond's eyes were adjusted to the dark already, and he had seen the other men coming forward and seen the long gleam of swords. Had he worn armor, he might have been tempted to fight. Without protection for his body or a friend to defend his back, he was too vulnerable.

He had intended to go out of the door as fast as he came in. Unfortunately, the twist that permitted him to avoid the man who had run at him from beside the door also carried him out of the direct line of the opening. In addition another man, who had been on the other side of the doorway, slammed the door shut before he, too, ran forward to attack.

Although he did not succeed in escaping, Raymond's swift action did take his attackers by surprise. The man he had so narrowly avoided jerked aside instinctively and, a second later—a second too late—thrust at Raymond. This caused him to bump into another man, who was rushing toward where Raymond had been, and to strike the sword of a third man. In general, as they converged on the spot Raymond had so swiftly vacated, all the men became entangled to a degree.

Their confusion did not last long. They were used to dealing with frantic efforts to escape, but the second or two necessary for reorganizing themselves gave Raymond time to draw his sword. This caused another brief hesitation. Most of the victims this scum of thieves and deserters dealt with were either paralyzed with fright at being trapped or unaccustomed to defending themselves. The second delay also worked to Raymond's advantage. He was able to swing his cloak off his shoulders, where it had hampered his movements, and whirl it around his left arm to use as a shield.

He was just in time. Two men sprang forward simultaneously. Raymond beat off one blow with his sword and tangled the tip of the other weapon in the trailing edge of his cloak. His counterstroke was aimed at the man whose sword was caught in the cloth, and he grinned wolfishly as a shriek followed his thrust. In general, Raymond did not use the point of his weapon much. In this situation, however, he was as eager to keep the attackers at a distance as he was to harm them. Thus he drew the sword back only enough to free it and then slashed sideways as he bent his knees to dodge a slash from the other man.

This move too was successful. Raymond's sword connected again, drawing another shriek, but neither attacker fell, and the strength with which their curses were uttered implied they were more surprised than hurt by Raymond's defense. He did not have time to be discouraged by such thoughts. The other men were pressing forward, slashing and thrusting.

It was immediately apparent to Raymond that none of the men was his equal in ability. It was also immediately apparent that his greatest danger was that he would soon be hemmed in so closely he would be overpowered by numbers and the inability to swing his own sword. The only counter he could make was to slash around him in a wide arc as hard as he could. He coupled this with snapping his cloak violently in the faces of the men to his left.

The action was partially successful. Raymond's blade made sharp contact with another, obviously of much poorer quality steel, which snapped. The cloak caused another man to jerk backward, catch his foot in an unevenness in the floor, and stagger sideways. The move was also dangerous. The spread of Raymond's arms bared his breast and throat. Two men, both immediately in front of him, thrust eagerly at the targets offered. Raymond jerked aside. The sword aimed at his throat missed; the other, directed at the broader target of his chest, struck the inner side of his left arm.

Because Raymond was moving in the same direction as the slash, its force was lessened. In the heat of the fighting, he hardly realized he had been wounded. He was more worried by his dodging, which moved him away from the door, than by the pain. Desperately he swung again and again, wildly, not aiming at any man or weapon, only striving to clear a space around himself. Made cautious by his violence, the four remaining attackers drew back a trifle. Raymond did not delude himself that he had cowed them. Obviously they were preparing to rush him all at once.

Mauger had had a lively night. He had not removed Elizabeth from the bed when he came up, ostensibly to watch by her through the night. He had felt a violent excitement when he saw her lying there bound and had fingered her body experimentally. The effect, however, had been disappointing. Elizabeth did not try to scream behind her gag or fling herself from side to side. She only opened her eyes, stared at him for a moment with blank indifference, and closed her eyes again.

Although he stopped handling her, Mauger was not entirely convinced by Elizabeth's apparent lack of reaction. Three factors made him let her alone. The first and most important was that he did not trust her. He remembered the swift stroke that had sent the "physician" careening across the room. In order to couple with Elizabeth, he would need to untie her legs. That would be asking for trouble, for a man is never more vulnerable to hurt than when his shaft is engorged.

The second factor reinforced the first. Mauger really did not find Elizabeth in the least attractive. He wished to soil her, to reject her. That made the third factor clear. His pleasure had come largely from displaying that he did not think her worth coupling—that he did not think her important enough, human enough, to need privacy from her when he performed the most private of all acts. Thus, he took Emma into Elizabeth's bed and, with her beside him, made love to his mistress. He found it remarkably stimulating. There was an additional pleasure in sleeping between the two women, an equal warmth on both sides.

Naturally, neither of Mauger's bed partners felt the same satisfaction. Emma had obeyed him in terrified, sickened silence, her helpless hatred growing greater and more bitter. Elizabeth, despite Mauger's belief that she was pretending, had truly been indifferent. She had reached the stage of despair in which nothing that happened to her had any meaning.

It was quite late in the morning before Mauger woke. He had Emma dress him and stuck his head out of the door to order that bread and cheese and wine—and broth for the invalid, a quick afterthought—be sent up. He made Emma attend to Elizabeth's physical needs and then eat the broth in front of her, but did not get the satisfaction he expected, even when he forced Emma to suck the liquid loudly from the spoon. Elizabeth never opened her eyes, and when he struck her and demanded that she do so, her gaze was blanker than any idiot's, showing no interest or desire. It was annoying, but Mauger told himself that she would not be able to control herself much longer. She simply was not hungry or thirsty enough yet.

That irritation sent Mauger down to inquire whether Egbert had left the keep. The information that he had done so soon after dawn was satisfactory but increased Mauger's discomfort. A glance at the sky was no help; the heavy clouds prevented him from judging the time. He went up to Elizabeth's chamber again and attempted to assuage his impatience to hear that Raymond had been killed by tormenting the women. This expedient was not particularly successful. Elizabeth remained limp. She did wince a trifle when he pinched her and pricked her with a knife, but he did not dare really mark her. Once she was dead, he would have to permit her women to wash her and lay her out. If there were marks of violence on her body, all his effort at making her death seem natural would be wasted.

There was little amusement to be obtained from threatening Emma with mistreatment. She was so exhausted by terror and weeping that she simply fainted. Mauger did not bother to revive her but stamped out of Elizabeth's room in disgust. He could not read and took no interest in the running of the estate, so he could not busy himself with those matters. Moment by moment his impatience grew to hear that the attack on Raymond had been successful. He willed Egbert to return from the town with the news he wanted to hear.

However, his will did not bring Egbert or news, but the thought of Marlowe town put Marlowe keep into his mind. Suddenly the look of frustrated impatience on Mauger's face was replaced by a smile. There was nothing to stop him from going to Marlowe keep. In fact, it would be an expected courtesy, since he knew William was not yet completely well, to go over and tell him what had happened after he left Wales.

Mauger's eyes lit with pleasure. A visit to Marlowe would be a delightful interlude. He could tell William that Elizabeth had fallen ill, implying that it was owing to her exhaustion from tending him. That would make William squirm. Also, the news about Raymond should come to Marlowe almost as soon as Egbert would bring it to Hurley. How delightful if it should come while he was there. He could watch that nasty little bitch Alys fall into a fit over her lost lover.

He would ride, he decided, and take the ferry. He did not wish to seem to avoid the town on the day that Raymond would be killed there—hopefully, had already been killed. It would be a mark of innocence in him that he rode through without pausing to speak to anyone.

When Mauger's horse was ready he mounted eagerly. In the back of his mind there was a faint feeling that he had forgotten something important. He sought for the thing, feeling that it concerned Elizabeth, but he knew she was bound and gagged and concealed behind the drawn bedcurtains. There could be no immediate problem, and the need for movement, for action of some kind, was so strong that he dismissed the slight nagging unease and concentrated on the coming delight of his visit to Marlowe.

A little while before Mauger left Hurley, Alys had told Martin that she was going there. "Do not tell papa unless he asks for me," she said with a worried frown. "Not only did Sir Mauger return yesterday, as you know, but I have heard that Lady Elizabeth is ill. I suppose she has taken to her bed to avoid her husband, but that maid of hers is a silly creature, and if Elizabeth *is* sick, I must look to her nursing."

"You may be sure I will say nothing," Martin replied with a nervous glance toward William's chamber.

"Let us hope papa will sleep until I return." Alys looked out of the window at the lowering sky. "Tell the men and have the boat made ready while I get my cloak. I will go the quickest way."

Usually it was quicker to go by the little boat than ride to the ferry, but the Thames was swollen with much rain in the past weeks and the current was faster than usual. The boatmen pulled lustily under Alys's urging. Still, it took them more than half an hour to drive the broad craft—designed for safety and comfort rather than swiftness—the two miles upriver. Thus, Mauger had already ridden ashore in Marlowe when Alys's boat tied up at the small pier at Hurley.

She did not stop to speak to anyone in the tiny village. They could not know the truth about what was going on inside the keep, and all she would get from them would be more disturbing rumors. It was best to hurry as fast as she could up the short road. The guards passed her without delay or hesitation. Alys thought one looked as if he wished to speak to her, but he, too, could know little if anything about what went on in the women's quarters and she did not pause. She hurried on up the steps to the main hall.

Here she did get news, the maidservants and men-servants crowding around her to tell her how Elizabeth had fainted when Mauger arrived and how he had been so disturbed that he sent for a physician. By the time the story was told, Maud had heard of Alys's arrival, and she came rushing down to confirm the tale and to add what she knew. Alys listened with growing horror, par-ticularly to Maud's romantic version of Mauger's dis-tress over his wife's illness. Alys discounted the ro-mance, but was much frightened by Mauger's concern. He did value Elizabeth as a manager, Alys knew. His anxiety might mean Elizabeth was really dangerously ill.

Alys began asking specific questions, drawing from Maud the fact that Elizabeth had been unconscious for a long time after she "fainted." That sounded very bad. Even worse was Maud's repetition of the conversation she had had with Elizabeth. If Elizabeth thought herself so ill that she was afraid the maid would take it and was apparently also afraid she would not be able to resume her duties in a few days, she was probably very sick indeed. She went upstairs immediately, telling Maud to obey her mistress and go back to her work. Her hand hesitated on the latch of Elizabeth's door for just a moment. What if she took the disease herself? Nonsense, she thought, lifting the latch. She had not sickened after caring for Harold and Martin, and Eliza-beth would warn her not to come near if the disorder was very violent.

A low whimper greeted the opening of the door. Be-fore she even looked for the cause of the sound, Alys hastily closed the door behind her. If Elizabeth was having fever dreams, Alys did not wish to alarm the maidservants with hearing her raving. The shriek that followed her action gave Alys good reason to fear the worst, but as she turned she realized the sound did not come from the bed.

"Go away!" Emma wailed. "Go away. He will kill me. I forgot to bar the door. No one is allowed in here. Go away!"

"Stop that!" Alys ordered sharply. "Sir Mauger has gone out. I have come to see Lady Elizabeth. I am sure Sir Mauger would not forbid me——"

"She is asleep!" Emma screamed, wild with terror. "She can see no one. She is sick!"

Alys looked toward the drawn curtains of the bed. Asleep? She swallowed nervously. Elizabeth must be unconscious or dead not to move or call out at Emma's screaming. Even as the thought crossed her mind, the bed curtains bulged and Elizabeth fell out of the bed tangled in the blankets she had had to pull with her as she rolled. Alys gasped with terror, thinking for a moment that the cloth that gagged Elizabeth had been used to tie up her slack jaws after death, but Elizabeth continued to roll toward her with desperate heavings. The blanket came undone, and Alys saw the bound hands and feet.

"Elizabeth!" she cried, leaping toward the struggling woman.

Emma screamed again, then rushed to the door and slid the bar into place. It was the only thing she could think of doing. Locking the door might delay her punishment a little while. Alys paid her no heed at all, kneeling to pull the gag from Elizabeth's mouth.

"Water," Elizabeth whispered.

Fortunately the remains of the watered wine Mauger had brought up to slake his thirst in the night were still in a jug by the bedside. Alys did not even look for a cup but held the vessel itself to Elizabeth's parched lips. After a few swallows she pulled it away.

"Let me unbind you before you have the rest. God, oh, God, how long have you been without food and drink? What happened? No, do not answer me. I will hear in good time."

Even as she spoke, Alys had drawn her eating knife and cut through the cloth with which Elizabeth was tied. Mauger had not tied her tight enough to stop the circulation and the cloths were too soft to bruise her badly, but her arms were numb from being in one position for so long and dropped limply.

"I will get you more to drink and some food."

"No," Elizabeth said. "Mauger—" She shuddered convulsively. "We must get away from here as quickly as possible. If Mauger returns—" She shuddered again. "Help me to dress, Alys. Emma is right. Mauger will kill—he will kill me too, not only her."

"No, no," Alys soothed, thinking that Elizabeth's reason had been disordered by terror. "He cannot harm you now that I am here. My men are below, waiting for me. Martin knows I have come to Hurley. Your husband would not dare harm me. Of course we must leave. You cannot stay any longer when he has treated you this way, but you must regain your strength."

While Alys was speaking, Elizabeth had been struggling to move her arms without much success. Her legs were a little better. Alys had helped her to sit up, and now she summoned Emma to help her lift Elizabeth into a chair.

"You must take me," Emma cried. "You must take me too. He will kill me."

"You treacherous slut—" Alys began, but Elizabeth stopped her.

"Of course we will take you, Emma. Stop crying now and come help Alys get me ready."

"Elizabeth," Alys protested, "she helped him!"

"Not willingly," Elizabeth said, biting her lips as fire and sharp pangs of cramp ran up her arms. "Believe me, Alys, Emma has already been very harshly punished for her sins. Go and pick out clothing for me, Emma, quickly. The sooner I am ready, the sooner we can go." She lowered her voice so that only Alys could hear. "She is very simple and very easily frightened."

"Simple!" Alys was outraged, but kept her voice low. "She left you bound like that, and did not even give you a drink of water!"

In her reaction from despair, Elizabeth's mind was working at top speed. She was well aware of Alys's distaste for Emma, but she knew Emma did not think much better than a dog. She had been too afraid to dare go near Elizabeth, not realizing that if the door

was locked Mauger could not get in and discover what
she was doing. And, gagged as she was, Elizabeth had
no way of explaining. She was sorry for the girl, but
she had no time to enlist Alys's sympathy for her. Even
if she could have done so by describing what Mauger
had done, Elizabeth shrank from soiling Alys with such
a tale. There was another easier way.

"We will need Emma to help us escape," Elizabeth
pointed out. "You are wrong when you say Mauger
cannot harm us. He can do what he likes with all three
of us."

"Elizabeth, he has frightened you out of your senses.
Do you think papa would permit me to be held against
my will? Or you?"

"Do not be a fool!" Elizabeth said sharply. "How
will your father know it is against your will? Everyone
believes I am very sick. Cannot Mauger say you stayed
to nurse me?"

"Oh, heaven!" Alys exclaimed. "I had not thought
of that. I even said to Martin—but papa will come at
once. You know he will."

"I do, indeed, know it," Elizabeth agreed, beginning
to shake with pain and fear. "It is just what Mauger
most desires. He told me—" She swallowed, unable to
continue for a moment but then forced her voice on.
"He told me he arranged the murder of my brothers
and planned to have your father and Sir Raymond
killed."

"Raymond!" Alys gasped. "I cannot believe it! Why
Raymond? If he hates papa—well, I understand that,
but Raymond. . . ."

"He does not hate your father because of me. He
did not hate my brothers. He had them killed because
he wanted Hurley. Your father and Raymond must die
because he wants Marlowe and Bix. To have them, he
must have you."

"Did Aubery—" Alys began, but she stopped when
Emma came to them, her arms laden with garments.

"Aubery knew nothing about this," Elizabeth said as
the two girls began to dress her. "He told your papa

that he did not wish to marry you. Love you as a sister, he does, but one does not wish to couple with a sister." In the midst of her pain and fear, Elizabeth had to smile. William had described his conversation with Aubery in detail, fearing that she would think her son had been hurt. "He said he did not know what ailed him, since you were the most beautiful girl he had ever seen, but he did not desire you for a wife."

"But if Aubery will not—"

"That is why I must die," Elizabeth said. "He did not say it to me, but I think Mauger plans to marry you himself."

Alys did not answer that directly. She was now nearly as frightened as Elizabeth. It was true that her father would come to Hurley as soon as Mauger sent word that Elizabeth was so sick Alys had stayed to nurse her. He would come alone, or with only one man, possibly Raymond, and he would be completely at Mauger's mercy.

Even if by some chance papa should be suspicious, what could he do? Alys's fingers trembled, making slow work of the ties and buttons on Elizabeth's dress. While Mauger held her and Elizabeth, papa would not blink an eye for fear Mauger would do them some harm. In the end it would come to the same thing. He, and Raymond, too, would come naked and willingly stretch their necks for the ax so long as she and Elizabeth were freed unhurt.

Seeing how the color had faded from Alys's cheeks and the heavy work she was making of the simple task of tying garters, Elizabeth realized the girl had come to a real understanding of their situation. Since Alys was no physical coward—as Elizabeth knew quite well from having bound as many cuts and bruises on the daring girl as on her adventurous sons—she knew the fear was for her father and lover.

"We are not helpless," Elizabeth said firmly. "The servants do not know that I was a prisoner. They will not interfere with us, and I do not believe Mauger would have told his men-at-arms anything either. The only one we need fear is his personal servant, Egbert. I do not know whether the men-at-arms would obey him, but he usually attends Mauger. Likely he is gone with his master. Help me to my feet."

Emma had slipped on Elizabeth's shoes and enough feeling had returned to her arms so that she could raise them and place one around Emma's shoulders, the other around Alys's. Thus supported she stood. Automatically Alys straightened the skirts that had been bunched around her. Falteringly Elizabeth moved one leg forward. Emma steadied her and she got the foot properly placed. She moved the other foot forward.

"Your maids will never let us leave carrying you this way," Alys sobbed. "They will cling around us—God knows what they will think."

Elizabeth gritted her teeth and took another step. "I will think of something to tell them," she said through set teeth. "I will think of something."

Upon the words, the latch of the door lifted and rattled violently. The three women froze, breaths held. Before they could even hope it was Maud or some other innocent person, a thunderous knock shook the door.

"Let me in, Emma. It is I, Mauger."

CHAPTER 19

Mauger would probably not have noticed Alys's boat making for the dock at Hurley even if he had not already ridden ashore. His attention after he led his destrier onto the ferry was taken up by the activity on one of the docks at Marlowe. He could see a fairly large riverboat tied up and unloading. Eventually he made out two figures standing side by side watching the work, one of whom wore a sword. Something in the attitude of the other man, who shouted orders from time to time, made Mauger feel pretty sure the one wearing the sword was William's hireling knight.

A slight feeling of irritation that Raymond was still alive passed. It was just as well he was not dead yet. If news of his murder preceded Mauger to Marlowe, there might have been too much excitement there for proper attention to be given to Mauger's news. Probably there had been too much activity at the docks for Egbert to have the young knight enticed away. Mauger looked up at the darkening sky. If it began to rain really hard, he might use that as an excuse to extend his visit in Marlowe. The previous day Raymond had been back in the keep well before dark. Perhaps his absence would be noted and Mauger could plant the idea that the merchants would have good reason to wish to silence him.

He rode well to the rear of the docks and spurred his horse up the steep road. There would be nothing suspicious in his eagerness. The weather was excuse enough for a man to hurry to shelter. Obviously the men-at-arms in Marlowe agreed with him. No one looked surprised when Mauger rode through the bailey right up to the door of the forebuilding. The groom who came running to take the horse cursed under his breath, but it was the weather and his fate that drew the obscenities rather than Mauger's action.

As he entered the hall he wondered whether Alys knew of the relationship between Elizabeth and her father. If so, would she try to prevent him from seeing William? It was the crippled steward who came to greet him, however. Ostentatiously Mauger looked elsewhere as Martin hobbled forward. When the steward continued to approach, Mauger waved him away. To his surprise, Martin did not scuttle aside and send a servant to summon Alys. He stopped where he was and bowed.

"You offend me," Mauger growled. "Take yourself out of my sight."

"I am sorry, my lord," Martin said softly, "but my master is abed and Lady Alys is not in the keep."

Mauger opened his mouth to call Martin a liar and say he knew William was up and about, but he remembered he could not explain that knowledge. "Sir William was not so severely hurt as to be still abed," Mauger snarled. "I have news for him that he will be most eager to hear."

"He *is* abed," Martin insisted, sidling between Mauger and the door to William's apartment.

He was desperate to keep Mauger away from William until Alys had seen Elizabeth and could assure her father that all was well at Hurley. He was intent on his purpose and it simply did not occur to him that a gentleman would use violence on another gentleman's servant. Thus, he was taken completely by surprise when Mauger stepped up to him, whirled him round, and shoved him away forcefully.

"Get out of my way, you loathsome filth," Mauger spat.

Unable to stop himself, Martin staggered halfway across the hall. A couple of the servants cried out and rushed toward him—they knew in what esteem their master held Martin—but it was too late. Mauger had already gone in through the door and was bellowing a greeting filled with spurious jollity.

"Oh my God," Martin breathed, rubbing his protruding chest, which had been bruised when he fell against a chair. "What can I do? What can I do?"

Impatiently he warned the servants away. They could not help. If Mauger told Sir William that Elizabeth was sick, Sir William would want to rush to Hurley. How to prevent him from harming himself? How? Then relief. Of course he could prevent Sir William from going. He need only mention at the right moment that Alys had already gone and would soon return with reliable news as to Lady Elizabeth's condition. Perhaps he could somehow hint that overeagerness on Sir William's part would be embarrassing or even dangerous to Lady Elizabeth. Martin moved as quickly as he could to the open door of Sir William's apartment, beckoning a servant and whispering that he should bring wine and cups.

Mauger's "cheerful" bellow had startled William awake. He had jerked upright, painfully wrenching his half-healed shoulder. This was not all bad because the expression of discomfort on his face hid all other emotions.

"Mauger!" he exclaimed. "Are you just come?"

"I am sorry to see you still abed," Mauger replied, without really answering William's question, "and still in so much pain."

Politeness forced William to swallow the retort that he had not been in pain until Mauger's stupidity had caused him to make an injudicious movement. The politeness was its own reward as he realized his apparent weakness would be a good excuse for Elizabeth's having lingered so long at Marlowe. Thus, he made no move to get out of bed, as he would ordinarily have done. He had been wondering simultaneously why Alys had allowed Mauger to walk in on him unannounced and then thought his conclusions might have been hers also. But he had to find something to say.

"The shoulder wound has been very slow to heal," William agreed obliquely. "I hope my men behaved well. There was no trouble?"

"None," Mauger responded promptly, "although there was no testing. The Welsh had fled away and nothing de Bohun or Clare could do would tempt them from their mountains. Some feints were made, but we did not have the force to take the large keeps. Mostly we just sat and waited. When our time of service was ended, de Bohun bade us go."

Having pulled his pillows up so that he could sit, William leaned back and nodded. "If there had been hopes of a decisive meeting with David, it would have been worthwhile to pay you to remain, but to chase an *ignis fatuus* through the Welsh hills, an army is more bane than boon. I suppose Hereford will remain with his own troops. Does Gloucester remain also?"

"How would I know?" Mauger asked, a tinge of bitterness in his voice. "I am not a confidant of the great."

William wondered uneasily whether the taunt was a deliberate reference to his relationship to Richard of Cornwall and sought for something to say that would be, all at the same time, soothing, unrevealing, and not untrue. The statement, however, was only meant to deflect William from further discussion of the Welsh situation.

To this end, Mauger did not wait for a reply, but said—smiling as if to take the sting from his words— "I had really come to quarrel with you, William, but now I see that I should not do so." Mauger's smile broadened as he saw William's color change. He was going to be richly rewarded in amusement, it seemed, for the loss of his wife's worthless affections.

"Quarrel with me about what?" William asked. He could not bring himself to add, as he knew he should, *I have done nothing to offend you.*

"You used my poor wife so hardly, she has fallen sick," Mauger answered, still smiling and speaking lightly as if in jest—but his eyes were hard and wary.

William was so shocked by the first part of Mauger's remark—made in that jesting tone—that he hardly heard and did not make any sense of the second phrase.

"Used your—used Elizabeth—" he choked. "What the devil do you mean?"

Before Mauger could reply, Martin hobbled hurriedly into the room carrying a tray with wine and cups. "Do you desire refreshment, my lords?" he asked blandly.

Mauger restrained an impulse to hit Martin, a restraint more easily applied as it was clear William had not been distracted by the interruption, and he certainly would be distracted if Mauger struck his loathsome pet.

"What could I mean?" Mauger asked merrily. "Only that she was so worn out with nursing you—"

"Some wine, my lord?" Martin interrupted, sidling up to Mauger and extending a filled cup. He set it down quickly as he saw the infuriated man's hand rise and hobbled past him toward the wall. "Will you not sit down, my lord?" He began to drag over a chair too heavy for him to move more than inches at a time.

The whining obsequiousness of the steward's voice, the unnatural and unwarranted intrusion, the futile, clumsy effort with the chair—all so unlike Martin's normal behavior—finally pierced William's shock. Once his mind began to work, several things leapt into it. Most important was that Mauger was deliberately baiting him. That meant Mauger must know—and yet he obviously did not intend to make a challenge of the matter. William knew he had given Mauger the perfect opening to challenge him, and Mauger had made a jest of that also. How had he discovered the truth? Elizabeth would not have . . . Sick! He had said Elizabeth was sick! William pushed himself upright only to have his view of Mauger blocked by Martin, who had abandoned the chair and scurried around the bed.

"Lie back, my lord," he cried urgently. "You would not wish to undo the work of the ladies. Lady Alys would never forgive herself if she knew you had risen from the bed when she was out. I promised her—"

"What do you mean Elizabeth is sick?" William demanded, paying no more attention to the steward, who was now clutching his arm, than if a fly had landed there.

"Lady Alys will know," Martin went on loudly before Mauger could speak. "We heard this morning that Lady Elizabeth was not well, and Lady Alys went to discover what was wrong and to make sure she was well nursed. You know Lady Alys is skilled in such matters. You remember how well she cared for me. . . ." Martin babbled on, not caring what he said, aware only of the fact that William was now staring at him.

"You are sure Alys went to Hurley?" he asked.

"Yes, my lord, certain, absolutely certain." Martin's voice was fervent, his eyes held William's, warning, pleading. "Stay abed until Lady Alys returns. There is nothing you can do. Lady Alys will know."

Both men were so intent on each other, trying to communicate what must not be asked or answered openly, that neither had any attention to bestow on Mauger. He had barely choked back a roar of rage when he heard that Alys had set out for Hurley. She would discover Elizabeth was locked in and come running back to . . . No. Alys would not come back to Marlowe at once. That nasty little bitch was too accustomed to getting her own way. Doubtless she would try to make Emma open the door.

An uneasy pang passed through Mauger. He realized suddenly that he had left Emma in a faint. He had not heard the bar being seated in its slots. Almost certainly Emma had locked the door as soon as she revived; however, would Emma be proof against Alys's insistence? What did it matter? Either way it would be a disaster. William would . . . Then Mauger realized that William could not do a thing! As long as Elizabeth was a hostage, that romantic idiot would not dare do anything, unless—unless Mauger himself were trapped in Marlowe.

"I am a great fool," Mauger said. "I should have thought to send for Lady Alys. I keep thinking of her as a child, but, of course, she is not. I will leave you now, William. Perhaps I can catch Alys before she leaves. She could then tell me whether the matter is serious."

"But what happened?" William asked frantically, "What did Elizabeth say?"

"She said it was nothing," Mauger assured him, now desiring only to get out of Marlowe. "She said she had been tired and worried about you. I would not have made a jest of the matter if I thought she was really sick. I am sure there is no need to worry. Alys will be able to tell you far more than I when she returns."

This was almost certainly true, William knew. Besides, he was so confused by the change in Mauger's manner that he merely nodded in response to the farewell Mauger was making and watched him dazedly as he walked out the door. Then he sighed with relief and sank back on his pillows. Mauger had not been baiting him about being Elizabeth's lover. He knew nothing. Doubtless he had found Elizabeth depressed and crying, and to excuse herself, she had said she was not feeling well. It was typical of Mauger that he should think that a subject suitable to joke about. William shifted restlessly, trying to convince himself that all was well. Finally he got out of bed and insisted on getting dressed, although he knew he could do nothing until Alys came back with news.

It was not until Mauger was out of the keep that he relaxed enough to think further on the subject of Alys's visit to Hurley. He rode as quickly as he could, absently noting that the large riverboat was unloaded and that Raymond did not seem to be anywhere around. As he led his horse onto the ferry, Mauger relaxed still further. His mind, freed from any concern with his own safety, fixed on the fact that he had not met Raymond leaving the keep or the road. So probably Egbert had already drawn him into the ambush and he was dead. One obstacle out of the path. But there would be trouble over this business with Elizabeth.

Damn that loudmouthed, nosy bitch, Alys. He would never be able to convince her of his sympathy and good will now. He would have to take her by force.

The ferry docked and Mauger went ashore and mounted. His eyes swept the river front. They passed over a small boat tied to the pier with two boatmen huddled under skins to shelter from the rain, which was becoming heavy. Mauger started his horse forward, eager to get to shelter before the few, heavy drops became a downpour and then reined the beast in sharply. That was the boat from Marlowe! Alys was still in Hurley!

All at once a complete, perfect plan was born. There would be no need to entice Alys or to force her. There would be no need for refinements or subterfuges to achieve William's death. Loosening his rein, Mauger dug his spurs deep into his horse's flanks. He could hold Alys, send a message to William that Elizabeth was very sick and Alys staying to care for her. That would bring William to Hurley, half-healed or not, and they would all be completely in his power.

He was so eager to close the jaws of his trap on Alys that he rode through the outer and inner baileys without a word, leapt from his horse, and rushed up into the hall. One sweeping glance told him that Alys was not, as he suspected she might be, furiously waiting for him to return so that she could demand he let her in to see Elizabeth. Possibly she was still upstairs arguing with Emma. He hurried up, stopped short, choking with disappointment. Alys was nowhere in sight and the maids were quietly at work.

Maud saw him and came across the room to tell him, with a pleased smile, that all would now surely be well with Elizabeth, since Lady Alys had come to visit her. Mauger gaped at her; he realized that Emma had not locked the door and Alys had simply walked in, so that the maids still had no suspicion that anything was wrong.

"She is still there?" Mauger asked breathlessly, hardly believing his good luck.

"Yes, and I am sure—"

But Mauger did not wait for her to finish speaking. He thrust past her, lifted the latch on Elizabeth's door, and pushed. The door would not open. Damn that idiot Emma! Mauger rattled the latch, hoping the girl would come and open it and the women would think only that the latch or door had stuck. When that did not work, Mauger lost his temper. What did it matter what a bunch of silly women thought. He pounded on the door violently, shouting, "Let me in, Emma. It is I, Mauger."

As the men attacking Raymond drew back a little to unify their rush at him, he leapt sideways, jerking at the latch of the door. It was a small hope, but it was his only hope. Although only four men ringed him now, all of them would be back in action soon, Raymond feared. He was proud of his fighting skills, but did not pretend to himself that he could hold off so many for much longer. They could afford to send a few at a time against him while the others rested until he was too exhausted to defend himself. Raymond knew he would die in that fetid room if he could not get out.

To his surprise, the door swung open. The men charged forward bellowing with rage, but it was too late. Outside, Raymond did not run. He swung round next to the wall of the place and brought his sword down from an overhead sweep as hard as he could. A blood-chilling scream rang out as the sword connected with the shoulder of the man most closely on his heels. Raymond wrenched his weapon back up fiercely. It came away more easily than he expected, having broken right through the collarbone and there being nothing but soft tissue above that. The wild backswing nearly decapitated the next man out, and he fell back into the inn, blood pulsing briefly from his throat before his brain died and his heart stopped pumping.

The others stopped where they were. Egbert, who had most to lose if Raymond escaped and had thus been the first out behind him, continued to scream—but more weakly. The sword had opened a four-inch-deep slash where the neck joined the body, and he was losing blood fast. As his voice weakened, the men still inside the inn looked at each other. Was it worth pursuing the intended victim? When Egbert was dead, they could strip him of whatever he had. Obviously they could not hope to obtain the bonus he had promised them even if they succeeded in killing this cursed "easy prey." Equally obviously he had lied to them. This was no merchant's clerk, even if he did check cargoes on a ship.

They consulted rapidly in whispers, arguing whether it was more dangerous to let Raymond live—in which case he could complain against them—or to try to kill him. Two men were hurt already, one was dead and another nearly so. It was not possible to take a chance on the front door, where that deadly sword might be waiting. They left the worst hurt man in the main room of the inn, talking softly to himself to make Raymond believe they were all still there, and carefully went through the back door to sneak up on him from behind.

The effort was all wasted. Raymond had not run, as they expected, because he was not in a panic. Although not as experienced in war as an older man, he had fought often enough and faced enough danger to keep a cool head. Nor had he remained by the door to take vengeance. He had only wished to discourage pursuit. Thus, when the man he had killed fell back into the inn and no one had leapt out over the body, he had waited no more than five seconds before running as silently as he could across the narrow lane into the shadow of another hut.

Here he had paused again, just long enough to look over his shoulder. Aside from the weakening screams of Egbert—now little more than moans—all was quiet. Raymond could only suppose that those who lived in the area were too callous or too frightened to bestir themselves over blatant evidence of violence. As far as he was concerned, this was all to the good, and he simply made haste to get as far away as possible. When he had passed down several winding alleys, Raymond stopped again. There was no sound of pursuit nor was there a person or an open door or window in sight.

None of this was surprising, as the rain had begun in good earnest.

Raymond leaned against a blank wall, wiped his sword on his cloak, and sheathed it. Then he used his knife to tear strips from his tunic to bind his left arm, hoping that would stanch the bleeding. He glanced around, but this alley looked exactly like any other. There were no stars, no moon, and the drumming of the rain was so loud that he could not hear the soft gurgle and chuckle of the river. Shakily he began to laugh. He was lost.

The paralysis of fear that had frozen the three women broke at Mauger's second thunderous demand to be admitted. Shaking with terror, Emma started forward. Just in time, Elizabeth's arm closed around her neck.

"He will break your nose and knock out your teeth," Elizabeth hissed.

"Even the dog boys and pig men will not want you," Alys added softly and viciously, "but if you help us, my papa will find you a rich lover who will value you and be kind to you."

"But what can we do?" Emma whimpered.

"Take me back to the chair," Elizabeth said. "I can stand with that support. Emma, call out that you are coming—say you are on the pot, quick!"

Once she was given a lead, Emma was able to obey. The trembling of her voice did not convey innocence, but that did no harm because Mauger already knew Alys was inside and expected her to sound guilty. He thought Alys was trying to hide and pounded on the door again. Elizabeth, leaning on the chair, turned to face the sound.

"Take off the bar," she urged, "and, as you open, stand behind the door. He will see me first and rush to subdue me."

Had Elizabeth not offered that hope of concealment and respite, Emma would have fainted. As it was, she was so frightened she could barely walk. She tottered toward the door, quite unaware that Alys had picked up a heavy bronze candlestick and had flattened herself against the wall on the other side. Mauger was shouting again, and Emma sobbed with terror, struggling to lift the bar with fear-loosened muscles.

As she had planned, the first thing Mauger saw was Elizabeth. "Where is she?" he roared, his eyes sweeping the room.

"Who?" Elizabeth asked calmly, as if there were nothing unusual in the situation.

Mauger took two steps forward, looking toward the bed, which was the most logical place for Alys to hide. He hesitated, unwilling to move far from the door lest Elizabeth dart past him while he tried to seize Alys, or vice versa. The pause was exactly what Alys needed. She leapt forward and swung the candlestick at his head with all the strength she had. Alys was no weakling, but she was a small girl. Although she hit Mauger, it was with less force than she desired because he was considerably taller than she. He staggered forward, roaring with pain and surprise, dazed but not incapacitated. Startled out of the few wits she had, Emma pushed the door closed and stood fozen with horror. Alys followed Mauger, raising the candlestick to strike again, but he turned with surprising swiftness and seized her arm. Elizabeth cried out and flung herself forward, but her weakened legs would not hold her and she fell.

Alys had brought her left hand into play, scratching at Mauger's eyes. It was a futile attempt. He seized that hand also. "You will wish you had not done that," he snarled. "When I have done with that idiot who disobeyed me, I—"

His voice cut off in a high shriek as Alys brought her knee up and caught him in the groin. Unfortunately the force of this blow was reduced by her long, clinging skirt. Mauger's yell was as much owing to shock and indignation as to pain, and he did not let go of her. However, she had hurt him enough so that he bent forward and stood quite still, gasping.

Something about the assault on Mauger's sexual organs woke in Emma the burning resentment that fear had suppressed. She had been schooled to docility to men. She had never, for a moment, considered resistance possible. Alys's first attack on Mauger shocked her; this second, when Emma had believed the other girl helpless, broke her paralysis. Before the sound of Mauger's shriek had died, while he was still bent over trying to catch his breath, Emma scuttled forward and brought the heavy bar of the door, which she had been too frightened to release, down on his back.

This second attack was so unexpected that Mauger let go of Alys to save himself as he fell forward. Alys had had a split second's warning, since she had been facing Emma and had seen her move. She skittered back out of the way of Mauger's falling body and hit him again with the candlestick. This time his head was lower than her hand and the impact was enough to knock him senseless.

He lay snorting on the floor while all three women stared, wide eyed, hardly believing in their success. Elizabeth, who had got herself back on her knees, was the first to recover. "Tie him. Alys, use the things you loosened from me or something else and tie him quickly before he regains his senses."

For a long moment Alys did not move, standing with the candlestick poised. Her common sense told her that she should not stop, that she should beat Mauger's head to a bloody pulp, spatter his brains so that he could do no more evil. She managed to raise the weapon higher, but she could not bring it down. It was murder. To strike and strike at a helpless body, that was murder. She could not bring herself to do it, even though she knew she was breeding grief for them all.

Alys dropped the candlestick, with a soft exclamation of regret for her weakness, and began to tie Mauger hand and foot. Meanwhile, Emma had let go of the bar and fled to Elizabeth, who praised her and comforted her while being lifted to her feet again. Alys added her thanks also, promising Emma—this time ungrudgingly—whatever reward she desired, for Alys was aware that the single blow the girl had struck had saved her father's and her future husband's lives as well as Elizabeth's and—eventually—her own. The sincerity of the praise lavished on her penetrated Emma's doubt. She grew quite cheerful and gleefully helped Alys drag Mauger to Elizabeth's bed and, heaving mightily, got him into it.

Emma's cheerfulness was not shared by Alys or Elizabeth. They had no idea whether Mauger had instructed his men-at-arms to prevent his wife and Alys from leaving. They feared that Egbert, who was usually in his master's confidence, might see them and give warning to hold them even if Mauger had not. If the women had heard Mauger's shouts, would they have run down to the hall cackling like frightened geese?

The last had not happened, although the maids were tense, not working, watching Elizabeth's door. There was a murmur when she emerged, walking waveringly, and Maud rushed over with a cry of joy mingled with consternation.

"Hush," Elizabeth said. "Mauger is furious because I must go back to Marlowe."

"Oh, my lady, are you strong enough?" Maud whispered, glancing nervously at the door.

"I was not really ill," Elizabeth said quite truthfully, "and would have been out of my bed yesterday by my own will. I do still find myself a little feeble, however, so you are to come with us. Fetch cloaks quickly."

Maud was silly, but she sensed something wrong. Obviously the reconciliation she had hoped for between her master and her mistress had not taken place. Possibly her lady was trying to be out of the way while the master worked off his bad temper. Emma's presence was a complete puzzle, unless Elizabeth's price for restoration of her favors was to be rid of Emma. Maud did not dare argue with her mistress and was relieved that she would not be left behind to face Mauger's wrath if he had not agreed to Emma's removal.

They crept down the stairs, supporting Elizabeth as well as they could, and bade Maud see if Egbert was in the hall. When she reported he was not, Alys called her men who were waiting there. They made their way down the outer stair, through the inner bailey, and around toward the small one-man gate in the rear of the outer wall. Although this was a kind of weakness, because the gate could be forced far more easily than the great front portcullis, it mattered little. The passage through the walls was so narrow that only one person could enter at a time. Thus, the postern could be easily defended or even stuffed with rubbish in time of war. As long as its placement was "secret," it provided a way for messengers to sneak out. In time of peace, of course, it was simply a shorter route to the rear of the keep.

By the time they reached the postern gate, they were all soaked and Maud was growing more and more frightened. She began to protest, crying that it was cruel and sinful that Alys should drag Elizabeth, weak and sick as she was, out into a downpour. It no longer seemed possible to her that Elizabeth's purpose could be to rid herself of Emma. There must be some emergency at Marlowe, but it did not seem to Maud that any emergency could merit such cruelty to her enfeebled mistress.

"Be still," Elizabeth hissed, slapping Maud. The blow itself was ineffectual; the fact that Elizabeth had dealt it stunned Maud into silence. "I am weak because Mauger was starving me to death and had me bound hand and foot for two days. Now come quietly and quickly before we are caught and killed."

Fear and tension had supported Elizabeth until they were out of the keep, but once free her strength failed rapidly. One of the men had to carry her as they proceeded along the wall back toward the road. For a little while, Elizabeth merely drew breath; after that she began to review what had happened and she gasped in horror at the mistakes they had made.

"Alys," she called, "we did not gag Mauger or shut the door!"

"What—oh, merciful Mary! When he regains his senses he will begin to yell for help and the women will have to release him." Alys held her breath and listened, but even as she did it she realized it was useless. The sounds of a full-scale battle might come over the walls, but nothing so insignificant as twenty or thirty men arming and mounting to catch a group of fugitives afoot.

CHAPTER 20

As Alys stood trying to decide in an instant whether it would be safer to go wide around the gate of the keep so that the guards would not see them or save time by taking the most direct route, Mauger was slowly becoming aware of the pains in his head and back. These were sharp and stabbing and drew attention first, but there was also a chorus, a duller, nagging pain in his arms and shoulders. He could not imagine how he had come to fall asleep in so weird a position and he lay considering that dully for some time.

Finally Mauger opened his eyes unwillingly—it was not morning! The bedcurtains were not drawn, but the room itself was quite dark. The bedcurtains—they were not *his* bedcurtains. Frantically now Mauger pulled and twisted, realizing at last that he was bound. He let out a bellow of rage even before he remembered the attack and then, as that memory returned, began to scream for help in earnest.

At Mauger's first shout the women in the outer room looked at each other questioningly. The women were not puzzled by the shout but by the need to decide who should answer it. None wanted to face Mauger in a bad temper. They looked doubtfully at the stairwell down which those who usually attended Mauger had disappeared. None of them had heard what Elizabeth said to Maud, but they had seen Maud fetch cloaks. It was odd that neither Elizabeth nor Maud had told one or more of them to attend Mauger if they expected to be gone long.

The second shout, followed in rapid succession by an increasing volume of sound, galvanized the women into action. Two middle-aged maids rose together and hurried into Elizabeth's chamber, excuses for their tardiness bubbling on their lips. What they saw when they entered the room, struck them dumb. They clung together, half minded to flee.

Angry as he was, Mauger was no fool. He realized that if he expressed the rage he felt he would frighten these maidservants so much they might run away without untying him. "Your lady is mad with fever," he said, moderating his tone with an enormous effort, "and that silly little girl from Marlowe believed what she said. Untie me quickly. If she goes out in the rain, she will surely die."

Both women sprang to do his bidding, greatly relieved by his moderate behavior. His explanation of what they had heard dimly through the door was convincing. While they worked at the knots, they bewailed the fate of their mistress, spilling the information that she had gone down more than a quarter of an hour before he called to them.

Mauger almost burst, but he did not waste time in venting his bottled-up rage on the women after they had served his purpose. He raced down through the hall and down again to cross the inner bailey. Mauger had intended to ask the outdoor servants which way the women had gone, but, of course, there were none in sight. The drenching rain had driven everyone to shelter.

As he ran across the outer bailey, Mauger said what he thought about his wife, his servants, the weather, the inhabitants of Marlowe, and his fate in general. Unfortunately, this did not really relieve his feelings much, so that when the guard at the gate swore the women had not passed that way, Mauger howled that he was lying and struck him. He might have gone further, but from the wall above two men added their confirmation. By then, the master-at-arms had come running from the shed in which he had been waiting out the rain. Mauger at once ordered that the outdoor servants be questioned and a general search of the grounds and keep be made.

One keen-eyed man-at-arms noticed that the bars were off the postern gate, but the man wasted time searching the outside for the fugitives. Since they were already hurrying through the village, this little delay could really have had little effect on the outcome of the search, but the man was fortunate he did not mention more than that the postern was open. Mauger was not certain this was not a ruse, but he took no chance and sent a dozen men out in pursuit while encouraging the search within the keep to continue.

Soon, however, Mauger realized that Alys, at least, would be clever enough to understand it would be impossible to hide in the keep or grounds for long. From that moment he knew in his heart that Alys and Elizabeth had slipped out of his grasp. His rage and frustration were so intense that they could not even find expression in violence of word or deed. For quite a long time Mauger stood staring into the fire. Then it occurred to him that Egbert had never come back with the news of Raymond's death.

Everything had gone wrong—everything. Fear swallowed anger so that when the men he had sent out returned to report the boat gone from the dock, Mauger only nodded. He had already known. His first impulse was to run—but there was nowhere to run to. Mauger was wise enough to know that the great men he had cosseted would be indifferent to him in his troubles. If he could grab estates and power, they would be willing to confirm his acts to win the gratitude of a rising man. None of them, however, would trouble to protect him when he was falling. He had no friends. Mauger did not bother with his equals or those less rich and powerful than himself unless he could use them.

Having reached the nadir of despair, Mauger began to add up what could be charged against him. Suddenly the picture looked less black. Obviously Elizabeth would cry out that he had confessed to her he had arranged the murder of her brothers and the attempts on William's life—but who would believe a wife who

fled to a lover from her husband's home? Quickly
Mauger ran over what he had said and done since
Elizabeth had "fallen ill." No one knew anything except
Emma, and she had gone with Elizabeth. Even when
he had sent the men hunting them, he had ordered
that they be taken unhurt and to the women he had
said he feared for Elizabeth's health.

Well! A new complexion began to cover the whole
series of events. All the men and women in Hurley
would testify that he had been a good husband—except
for having a mistress, and that was so common that
no one would think twice about it. He had never beaten
Elizabeth, never quarreled with her. Better yet, she had
always treated his mistresses kindly—which would
clearly show that she had not desired his marital attentions. Yes, he could say she had refused him her bed
and encouraged him to keep other women. And William had visited often; Elizabeth had also gone to
Marlowe—less often, but she had gone.

The story was now clear in Mauger's mind. While
he was away in Wales, his wife had gone to live openly
with her lover. No, that would not do if William was
sore wounded. But who knew he was sore wounded?
Only a hireling knight, a foreigner. Hereford knew also
—but Hereford was in Wales. Besides, he might not
have known how badly William was hurt. Mauger
thought Hereford had seen William only once, briefly,
before the fever started. After all, William was only
at the abbey for three days. . . . By God, that was
proof! One does not move a man half dead with
wounds. Mauger smiled.

It would run thus: William pretended to be sore
hurt so he could shirk his duty and run back to Marlowe to be with his mistress. Until he arrived at home,
Mauger had believed William to be an honest friend;
however, the story of his wife's unfaithfulness had
greeted him when he brought William's men to Marlowe. He had not wished to believe it and had questioned Elizabeth, whereupon she had fallen into a faint.
It all fitted together perfectly and, with the evidence

of the men and women in Hurley—which would be given without fear in the honest belief it was true—the story would be believed.

The only remaining danger was Egbert. If he was dead, that was fine. If he had been captured . . . No, it made no difference at all. Egbert would not speak unless tortured or threatened by torture. Taken out of William's power, Egbert would deny his guilt gladly; gladly say that he had accused Mauger only to save himself. Good. That settled that problem.

All that remained was for Mauger to make sure his version of the affair was the first men heard. Well, that was no problem. When a man's wife flies to a lover, it is natural for the man to complain and ask for help to retrieve her and punish her. Usually one would complain to one's overlord, but Mauger was in fee to an abbey. Was this the kind of tale with which one would sully the ears of a holy abbot?

Mauger nearly laughed aloud and had to check himself, remembering he was supposed to be sad and worried about Elizabeth. Unholy devil was more like the truth about the abbot of Hurley. Mauger doubted there was any depravity that abbot had not already tried in person. However, it was a good reason to carry his tale to a more practical listener. Who? William's overlord? That might be dangerous if Richard of Cornwall knew William; besides, Mauger remembered that Cornwall was still in Scotland trying to stabilize the relationship of the two countries to prevent future wars.

Then who? Hereford was in Wales and might know too much about William's injuries. Anyway, Hereford seemed all too enamored of William. Was there someone among the mighty who had a reason to dislike William? Then, like the sun rising, revelation burst upon Mauger. The king himself disliked and distrusted William. This time Mauger could not control himself and he roared with laughter. How could he have been so stupid, so bemused, as to forget that the hireling

knight Egbert had apparently failed to kill had been
sent by the king to spy on William?

Joy sang in Mauger's heart. Not only would he come
about from danger of total wreck, he would likely gain
all his purpose. Where did rumor say the king had gone?
London? Yes, London or Westminster, hard by. Even
if Henry was not there, the lords of the Exchequer
would know where he was. Mauger rose and made his
way out to speak to the master-at-arms in person. He did
not wish that the servants in the keep know his plans.
Let them think he had gone to try to bring Elizabeth
home.

Once Raymond had got over the humor of being
lost in a town that would fit into one quarter of several
of the larger cities he had navigated with confidence,
he did the practical thing. He looked about for the
neatest of the hovels around him and hammered on
the door. This was opened with caution, only to the
length of a sturdy chain. The neighborhood left much
to be desired and respectable people took precautions.
It did not take long for Raymond to convince the people within of his station and goodwill. He was invited
to come in.

Eventually, between gestures and broken English,
Raymond made clear that he only wanted a guide back
to the docks. He was afraid the men-at-arms might soon
report him missing. If so, it was an even chance that
Sir William would guess he had been set upon by some
disgruntled merchant. Then he would probably ride
into town himself to direct a search and investigation.
Alys will kill me, Raymond thought—and urged his
guide to hurry.

Raymond need not have worried. William was too
frantic about Elizabeth to think about anything else.
For some time he had been only normally impatient,
but as the time passed he became convinced that Elizabeth must be dangerously ill or in some other trouble.
In vain Martin pleaded it was no such thing, pointing

out the heavy rain and insisting that Elizabeth would not permit Alys to leave in such a downpour.

"Alys would know I was worried. She would send back a man to bring me word," William said, chewing his lips.

"But she did *not* know you would be worried, lord," Martin pleaded, hobbling after William as he paced the hall. "You were asleep when she left. She expected you would sleep until she returned. Indeed, she did not think you would ever hear Lady Elizabeth was unwell. You would not have heard if Sir Mauger had not . . ."

Martin's voice faded as William turned and glared at him. "And what else have I not heard?" he grated.

"Nothing! Upon my soul, nothing!" Martin assured him fervently. "I swear all else is well."

The hot glow of William's eyes dimmed, and he put a hand gently on the old cripple's shoulder. He was not convinced that all was well, only reminded of Martin's passionate devotion. The steward was deeply and truly religious. If he swore on his soul it was not a casual thing, as it might be for another. Martin would believe that if what he swore was untrue he had committed a great sin. Yet he would swear, willingly accepting the sin and the punishment he believed would follow if that sin would help his master.

But affection could not diminish the worry that gnawed at William. His hand fell from Martin's shoulder and he shook his head. "I must go," he said. "I cannot bear to wait any longer. Have Brun saddled and get me a heavy cloak."

"My lord, I beg you," Martin pleaded, "think! No sooner will you go out of the keep than Lady Alys will return. She will be so frightened for you. She will rush to follow you and bring you back. And what can you do at Hurley? It would not be fitting for you to go into Lady Elizabeth's chamber. I fear Sir Mauger is already suspicious."

It was true. William's doubts as to whether Mauger knew and had been baiting him returned. He paced the floor and soon became uncomfortably aware that his legs were growing unsteady. He tired so easily. He went to a window and pulled aside the skins that sealed it against the rain.

"You will get wet," Martin exclaimed.

William ignored him and leaned out. "The rain is less. Surely Alys would have come already."

"Wait a little longer," Martin cried. "By the time you ride to the ferry, Lady Alys will have left. My lord, my lord, Sir Mauger will think it very strange—"

Martin stopped abruptly. William's hands had suddenly gripped the frame that held the scraped skins so hard that the knuckles showed white and his whole body had tensed.

"The boat!" he exclaimed. "I think I see the boat. God in heaven! It is gunwale deep, and the river is wild."

Trained to act in times of emergency rather than stand frozen with horror, William burst away from the window and ran toward the stair, nearly knocking Martin down. The steward gathered himself together and began to follow but realized that was foolish. He could be of no help. Shaking with fear, he crept to the window and nearly fainted when he forced himself to look out and did not see the boat.

"No! No!" he whimpered. "Take me instead!"

As he spoke, the little craft, which had been hidden momentarily, came into sight. Martin breathed again. It was so heavy-laden it was not answering well to the boatmen's efforts, but it was still afloat. Simultaneously, he heard William bellowing in the bailey for horses to be brought down to the small dock and for strong swimmers to make ready. Martin pulled himself together. From the keep dock, one could see only a short stretch upriver. He called two lusty menservants to him.

"Watch the boat," he ordered one. "Call out to Paul what it does and where it is from moment to moment. And you, Paul, stand in the window above the dock and shout down to Sir William what Hugo tells you."

The shouted messages began as soon as Paul had

reached the short end of the keep above the river. Having done what he could to help in a practical sense, Martin sank to his knees and began to pray. This he did, more fervently every moment as Hugo's stentorian roar reported the boat was still afloat and coming closer. The minutes passed, slowly at first, dragged out by fear, and then quicker and quicker as hope grew strong. The hall started to fill as more servants rushed in to be closer to the news.

"It rounds the point," Hugo shouted.

A shrill chattering pierced Martin's concentration. The maids had come down from the women's chambers and were weeping and shrieking with mingled fear and excitement. Painfully, Martin climbed to his feet. Silly geese, honking away when they should be preparing for their mistress who would be soaked and frozen. He seized one of the older women by the arm.

"Fool! What do you do here? Go and send a woman to fetch a warm, dry cloak. Others should prepare a hot bath for Lady Alys. See that the fire is high in her chamber. Heat sand to be laid beside her if she has taken a chill and be sure her bed is well warmed."

Once they had orders, the women became less disorganized. But Martin had forgotten all about them. His words had made him conscious that he was as guilty as they. He had been on his knees praying while he allowed Sir William to stand out in that rain without a cloak. He rushed to Sir William's chamber, found the cloak, and hobbled down the stairs. Then he ran, an ugly, crabwise scuttle, around the building, through the small water gate. Here he stopped, holding his breath. The boat was in sight, tipping dangerously as the boatmen tried to bring it out of the fast, rain-swollen current. Two women were screaming hysterically, drowning out the instructions Sir William was trying to shout at the rowing men.

Suddenly a struggle erupted in the boat. Martin cried out in terror. Two cloaked figures seemed to be fighting while a third crouched at the knees of one rower and a fourth tried feebly to grasp one of the struggling pair.

One of the men-at-arms started to move; the boat tipped a gunwale under the water. A boatman shrieked a warning and the man threw himself back to trim the craft.

The hood fell back on the person nearest the stern, showing Alys's golden hair. In the next instant she had cast aside her cloak and swung a tremendous blow, felling the person with whom she had been grappling a moment before. Elizabeth, who had been trying to pull her fear-crazed maid away from Alys, after settling Emma's hysterics with a good slap, threw herself down on top of Maud. Both men-at-arms and Alys baled frantically. The boat rose an inch, so that water stopped slopping in with every movement.

Now that Emma's shrieks had been shocked into quiet and Maud's were muffled under Elizabeth, the boatmen could hear Sir William's voice. The horsemen plunged into the river carrying lines, and the crisis was over. Martin sank down on the wet stone and wept. William covered his face with one hand, shaking so badly he would have fallen in the river himself if one of the men had not steadied him.

The young are very resilient. As soon as Alys saw the lines made fast, her fear dropped away. By the time the boat was warped in, she was able to spring lightly ashore and run to her father, crying out that he was all wet and should go inside at once. He did not answer, only crushed her against him so hard that she could not find breath to say any more. A maid hurried forward with a dry cloak for her, and William let her go, prepared to give her the tongue-lashing of her life now that he had her safe. He never got the chance.

"No," Alys said to the maid, "I will take no hurt from the wet. Go cover Lady Elizabeth."

"Elizabeth!" William exclaimed, turning in time to receive her into his arms as a man lifted her ashore. "What . . . why . . ."

"Not now," Alys ordered sharply. "Let us get her inside. There is a long tale to tell, and horrible—simply horrible!"

It was some time, however, before William heard a

carefully expurgated version of Elizabeth's experiences. Dry clothing had to be exchanged for wet, and Alys insisted that Elizabeth eat before she explained. Fortunately before William had really absorbed the enormity of what Mauger had done and intended and worked himself into a great enough rage to ride to Hurley with a challenge to single combat, Raymond burst in on them, muddy and blood-stained, and a new spate of explanations began.

"Then it was he, not the merchants who attacked me," Raymond said thoughtfully. "Did you not say his servant's name was Egbert? The man who led me to that trap called out to 'Egbert' inside the inn."

"There is more than one Egbert in these parts," William pointed out. "Still, it would be rather a great coincidence. Elizabeth, can you guess what Mauger will do if this Egbert does not return or returns and reports that Raymond has escaped?"

"I do not trust myself to guess anything about him," Elizabeth remarked bitterly.

William leaned over and took her hand in his. "It is not easy for those with only good in their hearts to see evil in others. You do know him, my dear. You only need to add different intentions to this knowledge."

"He is not a coward," Elizabeth said slowly, "although he also does not wish to accept the results of his mistakes. Often he will blame them on others or seek to turn them in some way into a benefit."

"I am afraid that is all too true of most men—myself also." William smiled wryly. "What man likes to say *mea culpa?*"

"What I mean is that he will try to blame you for this. He will try to explain to the world that *you* deceived him."

That made good sense and William followed the idea to the conclusion that Elizabeth would not have thought of. "He cannot attack Marlowe directly. Even if he kept the mercenaries he hired for Wales, he does not have enough men. Obviously he knows I believe you because he has sent no messenger to demand your return. Yet I do not think Mauger a man to sulk and do nothing, particularly as you tell me his purpose all along was to gain hold of Marlowe and Bix. He will seek help from some great man to attack us and right his 'wrong.' "

"The earl of Cornwall?" Elizabeth asked.

William laughed aloud. "If he goes to Richard, we will be blessed. Could fortune so favor us?" He paused to think, then sighed. "I think not. He must know that Richard is in Scotland, and he would not take the chance of going there. Nor would he write to Richard, who might not know his name and might not look soon at a letter from a minor knight, not even his own vassal, when he is busy with affairs of state. No, he will go to some other great lord."

"Which?" Raymond asked eagerly.

It had come to him that his high connection could win Sir William what he wanted. Raymond could ask the king himself to punish Mauger or, at least, prevent him from attacking William and give Hurley back into Elizabeth's hands. But Raymond had not heard the king discussed for nearly six months without having a much better knowledge of him than he had started with. Henry would flick aside a minor knight who did not even have a powerful overlord to support him, but he would not confront a powerful man on Sir William's behalf. He would look the other way and bewail men's evil and dislike Sir William all the more for causing him trouble.

On the other hand, if Raymond went to whomever Mauger was trying to influence, identified himself as Henry's nephew-by-marriage, and hinted that the king would be ill pleased to have his brother's favorite affronted . . . Yes. Then Henry need not be troubled at all, except to agree that William was Earl Richard's close friend.

"That I cannot tell you," William replied. "Hereford would be most likely, because Aubery is obviously a great favorite with him, but Hereford is in Wales and all his forces are committed to dealing with David."

"The earl of Hereford would not listen to him anyway," Raymond said. "He thinks him an idiot because of the way he bungled that last action we were in. Also, he knows you too well to believe any ill of you."

William smiled indulgently at Raymond. "No man is free from all evil, and Hereford is too wise to think me a saint. I—oh, Diccon, take a squad of men into the town and see if you can find any men sore wounded or dead of sword blows. Likely they will be in that western part of the town you are forever warning your men to avoid or in some ditch or nearby waste ground. If you find such, bring them here. Do not rouse the town over this. It is not of great import. What is important is that I need a messenger to ride to Earl Richard in Scotland with all haste, and I mean *haste*."

Having waved his man away, William turned back to his companions. "Now I regret that I avoided Mauger at court. I have no idea who his friends may be. We must do what we can to protect ourselves here. Raymond, drop the matter of the merchants, and bring in every man who can hold a sword from the town and the farms. Alys, you and Martin had better see to stuffing and garnishing this place for war. I will speak to the men and warn them to be alert, and I will write to Richard, who will do what he can, but—"

"William," Elizabeth burst out, "this is madness! Let me go away. I can seek shelter in a convent."

He looked at her, and Elizabeth's eyes dropped. She was not frightened for herself. She was very willing to die with William if that was necessary, but she could not bear to think of Alys and Raymond being sacrificed to protect her nor that Marlowe should be ravaged on her account. Still, she said no more, and William's answer made any future objections hopeless.

"It would not help, Elizabeth. Mauger must have his revenge on me whether you remain here or not. Do not forget that it was Alys who freed you and helped you escape. You say Mauger wants Marlowe. He must take Alys to gain that end. We are all in this together."

Elizabeth closed her eyes, and Raymond stiffened,

but she did not weep or fall into hysterics any more than did Alys. William turned to Raymond, but only to see if he had a counter opinion.

"I will start gathering the men tomorrow," was all Raymond said, proud to be consulted and also that William no longer even thought of offering him the choice of leaving before they were attacked.

Raymond had realized he could not go off to counter Mauger's moves. He had not the faintest idea of where to go. In addition, Sir William was not yet strong enough to gather and train men for defense himself.

William levered himself out of his chair. "I will go write to Richard now." He bent over Elizabeth. "My love, come and lie down to rest until I am finished."

Raymond was somewhat shocked at the openness of this avowal, but he saw only amused resignation looked out of Elizabeth's eyes. William was truthful to a fault, but that was not the cause of his declaration. He had said often that he had waited long enough. Plainly, he intended to enjoy her openly in whatever time they had. She rose without comment. Perhaps he was right. In Marlowe, no one would dare look askance at her. Why then should they suffer the discomfort of sneaking a kiss or a coupling, fearing to be discovered.

Before Raymond could say anything after William and Elizabeth disappeared into his apartment, Alys said, "You need not think papa and Elizabeth have ever wronged Sir Mauger. They could not help what they felt. They have been in love with each other since they were children. Now that she is free, they may do as they like."

"It is none of my business," Raymond said quickly, hiding his amusement at what he believed to be Alys's innocence.

Sexual purity was not a matter of importance to him —except in his wife, of course, and Alys's "naïve" remark pleased him. In any case, he was more concerned with the question of whether and how he could use his true status to protect her father. This captured her attention at once, although she was as quick as he to see that he could not go before they were ready to resist an attack.

"If all is quiet when we are ready," she said, after a thorough discussion of who would be most susceptible to Mauger, "perhaps we had best tell papa who you are. Then you could go to London. Perhaps there you could find out to whom Mauger has appealed. And it is not so very far."

Raymond bit his lip. It was horrible to be torn between two necessities. If Marlowe should be attacked after he was gone, William would have to lead the defense—and Raymond did not think he would be strong enough. On the other hand, if it should take Mauger a long time to reach a major vassal's ear, he might be able to get to the man and discredit Mauger before any attack was started. And what of Richard of Cornwall? Could he finish his business in Scotland in time to help?

CHAPTER 21

The next morning, as soon as it was light enough to see, Mauger left for London, reasoning that, if the king was not there or at his favorite palace in Westminster, one of the officials permanently established in London would know where he was. He left Hurley sealed shut in the care of his master-at-arms with orders that no one, especially not his wife, should be allowed to enter. Mauger intended to ask Theobald of Hurley to get him a private audience with the king.

All the way to London, Mauger tried to devise a tale that could not be proved untrue and would make William out to be a sufficiently dangerous man for the king to send troops with Mauger to destroy him. The loss of Mauger's wife would not induce Henry to act; that was merely the overt reason for Mauger to complain. The exercise was of value, for it fixed the "facts" into Mauger's mind so that he could reel them off in any context, but the ground for his success had been laid in Scotland before Henry had brought his troops south again.

In general, the Scottish affair had been a brilliant success in Henry's opinion. There had been only one small unpleasantness. When it was clear that the danger of Alexander's attacking was over, Richard had urged his brother to take his hired troops and clean out Wales once and for all. Henry said loftily that it would be an affront to the earls of Hereford and Gloucester if he came with an army and took away the task he had given them, seeming to set their efforts at naught.

Richard did not think so—and said it, pointing out that he had never scorned help from anyone when he was at war. Because Richard was tired from arguing with "unreasonable" Scots, he suggested a little sharply that Hereford and Gloucester would be the best judges of what would affront them. At least Henry should send a messenger to ask whether they desired his help. But Henry was celebrating his escape from fighting a war; he did not even wish to contemplate another. This, too, he refused to do.

Henry was right—although neither he nor Richard knew it. What he should have said was that the Welsh would disappear into the hills and that the Flemish mercenaries, accustomed to fighting pitched battles in flat country, would be more nuisance than benefit. Moreover, a large army would be difficult to supply in such rough country. Richard might have been contented with a military reason for refusing, even if he did not agree with it.

Unfortunately Henry did not know a reasonable excuse for refusing existed. He had enjoyed his bloodless victory and was basking in the admiration of his northern vassals. He did not wish to risk his current status as victor in a contest with the unpredictable Welsh. This was not owing to personal cowardice. If Henry could have settled the war with a personal battle against David ap Llewelyn, he would have leapt at the chance. Such a thing was out of the question, and Henry's memories of being a war leader in Gascony and France were bitter and full of the humiliation of defeat.

It was those memories that had induced the king to go to the highly unnecessary expense of hiring the Flemish—which Richard had not approved but had understood and accepted without argument. Now that the money had been spent, however, Richard wanted to get some good out of it. Since there had been no war in Scotland, let the hired troops go to Wales and clean it out.

Thus, when Henry refused even to consider using the men in what Richard believed was a sensible fashion, Richard lost his Angevin temper. There was some excuse. He was short on sleep from many late nights and had an aching head from drinking too much good Scottish usquebaugh. He told Henry he was an extravagant fool who did not know how to use the expensive tool he had purchased. He told him he was lazy and luxurious, which had only enough truth in it to hurt because neither fault was developed enough to be a vice. He said a few other immoderate things also, all at the top of his lungs, before stamping out of Henry's presence without asking or receiving leave to go.

The next day they made it up. Richard was contrite for his bad manners, and after talking to some of his older vassals, Henry had the right reasons to offer for refusing to lead the army to Wales. Richard did not agree—he would have liked to try to bring the Welsh to heel—but he conceded that Henry might be right and begged pardon handsomely. Henry forgave his brother and kissed him fondly.

The trouble was that Henry knew Richard's outburst was caused by disappointment in him rather than by any real fears of the Welsh or the Flemish mercenaries. As a small boy, Richard had seen his big brother—the powerful and glorious king of England—as a hero. He knew better now—at least, his head knew better. In his heart, however, that glowing hero lived. When the real Henry—weak, vacillating, ineffective as a leader except for his disarming charm—appeared at the wrong moment, Richard's childish heart overpowered his adult head, and he flew into a rage of disappointment.

Henry did not understand enough, was not himself adult enough, to accept his own and his brother's weaknesses. He made the mistake of trying to ignore them. Thus, when he saw the disappointment and hurt under Richard's rages, when Richard tried to mold him by force into the hero he wanted him to be, the pain was greater than if his brother had wished to do him harm. Henry could not salve himself by believing Richard hated him and hating Richard in turn. He knew it was not true, and, besides, family ties were sacred to Henry. Thus, he sought a cause for Richard to hurt him.

Although all was well on the surface, inside the king

his brother's outburst still rankled. He was made even more uncomfortable by receiving a letter from Hereford. The earl did not openly ask for help but suggested that the army could be used to wage a different kind of war in Wales than he had attempted with the limited forces at his disposal. They could, Hereford wrote, as Henry's father John had once done successfully, capture all the cities and keeps. In the past that had often failed, but David did not have the kind of control over his people that Llewelyn had had. David needed his castles, and taking them could bring him down.

By then, however, Henry was only a few miles from London, from the comforts and beauties of the castle at Westminster, from the arms of his beloved Eleanor and the totally undemanding worship of his adorable baby son. He did not want to go to Wales. There was no reason, he told himself, to rush off to another primitive wasteland. It was ridiculous that a king should need to attend to these minor disturbances. Henry dispatched Hubert Fitz Matthew with three hundred knights and their attendant footmen to Hereford's aid and tried to put the matter out of his mind.

He did not send the mercenaries—somehow that was connected in his mind with going himself. And he told himself that he *had* done all that was necessary. Certainly Richard would not want him to be miserable; therefore, someone had put the idea into Richard's head. Henry could not see that Richard was not oppressed, as he was, with fear of failure and was not made miserable by going to war. Richard rather enjoyed war; Henry did not. But he did not think of that. He only wondered who was turning his brother against him again, and could find no answer to that question—not until a trusted clerk, Theobald of Hurley, begged an audience for the abbey's knight in fee, Sir Mauger of Ilmer.

The clerk could read Henry's irritability in his sharp gestures and periodic inattentiveness. He had already delayed several days in asking for the audience. At last, more to be rid of Mauger than in any expectation that

Henry would agree to see the man, Theobald made his attempt.

"Sir Mauger has been sore injured by a treacherous neighbor," Theobald hastened to explain, "by that same Sir William whom I once overheard—"

"Richard's favorite!" Henry exclaimed.

The whole thing was now fresh and clear again in his mind, although events had obliterated it for months. Henry remembered sending Eleanor's nephew to Sir William. Good God, they had never heard one word from him since he left! The king remembered also receiving a letter from Raymond's father and replying that Raymond had been with them briefly but had left the court without saying where he next intended to go. The king's face went pale with anxiety and then red with rage. Everything was falling into place. Richard had received a letter from Sir William, who was serving in Wales, just before he had begun to urge him to take the army there.

"Certainly I will see Sir Mauger," the king exclaimed. "I will see him now, if he can be fetched to me."

Since Theobald knew his master and was aware of Henry's impulsive nature, Mauger was very close. He was in the small closet where Henry conducted private business almost as soon as the clerk was out of it. He began to speak of his gratitude that Henry was willing to listen to his troubles, but the king cut him off with a gesture to ask about Raymond and whether he had come home safe from the Welsh war.

Henry had sent Raymond away with the thought of the joke they were playing on Raymond's mother uppermost in his mind. It had all seemed a merry lark. They had agreed that Eleanor should not be told her nephew would probably be engaged in a war. Eleanor was almost as silly about war as Raymond's mother and would not see the jest. Right now, Henry did not see the jest himself and wondered if he had been mad. How would he ever explain to his wife and to her sister-by-marriage if harm had come to Raymond?

His relief when he learned that the young knight was

home safe made him miss a great deal of the garbled story Mauger was telling him. He did not realize that once he had identified Raymond as his wife's nephew, Mauger had hastily revised and twisted the business of the merchants and various threats against Raymond into an elaborate plot concocted by William. Although he was very ready to believe almost anything against his brother's favorite, Henry was no fool and smelled something rotten somewhere.

"But what for?" the king asked at last.

"Because once William discovered who Raymond was, he believed he could use him—perhaps as a hostage, perhaps in some other way—to obtain a divorce for my wife and have her lands given to him instead of my holding them for my son to whom they belong by right."

That made sense. Henry could not believe that any minor knight, even Richard's favorite, would dare harm the queen's nephew. No, of course not. Raymond was Richard's wife's nephew also. Damn! No wonder the tale sounded idiotic, Henry thought—not knowing that Mauger had woven in all the threats of death to cover himself in case Egbert had been successful. Henry merely thought Mauger was a provincial fool, seeing things from his own petty point of view. Sir William was not any physical threat to Raymond; Sir William was trying to do to Raymond what he had already done to Richard—he was trying to turn Raymond against his own flesh and blood! Henry ground his teeth with rage. How could he have been such a fool as to send a young, impressionable man into the hands of one experienced in twisting and warping people to his own purpose.

"My lord," Mauger quavered, terrified by Henry's expression, "I did not mean—"

"Be still!" the king snapped, rising and starting to pace the small room. "Let me think."

First of all, Raymond was in no physical danger— that was certain. Doubtless Sir William was as tender of him as a father. Also doubtless, Raymond would come back to London singing Sir William's praises. He would be no use at all in raising the incubus from Richard. Probably he and Richard would sit together and croon praises of the detestable man. It was useless trying to collect evidence to convince Richard that Sir William was a snake—a venomous worm like that which had tempted Eve to sin. Such a creature should be killed outright. There was no other way to stop him spreading his corruption further and further.

Yet, if Richard heard his brother had any hand in . . . But Richard was in Scotland, and if the thing was done quickly enough, it would be all over by the time he returned. And here was this puling fool raving about his wife and a thimbleful of land. What better excuse could there be? A man whose wife is reft away has a right to avenge himself. So, if Sir Mauger led a force— which would actually be managed by experienced mercenary captains to avoid any mistakes—against Marlowe and killed the man who had cuckolded him, that could not be blamed on the king. Why should a king even have heard about such a minor disturbance?

Of course, Raymond was there in Marlowe keep. No matter. Sir William would not allow such a precious person to be endangered, and the captains Henry sent would instruct their men to protect at all cost the knight who wore a shield painted with a faceless head. Henry stopped his pacing and looked consideringly at Mauger.

"What is it you want of me?" the king asked.

Mauger wanted desperately to say, "Nothing," and run away, but he knew if he did that he would lose everything he had worked for all his life. He swallowed. "I want help—men or money to get the queen's nephew safe out of Marlowe and to revenge the dishonor done me by the treacherous monster I thought to be my friend."

"Very well."

Mauger was so surprised by the flat agreement that he stood with open mouth.

"I will give you five mercenary captains, and the troops they lead, of course. Together with your own men that should be enough to take a small keep. There are conditions, however. No one is to know that I have assisted you. If a rumor of my part in this comes out—I will accuse you of forging my order and taking the men without my knowledge. Do you understand?"

"I will obey, my lord. But I do not understand," Mauger got out.

He did not like this. The king had a way of turning on those he helped from time to time—but only, Mauger reminded himself, when he was blamed by others for what he had done. That made Mauger feel a little better. If no one knew, the king could not be blamed and would not grow angry. Also, Henry might well be inclined to look the other way when Mauger married Alys. He would not be afraid of Mauger—not that. He simply would prefer that Mauger did not confess how he came to have Alys in his power.

"It is simple enough," Henry replied blandly to Mauger's assertion that he did not understand. "I feel for your hurts and wish to help you. However, I do not wish that every man in the kingdom whose wife runs away should come to me to settle his affairs. Also, I hope that those in Marlowe keep will not be free to tell this tale either. . . ."

"I see, my lord."

Yes, indeed, Mauger believed he saw a great deal. Again, after all his uncertainties and disappointments Mauger saw the flower of success opening under his eyes. The king would never say it, but he wanted Raymond dead. That was the reason for all his anxious inquiries. That was why he frowned so angrily when Mauger said he tried to warn Raymond against Sir William. That was why he asked so eagerly what Raymond had said. Of course, Mauger knew that he must not, even by a blink of the eye, show he understood.

Mauger drew a deep breath. He would need to be careful, of course. A man who threatened a king died; but a man who knew something and did *not* threaten might be forgiven many little things for which others would be punished.

It never occurred to Henry that anyone, no matter how twisted his mind, could think he would urge harm to any member of his own or his wife's family. He said "those in Marlowe" because he was not sure what dependents William had who would, if they were not silenced, run to Richard. That Mauger could believe his vagueness included Raymond was unthinkable to him.

What Henry did explain in detail was that he had no intention of paying the men more than the term for which they had already been hired. Thus, Marlowe would have to be taken by assault within the next few weeks rather than by long siege. When Mauger had agreed to this with enthusiasm—people tended to get killed during an assault and explanations about it were not necessary—Henry told him to return the next day. He would then be taken to the camp and introduced to the mercenary captains who would be under his orders.

Throughout that day and the next, while Henry made the arrangements that would protect Raymond and seal William's doom, he was uplifted by a sense of a great coming freedom. So blithe were his spirits after Mauger had left, that his wife began to look at him askance.

Eleanor of Provence loved her husband dearly. She had been only fourteen when she had come to England, knowing only that she would be a queen like her sister and that her husband was more than twice her age. Whatever fears she had had at that time, not one had been fulfilled. Henry was handsome, tender, loving, delighted with her and with everything she did and said. There seemed, in fact, to be little difference in their ages. Henry would romp and play as eagerly as any child.

As the years passed, Eleanor grew older; Henry did not. There was much joy to be had from that. He was ever a gay companion, loving and laughing. But there was much to be feared in it also—the unbridled and unreasoning anger and spite of a child welded to the power of a king. Not that Eleanor feared for herself;

Henry was never a threat to her or to their son, and if he grew angry, he was as easy to soothe as the child.

Unfortunately, however, the great lords of England did not think of their thirty-seven-year-old king as a child. Eleanor did not interfere in the politics of England, although sometimes she thought if the barons would tell her what they wanted she could get it for them—but she watched her husband. She had heard what could happen when he took a spite and carried it too far. Just before she came to England the country had erupted into rebellion. It could happen again. Thus, when she could, she soothed him or explained away little things.

Eleanor had noticed that something was pricking under Henry's skin when he first arrived at home. It had faded, then flared up again. Now this sudden elation warned Eleanor that Henry had done something to "get back at" whoever had irritated him. She had asked no questions at first because, very often, simply being with her and Edward healed any small hurt, whereas talking about it might magnify it. Once Henry had spit out his spleen, however, it was sometimes possible to guide him into reducing the punishment he had ordered if it were too severe. He was vindictive only when he was afraid or still felt hurt and angry.

The task was a delicate one, Eleanor knew. To say openly that Henry had been cruel or unreasonable would only bring back the "wrong" he had suffered and make him more obstinate. It was necessary to approach the matter in a roundabout way and then subtly insinuate the idea that his generosity and magnanimity would be praised if he showed himself merciful once he had already overpowered those who offended him.

On the third day after Mauger had come, the queen led the king to play some of the laughter-provoking games he loved in the privacy of their own apartments. Naturally under Eleanor's management Henry always won. Later, when they were cooling themselves from their exertions with well-watered wine—Henry was no lover of drunkenness—Eleanor mentioned his high spirits.

"Is it some special news, my love, or only that you are happy to be home again?"

"Nothing special," he replied.

Eleanor judged his expression keenly. He did not pout—which meant that she had not half guessed a pleasant secret he intended as a surprise for her. There was no angry frown either,' to warn her away from a subject he did not wish to discuss. A slight shift of his eyes, a quiver in the drooping lid of the left eye— Eleanor specially loved that fault in her otherwise nobly handsome husband; it was an outward expression of the weaknesses that made him extra dear because she knew herself to be more necessary to Henry than she would be to a stronger man—those minute gestures hinted at uneasiness.

To press hard would be a mistake. Eleanor wished now to introduce a topic that was different but still connected to pleasure. "Then I am happy also, for your gladness means you will stay with us."

"Yes, indeed," Henry agreed firmly.

"Is Richard coming soon?" Eleanor asked. "I am very glad he and Sancia live so well together that he sent for her to come to him in Scotland after the danger of war was over, but I long to see her again."

To Eleanor's surprise, a clear expression of guilt crossed Henry's face. She drew in her breath and swallowed her desire to ask whether the brothers had quarreled again. She knew she must avoid any hint of knowing Henry had been disturbed. To cover her nervous gasp, she laughed.

"How strange it is," she said, "that I was separated from Sancia by many miles and years and only missed her a little. Now that she is so close and I see her often, I miss her dreadfully when she is away only a week or two."

"It will not be very long," Henry assured her. "A few weeks more should settle the business in Scotland, if it is not already done. Richard has a way of making peace seem more desirable than war so that men will keep a truce because they feel it is best, not out of fear. But it takes time to reason it all out and get all to agree with easy hearts and minds."

Whatever it was, Eleanor thought, Henry was not now angry with Richard. His warmth when he spoke of his brother assured her of that. Yet the uneasiness remained. What Henry had done would hurt or displease Richard, Eleanor guessed. That was bad. Eleanor liked Richard but more than her desire for her brother-by-marriage's happiness was involved. She knew Richard was better in tune with the thoughts and desires of the barons than Henry. Often what displeased Richard was politically dangerous. Eleanor did not dare approach such a topic directly. A wrong word could set Henry into a fit of stubbornness, and that might be a disaster.

On the other hand she could not abandon the topic of her sister too abruptly. She was about to say something about missing her mother also, when she remembered there was another member of her family closer by. Raymond! She had been worried about him at first, but then, when the Scottish war was announced, she realized what Henry had done. Sometimes he was remarkably wise and kind. She smiled tenderly at her husband and took his hand.

"And what about Raymond? I know you sent him away to keep him from fighting in Scotland. You are so clever, my love, and I am grateful. But surely that danger is past now. Can Raymond be recalled?"

Henry stood up abruptly. "In a few weeks also," he said. "I have already sent a messenger to him, but it may be he cannot come as soon as he wishes. He is quite safe, do not worry about him. And I have just remembered something I must attend to at once. I will come to you later, my dear."

Eleanor put a good face on—the half-pout, half-resignation of a loving wife abandoned for a duty she knows more important than her pleasure—and held it until Henry was out the door. Then she withdrew to her own chamber where her worried frown would tell no dangerous tales to anyone. The question about Raymond had obviously touched her husband to the quick, and it seemed—although on the face of it impossible— that it was the same sore spot as the one connected with Richard. How could that be? What could possibly connect Raymond and Richard? And what could she do?

Henry had indeed been touched on the raw. His blithe assumptions that Richard would not uncover what he had done and that Raymond would escape untouched in the battle to take the castle did not seem quite so certain upon reconsideration. Who the devil was this Sir Mauger anyway? Theobald had said only that he was the knight who held Hurley. He seemed to think Mauger a good man, but what could a clerk know of such matters? It was not as if Theobald was highborn and understood from birth and breeding, even if he had chosen the Church.

Perhaps, Henry thought, he should not have acted quite so hastily. Yet, what else could he do? If Mauger did not begin the assault on Marlowe within the next few days, he would never be able to reduce the keep before Richard came back from Scotland. And how else was he to rid Richard of that evil influence? A faint quiver of doubt crossed Henry's mind. He was not completely sure, now that no one was telling him what a snake William was, that William was the cause of Richard's fury. That letter that had come—it had been several days before Richard broached the subject of leading the Flemish into Wales.

If Sir William was innocent, it would be wrong to deprive Richard of his friendship. Yet if he were not innocent, he would soon drive Richard into some dangerous act that would cause everyone inestimable grief. Henry bit his lip, but then his brow cleared. There was no need to do anything in a hurry. Let Mauger march the men to Marlowe and set them up. It would take him a week or more before any attempt at an assault could

be made. In that time, Henry could write to Hereford—
who must know both men since they fought under him
in Wales—and find the truth about them. Then, there
would be time enough to recall the mercenaries if it was
necessary to do so.

CHAPTER 22

❖-❖

King Henry had an adequate knowledge of war, but only from the point of view of major actions. It was quite true that a week or more was needed to move a large army into position to set up a siege or assault on a major stronghold in hostile territory. However, it was not at all true that such a period was necessary to arrange an attack on a single keep where no counteraction need be feared. By the time Henry had dictated his letter to Hereford and ordered that a messenger ride out with it, Mauger had his men encamped around Marlowe and well advanced in the construction of scaling ladders and devices to bridge the moat.

Mauger had discussed the situation with the mercenary captains and found they were not only well primed for the task in hand but agreed with his plans. They were to go as quickly as possible and to cause as little disturbance as possible while passing. Mauger suggested that he send men from his own small troop ahead to the overlords of the lands they would pass and say they were marching additional reinforcements to Wales. This went well with the king's desire for anonymity and was agreed upon.

They arrived as silently as possible and at night, not for the sake of a surprise attack—they did not have ready the devices for an assault and Mauger had warned the captains how strong Marlowe keep was—but because Mauger wished to pacify the townsfolk and prevent them from running to the keep for protection. He left the captains to settle their men and rode into Marlowe town. Confidently he informed them that Marlowe keep was already invested. If they would victual his forces and make no attempt to aid those in the castle, he would not attack the town. If they attempted to defend themselves, he would turn his men loose on them.

There was ready agreement, which Mauger knew there would be. He also knew the merchants would begin at once to hide their valuables, even that many would escape the town by river, but he did not care. He had no intention of damaging Marlowe town if it could be avoided; after all, it would be his in the future to drain slowly dry. Much more would be made out of it in that fashion than by raping it now.

Mauger's troops had moved quietly, but not so quietly that the guards on Marlowe's walls did not notice. Diccon was awakened and peered through the dark while circling the walls. He did not see much, but what he did see worried him. He passed the responsibility to Raymond, who hurried from his bed with his mail drawn over unlaced shirt and chausses without cross garters. His eyes and ears learned no more than Diccon's, but both agreed troops were moving around the castle. Raymond's first instinct was to bid his men arm and ride out to attack them, but to do that was to risk every veteran in the keep. The other men, half-trained and some not even able to ride a horse, were useless. Although he hated to do it, Raymond went to wake William, whose right it was to judge whether to attack or endure.

William was tired. For eight days he had been struggling to regain his strength in arms and to train the men Raymond had gleaned from the farms and the town. His own strength improved more rapidly than he expected. The wound in his right side was well healed and did not much impede his swordplay. That in his left shoulder was not in such good case. It was tender and had started looking angry and swollen at the edges again. William knew he would be unable to use his shield as a weapon, as he was accustomed to doing. Nonetheless, he could hold it, and that was important. More important was that his legs no longer shook under him after a few hours of merely sitting or walking.

Nonetheless, by the end of each day, William felt half dead. He tumbled into bed expecting to be asleep as he lay down. Instead, through the aching fatigue, tendrils of heat stole, soon joining across his loins into a blazing need. The first night, William was as much surprised as Elizabeth by the hot lash of his passion. He had never thought of himself as a particularly lustful man, who needed to couple only because a woman was available, but he saw no need to deny himself either, watching her undress through half-closed eyes, relishing her surprise, her halfhearted protests that he should rest, her joyous yielding to his love play when he persisted. He was even more surprised when he woke just before dawn with an equally urgent need. Again Elizabeth yielded, but when he dragged himself from bed an hour later to work with the men, her eyes were worried.

The second night, Elizabeth drew the curtains of the bed as soon as William lay down so that he could not see her undressing. She idled over it also, trying to make sure he fell well and deeply asleep before she joined him. It made no difference. William was not sure whether he was awake and imagining or asleep and dreaming, but when Elizabeth's slender body settled beside him—he was already afire.

"Dear love," she sighed when they were finished, "I think I must seek a chamber in the women's quarters."

"Why?" William teased. "Have I not contented you?"

They laughed together. The one effect weariness seemed to have on William was to make his climax slow to come. Elizabeth had been twice convulsed with joy before he found his release.

"Because you will kill yourself this way."

William chuckled. "I cannot think of a better way to die." He felt her move and pulled her close against him again. "No. I do not believe it would make any difference. It is not because you touched me in the bed but because you are here, mine—mine without shame or guilt. If you settled above, either I would have to follow you there or I would lie here, listening to the siren's song—and I have done that for too many years."

His voice was slurring with sleep, and Elizabeth said no more. But after he had again wakened in the dawn to caress her awake, mount her, rouse her from torpor to lust, and satisfy that lust, Elizabeth began to think her exaggeration of the previous night was no exaggeration. If he continued this way, William *would* kill himself. They argued about it while she helped him dress.

"You cannot go on like this," Elizabeth warned. "You are too tired!"

"If I were *too* tired, I would not be doing it," William pointed out, laughing. Then more soberly he said, "That is true. Unless I am overburdening you, my love, let me have my way. The weariness passes. I am stronger each day."

"You are pressing yourself harder each day," Elizabeth said sadly.

William shook his head. "No. I am pressing myself to my limit each day—that I admit. But each day I can do more. Thus, I am growing stronger. My life—for you are my life—let me live my own way. If Richard comes home before Mauger finds the help he needs to attack us, we will come out of this scot-free. If he does not . . ."

He did not finish and did not need to. If Mauger found someone who would give him enough men to attack Marlowe and they could not hold off the attack, she and William would die. Perhaps William was trying to make up twenty years of unfulfilled longing in the short time granted them. It was foolish, but Elizabeth would not deny him anything that gave him happiness. She argued no more, responding to him each successive night with all the fierce joy engendered by her own long deprivation. *Dum vivimus, vivamus,* she thought, *while we live, let us live!*

It was not surprising, however, that when Raymond called from the outer chamber it was Elizabeth who awoke. William slept on, sodden with exhaustion. She pushed aside the bedcurtains, resolved to tell Raymond

that he should go about his duties as best he could and
let William have his sleep out. The darkness of the room
changed her mind. Raymond would never call William
in the middle of the night unless it was a real emergency. She shook her lover as Raymond called again.

The combined stimulus pierced William's deep sleep.
He got out of bed, cursing and groaning, promising to
murder Raymond if the sky had not fallen, but he fell
silent as he listened. To Raymond's question about
leading a force out to disrupt the invaders he shook his
head firmly.

"If we lose one or two men, it will do us more harm
than if they lose fifty. Nor is this a mercenary group
merely looking for pickings, as happened in the bad
old days; those could be driven away by a show of
force. If the castle is being invested, it is Mauger, and
he has come to take us."

He did not bother to dress, merely belted his bedrobe tighter around him and put on his shoes before
he went to the wall. He, too, walked all around it,
looking and listening, particularly westward toward
Marlowe town.

"Shall I call up the men?" Raymond asked.

"No. Why should they lose sleep before it is needful?
We will all be short enough on that before this is over.
They will not attack tonight. If that had been intended,
they would have come better grouped and begun already. No, I do not believe they will attack at dawn
or any time tomorrow, either."

Raymond looked surprised and, for the first time
since he had taken service with William, seemed about
to argue.

"I am not being deceived by my own wishes," William said. "If Mauger could have taken us by surprise,
he would have done so. Since he has not, I believe he
has not in hand what he needs for an immediate assault.
He will need time to build scaling ladders, to dam and
drain the moat. . . ."

"He could have left orders to build such things at
Hurley and then float them across the river with boats

or horses to guide them," Raymond suggested, looking out into the dark as if he expected to see such activity.

"That is clever, very clever," William said with admiration after a moment. "I would not have thought of it myself, and I doubt Mauger would have thought of it either. He must have been nearly beside himself when he left, if what Alys and Elizabeth say is true. I find it hard to believe he was thinking of anything clearly. However—yes, double the guard and tell them to watch the river especially."

"And alert the men? Even if we do not send them to the walls, should we not—"

"No," William said firmly, still looking out into the night. "We must not seem to be afraid, Raymond. If we take the heart from these inexperienced churls, we will be lost. Remember, these are not longtime men-at-arms who are accustomed to judging the odds for themselves, who know that four or five men are needed for assault to match every one man inside a keep. These will judge their chances from our manner and orders. To double the guard is a reasonable precaution—but to alert all the men will cause them to feel attack is imminent and make them fearful and nervous."

That made good sense. Raymond was well aware how woefully inadequate their preparations were. They had all worked as hard as they could, but there had not been enough time to make the keep ready for war. No one had believed there would be less than two or three weeks in which to bring the men from Bix, cart in grain, vegetables, and cattle from the farms, and teach the new men how to defend the walls. All the more reason, Raymond knew, to appear confident.

"I wish I knew how many there were," Raymond said.

William shrugged. "Mauger is not fool enough to come with fewer men than would make taking Marlowe possible. If he has the minimum, we may survive until Richard comes. If he has more . . ." He shrugged again. "Well, I think I will go back to bed and finish out my sleep. Tomorrow will be soon enough to worry."

Before William could turn, Raymond gripped his arm. "Sir—"

Fighting back an urge to scream, *Let me be. Give me time to face my despair so I can bear it like a man,* William only waited.

"I do not know how to say this," Raymond began. He felt William's arm stiffen under his hand; then the muscles went loose again with resignation.

"If you wish to leave before you are trapped, you have my—"

"No!" Raymond shouted.

"I beg your pardon," William offered promptly. "Do forgive me for such a suggestion, but you have so strange a look—"

"Oh, God," Raymond interrupted, "I do not know how I ever—I do not know how to tell you—but Alys—"

"I am not blind," William said gently. "Do not be so troubled. I am not guiltless myself. I meant you to have her. . . ."

His voice drifted, and he looked out over the wall again. Poor Raymond. But Alys was in no danger. The worst that would befall her was that Mauger would try to force her into marriage, but Richard would be back in time to prevent that.

"You do not understand," Raymond said. "I have something to tell you, something that might—not that I love Alys, which I do with all my heart. I am not ashamed of *that*. But—"

"Can it not wait until tomorrow?" William asked.

"No," Raymond replied, "because—because if I am to—No. You must listen to this now because you must tell me what to do."

"About what?" William found that he was shaking with fatigue and chill. He had not felt it while they paced the walls, but standing still made it worse. "Come in. Let us at least sit by the fire in my chamber."

Raymond was glad of the brief respite, and he lengthened it a little by closing the shutters of the window, lighting a branch of tapers, and renewing the fire. Before he had arranged in his mind what he wanted to say, Elizabeth appeared in the doorway. Looking at her, Raymond thought he knew where Alys had learned her strength. Elizabeth's eyes were large with fear, but her face was quiet and her voice calm.

"Shall I go and wake Alys and the women?"

"No, my love. Go back to bed. We are safe enough for tonight."

Their eyes locked, and Raymond looked away from the intimacy of that glance. There was such love, such communion between them. Although she must know she was the cause of this threat, there was no apology in Elizabeth's expression; there was no blame in William's, no look of *I do this, lose all, for you.* There was only a joy in being together for however short or long a time they were granted. Before he averted his eyes, Raymond saw a flicker of impatience cross William's face. Elizabeth moved back into the bedchamber. He realized how precious the few remaining hours of peace must seem to them, but what he had to say might give them a whole life rather than a few hours.

"There is no easy way to do this," he said harshly, the intimacy of that glance. There was such love, such can only tell you outright that I am the eldest son and heir of Alphonse, comte d'Aix, who is the natural son of Raymond-Berenger, comte de Provence, which makes me nephew—although by the bend sinister—to Queen Eleanor."

For a long moment William did not move or speak. His first thought was that fear had somehow unhinged Raymond's mind; but there was no fear in the dark face or the brilliant eyes that met his. There was determination in the firm lips and set jaw, unhappiness in the frowning brows. No, William thought, this is the truth he is speaking.

"You should have told me sooner," he said. "It was not fair to let Alys love you when you must have known—"

"It is nothing to do with Alys. I will marry Alys if it is the last thing I do in this life," Raymond said forcefully. "When we are safe, I will sue for her properly, and you can tell me what you think of me. I will accept any condition you wish to lay upon me so long as I can have her to wife, but—"

"But to achieve that you must live. I see. I also see that it would be most impolitic for the queen's nephew —no matter by what bend—to be slain in a little keep—" Raymond's face had crimsoned under the lash of sarcasm in William's voice, but suddenly William stopped and shook his head. "Nonsense!" he exclaimed, "I am talking like a hysterical woman. You risked your life for me in Wales more surely than here. Think of the royal favor Mauger could obtain by returning you unharmed to your aunt. So, you are not looking for a door to safety." He gave Raymond another, somewhat sour look. "Raymond, if you have kept me from my bed and my Elizabeth to ease your conscience, I will murder you here and now—in spite of my curiosity."

"No, sir," Raymond replied seriously, not able to smile in response. "That is what I meant when I said you must tell me what to do. I may have the key to a door to safety for all of us, but I am not sure how I would be of the most use to you. I am ready to stay and fight on the walls. I am not afraid. But if I went to the king, could he not stop Sir Mauger?"

"I do not know," William said slowly. "The king might be reluctant to offend whoever lent the men to Mauger and say it is not his affair to interfere in domestic quarrels—which is true. Even if the king sent a writ, I am not sure Mauger would obey it."

"I can convince my uncle to send a writ no matter whose men are here," Raymond assured William with the insouciance of youth. "It is the second question I need answered."

"I cannot answer it," William said. "It depends on the state of the assault when the writ comes. If we have thrown Mauger back with losses, he probably would obey and take his case, claiming seduction and so forth, to the Church. If he is near success, he would ignore the writ, take the keep, and apologize humbly to the king afterward. He does not know that Richard would hunt him. I never told him Richard was my friend."

Only half William's mind was on his answer. He could not help wondering more and more why Henry had sent Raymond to him. As if reading his thoughts, Raymond flushed up again. "Alys knows," he said. This made William laugh at his own forgetfulness. The personal affairs of the young are far more important to them than matters that can make or break nations.

"I wanted to tell you," Raymond continued earnestly, "but both she and Martin told me to hold my tongue."

"Why?" William asked, so astonished he himself forgot for the moment that besiegers were ringing his keep.

"They both feared you would object to my offer and might send me away before your wounds were healed. Then if some emergency should arise, you—"

William groaned. His loving daughter and steward were saving him from himself again. Very well, but why had Raymond's status been kept a secret in the first place? The question brought another deep flush. Raymond had realized that he did not dare tell the truth and he *would* not lie to William.

"I will tell you my part of it, sir. There is another part—and it is true that I am much ashamed of permitting myself to be involved in that, but I beg you will not seek to know it. There can be no benefit to you in knowing and might be some hurt. Alys knows."

"There could be no hurt in telling Alys but might be hurt to me?"

"Women have no honor," Raymond said simply.

That was clear enough. William's lips tightened. Raymond had come for some purpose that would be considered an insult deep enough to lead to a challenge for combat. But Raymond had come from the king. William had not thought Henry knew he was alive. Richard must have been talking about him far too much. Anger washed over William. It was useless and dangerous to be angry with the king, but the king's messenger . . .

His eyes lifted to Raymond, who had carried the insult, and there was a sullen glare in them.

"Alys accepted this insult?" William's voice was low and cold. He was not sure which hurt was paramount— Raymond's deception or the fact that his daughter's love was fixed so firmly on the deceiver that she would swallow her father's dishonor.

The color had faded from Raymond's face, and he swallowed. "Not—not easily." He remembered the way Alys had wiped her hand after touching him—as if he were something slimy and leprous. The things she had said . . . Sweat beaded out on Raymond's forehead.

The great distress apparent in Raymond's expression soothed William. Doubtless when she knew the king was involved, Alys had agreed to keep Raymond's secret. That would not be for the sake of the deceiver but for his own sake, William knew. And plainly she had exacted a high price. It was very unlikely that Raymond would be so careless again. Alys must have scorched his ears good and proper from the look of him. William began to laugh. The immediate hurt eased; he knew that deception was scarcely Raymond's forte. All the abortive "Sirs—" in Wales came back to him.

Now that his rage had passed, William did not want to know how the king was involved, but his curiosity as to how Raymond had been inveigled into one of Henry's harebrained schemes warred with necessity. As it had in every case that led man from a naked wanderer to a builder of castles—curiosity won. "Can you tell me your part in a few words?" William asked, trying to temper desire with need.

Raymond had relaxed when William began to laugh. He knew his future father-by-marriage well now. William would never try to find out what the king's reason was; he would never again ask Raymond nor would he permit Alys to tell him, even if she wanted to. He knew also this was no time to begin to explain the situation in his family that had led to his escape from it, but he did not wish to refuse to answer either. Amusement lit his pale eyes.

He pursed his lips and brought out: "My mother would not let me be a man, so I left home without saying where I would go. King Henry sent me here because he did not think it likely news of me would get back to Aix, and he thought I would enjoy the Welsh war. Is that few enough words, sir?"

There was a little silence while William struggled with himself. He would have been better off if Raymond had said it was too difficult to explain. Then there would have been nothing for his mind to pick at. The clever devil had instead given him two large bones well furnished with food for thought to gnaw on.

"You—" William began, unsure of exactly how he would finish the sentence, but revelation came to him and his face became suffused with a happy smile. "You will deserve what you get if we all come out of this with whole skins and you do wed Alys. She will teach you to play with words."

A very faint qualm passed through Raymond, a slight premonition that marriage to Alys might not be all wine and roses. However, he was too much in love to want to examine the idea. "I will learn whatever she wishes to teach," he said sturdily, in true courtly lover style— which made William guffaw and feel he had got his revenge for Raymond's summary of his arrival. "But you must tell me," Raymond said, ignoring William's laughter, "whether I will be of more use to you here or whether I should try to reach my uncle."

The laughter died. William stood up abruptly. "I cannot tell you. All I can do is assure you that whether you go or stay, Alys will be in no danger."

He turned away, but he was tired and slow and Raymond caught him by the arm. "Sir William, in God's name, tell me what is best for you."

"I cannot!" William bellowed. "You are like a pagan priest asking a mother which of her children she prefers to lay on the altar."

"What?" Raymond breathed, nearly stunned—as

much by the sudden change in William's mood as by what he said.

The cords stood out in William's neck as he fought for control. All through the talk about Raymond's purpose and the half-jesting exchanges about Alys, something inside William had worked over the essential facts. "You are asking me," he said more quietly, "to tell you to go, which might cost your life if you are captured, to sacrifice you and, thus, Alys's happiness, to save Elizabeth. If you stay, Mauger will not harm a hair on your head. He will send you to the king, and once there, you can prevent him from forcing marriage on Alys. Yet, if I tell you to stay and the keep falls, Elizabeth must die."

"My lord," Raymond said, coming up close and seizing William's arms, "my dear lord, you are building phantoms out of your weariness. I cannot be in any greater danger if I try to leave Marlowe. Surely if I were caught I would be brought to Sir Mauger for questioning. I can tell my tale then, just as if I should be taken within the keep."

William's strained look eased, and he put his hands up to rub at his eyes. "That is true," he muttered, very aware that he had been yielding to despair before he was beaten. "That is true. And God knows, if you fought on the walls, you might be hurt or killed. Men strike first in the taking of a keep and ask questions later. Yes, then, yes, it would be better that you go. God! What a fool I am to waste time with all this talk. You must go as soon as we can make ready. Let me think what way would be best."

"I have thought of that," Raymond said quickly. "I will take the boat. If I can get it midriver, I can let it drift with the current until I am past the encampment. Then I can either buy a horse or hire boatmen, whichever is quickest. But, sir, you will lose a strong arm on the walls and—and I fear you cannot afford it."

Without answering, William went to a chest and took from it his strongbox, which he opened. He began to count out silver and copper. Embarrassed, Raymond protested. William looked up at him in surprise. "What has friendship to do with money? You have served me well and honestly. I owe you your hire whether you need it or not. I pay my rents to Richard, although we love each other. Why should I not pay you?"

Raymond shifted from foot to foot, uneasily. William's remarks were unanswerable, but it still seemed wrong to take money for hire from the man who, he hoped, would soon be his father-by-marriage. Noticing the boyish foot shuffling, William smiled and stopped counting. He was not insensitive and recognized that what might be right between equals, like himself and Richard, might be wrong between father and son. He pushed all the coins together, grabbed a large handful of copper, a smaller one of silver, and added two gold pieces.

"I see you do not like my reasons. Very well. As a father, I will provide for your needs—and you will need money to get to London quickly. I do not know whether Henry is there, but the officials of the Exchequer will know where he is."

As he handed over the money and suggested how Raymond distribute it to save himself from tempting robbers, part of his mind wondered whether he had been unfair and unkind to Richard all these years. Had his pride been satisfied by demeaning Richard's? Had he the right to belittle his friend's kindness and generosity by tacitly forbidding him to offer freely tokens of love? Not now, William thought, pushing aside the uncomfortable notions. Now it is needful to stay alive until I see Richard again. Then will be time enough to think if I have injured him and offer amends.

"Do you wish to say farewell to Alys?" William asked.

"Yes!" Raymond blurted, but before William could move he caught the older man's arm. "No."

William waited, studying Raymond's expression. "She will not trouble you with weeping or pleading," he said after a moment.

"I know that." Raymond's voice was indignant, and

William could not help smiling. Of course, Raymond would think Alys perfect. "I am not concerned for me but for her," Raymond went on more softly. "Will it be easier for her if I go without seeing her?"

"I am not a woman. I do not know. I can ask Elizabeth," William offered.

"Yes, ask." Raymond agreed eagerly.

He wanted very much to look once more on Alys, even if she would not permit him to touch her. Perhaps Lady Elizabeth would be shocked and refuse—although Lady Elizabeth was almost as remarkable a woman as Alys. The thought was rewarded by the sight of Elizabeth running past him, obviously to fetch Alys down. Having got what he wanted, Raymond was no longer sure he wanted it. What could he say to her? Would she realize the necessity of what he was doing or think he was deserting Marlowe in its time of need?

William left, returned in a few minutes saying something Raymond could not concentrate on about Martin and boatmen. Raymond suddenly was uncomfortably aware of the disorder of his dress—his chausses hanging loosely ungartered, the strings of his tunic protruding untidily through his unlaced mail. He was fumbling with those strings, trying to tie them or thrust them out of the way when Alys entered. Her face was pale as milk, her eyes unnaturally large and bright.

"William," Elizabeth said, following on Alys's heels, "you will want to speak to the men who are to go."

"Yes," he agreed, smiling and sliding an arm around her waist. Tactful Elizabeth would not say, *Leave the poor things alone,* but he really did want to oversee the final arrangements and be sure the men who were half asleep overlooked nothing.

"You are dressed all by guess," Alys murmured. "Let me help you."

"It was your father's choice," Raymond said. "He thought it more needful that I go to my uncle and get a writ to curb Sir Mauger than—"

She came up to him and drew his head down to kiss him. "Do you think I could love you if I did not know

that without telling?" Alys sighed as she broke away.
"Let me get cross garters for you, beloved. You cannot go—" her voice quivered and she paused and then went on steadily, "with your chausses in folds around your ankles. God knows the king will be ill pleased enough to hear—no! He must not hear!"

Alys had been trying to make a jest about her reputation as a housewife being damaged by Raymond appearing like a scarecrow, but she suddenly realized that, if Raymond told Henry he wanted to marry her, Henry would certainly do nothing to help them. Likely the king would far rather see all of them dead and buried than have his nephew make so unequal a marriage.

"What?" Raymond asked. "Not hear what? I must tell—"

"Tell what tale you like, except about me. Do not mention me or your wish to marry me. Pretend I do not exist, that my father has no daughter."

"Why?" Raymond asked, his face crimsoning. "Do not tell me that King Henry was the man who desired you. I cannot—"

"No, no!" Alys cried, appalled. "I swear the king has never set eyes upon me or, if he has, did not care to ask who I was."

"Then why? I am not ashamed of you! And it is none of Henry's business whom I marry! And I do not care what anyone—"

He received another kiss in thanks for his passion but also because it was the most effective way to stop his mouth. "No," Alys agreed, realizing it would be useless and dangerous to explain the true reasons for what she had said. "But remember that papa has not yet agreed. To tell the king the matter is settled, to use it, perhaps to hasten Henry's decision, might seem a device to force papa's hand. Papa will not like that. There is something else too. The king and queen could not know you would be so idiotic as to fall in love in a poor knight's household, yet they will be bitterly blamed for what is no fault of theirs by your father and mother."

"It was not idiotic," Raymond growled. "There is

nothing idiotic in falling in love with the most wonderful woman in the world."

Alys took his face between her hands. "Love speaks. Others might not think I am so wonderful. In any case, before they know me your parents must think the worst of me if they hear of your intentions from the king or queen. Please, Raymond, do not mention me. When we are safe and papa has made terms with you will be soon enough to tell the world."

"You are right. My aunt would write to my mother as fast as she could seize a quill and set it to parchment—and it would not matter whether she praised you or cursed you. That Eleanor rather than I should write such news would certainly throw my mama into a despair—and that would set my father against me. Oh, you are right, my love. I will have enough to do without taking time to write long letters of explanation. I will hold my tongue."

His arms went out and she came into them, raising her face for his kiss. After a moment she pulled away and hurried into her father's bedchamber. There had been the taste of salt tears mingled with the sweetness of her mouth. He was thrilled that Alys would cry over his departure when she had not wept over her father's, but he dreaded an emotional storm. Before he could decide whether to follow her to comfort her, she was out again, carrying a pair of cross garters and seeming perfectly calm except for her pallor.

"Pull up those chausses," she said.

Automatically, Raymond did as he was told and Alys tied the garters, rising when she was finished to show him dry eyes and a smile—a little fixed and meaningless, but a smile. She tied his tunic, settled his mail hood into more comfortable folds, and melted into his arms one last time.

"You need not fear for me," he murmured. "I would be worth more to Sir Mauger alive than dead."

When he had explained, Alys's smile was more real, although she knew if the boat was seen and overturned Raymond would never have a chance to be taken prisoner. He must be armed, yet armed he would sink like a stone. A discreet cough in the doorway made her stand away from Raymond, but she still held his hand.

"You need not fear for me either," she assured him. "No man will have me but you. Aubery would not take me against my will—we are too good friends for that. And if Mauger thinks he can kill Elizabeth and have me himself—well, a man comes naked to his wedding bed and even a little eating knife stuck in the neck—just there—" she touched Raymond's throat—"will kill."

Raymond loved Alys, but he really did not know her very well. He smiled fondly at her ferocity. He could afford to smile because he was sure he would get to the king, convince him, and get back in time to save Marlowe. He was young.

In the doorway, Martin drew in his breath sharply. He also loved Alys, but he knew her very well. He did not doubt for a minute that, if necessary, she would put on a face of such submission and sweetness that a man would come naked to her—and she would kill. He leaned against the door frame to still his trembling. He was old. He did not believe Raymond could convince the king and return in time to stop Mauger. Alys, the child of his heart, who had kissed his ugliness even when she was a baby and had nursed him as gently as a daughter in his sickness, would be damned for the mortal sin of murder.

"The dock is clear," Martin said. "The boat and all other things are ready."

CHAPTER 23

William looked out at the scurrying activity in Mauger's camp through the thin mist of early morning. After two days of watching, he knew Mauger had fewer men than he had feared, but more than he had hoped. Thinking back on Mauger's deficiencies as a leader in Wales, William had determined to try to hold the walls. Mauger's men might be no better than his; the frantic and sometimes seemingly aimless way they buzzed about the camp certainly indicated poor leadership. William glanced right and left along the walls. What he saw gave him little comfort. The materials for resistance were ready, but the men . . .

They were not fools or cowards, not most of them, but they knew nothing. If Howard were alive and Sir Peter, and Raymond had been there as well, there would have been little danger that Marlowe would fall despite the fact that they were few and inexperienced. With someone to tell them what to do and give them heart and example, most would fight bravely. But there was no one except himself and Diccon, and no one man could be at all places at all times. Even if he had been completely well . . .

That was no way to think, William told himself. He was better, much better. Again he swept the wall with his eyes. The veterans, widely spaced out except for a few to guard special danger points, would help, but he still had not quite decided whether he should be at the point of greatest weakness or the place which, if taken, would lead to the greatest danger.

Here by the tower that controlled the drawbridge and portcullis? There was no need to fear the use of a ram. Mauger would need to fill the moat to use a ram and he was in too much of a hurry for that. Mauger would want to take the tower, of course, because that would make it easy to bring in his whole force with little loss and cut off the defenders' retreat to the keep. William could see several of the curved supports that would bridge the moat and hold the scaling ladders just across from where he stood. There were more ways than one to take the tower, however. Put enough men on the wall at any place and the defenders could be swamped. They were so few.

The weakest spot was where the moat ended. To the east, there was a huge outcropping of solid rock, the heart of the rise on which Marlowe stood. William could not see it with his eyes, but it was perfectly clear in his mind. Because it would have taken many years to break through that deep enough to continue the moat, William's father had compromised with a trench a mere ten feet deep. It had some water in it, perhaps enough to deceive a stranger, but Mauger knew Marlowe well. Although there was no sign that he intended to concentrate his attack at that point, William was sure that was a pretense. Should he be there instead of at the tower?

The one and only bright spot in a dark future was that William was reasonably sure Raymond had made good his escape. In the morning after the young knight had gone, William had called the men together and told them that help was on its way. They had only to hold out for a few days. He was not nearly as sure as he sounded, but it was necessary to provide some hope or even the experienced men-at-arms would begin to think about yielding rather than facing a certain defeat and probable death.

Suddenly William stiffened to full alert. The men in the camp had stopped their scurrying about and were gathering efficiently into groups. Calls came from around the walls warning that the form of activity of the enemy had changed all over the field. William watched for a second or two longer, hardly believing his eyes. Apparently Mauger was going to start the attack at once. William had thought it would take at least a day or two more to be ready. Cursing himself for a fool, he turned and bellowed for all to arm and take their places. From below, Diccon's voice repeated the order and the quiet bailey erupted into frenetic activity. Mauger was cleverer than he seemed, William thought bitterly, not knowing that the mercenary captains had done most of the planning. All that scurrying about had been a pretense to make it seem the attack was not ready. Behind that screen of activity the bulk of the men were arming and positioning.

Archers were already at the edge of the moat, kneeling to aim. A cloud of arrows rose. William half lifted his shield, but most fell short. The new men flinched and dodged, watching the sky instead of concentrating on the ladders being raised. Worst of all, the arrows flew only one way. It was a bitter thing to watch helplessly, knowing that archers on the walls could do ten times the damage. An arrow shot downward gained force. Had William had a hundred archers, it might have been impossible for Mauger's men to raise the scaling ladders at all. A hundred? He did not have twenty who could use a bow with effect. Those he had taken to Wales, and most had died there. The few archers he had were at work. Here and there around the walls a single arrow flew forth. One could hardly see them against the cloud coming in.

One man carrying the device to span the moat cried out and clapped a hand to his shoulder. Another took his place so swiftly that the heavy structure did not even tilt. The other men called jeers and insults. One lousy arrow could not frighten them. William ground his teeth, watching the attack move forward and knowing himself powerless to impede it. His own men were pelting up the stairs to the walls now. His head swung back and forth, now watching the moat spanners being moved into place, now checking on the defenders racing up from the bailey.

Diccon was still below. William could hear him roaring at the less agile—or more reluctant—to hurry.

Then the servingmen began to pour out of the fore-building and the sheds. They had knives and leather jerkins—those who had any form of armor or weapons at all—but they could push ladders, throw stones, help tip the cauldron of hot oil near the tower over onto those who were climbing the wall.

William flinched as an arrow struck his shoulder, but it did not bite through his mail. That was a piece of luck. The men who had taken up position nearest him took heart from the incident and looked out at the attackers rather than up above. There was now more noise outside the walls than inside them. Some spans were set and the men cheered and shouted to each other as ladders were maneuvered across and fastened to them to provide a path so that other ladders could be raised against the walls. William drew his sword.

The quiet around him was ominous. He had defended keeps before. Some men were always quiet before fighting, but most yelled and cursed at the attackers, either in real contempt or to keep up their spirits. There was not, William feared, enough spirit in these poor creatures gleaned from the town and the fields and hardly trained, to raise by any normal means. Well, at least he had not overlooked that problem.

A ladder was wavering upward some fifty feet away on the opposite side of the tower. The men near it stood still, as if mesmerized. William ran through the door on his side, crossed the tower, came out on the other wall bellowing obscenities and instructions. Roused by his voice, the defenders sprang into action. Two seized long poles with which they hoped to catch the ladder and overturn it. Three others converged on the area, drawing their weapons. One, with a terrified look behind him, ran for the wooden stairs that went down into the bailey. William's sword point caught him in the belly.

"One more step and you die long and hard. I swear to you, you have a better chance if you fight."

The man whimpered, then drew his own weapon and turned back seemingly now ready to fight. William let out his breath slowly, not daring to sigh lest someone notice and a new panic ensue.

"Watch that ladder!" William roared.

The men had thrust it away once, but it was rising again. William's order, however, was drowned in a series of crashes as all the wooden stairs were pulled sharply to the ground except the one running down the end of the wall that joined the southwest tower of the keep. There was a chorus of oaths and gasps of fear, but William smiled. No live man would come off the walls of Marlowe except through the gate tower or down the last stair, which Hugo and Artur, two long-time veterans, would defend.

"Now you fight or you die," William shouted, as Diccon burst out of the tower followed by the crew of veterans who had helped him demolish the stairs.

William clapped Diccon on the shoulder as they passed each other, and the master-at-arms smiled grimly but did not pause. He went around to the east to direct the men in the section William could not see. The veterans spread themselves thinly along the wall, Arnald and Rolf remaining near the door of the tower both to defend it from enemies and to discourage any of the frightened recruits from trying to escape down the stairs inside. William crossed back through the tower to his section of the wall. He was barely in time to avert another catastrophe.

The new men might be inexperienced, but the most intelligent that could be found with the proper physique had been chosen. They had quickly grasped the meaning of the demolished stairs. Now all had their weapons out and were determined not to allow an enemy on the wall, reasoning that the men on the ladders would be unable to fight back effectively. To a limited extent this was true, but in their fear and excitement they had forgotten that the best way to deal with scaling ladders was to push them off the wall before they were so weighted with men that they became too heavy to move.

"Poles," William bellowed. "Cod-sucking lumps! Push them off with the poles."

This galvanized about half the men into activity, while the others gaped, getting in the way. By the time they were organized, one ladder was solid with attackers. William sprang toward that shouting orders to the men with the poles to try another angle and attempt to tip the ladder sideways. He cursed them furiously when their efforts proved futile, but knew it was not all their fault. Bracing himself to meet the coming attack, William urged the pole wielders toward another ladder that was rising.

Tactical considerations aside, William was not sorry to face some living foes. For three days his feeling of frustrated helplessness had been bottled up, generating a rage to which he could give no expression. God knew, there was not a fault to be found with Alys or Elizabeth, and to rage at the men would have frightened them witless and made them even more useless.

The top of a helmet appeared at the crenel. William licked his lips as if he would taste the blood he was about to shed and drove his sword forward, just as the unprotected face showed. He had his blood. It spatted wall and blade as the sword broke through nose and cheekbone. The man did not even cry out, pain and shock loosening his handhold on the wall so that he toppled backward in silence. The next man could not be taken so easily. Warned that there was more than an inexperienced know-nothing above him, he was now coming up under his raised shield and William could not get at him from the side. However, there was no way to come over the wall without gripping it. Instead of slashing at the shield, William waited until the man put his hand on the merlon; then he cut the hand off. When the man screamed and jerked in agony, William took his head off.

Along the wall, things were not going equally well. Some ladders had been overturned, but some were disgorging men onto the wall while the defenders were busy in other places. Now William realized he should never have tried to hold the walls. This was as clever and deadly an assault plan as he had ever seen. Either

Mauger had hidden his true knowledge and experience very well for many years, or he had gotten very expert help indeed.

Desperately William strove to keep his own section clear, which was growing more difficult because a second ladder had been successfully raised nearby, and to shout orders and instructions. It soon became horribly clear that those were of little help. Unlike Raymond or Harold or Sir Peter, these men were not listening for his voice. There was too much noise, too many shrieks of agony, too many shouts of success, too much clashing and clanging as blows struck shields or went awry and metal met stone. The men were fighting better than he expected, desperation generating bravery, but it was no good. He must try to organize them for retreat.

William surged forward, striking down one man as he climbed over the wall and killing another by nearly decapitating him from the back. A third whirled to face him, and William held him for a few seconds, sword striking shield, until one of his own men came up and stabbed him from the rear.

"Keep together," he roared at the men. "You cannot keep them from coming over. Keep together and fight your way toward me."

He had temporarily relieved the pressure on the men nearest him, and they were transmitting his orders down the length of the wall. He could do no more for the men except keep the route of escape clear. Cursing, he turned back and cursed again as he saw the men coming up the ladders had been more agile than he had counted on. There was already an enemy man-at-arms between him and the tower door with two more half over the wall. He struck the nearest climber on the back of the neck with his shield, grunting with pain as he felt his shoulder wound tear open.

It was the beginning of the end for him, William knew, as the warmth of oozing blood spread with the pain. The loss of blood would add to his weakness and fatigue until his will could drive his body no further.

For now, it did not matter. William brought his mailed foot down as hard as he could on the face of the man he had felled, feeling a vicious satisfaction as the bones crunched. That one would not rise to strike him in the back. That stamp was all part of a single forward movement that brought his raised sword in reach of the second climber.

Bent, the man struck at William with his shield. He had no weapon in hand because one hand was necessary for holding onto the wall he was climbing over. William leaned back a little, just enough to avoid the edge of the shield, then snapped forward, thrusting at the man's unprotected breast. Instinctively he jerked back—but there was no back, nothing except empty air, and he fell, wailing. Perhaps he knew he had a minor revenge, that in trying to save himself his shield had hit William's violently, further jarring his sore shoulder. If he knew, perhaps he had a moment's satisfaction before he sank in the waters of the moat.

The man who was nearly at the tower door turned, realizing he could not get through in time to avoid William, who would surely thrust through his unprotected back. They traded blows, the man-at-arms far more anxious to defend himself than to harm William. Time was on his side. More of his comrades were already climbing up and would soon be over the wall so that William would be surrounded.

His caution undid him. William knew as well as his enemy that he had only a minute or two to finish his man and put the door of the gate tower at his back. He struck out furiously with shield and sword at his opponent's right side, blow after blow. Dodging and weaving, the man was driven to the left, more to the left. He saw that William was working his way around so that their positions would soon be reversed. Trying to avoid that, he advanced a step and struck out harder himself, but he was still buying time and safety, concentrating on the wall and the tower door. His attention was on guarding his right side; he was unprepared for William's sudden charge straight forward, for the strong forward thrust of William's shield. He staggered back and back again to avoid a sword thrust that brought the point rather than the sharpened edge to bear. He was puzzled by the gesture, which he caught easily on his shield—puzzled until William straightened his powerful right arm, lunged forward with the full strength of his body, and pushed him right over the inner edge of the battlement. He understood then, in the second before the terror of falling and the agony of ceasing to fall ended all understanding.

Before his opponent had disappeared, William whirled back to his post, only to confront still another man who had just come over the wall. He was still gasping with the effort of his previous furious attack, trying to dismiss the pain in his shoulder and the growing sensation that his arms were made of cold porridge while his sword and shield were weighted with lead. Desperately he looked down the wall, but none of the retreating groups was near enough to help him.

That bitter truth was a spark to relight the rage of hopeless frustration. William charged forward, no longer much aware of pain or weakness. It was fortunate his sudden action, after what had seemed an initial decision to wait for an attack to be made on him, so surprised his opponent that William's second backhand blow disabled him. However little he felt his disabilities, they were slowing him, making him clumsy. He caught another man at a disadvantage and disposed of him also. Then he was momentarily free.

He released the handgrip of his shield and sought the horn that hung around his neck. His grasp on it was awkward, the shield dragging painfully by its elbow strap. One half second longer he delayed to glance again down the wall and across—nothing had changed, at least not for the better. It was bitter, bitter, bitter to be driven from his own walls. But the sun—he had not noticed before that the sun had burned away the thin morning mist—the sun was glistening on more and more of the metal bands that strengthened the hardened leather of the common soldiers' helmets. If he did not blow now, he might never have another chance.

The horn came up. Pure and sweet William blew the *mort*. The hunt was done. The animal was dead— only this time Marlowe was the hunted animal.

On the same day that Mauger had finally been granted an audience with King Henry, both William's messengers found Richard of Cornwall in York. He had finished his work with the Scottish monarch and nobles and was riding south slowly, enjoying the early autumn weather and showing his young wife her new country. Surprised by two messengers, Richard read both of William's letters immediately. One had been written in the morning, the other in the evening of the same day. Apparently in those few hours, William's whole life had fallen apart and been remade. No, that was wrong, Richard thought, looking from the brief, stiff note of the morning to the tumbling, passionate words of the later letter. The stone facade of William's private life had been torn away, exposing the jumble underneath.

Richard had known of Elizabeth, of course. He had listened to William hour after hour and tried to comfort him over the first unhappy months of his marriage to Mary. Little by little the complaints had died away. Naturally enough, Richard had assumed that William had become accustomed to Mary and his feelings for his childhood love had grown into indifference. As the years passed, Richard had forgotten that Elizabeth ever existed. William had seemed perfectly normal, no more indifferent to his wife than most men.

Only, now that he looked back, Richard realized there had always been certain peculiarities in William's behavior. Right after he had been married, and for about five years after that, William had gone home to Marlowe as infrequently as possible and when he was at home any excuse would draw him away. Then, quite suddenly, that had changed. Richard looked at the second letter and nodded. Yes, ten years. The woman had returned to Hurley ten years ago, and just at that time William had developed a most peculiar reluctance to come to court, to go to war, to do anything at all that would take him away from Marlowe.

So, it had been the woman all along. Richard had assumed that William had developed a conscience about his estate just about the time that Richard had begun to realize his own duties and responsibilities both for his lands and for the realm at large. The question was what to do about it. How to avert disaster? A divorce or annulment on decent grounds must be obtained. That should not be too difficult. With the evidence that the mistress and the maid could give to force the husband to be compliant, he could be urged to discover a "prior contract" or something similar, something his father had done, perhaps, and not told him about that would permit an annulment and an arrangement for the sons to be legitimated.

The haste of the second messenger bothered Richard. The man had made up ten hours of time, riding for a day and a half without stopping except to change horses when the beasts tired. Yet William said nothing of any special need for haste and he knew how dilatory was the Church. It would not matter whether Richard spoke to Boniface today—which was naturally impossible—or next week. With all the prodding in the world, it would still take the Church several months, perhaps a year, to grant the decree. And it would be necessary to apply pressure to this—Richard looked at the letter again—this Mauger first.

Mauger—the husband! Richard got up from his chair suddenly. What an idiot I am, he thought. William believed I was still involved in the treaty arrangements in Scotland. He could not ask me to hurry that, but the husband will not sit there tamely waiting to be threatened. Naturally, he will try to protect himself. War? Not likely unless he could get help. Marlowe was very strong, too strong to be assaulted by one knight's forces. He would go to the Church or the king for redress—but which? Then he started for the door of the chamber. A stupidity to waste time asking himself such a question. If he went to London he would find both king and Church at once. Richard beckoned to his chief squire and told him to pass the word that they would ride on straight toward London tomorrow morning. It remained only to explain the matter to Sancia.

Here Richard expected some resistance. Since he set about Henry's business in the spring, Sancia had seen very little of him until about a week ago—and she did not hesitate to say that she did not like it. Of course, Richard was flattered by his bride's fondness for his company, but it was she who had suggested that they come south by easy stages, stopping here and there as it suited them for a few days. Probably she would not be pleased at the change in plans. Richard told William's story as persuasively as possible, with no caustic references to "the woman" or "sirens."

Sancia listened breathlessly. "For twenty years?" she repeated. "Has William really loved her for twenty years?"

"He says so, and I have never known William to lie." Richard answered a little stiffly, thinking Sancia was going to laugh, to belittle his credulity.

Instead her eyes filled with tears and she sighed. "Oh, it is just like the romances. Aucassin was true just so, and sought his love over the whole world. Of course, William did not have to seek Elizabeth, but he stayed nearby—did he not, Richard?"

"He most certainly did," Richard replied wryly. "God knows, I offered him everything—wealth, position, everything—to keep him by me, but he only wanted to stay on that little dish of an estate. Only when I ordered him to war or said I needed him would he come to me for longer than a few days at a time. I thought he was overanxious about caring for his lands." Richard burst out laughing. "Why the devil did he not tell me? I think I would have had the accursed husband *murdered* just to get William to act as marshal for me."

"He could not tell," Sancia breathed, her dark eyes

wide with romantic fervor, "for that would darken his lady's name. So true a heart would never tell."

"No."

Richard had no intention of saying anything to disturb Sancia's sweet dream of courtly love conventions come to life, but guilt lashed him. William would have told him if he had ever asked. He realized now that there had been times when he suspected William was carrying some heavy burden. He had told himself that it would be wrong to pry if William did not speak of his own accord, but it was not truly that. Richard knew he had been too much taken up with problems of his own—with his brother, with his vassals and estates. He had piled many of those problems on William and resented the fact that William would not carry even more of his burdens. This spring he had *known* William was in trouble, yet he had ridden back to Wallingford to spend the night in Sancia's bed rather than listen and try to help.

"You do not mind that he did not tell you? Oh, Richard, do not be angry. He could not—not because he did not trust you but—but—but it *must* be secret!"

Richard smiled at her. "No, my love, I am not angry—at least not with William."

"Can we help?" Sancia asked, her brow wrinkled with thought. "I know that the romances all end sadly, but—but these are real people. I like William. I do not wish to lament over his grave."

"Sancia!" Richard exclaimed, suddenly feeling cold. "William is in no danger of dying, nor Elizabeth either, since she is safe in Marlowe now. Of course we will do something. That is what I came to tell you. We must go to London as quickly as you can travel in comfort. I will speak to Henry and to Boniface and see if we can arrange a divorce or an annulment of Elizabeth's marriage in such a way that the sons are protected."

"Yes, indeed," Sancia's eyes brightened. "And I will get Eleanor to help also. She can do more with Henry sometimes—specially on a matter like this—than you could."

Richard burst out laughing again and swept his wife into his arms. Sancia was a perfect delight, a compendium of everything good in a woman—innocent, foolish, loving—and practical in strange, womanly ways.

CHAPTER 24

It seemed to Raymond in his haste and anxiety that everything had gone wrong from the moment he touched Alys's hand in silent farewell and stepped off the dock into the boat. The journey was a nightmare in slow time. Of course, Raymond knew objectively that each hour in his mind was no more than a few minutes in reality. He could see that the stars had not shifted in the sky and he could hear sounds from the shore—voices dimly and occasionally the clang of metal or the thud of a wheeled cart jolting over a stone. The sounds proved they were not past the men Mauger was bringing, but that hardly reconciled Raymond to their slow progress. He was beginning to believe that the armed train was miles long, that there would be thousands of men, that they had come prepared for war, perhaps with siege towers as well as ladders. If such a force were arrayed against Marlowe, it could not hold out for an hour.

When they were finally past the incoming men and silence was no longer imperative, Raymond urged the boatmen to speed. They did their best, but the river loops and bends, and there were obstacles invisible in the dark. Too often they struck, stuck, and needed to struggle to push the boat free, losing time. As soon as the sun came up, Raymond knew he could not endure the seemingly leisurely process any longer and told the men to make for land.

"Windsor, lord," one man said, pointing down the river and watching Raymond's face to see if he understood. "Windsor. The king stays sometimes."

After a moment's struggle, Raymond agreed. Apparently William had told the men to make for Windsor.

Of course, he must have. It was one of Henry's favorite residences, Raymond remembered, and William must have known they would reach it soon after first light. Even if the king was not there, perhaps someone would know where he was. And Raymond could almost certainly buy a horse at Windsor.

He was quite right on both counts. A clerk in the castle was able to tell Raymond that the king was in Westminster and was expected to remain there for a week or more. Raymond also found a good horse furnished with a respectable saddle. Raymond did not complain of the price, although he knew he was being grossly cheated. In spite of so quickly learning the king's whereabouts and finding a horse, Raymond was near frantic with disappointment. His hopes had been so high; he had convinced himself that the king would be at Windsor and that he could ride back to Marlowe that same day with the writ. Thus, he still felt everything had gone wrong and that he would be too late, long too late to help Sir William or save Alys.

Nonetheless, he rode off at once. He had not slept since the preceding night nor eaten for many hours. The landlord of the inn at Windsor had offered food to so generous a buyer, but Raymond could not choke it down and would not wait a minute after the saddle had been set on the horse's back. His haste brought him to Westminster just before the gates were closed at dark, but his anxious inquiries for the king coupled with his simple dress caused the guards to conceal smiles and direct him to a side office. The guards were accustomed to simple provincial knights who believed the king was available to anyone who asked to speak to him. Thus Raymond fell into the hands of an officious clerk, who passed him to another clerk.

It did not take Raymond long to realize that talking to this second pompous fool was getting him no nearer to Henry. He began to bellow with rage, and Theobald of Hurley, who was just leaving his writing table in an inner chamber to go to Henry, strode out to see who dared cause such a disturbance among the king's clerks.

His haughty announcement of who he was met with an even greater display of fury.

"I do not care who you are," Raymond screamed. "*I* am Raymond d'Aix, blood-bound to the queen. I must see the king. Now! At once! I do not know what idiot sent me here among a bunch of tonsured fools, but you will lack heads instead of just hair if you do not direct me to where the king is."

"Many men wish to see the king," Theobald said, raising his head and looking down his nose. "This is the office where such appointments are made. It is our purpose to spare King Henry importunity. All sorts of lies and threats—"

The statement ended in a squawk as Raymond vaulted the table behind which Theobald had been standing and took him by the throat. The other clerks set up a clamor, but Raymond had dragged Theobald out of the chamber, shaking him as a terrier shakes a rat. In the courtyard, he relaxed his grip enough so that Theobald would not lose his senses.

"Which building?" he grated. "We are going alive together, or I will leave you here dead and find another guide. I tell you I am nephew to the queen. If I am not, you will have your revenge."

Nephew! Theobald now remembered the king had mentioned a nephew of the queen's in relation to the business of Sir Mauger's. Merciful Mary, had Mauger done something to annoy the queen's nephew? Theobald began to utter a cringing apology, but Raymond's hand tightened on his throat again, and he gagged and scuttled in the direction of the king's private chambers.

Henry was sitting at his ease in the inner chamber, alone, for he had been expecting Theobald. He did not turn his head immediately when the clerk said, "Sire," and thus was utterly astonished when Raymond pushed past, crying, "Uncle Henry, I need help."

"Raymond!"

Before his uncle could rise and embrace him, Raymond flung himself down on his knees and raised his hands in the formal gesture of supplication.

"Good God, Raymond, what is wrong? What have you done? Stand up, boy, do not kneel there like a fool." Henry stood up himself and pulled Raymond upright.

"Done? I have done nothing wrong!" Raymond exclaimed. "And neither has Sir William, yet he is besieged without strength to withstand the attack and will die if you do not help him."

"Sir William again, eh?" Henry said, his face hardening. "Done nothing, has he? Has he not his neighbor's wife in his keep?"

"Yes, Lady Elizabeth fled to him because her husband held her prisoner and wished to starve her to death. Sire, the man is a monster. I have a tale to tell of his doings that is years long, but there is no time for that. You sent me to Marlowe to test Sir William's heart. I tell you it is the truest heart in the realm."

"Sir William loves me well, does he?" Henry asked sardonically. Raymond's slightly hysterical exaggeration was pushing him into Mauger's side again. It certainly implied a warping of Raymond's judgment. "No doubt he speaks widely of my wisdom and goodness."

"No, he does not," Raymond replied, swallowing nervously. He was so frantic that he did not recognize the trap that Henry had laid for him, but he had been set a task and had agreed to do it. His answers must be as honest as he could make them. "I do not remember that he spoke particularly of you at any time, except once when Earl Richard was visiting—"

"Richard visited Sir William? When?"

"In the spring. He wished Sir William to act as quartermaster to the force he was sending to Wales. At that time, Sir William spoke of you just as he should—he said that you did your duty as king. Sire, I will answer your doubts at large later. I swear to you the man is honest and loyal. He stinted neither men nor service in Wales but went gladly—"

"And returned more gladly, saying he was wounded to death for a scratch or two—"

"Scratch?" Raymond gasped. His voice rose as he

forgot in his surprise and indignation to whom he was speaking. "He was near death! I dressed his wounds on the way."

"A man near death does not ride hundreds of miles," Henry snapped.

"He did not ride, Sire." This time Raymond spoke respectfully. Partly he remembered William remonstrating with Richard about his manner to the king (and feeling considerable sympathy for Richard suddenly) and partly he, himself, realized that angering Henry would scarcely accomplish his purpose. "Nor was it Sir William's decision to leave Wales," he continued quietly. "He was, by that time, too ill to decide anything. It was the earl of Hereford's decision. There had been several attempts on Sir William's life—"

"Raymond, you are bewitched! I swear the man is a sorcerer. All he does is good, whatever it is, even to taking another man's wife."

"Bewitched?" Raymond was shaken for a moment, thinking of Alys's beauty. Was he seeing her father through her eyes? But how could Henry know about Alys? For that matter, how could he know about Lady Elizabeth. "Has Sir Mauger been here before me?" he asked.

Henry turned away without answering. A king does not have to explain himself to others!

"Sire, I beg you to hear both sides," Raymond pleaded. "At least stop Sir Mauger's attack until the evidence against him can be heard. Summon Sir William and examine him yourself. Ask the earl of Hereford about his service in Wales and his wounds."

Henry had been standing with his back to Raymond, but at the mention of Hereford he turned to face his nephew-by-marriage. Here he was on firm ground. "I have already written to Hereford—many days ago." That was not true; it was only four days, but Henry wanted Raymond to believe his next statement. "I expect a report from him at any moment. When that comes, I shall be better able to decide."

"Thank God!" Raymond exclaimed with such fervor

that Henry became decidedly uneasy. "But if you do not stop Sir Mauger's attack, it may be too late to do Sir William justice. I tell you, Marlowe is near naked. We had, perhaps, fifty veteran men-at-arms, and I found near a hundred more men willing to serve, but they were all untrained. Sire, I beg you, give order that Sir Mauger hold his hand."

Henry was growing more and more uneasy. Raymond's enthusiasm for Hereford's judgment certainly meant that Sir William had been severely wounded and Hereford had sent him home. That meant that Mauger had lied about that. Probably the man had lied about everything except his stolen wife. Then he was seized by a sudden dreadful qualm. Richard must be in London by now. He had not seen his brother yet, but Sancia had written to Eleanor to say they were only a day's ride away. When had that been? Yesterday? The day before? If Richard and Raymond met . . .

But there was a way out of the dilemma. It was obvious from the way Raymond was phrasing his plea that he did not know the men with Mauger were the king's own mercenaries. All Henry need do was recall them and keep Raymond and Richard both in London until the men dispersed. If Mauger had lied to him, he deserved to be deserted. Henry felt he had a right to be avenged against such a liar, who had led him into an unjust act against his brother's dear friend. Sir Mauger must suffer for that crime! And if Sir Mauger—instead of Sir William—was dead, he could never mention that the men were the king's.

"Yes, you are right. I will," Henry said.

"Thank you, uncle, thank you," Raymond cried, going down on his knee and kissing Henry's hand.

Henry smiled at him, puffing his chest out a little. He had decided the right thing now. Raymond was behaving most properly and Richard would be very pleased. No doubt the suspicion against Sir William had been planted in his mind apurpose. He had been very wise to send Raymond to sift out the truth without acting against Sir William.

"Will you have the writ prepared now so I can take it back?" Raymond begged.

"You take it? By no means!"

"But I must go back, I must!" Raymond's voice rose hysterically.

Because Henry had convinced himself he was blameless, he was free of preoccupation and really saw Raymond, saw the travel-stained garments, the sunken eyes, the greenish tinge under the swarthy skin that betrayed the young knight's exhaustion. The king, who was truly kind of heart when his childish pride and spite were not roused, put his arm around Raymond's shoulders.

"Now, now," he soothed, "let me go about this in my own way."

"Why cannot I go? I must see what has befallen them."

"And so you shall," Henry agreed patiently, seeing his way clearly now and well pleased with himself, "when you are rested. When did you last eat or sleep, Raymond?"

"What does it matter? I will not fail, I promise you. My horse is foredone, but if you will lend me another——"

"Raymond, have some sense," Henry laughed. "Sir Mauger knows you as Sir William's hireling. If you come with a writ from me, would he believe you? Would he not more likely think it was some forgery? a trick? Certainly he could say it was—and who would fault him?" Henry knew that was not true. He had identified Raymond as his nephew, but Raymond did not know that. "When truce is declared, you can go back," the king promised.

"But I will not know if the writ came in time. Let me go back with your messenger. Let me——"

"No. You look like a wakened dead man. You must eat and sleep. Then we will see. Now do not argue with me, Raymond, or you will make me believe Sir William *has* ensorcelled you. And the more time I spend arguing with you the later the writ will be prepared."

That silenced Raymond and he stood biting the knuckles of his hand while Henry went to the door and bellowed for Michael Belet, to whom he introduced his nephew-by-marriage. Belet was not pleased at the arrival of another of the queen's relations, although he did not remember having seen Raymond before. Nonetheless, he bowed politely as he received the king's orders that Raymond be suitably lodged, fed, and clothed.

"Go," Henry said, shoving Raymond toward the door.

"The writ," Raymond begged.

"Yes, yes," the king soothed and told Belet to fetch Theobald first.

As he said the name of the clerk, a bell rang in the king's head. It was Theobald who had told him the tale about Sir William in the first place and who had brought Sir Mauger to see him. A black frown darkened Henry's face as the clerk entered and Belet led Raymond out. Henry trusted Theobald, and he did not like to have his judgment shown to be mistaken.

Seeing the scowl on the king's face, Theobald made an instant decision to cast Sir Mauger to the wolves and save his own skin. He had had considerable time to think, and his explanation of the entire matter was very smooth. By the time he was done retracting and withdrawing and apologizing, Henry was preening himself and feeling he was not at all a fool if his clever clerk had been deceived and, unknowingly, had deceived him. He forgave Theobald, who was humbly begging pardon. Then, glowing with righteousness and magnanimity, he told Theobald to send one of his squires for Philip d'Arcy and to obtain materials and prepare his Great Seal for a writ bidding Mauger to abandon his attack on Marlowe.

In the outer chamber, impervious to Belet's pleading, Raymond waited. "Let me be," he snarled at the royal butler. "I will choke on food and lie sleepless anyway until I see done what must be done."

This was most uncomfortable hearing, and Belet slipped away to inform a group of his friends that another relative of the queen was waiting for some grant from the king—and, from his nervousness, it must be a great matter. There was a general helpless gnashing of teeth and glaring at Raymond—who was totally unconscious of the violent feelings he had aroused. Then, one of the men remembered that Richard of Cornwall was in London, a few minutes away, and he rushed out to fetch the king's brother. Perhaps Earl Richard could dissuade Henry from giving away too much.

Richard came at once. He had intended to present himself the following day, not wishing to seem to rush in only to ask a favor. "There is the man," the courtier who had summoned Richard hissed, pointing, "the queen's nephew."

Richard glanced quickly in the direction indicated and stopped dead in his tracks. "Raymond!" he bellowed. "Raymond d'Aix! Damn! I knew I had seen that face before."

Raymond swung around from his fixed concentration on the door of the king's inner chamber and uttered a cry of joy. "Earl Richard!" He rushed across the room, stumbling with weariness. "Thank God you are come! Thank God! Marlowe is under attack and cannot stand."

"What? But William never—"

"We were not under attack when Sir William wrote," Raymond hurried on breathlessly. "We hoped Sir Mauger would not be able to find the men or that it would take him long—but it happened so fast. There was no time to—"

"What are you doing here if Marlowe is besieged? When did this happen?"

"The men came last night—was it last night? I have lost count of time, my lord. When I saw there was no hope of driving them away, I told Sir William that I was the queen's nephew and—"

In the shock of hearing about the attack, Richard had forgotten why he had been summoned. "What was the queen's nephew doing, acting as a hireling knight? Why did you lie to William? to me?"

Raymond wavered on his feet. "It is so long a tale," he sighed.

Suddenly Richard's black eyes were cold and calculating. "My brother sent you," he said softly, remembering what William had told him. "And he would not send his nephew-by-marriage to be trained to take the place of castellan in the little keep of Bix, which is of no importance. Nor do I remember ever having mentioned William's need to Henry. Why were you sent to Marlowe?"

Tired as Raymond was, the deadly cold anger in Richard's voice sounded alarm bells in his head. That the rage should fall upon him was not so bad, but it could not touch him without touching Henry—and that would be a disaster for everyone. Raymond did not like to lie, but to bend the truth just a little to accomplish a great good could not be wrong.

"The king had heard a lying tale about Sir William—wait, my lord," Raymond cried as Richard's lips drew back from his teeth in a vicious snarl. "Do not think ill where no ill was intended. I *was* sent to watch, but to watch for enemies of Sir William as much as to watch Sir William. My lord, the king *could* not take the chance that someone had perverted a man you love so dear—and he would not take the chance that someone intended harm to your dear friend either."

"But why the stealth?" Richard wanted to believe Raymond's explanation. His voice was eager now instead of angry.

"How could he do otherwise?" Raymond asked. "If the king said to you he had heard ill of Sir William, would you not have flown into a rage? You would have listened to neither side—not that Sir William was to blame nor that another wished ill to Sir William. As now, you would have blamed your brother for listening at all. Yet, someone did wish Sir William ill. When the lying tale seemed to have no effect, Sir Mauger tried three or four times to kill him in Wales. I cannot say I saved Sir William's life. He is a strong man and saved himself—but I helped him, at least, and there would not have been any help if the king had not sent me."

"That is true," Richard admitted wryly. "I would have jumped down poor Henry's throat before he could explain." Then he frowned. "But all this does not explain what you are doing here now. You said Marlowe was besieged?"

"Yes. Sir William sent me out before the net was drawn tight. I came to ask the king to forbid the attack until the evidence concerning Lady Elizabeth could be sifted. That, too, is a long tale—and horrible."

"I know about that. William's letter was full of it. But what are you doing here in the antechamber? Has Henry refused to see you?" Richard's dark eyes were dangerous again.

"No, no," Raymond said hastily. "He saw me at once and the writ is being prepared now, but—but I could not go to eat and sleep as the king desired. I cannot rest. I fear Marlowe is fallen—and if it is," Raymond's voice shook, "Mauger will kill them."

"So bad as that?"

"We had nothing. It happened so fast. The men I gathered were all untrained louts, and there was no time for the trained men to come from Bix—" He covered his face with his hands and fought sobs. "It cannot stand! It cannot!"

What Raymond said was very serious, but Richard realized that Raymond was near hysteria and collapse from worry and fatigue, and he discounted more than half his urgency. No doubt attackers had ringed Marlowe and the keep was not well prepared, but Marlowe was very strong and William knew his business in matters of defense. Also, it was not possible to assault a keep five minutes after the attacking force arrived. That was all fear in Raymond's mind. If Henry's writ went out tomorrow there would still be plenty of time to stop the attack.

Richard looked kindly at the overwrought young man. "Do you believe I love William?" he asked.

"Yes, of course."

"I swear to you that I will make sure the writ goes out in time, and I will summon my own men from Wallingford and the keeps round about there to gather at Marlowe, and I will go in my own person to see that the writ is obeyed. Believe me, no harm will come to William or anyone else in Marlowe."

"But it must be soon, very soon," Raymond begged.

"This very night I will begin," Richard promised.

Raymond sighed and seemed to sag. Richard gestured Belet to him and said that Raymond was now ready to rest and eat, and Raymond followed the puzzled royal butler without argument. Belet and his friends had overheard some of the talk. They had been wrong in assuming Raymond was being given a grant of some kind—at least at present.

As Raymond staggered out one door, Richard entered the inner chamber. Theobald was scratching away at a copy of the writ he had completed and Henry was finishing his instructions to Philip d'Arcy. Richard's lips thinned when he saw d'Arcy. He did not like the man and never had liked him. He did not think Henry liked him either. But he used him. Suspicious, Richard picked up the writ, but it was just what Raymond said it would be. Richard felt contrite. He was far too often suspicious of Henry without cause.

"You are so kind, Henry," he said warmly, going toward his brother.

Henry started with surprise. He had been so intent on his low-voiced orders to d'Arcy that he had not heard his brother enter. Now if Richard had not thrice suspected Henry and thrice been proved wrong, he would have read the guilt on the king's face immediately. As it was, he blamed himself for seeing evil where there was no more than surprise and took Henry's hand and kissed it.

"You are very good," Richard went on. "You do for me what I would have begged before I even ask. Thank you, dear brother."

Henry was so relieved and delighted that Richard seemed to know and yet know nothing, that he clasped his brother in his arms and assured him passionately that he always wished to please him. He gestured for d'Arcy to go and wait for the writ to be delivered to him outside, and then urged Richard to a seat and asked if he would drink or eat.

"I have no need," Richard replied, smiling, "and I have finally sent that young idiot Raymond off to bed. I wish to thank you again, Henry, for what you have done, not only in sending this writ so swiftly but in sending Raymond to Marlowe."

"Well, I—" Henry faltered, stunned. It seemed that Richard knew everything, and was *pleased*.

"You were perfectly right to send him without my knowledge," Richard continued. "As Raymond pointed out, I would have stormed and ranted, thinking the worst, when you intended—and, indeed, accomplished —the best. Sometimes I think myself so wise that I am the more a fool."

"No, no," Henry assured his brother, "you are mostly wise, Richard, but you are a little hasty sometimes."

He was glowing with pride and satisfaction, pleased with Richard, with Raymond, even with Sir William. In a sense he was pleased with Mauger, too, for proving to be a villain who deserved punishment. Everything was working out perfectly. Although Henry suffered a little prick of anxiety when Richard mentioned gathering an army to enforce his brother's writ, he was able to smile and approve the move after Richard mentioned it would take about a week. By then, Henry knew, Marlowe would be clean of Mauger and his mercenary troops.

CHAPTER 25

To go from Marlowe to London, a man can ride cross-country and save many miles, even if he does not know the way. From London to Marlowe is not so simple. Thus, when Philip d'Arcy left with his troop at dawn he knew it would be necessary to follow the river Thames all the way. He had never been to Marlowe in his life and took the surest road, knowing it would waste more time if he missed the keep and lost himself.

His group rode with haste but not with dire urgency. Philip d'Arcy knew they could not come to Marlowe by any exertion before nightfall, and he had no intention of approaching an armed camp after sunset. Thus, when a horse cast a shoe, Philip did not go on, leaving that man behind. He allowed the whole troop to rest while they found a smith and had the animal reshod. It was not in his opinion a serious matter.

It was just about the time the shoe was cast that William blew the *mort*. Inside the keep, they heard, for they had been warned and were listening. Alys and Elizabeth stopped what they were doing and looked at each other.

Both had been very busy, Elizabeth preparing for the treatment of the wounded and Alys for the last-ditch defense of the keep itself. Both had feared it would come to this, but it was a shock that the defense of the walls had failed so quickly. Still, both were calm. Alys knew there was nothing to fear for herself; her plans were made. Elizabeth also had little fear. She would live or die with William. She wished to live, but she did not fear to die with him.

The horn was a signal for a furious spurt of activity.

The great wooden shutters that closed the windows of the keep were braced with heavy bars; pails of water were poured over the iron-bound foot-thick wooden door that closed the hall off from the outside stair; the tops were knocked from several barrels of oil that stood just outside on the landing of the stair that rose into the keep in the forebuilding. These stairs, unlike those of stone that connected the floors of the keep inside one tower, were made of wood. Torches were thrust into the fire and carried to holders on each side of the doorway; others were laid ready.

All this was work for the ablebodied. The old men and women clustered together, pounding herbs and preparing medicinal draughts and ointments according to Elizabeth's instructions. Those too feeble for this work prayed. Martin had been among the latter group. He was not so feeble as to be unable to prepare for the wounded, but he never did such tasks because of his deep fear that he was an unclean thing whose evil would somehow contaminate the healing materials and make them ineffective or even deadly. Although Martin fought the feeling, telling himself that God was good, it always lay in him, ready to rise and choke him. At the sound of the horn, Martin's prayer faltered and he fell silent.

For a few minutes he remained kneeling, then looked blankly around at the seeming chaos that was swiftly readying Marlowe for its final stand. It was his fault, Martin thought dully. Abbot Martin and Abbot Anselm had been wrong. They had tried to believe and to teach him that the outward form does not reflect the inner soul. He had struggled all his life to believe that, struggled to root out all evil from his soul so that it should be straight and beautiful in God's eyes even if his body was ugly and crooked.

Until a few weeks ago, Martin had continued to hope that the abbots who saved him and were kind to him were right. When Abbot Paul had cast him out, he had said that the soul in so warped a body could not be saved except by death immediately after baptism.

It was a soul created by the devil and oozed evil. It was the evil in Martin that had corrupted the abbey, Abbot Paul claimed, not his own laxness.

When he lay dying in the road, Martin had wondered if that could be true. But then Sir William had found him and his life had been filled with richness and kindness and love. He had thought little of Abbot Paul's cruel words, preferring to believe that God had afflicted him, found him worthy, and brought him in His own mysterious ways to a place where he could perfect his goodness and die in peace. Now, standing and watching everyone make ready to die—although they did not yet know it—Martin wondered if his rescue and years of happiness had been another snare and delusion of the devil.

Had evil oozed from him and little by little rotted Marlowe? It seemed so, indeed. After long years of resistance, Sir William, his greatest benefactor, had yielded to sin and committed adultery with the woman he had loved purely for so long. Little Alys, as pure and stainless as gold, had overthrown the meekness and obedience required of women and said in a voice of adamant and with eyes glittering with the flame of hatred that she would commit the mortal sin of murder. And now Marlowe itself and all in it were about to be destroyed. Had all this corruption come from him?

Was there no way, Martin wondered, to redeem the evil he had wrought? He knew God was stronger than the devil. He knew he did not will evil—not even to those he hated, much less to those he loved. Surely there must be a reason that God had permitted him to be born, even if the devil planned it. God was the stronger. If there was no reason, there was no God. Yet man had free will, and it was his duty to find his own way, to find the reason that made sense of life. So, Martin thought, retreating instinctively to a dark corner where he would not be in the way, he must discover the reason for himself—since surely God did exist.

Only it was very hard to think when his own guilt

and his hatred for Mauger, who was surely more evil than he because evil clothed in fair form was more deadly than naked evil. . . . That was the answer! The evil that was nakedly foul—himself—was put in this place to rid the world of the evil that was outwardly fair. How right! How just! How good was God!

Suddenly all was clear. Martin began to inch his way along the wall, sliding into Sir William's chamber to pick up a long-bladed, razor-sharp hunting knife which he tucked into the bosom of his tunic. Then he sidled along the wall again, closer and closer to the stair, unnoticed, waiting until he could slip out. He felt strong and light as he never had before, sure at last, if not of redemption, that he understood the reason for his damnation.

If he did not stop the fair-seeming evil that was Mauger, it would spread corruption far and wide. Martin realized now that he had not corrupted Marlowe; nonetheless, he was still at fault. He should have seen his duty sooner and done it—but the evil was so fair-looking, Mauger being tall and blond and handsome with a ready smile—that he had been blind. Thus Mauger had corrupted Marlowe. Lady Elizabeth, being good, had sensed the evil under the fair looks and had been unable to love her husband. That fact had called to Sir William like a siren song over the years. Mauger had threatened to force marriage on Alys, and that had turned her from womanly thoughts of love and devotion to hatred and murder.

So all was clear. Since he had been so blind, Mauger had at last openly committed evil. God did not ask the impossible of any but the saints, so God had made it possible for him to understand and to deal with the evil that endangered man and to keep clean the sweet, pure souls of those in Marlowe.

Then all was ready at the stair and Alys called the servants away so that none would block the passage when those men who could fled the walls and began to retreat into the keep itself. As swiftly as he could, Martin made his way down the stair. He was only just

in time and slid aside into the darkest part of the forebuilding as the groaning wounded stumbled in through
the door to the bailey.

They were the first to come, let through by Hugo to
crawl down the stair by the side of the southwest tower.
Others, Martin knew, must be coming down the gate
tower, which Sir William had been defending. All the
men of Marlowe keep were drawing together, trying to
fight their way through their enemies to one stair or the
other. Although he could not see it, Martin could
imagine the attackers pouring over the wall as the defenders yielded or retreated, trying to overwhelm them
before they could escape into the great keep itself.

Through the relatively flimsy wooden structure of the
forebuilding, which was a shelter against the weather
and not meant to be defensible, Martin could hear the
tempo of the battle increase. He could not understand
this. It seemed to him that as men left the fighting, it
should grow less. He was not worried, however. He
knew that Sir William would come last, shepherding his
men. Then there would be time for him to get out.
He knew just where to hide.

There was nothing mysterious about the increasing
noise of battle. The defenders were bunching together,
coalescing into larger and larger groups—those who
could. This permitted them to dispose of any attackers
between their groups as each group strove to reach
the tower or the stair. They could overthrow the ladders
that intervened because a few fought on the periphery
of the group while the others had time to denude the
ladders of climbers by pouring hot oil or sand or dropping rocks on them and then pushing the ladders over.

As the groups grew, however, more and more of the
wall was left completely undefended. The attackers
poured into these areas without resistance, and they
did not stand idle. They charged with desperate ferocity,
doing their best to break up the defenders, to get to the
stairs and into the tower before the defenders could.
These men were nearly all experienced mercenaries.
They knew that taking a keep was both the most dan-

gerous and most profitable of the various types of war. But to gain the real profit, the women, the rich drinking and eating vessels, the jewels and money and cloth, one had to get into the heart of the keep itself. If William and his men could get off the wall and inside first, it would take another desperate and even more dangerous assault to win.

In a very short time, there were many more of Mauger's men on the walls than William's, and many groups were broken. The only reason that all the defenders were not immediately overwhelmed was that the battlements were only wide enough for four men to stand abreast—and if they did they could hardly move. Thus no more than three of the invaders could confront three of the defenders at any one time or place. Still, the numbers told heavily against William's men as did the need to carry with them as many of their wounded as they could. Mauger's force could replace those who were wearied or only a little hurt with fresh men; there was no relief for William's people.

The mercenary troop leaders knew their business. As soon as it was clear that the intention of the defenders was to escape, they began to bellow for the archers to come up. Protected by the heavily armed men-at-arms, the archers could shoot at those defending the tower and stair with little danger of hitting their own comrades. For William's men there was also the danger of watching for the shafts. Many fell to sword strokes because their eyes were elsewhere at the wrong moment.

William, himself, who knew better, had to fight the temptation to watch for arrows. The memory of being struck was still green. He fought with the strength of desperation, panting for breath as fatigue and loss of blood seemed to deprive him of air. He struggled, too, to call encouragement to those who still strove to reach him. Many did not. Caught between terror and terror, many of the recruits threw down their arms and cried for quarter.

At last it seemed to William that he and the few veterans who fought beside him were all the resistance left on his side of the tower. He shouted, "Down! Down!" and began to back toward the door. He would have been last in, but his men saw his weakness and closed up before him, thrusting him back. A flash of pride was drowned in reason. William stepped back into shelter and stood leaning on his sword, fighting off the desire to let everything go and drop.

He had little time to gather strength. The last of the men who had won their way around the walls were coming through the other door. Close behind them pressed the attackers. William stopped the last of his men, shouting that one should grab the door bar, the others should pull the closest opponents through to them, then slam and bar the door. Briefly William was engaged again in killing one of the too-eager attackers. Then the bars were fast. Blows battered at the heavy wooden door, shaking the thick bars, but it would take more than men's bodies to burst through that obstruction. A ram would be necessary.

His energy restored a little by this success, William turned to the side he had been defending and shouted at the men to come through. One, then another came. William braced himself to fight again, and found Diccon beside him, yelling about the stair at the other end.

"Can you hold and bar this door?" William asked.

Diccon was so spattered with blood that William could not tell whether it came from the master-at-arms's body or from other men. There was no hesitation, however, in Diccon's assurance that he could nor any lack of energy in the way he sprang toward the still-open portal. If the defense of the stair near the keep failed, they would have to fight their way across the bailey and might find the forebuilding held against them. Worse, Alys and Elizabeth would never close the keep while he was outside, and the attackers might get in.

William ran down the stair of the tower, only just catching himself before he toppled over in his haste. He managed to stay upright, but he was sweating and grinding his teeth with fear before he came out into the bailey and saw there was no fighting there yet. He bellowed to the men running toward the forebuilding to go to the stair. Most of them paid no heed, being blind and deaf with fear and fixed on reaching safety. Two or three understood, and those who were following him down the tower steps were all veterans and came with him.

They were in time, although barely—but barely was enough. The tide of attackers gathering to pour down the stair as the plug that had defended it so long failed, met a new, firm resistance. The last of the wounded hobbled, staggered, crawled, or were dragged into the forebuilding. For a minute, two, William and the men with him, who now included Diccon, held on, not realizing those left in the bailey were already dead or too far gone to move. In those two minutes, Martin sidled through the door, flattened himself against the wall of the forebuilding, and slipped around the side toward the northeast.

No one noticed the single bent figure in dark clothes hobbling along. If a man or two did see him, they dismissed him from their minds as another of the wounded. The scuttling form paused a moment in the dark angle between the forebuilding and the northwest tower, rounded that, and made a wavering dash for a low stone shelter built out from the wall itself. He might have been seen then, except that shouts of fury burst from the men fighting on the stair as William's party suddenly broke contact and ran, with every bit of strength left in them, for the forebuilding.

All attention was fixed on the race between William's bloody, weary group and the attackers who bounded after them, still hoping to catch the master of the keep who would then be used to force those inside to yield. They had no doubt who was their quarry. William was the only man in mail, and the device on his shield identified him even more surely. There were fresh men in the bailey also, let down on ropes from the walls when they found the tower doors barred to them.

The efforts were vain. The last of the defenders leapt

up the stairs with the inhuman energy of finality, toppling into the hall to be dragged aside out of the way by those waiting. William fell forward, aware of little beyond the bursting pain in his chest, and Diccon, one step behind him—the last of all—was in little better case. Fortunately the women of Marlowe keep were in no need of instructions from anyone.

"Now!" Alys shrieked, grabbing a torch from a wall holder.

Men and women ran forward, shoved hard on the two barrels of oil so that they toppled forward, spilling their contents down the steps and rolling down themselves, splashing the walls as they bounded and emptied completely. As the barrels went over, Alys cast her torch down to the bottom of the steps, seized another from Elizabeth just behind her, and threw that after it, and then still another. The stairwell burst into a roaring inferno. One last torch Alys dropped right on the landing just in front of her feet and leapt backward barely before her dress caught fire.

As she came in, the heavy door was slammed shut behind her and its massive bars were set into the broad iron slots to hold it closed. Still, shrieks of agony could be heard from the stair and forebuilding. Alys closed her eyes and prayed the cries came from unwary enemies, who had been close on her father's heels, and not from their own wounded, who had been too weak to climb the stair. The sound died, swallowed by the hungry roar of the fire. Alys sighed. It was too late to worry, too late to do more than pray for them, whoever they were.

Martin had gained the safety he sought. He burrowed far back into a bin of musty last-year grain, heaping it up in front of him as well as he could. Then he lay still. For a time he heard excited shouts and calls, then the groans and clanks as the portcullis went up and the drawbridge came down. After that, the sounds were harder to interpret. He had never been in a similar situation, but he had heard Sir William talk and guessed that the invaders were searching for concealed enemies and examining the animals and stores in the bailey. He ground his few remaining teeth in futile rage, knowing himself helpless to prevent the despoiling.

Mauger was almost as angry as Martin, although not at the despoiling of the cattle and other stored foodstuffs of Marlowe. He was furious because the men had failed to penetrate the keep. A few harsh words were exchanged with the captains under his orders, particularly because they had not been quick enough to quench the flames that were now avidly destroying the forebuilding as well as the stair, which was the only way into Marlowe keep.

"It does not please me any better than it pleases you," one captain pointed out with a marked note of contempt in his voice for Mauger's stupidity. "Do you think we do not desire what is within? I tell you the men did their best. The defense was desperate and well designed. This Sir William knows much of war." The captain's eyes said, *Much more than you,* but all his mouth gave out was, "I hope he does not have any more surprises for us."

"He cannot have," Sir Mauger said sourly, aware that he was being blamed for underrating William's ability to the captains. He took a grip on his temper. "You saw how few men he had. He can do no more."

The reasoning calmed Mauger if it did not convince the captain. Really all Mauger cared about was killing William and getting Alys, and there should be time enough, in spite of Marlowe's strength, to break it open. William's own mangonels and trenchbuts could be turned against him and those from Hurley added. Mauger thought about ordering the men to begin taking the devices apart so that they could be moved to new positions, but he curbed that impulse also.

Tomorrow would be soon enough for that and to begin to build the platform, which could be rolled against the door to bring a ram to bear on it. He had promised the men they could loot the keep completely. Let them have a taste of his willingness to permit them to enjoy the fruits of their victory. Let them slaughter

William's cattle and have a feast; let them get drunk on the beer in the vats in the brewhouse. It would whet their appetites for the dainties within—the women whom, all except Alys, they could use as they pleased— he was reserving Alys for himself; the wine in the cool lowest level of the keep; the fine embroidered cloth— and whatever else they desired.

Having made this announcement without consulting the captains, with whom he was annoyed and to whom he wanted to display his power of command, Mauger made a brief tour of the bailey. He nodded indulgently at the men who were already slaughtering cattle and pigs and chickens and dragging what vegetables they best liked from the sheds. He ordered his own servants to set up his tent, choosing the angle made by the stone shed and the wall as its site because that was safest from any arrows that might be shot from the keep.

There had been a cursory search for hidden enemies, but it was soon clear that no large force was concealed. The invaders did not care if one or two servants or wounded men-at-arms were crouched in corners. They could do no harm and would eventually die of themselves or creep out for food and water and be discovered. Thus no one did more than stick a lighted torch inside the door of Martin's hideaway and peer around.

Not very long after that, the feasting began. Martin heard the shouts and laughter, which completely drowned the groans of the wounded and dying. Still he waited. When the light coming in at the open door began to dim, he dared creep forward, clinging to the deep shadows along the walls. Crouched in the corner nearest the door, he listened.

He heard nothing of interest for a very long time. The snatches of talk he did hear horrified him— Martin had no cause to mingle with William's men-at-arms, and he had been raised in an abbey. Often enough, the talk became argument and a captain would shout for peace. Dark came. The drawbridge was lifted and the portcullis let down. A few men were called from their revelry and ordered to the walls as guards. Torches and fires blazed in the bailey.

As the beer in the vats diminished and the marked bones rolled in torchlight or firelight, there were more and more acrimonious differences of opinion as to what the marks showing were. One quarrel, quite near where Martin hid, became violent, and the cripple drew back a little. A captain shouted, but the argument had gone too far. A blow was struck, and then another.

"Damn you all to hell!" Mauger roared, stepping out of his tent. "Have you not had enough fighting this day? Peace, I say."

He strode into the firelight, past the door of the stone shed, to apply the flat of his sword to the combatants until their slightly more sober comrades could get hold of them and quiet them.

"That is enough," he said to the captain, who had also come over. "I do not want them killing each other over the treasures they have not yet won. Put an end to this freedom."

Since the captains had long since thought it was enough, they did their best, cursing Mauger's desire to indulge the men. It took some time before the torches were doused, the fires allowed to burn away to embers. All the time it took to restore order, Martin knelt in prayer, thanking God for placing Mauger so close and letting him reveal himself and begging for the strength to do what he must do.

Inside Marlowe keep, surprisingly enough, there was little despair. When the door had closed on the blazing stair and forebuilding, Elizabeth and Alys had run to William. They found him on his feet, not far behind them, breathing hard still but smiling grimly.

"That was well done," he remarked. "Perhaps I should have had you two on the walls to give orders to the men."

"You are covered with blood, William," Elizabeth said.

"Yes, but most of it is other men's. I have opened my

shoulder and may have some nicks and scratches I do not yet feel, but I am not hurt." He turned and looked at the mass of men and women behind him, huddled together, too silent, and he smiled. "The first thing is to put some heart into these ninnies. Come."

Because people want to believe in safety, William had no difficulty convincing everyone. Marlowe had never been broken, he pointed out, and help was on its way. He then gave orders about the care of the wounded and the disposal of those who died, and ended, "As soon as the wounded be tended and the dead laid away in decency, we will eat. There will be wine for all, for all of you have served me well this day."

That brought a short burst of cheers, and William stepped down heavily from the bench he had been standing upon, remarking quietly to Elizabeth, "Yes, and because I have ordered it, they will forget for a while that they drink wine because there *is* no beer." He paused and sighed. "I am tired. My love, once I said I could protect you, but . . ."

"I am content," she replied, "and more than content. Must I remind you, William, that if I had not run to you in my fear and my need, this would never have happened?"

"Do not flatter yourself," William said, smiling at her tenderly. "If what you have said about Mauger is true, you have doubtless saved my life rather than brought trouble upon me. I own, I never liked him— but you can guess the cause of that—and I blamed myself for it, and *would* not think ill of him. Thus, as soon as I denied him Alys, he would have taken me unaware and slain me. Or, if I escaped him, he would have found some reason to attack Marlowe even if you were meek, mild, and loving as a lamb."

Elizabeth did not answer that directly, but she was greatly relieved. Aside from the first moment when she cried out against what she saw coming, she had felt no guilt, because she knew what William had just said was true. All that had troubled her was that, perhaps, it was out of love that he did not blame her for his loss and his trouble. That would not have pleased Elizabeth. Love, even as great a love as William's, could be strained by such a burden. Now she was sure reason as well as love judged her innocent, and she was truly content.

"Come," she said softly, "let me unarm you and tend your hurts, beloved. Then you can rest while I help Alys with the other wounded."

Lying still, drifting into sleep, William found his despair was gone. Now that he was recovered from the shock of losing his hold on the walls, William began to think their chances were not so very bad. Even if Raymond could not get a writ from the king or Mauger would not obey it, Raymond was not the type to sit wringing his hands and weeping. He would seek Richard—and Richard would come. On that pleasant thought he slept to be awakened about an hour later by Alys.

"Papa," she said when his eyes opened. "I cannot find Martin."

"What do you mean, you cannot find Martin?" William asked irritably, too aware of his aching body. "Look in the darkest corner of the chapel. He is always there if he is not in his chamber or the hall."

"Papa, I have searched that chapel well enough to find every mousehole—and I have even looked in those. He is not in the keep."

"Drat the man," William groaned, not wanting to believe her, "he must be below seeing to the stores. Doubtless he thinks every man must now do double duty. He will do himself a hurt. I will—"

"He is not there!" Alys exclaimed, her voice rising. "I have searched myself, *everywhere*. I tell you he is not in the keep at all, unless—"

"Not in the keep? Surely he was not on the wall!"

"No. He was here during the battle, praying. I remember because I thought that if anything could bring us God's help it must surely be Martin's prayers. God must listen to so pure a soul, so cleansed by suffering. After that, I did not think of him at all until I went to ask him for the keys to the wine store. Papa, they were in his chamber, on the little table under his crucifix with a candle lit beside them so that I could not fail to see them—all his keys were there." Her voice caught on a sob.

All William could think was that Martin might have left the keep so that there would be one less "useless" mouth to feed during the siege. He did not say that to Alys. He did not need to say it. The fear of it was already in her eyes. Instead he said some meaningless words of comfort.

More practical, Alys asked, "Are there no secret places? No passages you would not show to me for fear I might be trapped?"

William shook his head. "Only the one you know of. The tunnel to the river."

"I have looked there. The outer and inner doors are locked and barred."

"He must have gone out during the fighting," William guessed, "near the end, when he knew we could not hold the walls. Fool that he is to add to our grief more than his small stomach could ever keep from our mouths—but love makes fools of men. Do not despair, Alys. He is very small. He could hide where a man could not. Perhaps when we come out of here, we will find him safe."

And safety was, indeed, in Martin's mind as he watched the fires die and heard the voices of the invaders drift away into silence. There were sounds, however: the wounded and dying moaned and wept; the drunk and exhausted snored; occasionally a clink of metal on stone came from the walls where the guards passed. There was enough sound to cover any small noise he would make, Martin knew, and he was not concerned that any guard would notice his movement; they watched only outward.

Softly, slowly, Martin eased himself to the doorway and out. He leaned against the stone for a little time to steady his legs, which were weak and shaking with having knelt so long in prayer. When he was ready, he slipped between the tent and the shed so he could come around the back out of sight. No one noticed the dark figure—a distorted shadow among other shadows. Buoyed up by success, Martin lifted the tent flap and crept inside. He could see before he entered that a light was burning, but most men slept with a night light. However, the hope of coming upon Mauger unaware was not fulfilled. As Martin entered, Mauger turned on his cot and called sharply, "Who is there?"

"Do not cry out, lord," Martin whispered, "I have a secret to sell."

Mauger sat up abruptly, reaching for his sword, but his hand dropped. He could see the twisted shape and knew at once that it was William's crippled steward. He did not ask how Martin came to be there, assuming that the foul little beast had deserted his master as soon as danger threatened. Now the creature would want to buy new protection.

"Sell," Mauger sneered. "I do not need to buy. You are in my hands and I can wring from you whatever I want. Say what you have to say quickly. If it is worth something, perhaps I will let you live."

"Yes, yes," Martin agreed eagerly. "I have good news for you. You will let me live and reward me also, but allow me to approach closer, my lord. One thing I have to say," he lowered his voice to a hoarse whisper, "should not be heard by too many."

"What do you mean?" Mauger asked, but he gestured Martin closer, hoping for what he was about to hear.

"In the years when my lord's father guarded Wallingford, he got much good," Martin began suggestively.

"There is a hoard in Marlowe?" Mauger whispered. "Where?"

"Is it worth my life to know of it, and of a secret way into Marlowe keep? But it is not so easy to find," Martin tittered horrid laughter. "Let me bring the table and the light nearer so I can show you something that will bring you the reward you deserve for your mercy and your generosity."

The creature must have a map, Mauger thought. No wonder William never complained about need of money. He was so excited he never stopped to wonder why Martin should be so stupid as to show him a map that would make Martin himself unnecessary as a guide. Mauger knew he could have wrested the map from the old man, but it suited his sense of humor to allow the cripple to struggle painfully to drag the table across the room.

Solicitously Martin arranged the table so that it fit over Mauger's knees and blocked his path to grip his sword. Then he carried the candle over and set it by the table where it made a little pool of light. When he stepped to Mauger's side, close enough that Mauger would need to twist his neck uncomfortably to look at him, Mauger instinctively looked down at the little pool of light. It would be there that Martin would lay whatever he had to show.

That instant Martin's hand slipped into his breast, drew the knife, and struck. Blood spurted wide. Mauger howled and reached out, twisting to grip his attacker, but the table held him down momentarily and Martin clung to the knife, pushing against it and weeping with horror and terror.

In the end it was Martin's fear and Mauger's rage at the insolence of the inept attack that killed them both. Martin had never in his life used violence against any living thing, man or beast. He was so terrified by the actual fact of what he had done that he was frozen. Mauger, on the other hand was so convulsed with rage that he lunged forward, which drove the knife deeper. Then he tore at Martin's hands, lacerating his throat more and more while he struggled for the knife. And when he had it, he stabbed and stabbed and stabbed at the unresisting cripple while his lifeblood poured away.

CHAPTER 26

Raymond waked as the sun rose, about half an hour after Philip d'Arcy rode away from Westminster. He lay for a few moments trying to reorient himself. The huge, soft bed with its elaborate curtains had cast him back to Aix. He had not slept in such a bed since he left home. However, in seconds he knew he was not in Tour Dur, and memory came rushing back. Then began one long battle against himself. All he wanted to do was ride back to Marlowe, but the king had forbidden it, and Raymond did not wish to annoy the king, who had done all he could already.

He managed to eat, but he could not endure the talk of the courtiers around him. All he could think of was Marlowe. His need brought him out to the stable where, after some trouble, he found the destrier that he had bought. When a groom hurried forward and asked if he should saddle the beast, Raymond agreed eagerly.

Then he felt a fool. Where could he go? The only place he wanted to be was Marlowe. It came to him then that there was one other person nearby who was as interested in Marlowe as he—Richard of Cornwall. The groom was able to give him directions, and Raymond rode off feeling less as if he were stifling. He found the earl awake, at breakfast, and was welcomed kindly despite the fact that there were several clerks waiting for Richard's attention.

"I am intruding on your time of business," Raymond said.

"All times are times of business for me," Richard responded sourly. "I am again without a marshal. The lands are so great that they are a temptation to avarice and power. It is a hard post to fill. This is all non-sense." He gestured with his head at the clerks. "Stu-pidities of receipts and disbursements that should be seen to in a round of visits to the estates, but I am sent hither and thither by Henry and I do not complain of that for it is needful and right. However, I cannot be in two places at once." He sighed. "You have met Lady Elizabeth. Do you think—" He looked at Raymond, who had jumped as if he had been stung. "What is it?"

"I do not know," Raymond sighed. "I am so uneasy. Lord Richard, what if Mauger will not obey the king's writ? Sir William said that if Marlowe was near to falling, Mauger would take it first and apologize later to the king. But it is not a question of the keep or goods, which can be restored. Mauger will have Sir William and Lady Elizabeth killed if he can lay hands on them. I know it."

"Marlowe will not fall so quickly," Richard soothed, and began to explain that it took time to build engines of war.

"He does not need to build them," Raymond pointed out, reminding Richard how close Hurley was and con-tinuing to describe the situation. By the time he had enumerated the weaknesses in William's situation, Rich-ard was beginning to look as worried as Raymond felt.

"I have not men enough with me," the earl muttered.

"Are there no free mercenary bands in so large a city as London?" Raymond asked. "If you will lend me the money to hire men, my lord, I will repay you. I am heir to Aix, and I have some small estates of my own."

Richard pursed his lips thoughtfully. "Do not be silly," he replied. "Why should you pay for that? William has been my friend for thirty years. No, no more than my own troop should be needed. Mauger might ignore a king's messenger and a king's writ, but he will not ignore *me*. Idiot that I am, but I did not know. . . ."

Richard got to his feet and the clerks surged forward. He cast them a glance of exasperation and waved them away, shouting for a servant to tell his troop to arm. Raymond jumped up also begging to go along. Richard cast him one slightly quizzical glance, remembering how the young man had jumped when Lady Elizabeth had been mentioned. Was that the reason for Raymond's surely excessive devotion? Had he too fallen under the spell of the siren who had held William in thrall for twenty years? What a beauty this must be! However, he said nothing of that, merely nodding and telling Raymond to ride back for his arms while he told Sancia that he would be away for a few days.

"Do not say anything to anyone about this," Richard warned. "We are going to Windsor to hunt—if anyone asks. My brother would be hurt if it seemed we did not think his writ of sufficient power to work on its own."

There were enough screams from the wounded that Mauger's shriek of pain and rage brought no one. When Martin fell from his weakening grasp and his rage was spent, Mauger's eyes were already dimming. He squawked for help, but many men cried for help, for water, for ease. No one noticed one more gasping wail. He started for the door, stumbled over Martin's body, and fell. He tried to crawl, but the humpbacked corpse twisted and rolled under his feeble hand and he fell forward and lay still.

In the morning when they were discovered, the captains were aghast, fearing they might be blamed. Then there was the question of the keep. They looked at it hungrily and then, with far more interest in the direction of the town, which they had not been allowed to plunder. Mauger had assured them that there was little in the town; that William drained it dry and kept all he got for he was a miser. Should they try to break into the keep, which would take time and lives or should they take what little there was in the town—there were always women, at least—and then hurry back and report Mauger's death.

At dawn, watches had been set inside Marlowe. Two

of the shutters facing into the bailey from different angles had been opened enough for an experienced man-at-arms to keep an eye on what the troops were doing. The guards were surprised that they seemed to be doing nothing at all. This rather suspicious circumstance was reported to Diccon, who snorted with contempt. Probably Mauger was giving them another day and night to drink themselves into insubordination and grudge fights. Nonetheless, Diccon warned the men to keep close watch, reminding them of Mauger's treacherous nature and that he might be preparing another trick.

When the men started to strike their tents and pack their gear, William was at the window in minutes. He watched, his brain spinning as he sought a reason for the unreasonable. They *were* leaving; his horses were being led from the stables, the cattle were being driven from the pens, the grain and smoked meat available being loaded on carts. The portcullis went up, the drawbridge down. Some units marched out. The loot, such as it was, and the carts carrying the wounded followed.

"What is it, William?" Elizabeth asked softly, seeing his knuckles white as they gripped the shutter.

"They are leaving," William said thickly. "I cannot believe it, but they are leaving."

"It must be a trap," Alys warned.

"What sort of—" William began, and stopped.

Men were backing off the bridge to make way for eleven horsemen, one a knight in elaborate dress. When he swung around to face the three men who came up to him, his shield came into view, and William gasped, "It is d'Arcy."

His voice was grim, but he said no more. There was no sense in telling Alys and Elizabeth that d'Arcy was customarily employed by Henry to do his more unsavory errands. William continued to stare into the bailey where, obviously, some argument was taking place. Was d'Arcy urging the men to return and assault the keep? Why was that necessary? Where was Mauger? William called back into the hall to ask if there were any who were longsighted. Having described Mauger to the man who limped forward, he waited for him to scan the area, but he could not see Mauger anywhere either and he assured William that Mauger was *not* one of the three talking to d'Arcy. The argument seemed to be growing more intense, the mercenaries moving restlessly as if they were itching to discard their packs and seize their arms. They were; d'Arcy had forbidden the attack on Marlowe town, wanting them clear of the area quickly.

Then there was another furor. William had thrown open the shutter by now and was leaning out of the window as far as he could. He heard horns blowing a warning from the road outside, and another man came galloping over the bridge to fling himself off his horse and draw aside the three captains who were talking to d'Arcy. This time the colloquy was brief. All hell broke loose. The men began to march over the bridge in quick time. Two of d'Arcy's men dismounted and walked toward the stone storage shed. D'Arcy himself rode hastily out again.

It was then William noticed that Mauger's tent was there. He knew it well from the time in Wales. The troops were leaving, but Mauger remained? That was impossible. However, he did not have time to think about it because something even more impossible was taking place. His cattle and horses were coming back over the drawbridge, herded with shouts by several of d'Arcy's men.

"I am going mad," William groaned. "Do you see what I see?"

Elizabeth laughed and kissed him. "William," she cried, "I am going up to tell the wounded men that we are saved. Joy is the greatest healer of all. Let them have that to ease their pain."

Alys did not bother to answer. Her eyes were alight. It was obvious to her that Raymond had succeeded and saved them. It was obvious to William also, but he could not understand the return of his property. Even if the king had forbade the attack, what had been taken before the order arrived could usually be counted as lost. Probably that was what the argument with d'Arcy was about. It surprised him that d'Arcy had not shouted for him, that he had ridden out again. That made William a little uneasy, but the last of the troops were marching away and did not turn back.

William was just about to leave the window to order the unbarring of the door and a ladder to be let down when d'Arcy returned with Richard and Raymond beside him, and all three rode into Marlowe. Then, of course, there were no more doubts. All the shutters were flung wide, the door was unbarred, the ladder let down. As William prepared to descend, his daughter dragged him back.

"Oh no! Let them come to you. You will open that shoulder a third time and it will never heal aright. There, papa, see. Richard is coming." She leaned from the door to shout a greeting and bade the earl come up before her father jumped down.

But the beaming smiles that met Richard dimmed at the trouble in his face, then vanished as he told them what lay in Mauger's tent.

"Martin?" William said. "I do not believe it. That Mauger could—could torture *him*—yes. But that Martin could wrest the knife from him and strike back—no. Even if he had the strength, which he did not, he *would* not. Not Martin."

"Martin struck first, William," Richard said softly. "The knife is yours—that with the staghorn handle carved like a wading bird. You say Martin would not— not for himself, I agree—but for you and Alys?"

"Murder? Martin? No!" William insisted.

"You did not commit murder when you fought the men on your walls. Likely Martin thought what he did an act of war—the only act of which he was capable."

"I do not care what he thought," Alys said. "You are right. He did it for us. Papa had talked about these men being hired men, not bound by loyalty. Martin understood that if he killed Mauger and there was no pay, they would go away."

"Yes," William agreed. He hid his face in his hands

for a moment. "I shall miss him. He was an other self."
Then he turned and roared across the hall for the
carpenters to get themselves down the ladder and knock
up a staircase. He made as if to go down and Richard
held him back, saying that Raymond had stayed.

"But he cannot make him decent," Alys said, "and
he will be needed for other things. I cannot let Martin
lie all bloody. I will go down. No, you will not, papa.
Do not make more grief for me and labor for Elizabeth
by doing yourself a hurt. He will not be impatient if
you do not come right away." Her voice broke on the
words and she leaned against her father, sobbing. "I
will not weep," she said after a moment, pulling away.
"He could not bear it when I wept—or you either,
papa. So let us not."

"No," William said slowly. "There is nothing to weep
about, Alys. The dearest wish of Martin's heart was to
repay me for saving his life. He must have died very
happy, love, believing he had done so. It was his choice.
We must be content with it."

She called some women, sent one up to summon
Elizabeth from the wounded to comfort her father and
bade others gather vessels and cloths for washing the
body. William stood looking out the window toward
Mauger's tent for a little while, then dried his own wet
eyes. Richard had walked toward the hearth where the
family sat to give William time to control himself.
There, seated on a chair, looking idly into the fire while
everyone else ran about busily, was the loveliest creature he had ever seen in his life. No wonder William
was bewitched and Raymond jumped at her name.

"Madam," Richard said, bowing, "I have news." It
was awkward, he realized, to announce the death of a
husband to a woman who must regard this as the best
of good tidings. Nonetheless, it was better for him to
tell her than for William to do so. "Sir Mauger is dead,"
he said simply.

"Oh? How delightful!" Emma crowed, jumping up
and clapping her hands.

Richard felt sick. The large blue eyes had fixed on

him now and he saw their emptiness behind the surface joy. Was this what William had loved for twenty years? Even as the revolting question rolled through his mind, he realized that this girl could hardly have been alive for twenty years. In the same moment, William came up behind him and snarled, "What the hell are you doing here?"

Emma sidled over and leaned against him suggestively. "My chamber is full of wounded men bleeding and groaning," she simpered. "There is not a clean or quiet corner up there, so I came down to be near you."

William choked, then took a breath as if to blast a reprimand, but instead he merely pushed her away gently. Richard blinked, completely at a loss.

"Oh, Emma, my dear," a soft voice said, "do make your curtsy. This is the earl of Cornwall, and he may know someone who would like your company. Someone very rich."

Emma dropped into a deep curtsy at once, all smiles, but Richard was looking over her head. This was the siren? Her wimple was crooked and the hair that escaped from it curled wildly about her face, her gown was laced up all wrong, and one edge had caught in her garter so that a graceful leg and neat ankle were exposed. Then he saw the great, luminous eyes and the sweetness of her smile, and her hand came out in a gesture of such grace that he was enchanted. William's face lit with a deep, inner joy that wiped the pain from it. Compared with Emma's face, Elizabeth's was brown and plain, but already Richard felt warm and comfortable in her presence.

"Now you must go away for a while, Emma," Elizabeth continued placidly, "so we can decide what is best for you."

Emma looked toward William, but the fixity of his attention on Elizabeth was so palpable that even she recognized it. "I want to live in London," she reminded Elizabeth. "I do not wish to be imprisoned in a keep in the country."

"Yes, yes, I remember," Elizabeth assured her hastily, hearing a growl begin in William's chest, "but go up above and help Maud cut cloth for bandages. You must show you are good and obedient."

As soon as she was gone, Elizabeth dropped a deep curtsy before Richard. "I beg your pardon, my lord, for using your name in such a way, but—"

"Never mind that, Elizabeth," William interrupted. "I must tell you that Martin and Mauger have somehow killed each other."

Elizabeth's eyes grew enormous and she reached for William's hand. "Martin? How?"

"We do not know exactly," William said and then Richard told her what had been found.

"Do not grieve for Martin, beloved." Elizabeth's voice was not steady. "For such a soul there cannot even be purgatory. He must, at last, be straight and beautiful and at God's very knee." Then she was silent. "Mauger," she sighed, "I hope God may have pity for him—although there is little of it in me. He died with many black sins on his soul."

They had little more time for private talk. All were fully occupied restoring Marlowe to as near normal as possible. Much discussion did not clear up the problem of the queer behavior of the mercenaries. Even d'Arcy blandly asserted he could not understand, and the subject was abandoned after a time as a mystery that would never be solved. Martin was laid out; Mauger's body was sent back to Hurley to be packed in brine and transported eventually to Ilmer. There was so much to be done that they did not even sit down to dinner and, as soon as it was dark all tumbled into bed and to sleep, Elizabeth somehow having found time to prepare chambers for Richard and d'Arcy and pallets in the hall for their men.

The next morning d'Arcy left early to inform the king that his writ had been obeyed—Richard had suggested that he say nothing of his presence, and the suggestion was accepted gladly. By dinner time a close approximation of normalcy had been restored.

William and Richard came to sit by the fire and found Emma there again. William's outraged roar as the girl plumped herself down in his lap brought Elizabeth, who sent her away again.

"I must apologize for Emma," she sighed in answer to Richard's exasperated question and explained the circumstances of bringing the girl to Marlowe. Then she looked at him piteously. "I can only hope that you do know someone who would be glad to keep her. She means no ill—really, she is so stupid that she could not *mean* anything—but she is *totally* useless except in bed. Do you know a rich merchant or even—even a—a house where such girls are kept. . . . It would not be a cruelty. She was in such a place before Mauger bought her and speaks of it with—with longing. And she will drive William mad if she remains here much longer."

"Do you mean to let that creature loose on the world?" Richard asked with twitching lips. "William seems immune to her. Perhaps she is safest here."

Elizabeth's rich chuckle rewarded him. "You do not know how persistent she is," she sighed, although her eyes twinkled. "She *cannot* believe William could prefer me to her and pursues him whenever she can."

"If you would let me beat her soundly," William suggested drily.

"No," Elizabeth pleaded. "It would be cruel! She is so simple, like a stupid child. And she did save my life and Alys's."

"Well, *I* cannot take her home," Richard said, horrified as he saw where this was leading. "Sancia is very young. She would—er—never understand I was only doing William a favor."

"Brothers," William remarked with a malicious grin, "should share their troubles."

"Do not be such a tease, William," Elizabeth laughed. "Of course you cannot take her, Richard, but you could ask about."

"But William must go to London, too, to thank the king for his kindness."

Richard spoke gently, but he was worried. Did Elizabeth intend to keep William pent on these small estates? Was she too timid or lazy to go out into the world? If so, his hopes that William would be willing to take on the position of marshal of his lands would probably be at an end. Once he was married to Elizabeth, he would be even less eager to spend much time away.

"London?" Elizabeth said. "Are you going to London, William?"

"You will not come with me?" William asked rather anxiously.

"You have not invited me," Elizabeth rejoined, her eyes laughing again. She simply had not thought of this solution. "Perhaps you wish to take Emma there on your own. . . ."

"Imp! Evil imp!" William exclaimed. "How dare you tell me not to be a tease."

It was now Richard's turn to grin maliciously. "But if William is going to London, and you are willing to trust him to take Emma, I do not hesitate to say that he knows as well as I where to show her off."

"Traitor!" William groaned, and was about to complain further when Richard's expression made him turn his head.

Alys was coming, hand in hand with Raymond. It was clear that somehow Richard had not previously noticed their attachment in the hurry and bustle of the past day and a half. The earl drew a sharp breath. How had he been such a fool as not to think of Alys immediately when he wondered what inspired Raymond's devotion?

"He is the queen's nephew," Richard said under his breath, but his eyes were on the radiant young faces, and he suddenly remembered how Henry had cried, *What could I do?* when his sister and Simon de Montfort had wanted to marry.

"I know now," William replied to Richard's anguished protest, "but I did not know when I first saw they loved. You wanted her to make a great marriage.

I only wanted her to be happy. I thought it would be no bad thing, even if he had nothing. Elizabeth was not free then. I did not expect to marry. I thought they would have Marlowe and Bix and that would be enough for them."

"Have you given your approval to this?" Richard asked stiffly.

"You know I have not. Raymond only told me after we were besieged. We did not have time. . . . I only said he was unkind to let Alys love him—"

"And I said that I would marry Alys if it was the last thing I did in this life." Raymond had come up to them during the last words William spoke. There was no deference in his voice.

"Marriage for the heir of Aix is not a matter of personal preference," Richard protested—but his voice was less certain than Raymond's.

"I have a brother," Raymond replied. "There is no need for me to be heir of Aix."

"Do not be ridiculous!" Richard snapped. "Can you imagine the troubles that could arise in Aix and in Provence if your father tried to change the succession—not to mention the bitterness that could be caused between England and Provence if my brother countenanced this marriage?"

"What troubles? Are you implying that my grandfather would make war on England because the son of his natural son is, in his opinion, a fool?"

"I said this would not work, Raymond," Alys said stonily. "I am not fit—"

"You are fit for anything," Richard interrupted in an agonized voice. The bleak resignation of her words, the way her brilliant eyes had dulled and her face slipped into lines of grief were unbearable. "It is nothing to do with you, sweetheart. You are fit to be a queen, but—"

"Then do not tell us that what we desire is impossible, and seek for a way to *make* it possible," Raymond snarled.

Both Richard and William looked at the young man in amazement. He had always seemed soft and pleasant to William. Even when Raymond fought, he had been easy, without bitterness or hatred. Richard had seen him nervous and distracted by worry in a situation, in which he was truly helpless. This was different. It was something that *was* in his power to obtain and it was quite clear that Raymond intended to have his way even if every throne in Europe toppled for it and gall flowed in the rivers of England and Provence instead of water. Richard whistled softly and William bit his lip. Both saw Raymond-Berenger in his grandson—and Raymond-Berenger ruled Provence like a king in the teeth of the displeasure of Louis of France.

"I think," Elizabeth said softly, "that Raymond is quite right, and Richard also. Alys has the manner and bearing to fit her for his wife. Some arrangement could be devised, surely, that would make her acceptable—"

"Faugh!" Raymond exclaimed, his eyes blazing and his hand on his sword hilt. "Is there no one here but myself and one woman that has more courage than a hen?"

"Raymond," Alys said softly, "let them think. All here love us. Your quarrel is not with my father or Uncle Richard."

"No?" Raymond asked, staring at Richard.

"No," William said. "You must know, Raymond, that no one here would try to prevent this marriage if it were welcomed by *your* parents."

"My lord?" The question was addressed to Richard and it was a challenge.

The earl chewed his thumb. "I have an idea," he said and, when he raised his eyes, to everyone's surprise they were laughing. "William, I have you at last in a cleft stick, and I will have my way with you. I will be happy, and you will be powerful enough, and soon rich enough, to make Alys quite acceptable. At least, Alphonse will certainly think twice before refusing. William, you are now—as of this moment—hereditary marshal of the lands of the earl of Cornwall. We can find you a title somewhere too, if—"

"Oh no! You can make me mind your clerks and bow and scrape at court—if that is what I must do to buy my ugly daughter a husband," William said, "but you are not going to make me any jumped up lord of this or that. I am too old. I would never learn to answer to my new name."

Elizabeth giggled. "I can just see it, the herald calling 'Baron Bogus of Nowhere,' and William looking around to see who this new Baron Bogus is. . . ."

"If I ever came across a more ungrateful set of people!" Richard exclaimed, as Alys began to giggle also, and Raymond caught her into his arms and kissed her soundly. "But it will work, I think," he continued, his eyes softening as he watched the happy couple embrace.

"I will work, you mean," William said, but he put out his hand and clasped Richard's. "I should have done it years ago. I know I should, but . . ."

"Do not blame yourself. If I had asked, I could have bought him off and saved you years of grief—it was my fault!"

"It is over," Elizabeth said. "We are happy now."

Richard glanced at Alys and Raymond, who had moved away and were talking eagerly. "Yes, I will make it work. Sancia and Eleanor will talk Henry around. You will bring Alys to court when you come, William; she will be set high among the queen's ladies as the daughter of my marshal, and Alys—if she likes—can charm the birds off the trees."

Raymond came back toward them, leading Alys by the hand again. "If my aunts, Eleanor and Sancia, will write to my mother . . ."

"Yes," Richard agreed. "And Henry will write to your father and grandfather. . . . Yes, and if you talk softly, Raymond, and do not clap your hand to your sword hilt and roar at your father in public—"

William almost fell off his chair laughing. Alys whooped aloud. Raymond and Elizabeth choked, trying to be polite.

"What have I said that is so funny?" Richard asked. "It is very good advice."

"Yes, indeed," Elizabeth agreed, "and if everyone would take it, we may all end like the fairy tales—so they lived happily ever after."

Four Best-Selling Authors of Sweeping Historical Romance

ANDREA LAYTON

___16489	SO WILD A RAPTURE	$1.95
___16455	LOVE'S GENTLE FUGITIVE	$1.95
___16532	MIDNIGHT FIRES	$2.25

STEPHANIE BLAKE

___16516	SO WICKED MY DESIRE	$2.25
___16462	BLAZE OF PASSION	$2.25
___16425	DAUGHTER OF DESTINY	$1.95
___16377	FLOWERS OF FIRE	$1.95
___16610	WICKED IS MY FLESH	$2.50

BARBARA RIEFE

___16796	TEMPT NOT THIS FLESH	$2.75
___16480	FIRE AND FLESH	$2.25
___16444	FAR BEYOND DESIRE	$1.95
___16396	THIS RAVAGED HEART	$1.95
___16658	SO WICKED THE HEART	$2.75

ROBERTA GELLIS

___16814	ROSELYNDE	$2.75
___16468	ALINOR	$2.25
___16490	JOANNA	$2.25
___16531	GILLIANE	$2.50
___16701	THE SWORD AND THE SWAN	$2.75
___16364	THE DRAGON AND THE ROSE	$1.95